SWOONY BILLIONAIRE

THE KLINE BROOKS COLLECTION

max monroe

Swoony Billionaire: The Kline Brooks Collection
Published by Max Monroe LLC © 2021, Max Monroe

ISBN: 9798598610534

Editing by Silently Correcting Your Grammar
Formatting by Champagne Book Design
Cover Design by Peter Alderweireld
Photo Credit for *Swoony Billionaire*: to David Vance Photographer

Author's Note:

WARNING: You are about to meet Kline Brooks, the swooniest billion-aire of them all.
Please prepare yourself in advance to laugh, to swoon, and to fall head over heels in love because your new favorite book boyfriend is right here, officially in your hands.

Swoony Billionaire: The Kline Brooks Collection includes the following books:
Tapping the Billionaire
Tapping Her
Plus, a brand-new, hilarious novella—***Be My Billionaire Valentine***

And, because you're so special—*and because Thatcher Kelly is bound to be locked in your brain like a (charming) parasite by the time you reach the end of this collection*—we've included an excerpt from ***Banking the Billionaire***, the next book in our best-selling ***Billionaire Bad Boys Series*** and a standout reader favorite since its release.

Now that you know, please don't buy a voodoo doll in our honor because ***Swoony Billionaire: The Kline Brooks Collection*** concludes at around 90%. We're not very good at writing through any kind of pain. And trust us, once you finish this sexy and hilarious collection, you're going to be ready for *more* Max Monroe billionaires and romantic comedies, and if you hit us with some kind of voodoo lightning strike, there'll be no one left to write them.

Also, due to the hilarious nature of this book's content, reading in public is not recommended. And we strongly suggest that you reconsider (aka: don't do it) eating and/or drinking and/or operating heavy machinery while reading.

Happy Reading!
All our love,
Max & Monroe

DEDICATION

This collection—*my collection*—is dedicated to every woman who
has never had
a book dedicated to her.

This is for you, sweetheart.
Well, you *and* my Georgie. Because I value my life, and in order to
keep it, I have to uphold my promise to value her above all other
women.
But I can promise you this: You're all in good company.

All my love,
Kline Brooks

TAPPING *the* BILLIONAIRE

BILLIONAIRE Bad Boys

BOOK ONE

max monroe

DEDICATION

Fuck you very much, Leslie.
You always manage to ruin everything, but you didn't ruin this.

Disclaimer: You are NOT the Leslie we're talking about. No, really.
You're not her. We swear. It's another Leslie. One you don't know and
have never heard of. Camp Love Yourself Scout's honor.

I'm Kline Brooks.

Harvard graduate.

President and CEO of Brooks Media.

Net worth: $3.5 billion.

Devilishly handsome. How do I know this? I was prom king two years in a row.

Highly intelligent. Proof? I can solve any Rubik's Cube, in front of your face, with *magic* fingers.

Certified master of female orgasms. My fingers, my tongue, my cock—I can make you scream, *"I'm coming!"* before you even realize I've removed your panties with my teeth. Not the almost orgasms that spur a pathetic moan and half-ass whimper. *No.* I'm talking toe-curling, back-arching, earth-shattering Os that will leave your voice hoarse, your body shaking, and pack a punch so powerful you'll be left a sliver of intensity short of unconscious.

Am I piquing your interest?

Should I mention my cock is the kind of cock that's actually dick-pic worthy? I'm not talking an average six-inch shaft. I'm talking big. Thick. Smooth. And hard. Especially when there's work to be done.

Or maybe all I've done is turn you off. Are you thinking I'm like every classless man out there who's literally a disgrace to my gender?

The type of spineless dicks who won't call the next day. The guys who specialize in late-night booty calls but refuse to take a woman out on an actual date. Yeah, you know exactly who I'm talking about. Those idiots who have women thinking staying single for the rest of their lives is a better alternative than dealing with the bullshit that's running rampant in the dating world.

Well, I'm not that kind of guy.

I say what I mean and mean what I say. I don't kiss and tell. I call the next day. And if I'm interested in a woman, I *will* take her out on a date. I'll open doors for her. I'll pull out her chair. And I'll never be the kind of horny bastard who texts dick pics—unless the right woman begs me for them.

Bottom line, **I'm a gentleman**. I prefer monogamy to serial dating and fucking my way through New York City. I've spent the past few years avoiding the kind of women most would label "gold diggers" and trying out a couple of girlfriends in between. I've looked for the kind of woman I want, but lately, I have to admit I haven't put in as much effort. My focus has been on my company—building it to what it is and then keeping it that way, not only for me, but for all of the people who work so hard for me.

Until Georgia Cummings.

She's fiery, beautiful, has this sassy attitude that demands attention from everyone within her orbit, and is worth way more in value of character than I am in money.

I don't know how I missed her.

I don't know why it took me so long to *really* see her.

Two years, right there in front of my face as my Director of Marketing.

Maybe it's because I need to stop drowning myself in work so much. Maybe she didn't want to be seen.

No matter the reason, it only took one spur-of-the-minute decision for this remarkable woman to come barreling into my world.

I wasn't prepared for her.

And I sure as hell had no idea she'd knock me on my fucking ass.

Because the nice guy who believes in real love enough to build his entire fortune from a dating website?

That's me.

And this story?

Well, that's us.

CHAPTER 1

Georgia

*M*y eyes! Dear God, my eyes!

There were things in life that, once seen, were damn near impossible to forget. A bleach scrub…acid straight to the retinas… three hours of perfect porn GIFs…hell, even a lobotomy wouldn't remove those kinds of images.

Lucky for me, I had come across not one, not two, but *four* day-destroying pictures. Dick pics, to be more specific. And let's just say this latest one was *not* pic-worthy. Not by a long shot. Or a short shot, if I took size into consideration. This was the kind of pic that would leave any woman wondering why. *Why? Why would anyone want to advertise they were the owner of* this?

It was the gremlin of male members—and the sole reason my night had taken a turn for the worse. What was supposed to be a nice evening in, watching TV with my best friend and roommate, Cassie, had turned into a nightmare of pubes, wrinkled balls, and a crown that was not fit for a king.

I banged my fingers across the keypad with a response.

TAPRoseNEXT (11:37PM): Is that your dick? Really? REALLY?

TapNext was the latest and greatest dating-site-turned-app for single men and women to meet, chat, and, hopefully, find their next date. Generally speaking, it was a better alternative to nights out at a bar or club. Because, for me, those nights had the same ending—politely declining the thrilling (insert *heavy* sarcasm) offer of hooking up with some random dude at his apartment, one hell of a hangover, and weird guys with names like Stanley or Milton sending me texts for late-night booty calls for the next month. Which I *always* ignored.

My business card said *Director of Marketing, Brooks Media*. It was a hefty title for someone just starting out in their career, but I had earned it. I worked harder than anyone else in my department, and it also may have helped that the man who held the position prior to me had been fired after being arrested for picking up a prostitute in one of the company cars. Why he had even been driving a company car in the city was still confusing to me. Seriously, even hookers cabbed it in New York.

Since Brooks Media owned TapNext, it was easy to understand why I was well versed and highly invested in the app's success. It was a requirement when hired—all single employees had to create a TapNext profile. Staff were strongly encouraged to use the app and give honest feedback about their experiences. Profile names were kept top secret and on penitentiary-style lock-down with Human Resources. And feedback stayed anonymous.

Translation: *Don't worry,* ***TAPRoseNEXT****, your boss doesn't know about your pervy play on words.*

At first, I'd felt it was an odd way to handle business, but after two years of working at Brooks Media, I'd found that my TapNext profile was a damn good way to do research and find promotional ideas.

My phone pinged with the offender's response.

BAD_Ruck (11:38PM): …

Did he just ellipsis me? Really?

TAPRoseNEXT (11:38PM): Creep Threat Level MOTHERFUCKING Red.

There was no immediate response, but the rest of my rant would not be contained.

TAPRoseNEXT (11:39PM): Don't any of you know how to start conversations anymore? Jesus.

Cassie sighed beside me. "Stop slamming everything around, Wheorgiebag! I'm trying to watch *American Ninja Warrior* and you're totally messing with my pumped up vibe."

I ignored her, still focused on finding a way to erase the offending images from my brain.

She peeked over my shoulder before I could pull my phone away. "Whoa. Whoa. *Whoa.* Is that *my* picture on *your* profile?"

Creamy, perfect-skinned thighs on display, she was bent over with her dark brunette head peeking through the space between her open legs. Her hooch just barely escaped making an appearance.

"Paybacks, Casshead."

"And what did I do to deserve being your pro-bono photo ho?"

I cocked an eyebrow. "Do I have to choose just one?"

"Go ahead, give me one example. I dare ya."

"College. Sophomore year. I told you not to post those pictures on Facebook, but did you listen? Of course not."

She grinned. "Ahhhhh, yes. I remember those. I thought you looked really cute that night."

"My head was in the toilet."

"But you had those cute puppy dog eyes going on." She glanced at my phone again, dusky gray eyes hitting the phallic bull's eye. "Holy hell, what is that? Is that Quasimodo's dick?"

I stood up from the couch and began to pace in front of the TV. "Four dick pics today, Cassface. *Four!*"

Cassie scrunched her face up. "And what? You were hoping for five?"

My expression was a combination of disgusted and puzzled.

"You know," she explained, "one to fill all the holes and one for each hand." Easy to interpret and equally graphic hand gestures matched her words as she spoke. "Although, I'm not sure I'd want DP from The Hunchcock of Notre Dame." One look at my face and she coughed out a laugh. "You're not really a prude, but right now, you're playing one on TV."

I groaned and gave in, planting my ass back on the couch and burying my face in my hands. "I guess it's because this profile is for work research. I have this unjustified sense that it should be more professional."

She shook her head and smiled, propping her mismatched-sock feet on the arm of our couch. "I gotta say, that wiener is pretty fucking awful. But, Georgie, you work for a company that specializes in an app called *TapNext*, not the White House."

After a brief beat of silence, we laughed at the same time, and I raised one eyebrow in question. "You're comparing *TapNext* to the *White House*?"

"You're right," she agreed. "Bad analogy. There's probably *more* dick pics there." A giant, mischievous grin consumed Cassie's face as she grabbed the remote.

"*Cassie…*" I pointed in her direction, but it was too late. She was already standing on top of our coffee table, using the remote for a microphone.

My best friend had this thing with making parody songs out of pretty much anything when inspired. And she didn't do it quietly. No way, quiet was not Cassie's style. She sang like she was Adele performing at the Grammys.

"I call this one *White House Lovin*'," Cassie announced.

I groaned but secretly couldn't wait to see what she would come up with. Think Kristen Wiig on *Saturday Night Live* kind of hilarious shit. That was Cass.

"*Blue-dress intern, found my pants fast...*"

"*White House intern, it was a blast...*"

She was singing her little heart out.

"*This girl, she was crazy for D...*"

Snapping fingers. Pelvic thrusts. Head bobs. Cassie wasn't missing a beat.

"*Met the prez, down on both knees...*"

One verse in and the dick pic bandit had been forgotten. I hopped off the couch and tackled her to the floor. She screamed. I laughed. And five minutes later, Cassie was back on the coffee table while I sang backup to the rest of her ridiculous song.

Tell me, whore... Tell me, whore...

Admit it, you're singing it too.

Later that night, once I had cozied myself in bed and was so very close to reaching that heavenly REM cycle, the ping of my phone pecked at me. I groaned my way out of Dreamland slowly. God, it was time to make some major life changes. For example, the alert settings for my TapNext profile in my phone. It was either that or murder, and I'm the kind of person who likes to dip a toe in the pool water to test it rather than cannonball my way in.

Rubbing a hand over my face, I forced my eyes opened and snatched the phone off my antique nightstand. I barely resisted the urge to slam it back down, thus breaking it into a million tiny pieces. Luckily, my rational thinking wasn't as sleepy as the rest of me and realized the amount of work that would result from such an impulsive decision.

Cleaning and shopping and transferring my contacts, oh my.

Yeah, *screw that.*

BAD_Ruck (2:09AM): It's NOT my dick.

It's not his dick?

What the double actual fuck?

No. Nope. This was *so* not the right time to deal with this bullshit. Not. Answering.

The sides of my pillow exploded upward with the force of my punch and made the perfect cushion for my face when it slammed down beside my hand. I had so much shit to do at work tomorrow, and dealing with **BAD_Ruck** and his proclivity for awful crotch selfies and unintelligible responses was not going to be on my agenda.

I was focused on getting shut-eye, confident that sleep and I would spoon the fuck out of each other until the sun rose the following morning. I channeled Buddha for my inner Zen, humming my way toward unconscious bliss. It was either that, or grab my vibrator and participate in a ménage à moi.

Thankfully, my return to sleep came easily that night. No hands-on approach required.

The next day, while I was getting ready for work, I decided to give **BAD_Ruck** a piece of my mind. I spit toothpaste into the sink, rinsed my mouth out with water, and turned off the faucet. Striding into my room with purpose, I grabbed my phone off the nightstand and sent the dick gremlin a response.

Suck. On. That. Buddy.

CHAPTER 2

Kline

TAPRoseNEXT (7:03AM): Then it's someone else's dick? WORSE. Threat Level EXPLODED.

"Good morning, Mr. Brooks."

"Good morning, Frank," I replied, picking my head up from the crime scene on my phone just long enough to meet his honest amber eyes before sliding into the soft leather seat of my Town Car.

Fucking Thatch.

I swear, somehow he took doing what would already be really fucking annoying and advanced it to the next level. If he didn't have the same ability with money, I probably would have dropped him by now.

To the bottom of the ocean. *With a cinder block attached to his ankles.*

She was right, of course. Sending a picture of someone else's dick *was* considerably worse than sending a picture of your own.

Especially this one.

Three rings trilled in my ear before his sleep-laden voice forced one hungover syllable past his lips. "'Lo?"

"A dick, Thatch? Really?" I asked immediately, pinching the bridge of my nose to stave off a headache.

No amount of lingering alcohol could stop his answering laugh.

His throat cleared a little more with each chuckle, and by the time he responded, he was speaking clearly. "You're the one using my picture for your profile, bro. It was only fair that I unleashed the gargoyle dick."

Gargoyle dick. Too fucking right. A winglike knob, a hunchback, and questionable coloring all lent themselves to his description. I'd left my phone on the bar without hawk-eyeing it for *two fucking minutes*, and the asshole had somehow managed to send one of the world's worst illicit pictures to some poor—now blind—woman in that time.

"That profile was only payback for the last awful thing you did to me."

"Which was?" he asked, altogether too amused.

"Who knows," I admitted, staring up at the passing high-rises and shaking my head. "I can't keep up."

"Then join in, K. Live a little, for fuck's sake."

The burgeoning sun glinted off of a pane of perfectly smooth glass at the top of a building and reflected a rainbow right into the window of my car.

"I'm living just fine," I argued.

"Yeah." He laughed and scoffed at once. "Say hi to Walter for me."

That was Thatch's version of calling me a cat lady.

"Hey, fuck you!" I said, only to be met with dead air. I pulled the phone away from my ear to discover he'd ended the call.

"Fuck that guy," I muttered, somehow calling more of Frank's attention to myself than I had with all the yelling.

"Sir?"

"No worries, Frank." I paused for a second and looked back out the window. "You wouldn't happen to know a hit man, would you?"

I glanced up front in preparation for his reaction.

"Um," he murmured hesitantly, flicking his eyes between me and the road in the rearview mirror. "No, sir."

I shook my head as I smiled, a brief chuckle tickling the back of my throat.

"Good. That's good," I remarked, just as we pulled up to the curb in front of my building.

Flexing the door handle in my hand, I shoved the door open with the toe of my shoe.

"Mr. Brooks," Frank started to protest, as usual, jerking into motion in order to hop out to help me, but I just couldn't get into the mindset where his *and* my time was well spent waiting on him to walk around the car just to do something my opposable thumbs and lack of paralysis made shockingly simple.

I smiled in response before he could get out, meeting his eyes in the rearview mirror before exiting.

"Have a good day, Frank. I'll see you at six."

With the slam of the door, I buttoned my suit jacket as I walked, twenty audible smacks of my soles eating up the concrete courtyard in front of my building in no time.

New Yorkers buzzed around me, continuing a marathon life that started the moment they opened their eyes. That was the vibe of this city—active and elite and totally fucking focused. No one had time for each other because they barely had time for themselves. And yet, each and every single one of them would still proclaim it the "best city on Earth" without prompting or persuasion.

As my hand met the metal of the handle, I surveyed the lobby of the Winthrop Building, home to Brooks Media, to find the front desk employees and security guards scurrying to make themselves look busy when they weren't.

I bit my lip to keep from laughing. I'd never been the kind of boss to rule with an iron fist, and not once had I uttered a word of micro-management to loyal employees like the ones practically shoving their hands in their staplers in order to look busy.

But being CEO of a company of this size and magnitude had a way of creating its own intimidation factor, whether it was intended or not. And, sometimes, the weight of unintended consequences was heavier than gold.

"Morning, Paul."

He nodded.

"Brian."

"Mr. Brooks."

The button for the elevator glared its illumination prior to my arrival—more help from the overzealous employees, I'm sure—and the indicating ding of its descent to the bottom floor preceded the opening of the shiny mirrored doors by less than a second.

I stepped in promptly without another word, offering only a smile. I knew anything else I said would only cause stress or anxiety, despite my efforts to convey the opposite. For a lot of people, their boss was never going to be a comfortable fit as a friend—no matter how nice a guy he was. The best thing I could do was recognize, accept, and respect that.

I sunk my hips into the rear wall as the doors slid closed in front of me and shoved my hands into the depths of my pants pockets to keep from scrubbing them repeatedly up and down my face.

I rarely overindulged, so I wasn't hungover, but Thatch's antics, both in person and online, were wearing me out. It wasn't that I didn't think the gargoyle dick was funny—because it *was*—but it was really one of those funnier-when-it's-not-happening-to-you things.

In fact, that rang surprisingly true for most of Thatch's prank-veiled torture.

The direction of my thoughts and the weight of my phone bumping against my hand had me pulling it out of my pocket against my better judgment.

I hovered my thumb over the TapNext app icon.

With one quick click, I had the ability to make a bad situation worse.

The screen flashed and the app loaded as soon as my thumb made contact.

BAD_Ruck (7:26AM): Despite what the gargoyle dick conveys, I promise I'm NOT a sexual terrorist.

Clutching the phone tightly in my fist, I shamefully knocked it against my forehead multiple times.

"Fucking brilliant."

I should have just dropped it. Moved on. I didn't fucking know this woman, for God's sake, but I couldn't help myself. I couldn't stand for even my fake dating profile persona to be remembered like this.

Here lies this man to rest. He will be remembered: Sexual Terrorist, Social Media Nuisance, Unfortunate Genital Development.

The elevator settled smoothly to rest on the fifteenth floor, and as the doors opened, I stepped out. My receptionist stood waiting with a stack of messages, having been warned of my arrival by the staff one hundred and fifty-some-odd feet below.

Neat and conservative clothes encased her sixty-eight-year-old frame, and stark white hair salted its way through her dark mocha bun.

Her smile was genuine, though, years of age, wisdom, and experience coloring her view of her thirty-four-years-young "boss." When it came to the infrastructure and real office inner workings, she ran this show.

The ends of my lips tipped up, forming wrinkles at the corners of my eyes.

"Good morning, lovely Meryl."

She clicked her tongue. "You better find some other roll to butter up, Mr. Brooks. It may be early, but my allowance of saturated fats is all used up for the day."

"Geez." I winced, clutching my chest in imaginary pain. "You wound me." A grin crept onto one end of my mouth and a wink briefly closed the eye on the same side. "And it's Kline. Call me Kline, for shit's sake."

"Ten years. Same conversation every day for every single one of them," she grumbled.

"There's a lesson in there somewhere, Meryl, and I think it has to do with bending to my will." I took the messages gently from her hand and bumped her with just the tip of my elbow.

"I'm consistently persistent."

"So am I," she retorted.

"Don't I know it."

"Four urgent messages from new potential investors on top, and multiple urgent IT problems below those," she called to my back as I walked away.

I shook my head to myself. Potential investors were always urgent.

Pausing briefly and turning to look over my shoulder, I asked, "And *you're* giving me the messages from IT, why?"

Things like that normally came from my personal assistant.

"Because I am," she called back, not even looking up from her desk. "And because Pam is at home with a sick baby."

I leaned my head back in understanding and bit my lip to stop a laugh from escaping.

"Ah. And we all know the only soft spot in your entire body is reserved for the babies."

"Precisely," she confirmed unapologetically, looking over the frames of her glasses and winking.

I turned to head for my office again, but she wasn't done talking.

"But don't you worry—"

Shit. Anything that started with Meryl telling me not to worry meant I should worry. I should *really* worry.

"Leslie's here to pick up her slack."

I shook my head. I didn't know if it was in disbelief or resentment, but whatever it was, I couldn't stop the motion.

Meryl's eyes started to gleam.

"And since *you* hired her and all, I figured you wouldn't mind taking her directly under your knowledgeable wing for the day."

Fuck.

I let my head fall back with a groan briefly before resigning myself to a day from hell and getting back on my way.

One foot in front of the other, I walked toward my doom, knowing the only people I had to blame, other than myself, were my family. And I couldn't even *really* blame them. I was an adult, a business owner, and the leader of my own goddamn life. It had been my choice to hire the airhe—*Leslie*—whether I had done it out of obligation or not.

Still. "Fuck."

"Good morning, Mr. Brooks," she greeted as soon as I rounded the corner, the last syllable of my name trailing straight into a giggle.

God, that's painful.

Her eyes were bright, lips pouty, and her forearms squeezed into her breasts. Her black hair teased and sprayed, several curls rolled over her shoulders and hung nearly all the way down to her pointy nails. And she eye fucked me relentlessly, pounding me harder with every step I took.

I plastered a smile on my face and tried to make it genuine. She was really a nice person—just devoid of each and every quality I looked for in both lovers and friends.

"Come on, Leslie." I gestured, turning away from her nearly exposed—completely office inappropriate—breasts and walking straight into my office with efficiency I knew Cynthia, my head of Human Resources, would appreciate.

The boss in me wanted to tell her to put them away. The man in me knew I wouldn't be able to do that without opening some sort of door for a sexual harassment suit. Situations like this were ripe for postulation.

"You're with me today," I went on, walking straight to my desk and shucking the suit jacket from my shoulders to hang on the hook to the back and right of me.

"Here," I offered when she didn't move or speak, holding the messages from potential investors Meryl had handed me not five minutes ago out to her. "Take these to Dean and have him make some precursory calls. He can schedule calls for me this afternoon with any of them that show signs of legitimacy."

A fake-lashed blink followed by a blank stare.

I even shook them a little, but she didn't respond.

Right. Small words.

"Ask Dean to call these people back. He'll know if it's worth my time talking to them, and if it *is*, I'm free to do so this afternoon."

"Got it!" she said with a wink, jumping from one heel to the other, spinning, and sashaying her way out of my office.

I wasn't a psychic, but one thing was increasingly clear—I was going to need to stop and buy an extra bottle of scotch tonight.

CHAPTER 3

Georgia

I dove through the subway doors mere seconds before they crushed me to my death.

Okay, maybe that seems a tad dramatic, but if you lived in New York, you'd understand the sentiment I'm trying to portray.

The subway waited for no one. It didn't care if you were the next big shark on Wall Street. If you didn't reach those doors in time, *fuhgeddaboutit.*

I loved my job. I loved working at my job, once I managed to get my "never on time" ass there. It was that whole getting out of bed thing that caused me the most grief. Morning person, I was not. My body preferred to wake up on its own time. Therefore, my snooze button was ridden hard and put away *extremely* wet.

Every day was a race against time, and today was no exception.

I found a seat across from a thirty-something-year-old guy whose nose stayed buried in a book. He was hot by all accounts—brooding eyes, red flannel shirt, beanie-adorned bedhead, and cheekbones that would make Michelangelo's David look soft.

His book: *Sex, Drugs, and Cocoa Puffs: A Low Culture Manifesto* by Chuck Klosterman.

I knew that book well. I'd fiddled around with it during under-grad at NYU. It was a handwritten bomb of pop culture references and reflections on pretty much anything that mattered to young people. *The Real World*, porn, kittens, *Star Wars*, you name it and Klosterman discussed it. His witty take on American culture was supposed to be ironic in an existential kind of way. But I wouldn't say any of the top-ics were deeply examined, which was probably why the book had left me with a Tumblr-like aftertaste in my mouth.

Translation: *Total hipster.* Although insanely good-looking, this guy would probably end up an NYC transplant in Portland within the next year. But I wasn't ruling out seeing his gorgeous mug on one of my favorite Instagram accounts, *Hot Dudes Reading.*

Because who doesn't love seeing man candy nose deep in a book?

My ogle time came to an end as I jumped off at my stop. Brooks Media headquarters was located on the prestigious Fifth Avenue, smack dab in the center of Midtown. This part of Manhattan was the central business district of the city—hell, even the country. Name a successful business, and it was probably located here. And lucky for me, my apartment in Chelsea was only a ten-to-fifteen-minute sub-way ride away.

Doesn't explain why I'm running twenty minutes late.

Following the hustle and bustle of sidewalk traffic, I maneuvered past as many map-reading tourists as possible. Street vendors littered the sidewalks. A guy on a bike missed getting hit by mere inches, ele-gantly flipping the driver off over his shoulder.

It was a weekday in New York, and it was fucking beautiful.

I loved my city. I loved the ebb and flow of its many eccentric-ities. Heels click-clacked against concrete, headed for Fifth Avenue's upscale boutiques. Loafers tip-tapped their way toward the Financial District. Taxis honked. Delivery trucks unloaded their goodies with clashing bangs and swift maneuvers. It was the New York song and dance. Everyone was on a mission to start their day. And nothing would stop them.

I strode into the Winthrop building, the spacious lobby greeting me with its gorgeous marble pillars and floor-to-ceiling windows. It was breathtaking. The office space was just as exquisite—wide hallways, natural stone floors, and the perfect amount of light coming in through large windows and skylights. Brooks Media had definitely shelled out some cash for this prime piece of real estate. By all accounts, it was stunning.

"Morning, Paul. Morning, Brian," I greeted the front desk security guards.

"Well, hey there, pretty lady." Paul smiled. "I see someone is still having issues with getting here bright and early."

"Oh, shut it, Paul. Not all of us can look as good as you without a little work in the morning." I grinned and batted my eyelashes.

Brian laughed. "She's got your number, dude."

"I *wish* she had my number," Paul interjected. "C'mon, Georgia, let me take you out to dinner."

"We've been going through the same conversation at least once a week for the past two years, Paul. My answer isn't going to change," I called over my shoulder as I made my way to the elevator.

"It will change!" he yelled. "One day, it will change!"

The elevator pinged and I stepped on, giving Paul a little wave before the doors shut.

He was an adorable guy: mid-forties, hard-working, and sweeter than honey. But I didn't mix business with pleasure. And Paul from security wasn't my kind of guy. One day, though, he'd meet the right kind of lady who'd wash his socks and make him beer-cheese dip for Monday Night Football. He needed a woman who was just as good in the kitchen as she was in the bedroom. I could sixty-nine with the best of 'em, but I was useless when it came to home-cooked meals. Talented chef would never be on my résumé. My oven was better used for storing shoes.

"Well, look what the cat dragged in. Fashionably late today, Georgie?" Dean winked, passing me in the hallway.

Shit. My late arrivals were starting to mimic the walk of shame. I seriously needed to get my shit together.

"I was only trying to impress you with my new A-line skirt," I called over my shoulder, sashaying my hips a little. "Vintage. Vera Wang. How 'bout them apples, cupcake?" Should I have mentioned I found the skirt at a secondhand shop in SoHo? Designer digs were great, but I refused to pay designer prices.

"Someone is fierce this morning. Go on with your bad self, little diva," he teased, snapping his fingers. Dean was one of my favorite people in the office: hilarious, flamboyantly gay, and smart as a whip. What more could a girl ask for?

He turned in my direction, stopping in his tracks. "Lunch today?"

I paused at the entry to my office. "I'd kill for a chicken salad sandwich from the deli across the street."

Dean grinned. "No homicide needed. We'll grab it to go."

"Let's eat there. My office, quarter till one?"

He blew me a kiss. "It's a date, lover."

Another day, another dollar, yadda yadda yadda. My mantra, even though I would have preferred staying wrapped up in my comforter and sleeping until noon. Some days, adulting was too much responsibility. Get up for work. Brush your hair. Pay bills. It was an endless list of too many things and not enough time. The struggle was real, my friends.

But rent in Chelsea wasn't a Sunday picnic in Central Park. A two-bedroom space with an elevator and doorman was pricey. Bottom line, I *had* to adult. No ifs, ands, or buts about it.

I settled into my day, checking emails and making follow-up calls to a few marketing prospects. The TapNext app had skyrocketed in success over the past year. I'd developed an ad campaign that had brought in several companies wanting to advertise within the windows of our app. And these scrollbar ads had become quite lucrative for the company. Businesses not only paid us a nice advertising fee, but they also agreed to some form of promotion for Brooks Media. We scratched their backs, and they gave us a full body massage. Although I was no use in the kitchen, I was *very* persuasive in a boardroom.

"Knock, knock," Leslie announced her arrival. Her curvy frame swayed into my office, seemingly aloof to the fact I was in the middle of a conference call with Sure Romance.

"Uh, Georgia, like, there's birthday cards you need to sign for people in the office," she continued, tossing the greeting cards onto my desk. They spilled over my laptop, stopping my busy fingers from making much-needed progress on the current contract I was discussing.

I held up a finger, pointing to the Bluetooth in my ear.

"Georgia? Hellooooo, Georgia?" she repeated, tapping the toe of her stiletto in six quick, impatient movements.

Leslie was a horrible nightmare of ditzy responses, poor time management skills, and cleavage-revealing tops. And she was new to the company. But *for fuck's sake*, how hard was it to see that I was currently in the middle of something?

"I'm so sorry, can you hold on for just a second?" I politely asked Martin, Sure Romance's Director of Marketing.

"You know what, Georgia? I've got about three minutes to get to another meeting. How about you make the changes in the contract and send them over to legal? Let's shoot for another call on Friday to review everything and find a middle ground we can both be happy with."

Goddammit. This, my friends, was a perfect example of how to lose valuable footing in a business deal.

"Sure thing, Martin. And since Mr. Brooks wants to be on that call Friday, let's plan on it being a video chat." My boss knew nothing about that call. But this was me calling Martin's bluff. My persuasion skills were top notch, but there was a reason Kline Brooks was President and CEO of his own company. The man could talk an Eskimo into buying ice.

"Oh, okay." Martin cleared his throat. "In the meantime, I'll try to get legal to review everything over the next twenty-four hours. The sooner we can sign off on this deal, the better."

Translation: I'd like to avoid a video chat with your boss.

"Perfect. I look forward to hearing from you." I ended the call and used all of my strength to plaster a neutral smile on my face as I looked up at Leslie.

"So, like I was saying, you need to sign these," she repeated, still clueless.

God, I didn't even care if I had resting bitch face. Hell, I wanted to active bitch face this chick so bad. She'd been with the company for a hot minute, and I was already done with her.

"Okay, Leslie. Just give me a second and I'll sign them so you can go about your day," I responded through a fake smile. I wanted to berate her. I wanted to let her know just how much her interruption could have screwed up an important business deal. But it would've been useless. My words would have gone straight through the giant hole in her head.

I gripped my pen, scribbling half-assed sayings about celebrating and happy birthday and have a great day. Five cards later, I handed them back to Leslie and sent her ditzy ass on her way.

I was twenty emails deep before another interruption peeked in my door.

Kline Brooks. He was the kind of man women fantasized about. A quintessential billionaire bad boy—styled, short dark hair, muscles for days, and a panty-dropping smile.

Except—he *wasn't.*

His smiles were genuine and his orders gently delivered. He kept to himself, from what I could tell, and didn't appear to sleep around. Despite his crazy good looks and net worth, I'd yet to see him land an "NYC playboy" spot on Page Six. I'd never seen him execute a salacious glimpse at a single employee—male or female. He was a mystery, hidden under all of that quiet direction with absolutely no chance of being uncovered.

As an employee, he wouldn't touch me with a ten-foot pole. Honestly, I wasn't sure he knew I had a vagina. He treated me as an equal and seemed to truly value my opinion on all things business and marketing. His eyes never strayed to my tits. His mouth never flashed a devilish grin.

And I stood strong in my beliefs that business and pleasure may as well have been oil and water. Kline was business, plain and simple.

Plus, he wasn't at all what I was looking for.

And yes, I can practically see the word billionaire flashing in front of your money-hungry eyes and feel the judgment rolling off of you in thick, disdain-filled clouds.
But this isn't actually about him. Not really, anyway.

Despite my inexperience with relationships, I knew myself enough to know I liked a straight shooter—both in conversation and the pun that intends. And I wasn't willing to settle—even if it was on a big, comfy pile of money.

Christ, there had to be a middle ground between soft talkers like Kline and dick pic bandits like **BAD_Ruck**. *Didn't there?*

"Good morning, Georgia," he greeted with that professional yet handsome smile of his. "Just wanted to check in and see how the Sure Romance deal was doing."

"Even though I had to threaten Martin with your presence on a video chat, I think we'll walk out of the deal with a million more than we anticipated."

"Nice work. Keep me abreast on the progress and let me know if you need backup."

My mind went straight to the word *abreast*. I knew my boss wasn't referring to my breasts, or breasts in general, but I couldn't stop my thoughts from wandering there.

I doubted Kline Brooks had ever thought about my breasts.

That would have been weird, right?

There was no way he saw me *that* way. And of course, I didn't think about him like that either. But it didn't hurt that he was easy on the eyes. Well, not *my* eyes, but other women's eyes. I was sure he was easy on *their* eyes. My eyes *knew* not to look at him.

I wouldn't deny my eyes were thankful he didn't have a weird comb-over or nose hairs or crusty lips. But Kline Brooks was business, *not* pleasure. He wouldn't touch me, and I sure as hell wouldn't touch him.

"Georgia?" he asked, pulling me from my rambling inner monologue.

Shit.

"Sorry." I shook the awkward thoughts out of my head. "I will definitely keep you updated on the Sure Romance contract, Mr. Brooks. I'm planning on signatures being finalized by the end of this week."

"Good to hear." He rapped his knuckles twice against the doorframe in that way only a man can pull off. "Thank you."

And with that, through the glass walls of my office, I watched as Kline Brooks strode down the hall with purpose. I knew that look well. Either someone was ready for lunch or they were about two minutes late for a meeting.

Before I could resume the task of responding to the morning's emails, Dean walked into my office, a shit-eating grin plastered to his face. "Got a minute, sweet cheeks?"

"Of course." I shut my laptop, giving him my full attention.

He plopped his Prada-wearing ass in the leather seat across from my desk. Dean kept grinning like the fucking Cheshire Cat as he slid a Hallmark card across my laptop.

I raised an eyebrow. "Why are you smiling like that? It's creepy, dude."

"So, Tits McGee put this card on my desk," he sing-songed. "Of course, this was after she practically shoved her cleavage in my face." The wide smile turned to irritation. "That girl has about the worst gaydar I've ever seen."

"Aw, poor Dean. So attractive that single women are throwing themselves at him," I teased.

"Well, you're about to be thanking poor Dean here in a minute." He nodded toward the card. "Go ahead and read it, sassy pants. I think you might want to make some changes."

Huh? I glanced at the front, reading the sentiment. It was, by all accounts, a sympathy card. Someone in the office must have had a death in the family. I opened it and read through everyone's thoughtful responses.

I'm so very sorry for your loss, Mary. -Patty
You're in my thoughts and prayers. -Meryl
Please let us know if there's anything we can do. -Gary

My coworkers were really sweet. That much was apparent.

Lots of love and prayers being sent your way through this difficult time. -Laura
HAPPY! HAPPY! JOY! JOY! Have a great day celebrating! -Georgia

Oh, fuck.

I read it again just to make sure my eyes weren't playing tricks on me.

Shit.
Shit.
Shit.

My *Ren & Stimpy* reference wasn't all that funny when written in the center of someone's CONDOLENCE CARD.

"*Fucking Leslie,*" I spat. "She threw a bunch of cards on my desk and said they were *birthday* cards."

Dean proceeded to lose his shit, his cackling laughs echoing inside my office.

I glared at him. "It's not *that* funny."

"Oh, hell yes it is. You referenced *Ren & Stimpy* on a sympathy card," he wheezed.

Seriously, fuck you, Leslie. Fuck you, hard.

I was convinced I could blame her for everything wrong in my life.

Lost my keys? *Goddammit, Leslie!*

Missed the subway? *Fuck you very much, Leslie.*

Another awful dick pic sent to my phone? *You're such an asshole, Leslie.*

I sighed. "I'm not even sure how to fix this."

"White out?" he suggested, still laughing like a lunatic.

"Please." I waved my hand at him. "Continue to giggle your ass off at my expense."

"This was literally the highlight of my day. When I read it, I about fell out of my chair from laughing so hard. Pretty sure everyone in the office heard me. Even Meryl was giving me the stink eye."

"Glad to know I'm brightening someone's workday."

He smirked, standing up and snatching the card out of my incompetent hands. "Let's just throw this card out. I'll have Meryl send flowers to Mary's house from everyone in the office."

I let out a breath of relief. "I'm in full support of this plan. I'll even chip in fifty bucks."

"Perfect."

"Hey, you're throwing that card out, right?" I asked before he made his way out of my office doors.

He only responded with a shrug and a few more cackles.

Dean was such a bitch. If I didn't love him so much, I'd have definitely disowned his designer-tag-wearing ass.

As his laughter faded, the annoying crescendo that signaled a text on my phone built.

I grabbed it quickly, knowing if I didn't read it now, I wouldn't remember it until the end of the day.

Cassie: *I just watched the police arrest two guys for fucking right up against a wall on Broadway.*

Not sure how to respond, I said the only thing that came to mind.

Me: *Well, it is the Theater District.*

I exited my messages, and before I locked the screen, I noticed the little red notification on my TapNext app. A message from **BAD_ Ruck** from this morning made promises of sexual normalcy despite his indiscretions. A truce was in order.

TAPRoseNEXT (12:14PM): Awkward apology accepted.

His response came two minutes later.

BAD_Ruck (12:16PM): Thank God. Though, to be fair, your profile name really does nothing to discourage bad behavior.

CHAPTER 4

Kline

TAPRoseNEXT (12:19PM): Ugh. Don't remind me. I owe it mostly to a bottle of wine and an ill-advising roommate.

I chuckled to myself and then glanced at my watch, compelled to double-check the time even though the display on my phone told it to me just fine.

A pastrami and corned beef on rye from the deli on the corner was calling my name, yelling louder with each passing minute, but every single action of the day seemed to move as if it were coated in molasses.

"What are you laughing at?" Thatch asked from the screen in front of me.

I'd nearly forgotten I was on a video call with him.

"Your ugly mug," I countered, pointedly electing not to tell him I was having any further conversation with **TAPRoseNEXT**.

"This face? No way. This is my moneymaker, son."

"You sound like the biggest douche on the planet right now. Can we work, please? I'd like to eat lunch sometime this century."

"You and your delicate stomach."

"It's not fucking delicate," I argued grumpily. But he really couldn't blame me. I *was* hungry after all. "It's manly and it needs food on the regular. There's nothing wrong with that."

"Right. Now you're justifying your PMS symptoms—"

"Yes, Leslie?" I interrupted Thatch as she pushed open the door to my office.

"I just finished moving all of your meetings from this morning to this afternoon," she purred, smiling at me like I should praise her. *She* was the one who'd told Dean to schedule the investor calls for that morning rather than this afternoon, necessitating a schedule flip in the first place.

"Thanks," I said through gritted teeth. Catching sight of Thatch's "Duran Duran" face on the screen in front of me stopped me from rolling my eyes. Operation *Cockblock Hungry Wolf* superseded my needs.

"You can just leave the new schedule by the door and head to lunch," I offered, hoping she'd telepathically understand what I was trying so hard to communicate—*get out.*

She giggled.

Nope. Life wasn't that easy.

The tile of my office floor turned into a runway, her dramatic, foot-crossing steps designed to amplify the swing of her hips and elicit a man's attention.

And for any other man, it probably reached into his pants and hardened the attention right out of him.

I, however, was too busy cleaning up her mistakes and trying to finish a phone call so I could go to goddamn lunch.

Tits suddenly filled the frame of my vision, and I practically had to slam my head back into my chair to keep from eating them by accident.

No, I wasn't *that* hungry. That was how close she had placed them.

"Here you go."

"Yeah, thanks," I said, dismissing her and averting my eyes as much as possible. It wasn't a battle of wills, but rather, strictly a game of proximity.

The day I was willing to subject myself to that kind of pussy was the day my cock would rot off and my office would burn straight to the ground. I was sure of it.

Come hell or high water, I was done being this amenable to my mom's suggestions. Leslie needed to be gone by the beginning of next week. Soon, but not soon enough that I couldn't talk my way out of it at family dinner.

I watched as she walked, counting the seconds and praying he'd wait until she left the room.

"Ho-ly hell—"

"Thatch—" I attempted to interrupt, recognizing his tone from experience and knowing it would only lead to bad things.

"Where the hell have you been hiding that one?"

"Don't say another word," I warned, just as the door shut blessedly behind Leslie.

"Fuck me hard, fast, and dirty, Kline-hole. Did you see the tits on her? Seriously, let her know she can swaddle me up and ride me like a cockpuppet any fucking time she wants."

I picked up a pen and pretended to scribble on a piece of paper.

"Ride...you...like...a...cockpuppet. Got it."

The muscled chords of his throat flexed with a bark of laughter, and recognition of his absurdity flashed in his eyes.

"All right, point taken." He raised his hands and winked, his fingers in air quotes, mocking, "Business."

I didn't waste any time getting back to it. "I've got two investor meetings in L.A.—"

"And you want me to be there."

"Yeah."

He sat back in his leather chair and crossed his thick arms. "Done."

"You don't even know when they are," I pointed out. I reached forward and took hold of my mouse to double-check the timing, but he didn't wait.

"For you, my love, no time is a bad time." He blew me a kiss.

"Why do I put up with you?" I asked, sitting back again and raking a hand through my hair.

His response was immediate. "I personally think it's because you like a reminder of the fine male specimen you'll never live up to."

I shook my head and smirked, knowing I'd never be the six-foot-five monster he was and not struggling to swallow it even one little bit. My leaner but no less toned six-foot package hadn't failed me yet.

"I'll see you in L.A. tomorrow night, Adonis."

"No way. I'll see you here, at the airport, so you can hold my hand during—"

Raising my middle finger in salute, I clicked the button to end the call.

Thatch's ability to bounce back from a night out was almost unfathomable. I needed more than four hours of sleep, and I needed to do it for some other reason than being blackout drunk.

My best friend and money man could go several nights in a row without, it seemed, and holding his liquor had practically been his first childhood milestone.

Nights out were dwindling for both of us, though. My tendency to be "an old man," according to Thatch, and his secret rendezvous with every available pussy in Manhattan pretty much soured the deal.

It's not that I didn't enjoy nights out or the company of a beautiful woman. I loved women. I loved every fucking thing about them. I just didn't love the idea of having drunken sex with some chick I picked up at a bar. I wasn't a fan of Pussy Roulette, and when I ate one, I wanted to be able to remember the taste.

My phone rang on my desk as though the call had been put straight through without a heads-up from a lunch-eating Leslie. Normally, Pam rolled my calls to voicemail when she was away from her desk, sorting through them and passing along worthy callers upon her return.

Every ring made it that much more painfully obvious she was out, a duck-lipped, inexperienced seductress in her place.

"Brooks," I answered, putting the phone to my ear.

"Yo," Thatch greeted. "I forgot to ask. Do we have BAD practice tonight?"

I covered my groan. I'd forgotten about rugby practice.

That didn't stop me from busting his balls. "Yes, Princess Peach. We have practice every Monday night."

"Yeah, but with it being football season and all, I thought maybe Wes was busy cheerleading or whatever."

Wes was the third member of our bachelor trio and the owner of the New York Mavericks. We teased him relentlessly, but in reality, it was *cool as fuck* to know somebody who owned a team in the National Football League. A little sweet-talking got us tickets anytime we wanted and field time with the players.

"I take no offense, by the way. Princess Peach is a badass bitch."

"Most of their games are on Sunday. You know, like the one you talked me into going out to watch last night. I'll see you at practice tonight," I said, shaking my head at another ridiculous conversation.

"Geez, Diva. Eat a Snickers."

I pinched the bridge of my nose. "You know, you force me to say *fuck*, as in *fuck you*, way more than I ever dreamed in a business environment."

His answering chuckle was dry. "Just one of my many talents, K. Most of the others involve a lighter, a forty of beer, and my cock—"

I ended the call before he could finish.

Jesus. Is this guy really my best friend?

The short of it was, yes, he *was* my best friend. And I wouldn't change it despite his ability to produce migraines. I was never short on entertainment, that was for sure. But my well of patience had run dry for the day. Simple as that.

Standing quickly, before I could be interrupted again, I yanked the skinny end of my tie from its knot, unwound it from my neck, and hung it on the hook next to my jacket.

I dropped my keys with a clang into my pocket and slid my wallet snug into its spot in the one in the rear.

Retracing my steps from several hours earlier, I passed Meryl with a nod and escaped the building without having to do more than smile politely at passing employees.

The sun nearly blinded me as I pushed the front door open, and the sounds of an active fall lunch hour overwhelmed my office-trained ears. Horns honked and cabbies yelled and pigeons took off in a rush as a toddler ran screaming through the middle of them.

I popped the buttons on my sleeves as I walked, rolling them up to expose my forearms and bask in the dramatically warm weather, and faded into the crowd of pump-wearing women and suit-clad men.

Indian summer, I think they called it, the desertlike arid heat settling deep into my bones and radiating from the inside out.

I could see the sun and city from the wall-to-wall windows of my office, but my lunch hour was pretty much the only opportunity I got to *feel* it.

That was the real root of my grumpiness, I guess. I worked hard from sunup to sundown, and one simple hour in between was what helped keep a happy head on top of tense shoulders.

"Kline!" the owner of my favorite little mom-and-pop deli called as I pushed my way inside the door.

"Hey, Tony!" I answered, gently making my way through the standing-room-only crowd to shake his hand over the counter.

"Here, here," he urged, moving some old memorabilia to unearth the one empty seat in the place.

"No way," I denied with a smile and a shake of my head. "I'll wait for a table like everybody else. I could use the extra time to clear my head today."

"Sit, sit, sit," he said over me, his refusal to let me stand in the crowd and wait a regular occurrence. But he didn't do it because I had money. Tony didn't even *know* I had money. All he knew was I'd been coming in every workday I was in town for the last ten years, and I looked him in the eye and shook his hand every single time I did.

"Thanks, Tone." Giving in was the only option.

"We got a sandwich for you today, buddy," he said as I slid my butt onto the seat.

"I hope it's a pastrami and corned beef on rye. I've been fantasizing about it all morning."

"Ah," he said with a shout and a wink. "For you, I've got just the thing!"

And the truth was, he did—a warm smile, familiarity, and a genuine exuberance. Stuff I needed way more than a sandwich.

CHAPTER 5

Georgia

"**F**inally!" Dean remarked as he slammed through my door half an hour later.

I'd just finished finalizing and faxing the *original* Sure Romance contract. The one where a little quick talking had prevented Leslie's ill-timed interruption from ruining my life and dragging the company over a swath of hot coals. *The one I was shoving down Martin's throat whether he liked it or not.*

Meanwhile, my stomach was working on chewing a sandwich-sized hole through itself.

"I swear that evil trampvestite is the bane of my existence."

I raised a single, perfectly plucked eyebrow in amusement. If Cassie was the expert of parodies, Dean was the single-most talented nickname giver I'd ever encountered. No two people were alike and no name was deemed off-limits in the name of political correctness. Basically, Dean did the dirty work and I reaped the benefits.

"Trampvestite, huh?"

"Oh, yeah," he confirmed, pointing to his fluttering eyes. "Fake lashes to here." He held both hands out generously in front of his chest. "And fake tits out to there."

I didn't bother to conceal my laugh.

"She's had me running all over this goddamn place this morning, putting out fires and sweating through a five-hundred-dollar shirt."

"You know what will make you feel better?" I cooed.

His green eyes twinkled under the fluorescent lights. "Twenty million dollars and a private island with Brad Pitt?"

"A hot turkey sandwich."

"Hmm," he mumbled as he pretended to consider it. "I guess that'll work."

I slid the bottom drawer of my desk open with ease, yanked my purse out, and slammed it shut with a bang.

"Let's go. Feed me. Regale me with all of your tales of woe."

"She's been annoying you too," he argued as I slid my arm through his at the elbow.

"She has," I agreed. "You just play a much more convincing victim than I do."

A small blush stole through his cheeks, and he leaned down to smack a kiss on mine. Compliments always cheered him up.

"I've had more practice," he comforted me. Not that I *needed* to be comforted. This was still all about Dean and giving him what he needed. I didn't have a dick, but I could do drama.

"Ah, yes, the struggles of an attractive gay man."

"They're like wolves, Georgia! One innocent cherub like me in the club and they swarm like bees."

"Wait. I'm confused. Are they wolves or bees?" I teased as he pushed the button for the elevator.

"Shut your crimson lip-stain-covered trap!"

Perfect.

A distraction of *cosmetic* proportions.

"You like the color?" I asked as I backed into the rear wall of the elevator, propping my chin up on a posed hand and pursing my lips.

"Hmm." He pretended to inspect me, fluffing the hair on both sides of my head. Consideration turned into a quick smile, and a wink popped his left eye closed. "Love!"

"Thanks," I offered with a return grin.

While Dean proceeded to gab about his recent rendezvous with a cute bartender, I couldn't shake a question that'd been nagging me. I needed an answer.

TAPRoseNEXT (12:52PM): So, if that wasn't your dick, whose dick was it? I think I want to know the answer to this, but there's another part of me that's a little afraid…

BAD_Ruck (12:53PM): Afraid I'll reveal that I've got a stockpile of other dudes' dicks on my phone?

Hells bells, that answer was *not* reassuring.

TAPRoseNEXT (12:54PM): …

TAPRoseNEXT (12:55PM): For real "…" is the only response I have to that.

Okay, seriously, if he didn't respond in the next two minutes, my trigger finger was going straight for the block button.

TAPRoseNEXT (12:56PM): …! (If I could use shouty caps for ellipses, I'd be doing it RIGHT NOW)

BAD_Ruck (12:57PM): I don't make a habit of collecting other dudes' dick pics or taking my own. But I do have a friend (who's a bit of a prick) who loves "gargoyle dicking" people as a prank.

TAPRoseNEXT (12:58PM): My friend (who's pretty hilarious)

referred to the dick in question as, "The Hunchcock of Notre Dame."

BAD_Ruck (12:59PM): If I were the kind of guy who used text acronyms, I'd definitely be responding with LOL.

TAPRoseNEXT (1:00PM): Question: were you purposefully withholding important information to get me worked up?

We crossed Fifth Avenue, heading straight for my favorite family-owned deli. The sidewalks were bustling with energy, but **BAD_Ruck** had become quite the distraction. I only willed my eyes to look away from our message box to avoid being run over by a taxi or knocking over my fellow pedestrians.

Dean cleared his throat. "Excuse me? Are you even listening? Or am I rambling on about Sir Sucks-A-Lot for no reason?"

"Sir Sucks-A-Lot?"

"Jesus." He sighed. "What in the hell are you doing? Are you texting someone?"

I shrugged. "Just checking work emails." No way in hell would I give Dean any kind of ammunition regarding TapNext. I'd never live that down.

He stopped in the middle of the New York sidewalk traffic, nearly causing a woman with her dog to trip over the leash. "Work emails? You're so full of it."

Uh-huh. I hid the screen of my phone. "What? I've got that big deal with Sure Romance I need nailed down by the end of the week…"

"You're the worst liar. Seriously. It's like you're so bad at lying that I honestly wonder if you're doing it on purpose."

"I'm not lying," I said, fighting a smile.

Dean pointed to my mouth. "Says the girl who's notorious for smiling or giggling nervously whenever she's lying."

Shit. I covered my mouth.

"Honey, you are too much," he teased, placing his hand at the small of my back. "Now, let's get your lying ass inside that deli so I can fight the starvation that's threatening to take place."

"This place is insane," Dean whispered in my ear as we stepped in the door.

The restaurant was packed. Every table was filled, and the line to order reached the door. But I didn't care. My nostrils had already been seduced by the delicious aromas of freshly baked breads and soups. I'd wait two hours if I had to.

"I know," I agreed. "But it's like this all the time." My eyes scanned the tables for any open seats. "It looks like that woman in the corner is about to get up."

"Perfect. You grab it. I'll order," Dean suggested. "The usual?"

I cocked an eyebrow. "Like you even have to ask."

"Chicken salad. Lettuce. Light mayo. Hold the onion and tomato."

I nodded. "I swear if you didn't have an aversion to vaginas, I'd beg you to be my husband."

He smirked. "Plenty of women are beards to their fabulously gay husbands."

"Yeah, but we'd fight too much over our clothing budget. You'd shop us out of food and rent money."

"I bet you wouldn't be complaining too much when your curvy little ass was decked out in designer duds."

Laughing, I held up both hands. "Fine. You've convinced me. If I reach the age of thirty-five and neither of us is married, I'll be your beard."

"Fabulous." He winked. "Now go snatch a table while I grab the food."

Since Dean was a diva from way back, I did as I was told. I

pretended to mosey around the joint, casually stopping to look at the memorabilia on the walls, but in reality, I was watching some woman with a red turtleneck and Crocs like a hawk. By the time she gathered her trash and was getting ready to hop to her feet, I had strategically placed myself a few feet away from her table, carefully planning my descent onto her chair.

The second Turtleneck's butt cheeks left the seat, I slid into her place with the finesse of a gazelle. Well, in my head, I looked like a gazelle. The guy whose head I nearly took off with my purse probably would've called it more *bull in china shop*, but whatever. Tomato. Tomahto.

My phone pinged inside the front pocket of my purse.

BAD_Ruck (1:12PM) Question: Is now the time to confess you're pretty adorable when you get worked up?

TAPRoseNEXT (1:13PM) Egging me on for your own amusement? That's not very gentlemanly of you.

BAD_Ruck (1:14PM) I can assure you, I'm a gentleman in all the ways that count.

TAPRoseNEXT (1:15PM) Are you flirting with me?

BAD_Ruck (1:16PM) If I am, is it working?

TAPRoseNEXT (1:17PM) A lady never kisses (or flirts) and tells.

BAD_Ruck (1:18PM) Neither does a gentleman.

TAPRoseNEXT (1:19PM): I think you might be BAD news.

BAD_Ruck (1:20PM): BAD in the best kind of way, sweetheart.
TAPRoseNEXT (1:21PM): You're definitely flirting with me,
Ruck.

BAD_Ruck (1:22PM): You've got a keen eye, Rose.

"I'm convinced. You're sexting someone."

I glanced up from my phone, meeting Dean's knowing look. "Don't be ridiculous. Why would you think I'm sexting someone?"

"The fact that you're smiling like a loon and haven't noticed I've been sitting here for a good five minutes with our food."

He had a point. I was too wrapped up in **BAD_Ruck**'s responses to notice anything else. I couldn't deny, the man intrigued me. But I also couldn't deny that if I didn't set my phone down and give Dean my undivided attention, it might be grounds for a full-on catfight.

TAPRoseNEXT (1:23PM): I've got a growling stomach and
an impatient friend who's staring at me from across the table.
Rain check (on the flirting)?

I set my phone on the table, eyeing the goodness set before me. The aroma of chicken salad and greasy French fries called my name. "This looks like heaven ready to explode in my mouth."

"That's what Neil said last night when he was taking off my navy Gucci dress slacks."

My hands stopped at the halfway point of sandwich-thrusting into my mouth.

"Simply stating 'my pants' would have been sufficient. And who the hell is Neil?"

"Sir Sucks-A-Lot," Dean said, taking a bite of his Greek salad. "And honey, those weren't just any pants. They were Gucci's twill blended wool. And they make my ass look fabulous."

"I guess that explains why Neil was taking off your pants in the first place."

Dean grinned. "Truer words have never been spoken."

A jolting bump forced the sandwich to fall from my hands and land half open on the kitschy diner table. *What in the ever-loving hell?* If Turtleneck was coming back for her seat, it was about to go down.

"Excuse me," was muttered over a man's shoulder as his dress-slack-covered ass—fantastic ass, mind you—moved past my chair and toward the doors. His face was too buried in his phone to realize he had just barreled through my lunchtime fun.

"*Jesus,*" I grumbled. "Does everyone in New York have to be so pushy? I mean, how hard is it to watch where you're going instead of knocking into everyone?"

Dean tilted his head to the side, eyes focused toward the front of the restaurant. "I think that was Mr. Brooks."

"What?" I turned in my chair and watched as my boss's tall frame walked out of the restaurant and onto Fifth Avenue.

An incoming TapNext message icon lit up my screen.

"Yep," Dean agreed. "That's definitely him. I'd know that body anywhere. Broad shoulders. Sexy forearms. Perfectly toned ass. The things I'd do to that man."

"Horny much?"

"Nah." He waved me off. "I'm still recovering from having all the horny sucked out of me last night."

"On that note," I announced, standing from my seat. "I think I'll go order another sandwich. Be right back."

"I'll be here, doll face."

While I stood in line, I took a gander at what else Ruck had sent my way.

BAD_Ruck (1:25PM): Can't wait. Enjoy your lunch, Rose.

Two things stood out in my mind.

1. I wanted to chat more with **BAD_Ruck.** Which was crazy, considering we had been introduced by a gargoyle of dickish proportions.

2. How had I not known Kline Brooks had such a tight ass? And more importantly, if his ass looked that good *in* pants, what did it look like without them?

CHAPTER 6

Kline

"I found the perfect date for you Friday night," my mom claimed in my ear as I walked out of my office to head home for the night.

I didn't even have to think about it.

"No."

I pulled the door shut behind me and walked slowly down the hall and around the corner to the main office space.

"She's twenty-nine, long dark hair, well kept and attractive—"

"No."

"Her name is Stacey Henderson. I don't know if you've been at any social engagements that she's attended in the past—"

Stacey Henderson? Oh, *hell* no.

She *was* well kept and extremely attractive. And an eleven in vapidity on a scale from one to ten.

"Mom. *No.*"

"She's really excited—"

"Mom—"

"Said she had just the thing to wear—"

"Mom," I snapped, finally speaking firmly enough to earn her attention.

"What?"

Excuse. I needed an excuse.

My marketing director's back and bright red hair caught my attention from across the office, and the words left my lips before I could think of anything else.

"I already have a date."

"Oh. Oh dear. Well, I guess I'll have to call Stacey and cancel, then—"

"Yes!" I agreed eagerly. "Cancel Stacey."

Her voice turned suspicious.

"Kline—"

"Gotta go, Mom. Have to touch base with my date."

Convince her to go with me.

"Kline—"

"Loveyoubye."

With a tap of my thumb, I hung up fast, hoping I wouldn't find myself in too much hot water for ending the call so quickly but desperate enough to end the conversation that I didn't care.

Thirty-four years old and, if anything, my mother was "mothering" me the most she had in my entire life. Wanting a respectable woman to take under her wing and claim as her own was a powerful motivator, apparently, compelling her to meddle like she'd never meddled before.

Most of the time I gave in, but living with Walter on a day-to-day basis was a pretty unforgettable lesson. The grumpiest cat in Manhattan—if not the world—lived with me, and it was all my mother's fault.

I don't want you to be lonely, she said.

We're traveling too much to take care of him, she said.

You'll love him, and he'll love you, she said.

Ah, to go back in time.

There were days I actually avoided going home—to *my* apartment—because Walter lived there.

But that was a subject for another time.

I crossed the office quickly, my shoes slapping out a muted rhythm on the marble tile and a whistled tune flying from my lips.

Georgia Cummings.

My employee and the cure for my Stacey Henderson-themed nightmares.

She'd been working for my company for a couple of years now, but as I approached, I realized I'd never actually *looked* at her in all that time.

A glance here, a smile there, a professional exchange every week or so. But I'd never studied her body the way I was now.

I knew I hadn't.

Because I sure as fuck would have remembered.

Petite in stature but curvy in shape, her body was a perfect pint-sized hourglass perched precariously on top of razor-thin five-inch stilettos.

Her goddamn calves looked like they had been carved out of granite, and the rounded cheeks of her ass grabbed on to my eyes and refused to let go.

She moved slightly as I got closer from behind, and she bent at the waist to do something in the filing cabinet in front of her.

The gloriously short filing cabinet.

I watched as she went about her business, wondering how I'd managed to so effectively blind myself to her. I worked really hard at treating every single employee with fairness and without prejudices. I could remember the looks Dean had given me when he'd thought I wasn't looking, and the friendly crinkles at the corners of Pam's eyes. *The devil was in the details*, my dad had always told me, and I did my best to notice them. Except for hers.

As I tried to picture her smile from memory—*and couldn't*—I knew all of my compartmentalizing engines must have been running at full fucking steam to protect me from getting into something I shouldn't.

But those engines weren't running now, the override switch

turned and fully engaged thanks to Meddling-Mom-Maureen, and as the fabric of Georgia's creamy white dress pulled tight over her ass, alarms started blaring.

"My neck."

A sway of her tight-white-fabric-covered hips accompanied her off-key singing.

Something told me she didn't know I was standing behind her.

"My back."

More torture in the opposite direction.

"Lick my pussy—"

Ears bleeding. Pants tightening.

"—and my crack."

Holy. *Fuck.*

I had to stop her before it got even worse. *Better.*

Quickly, I shook my head to clear it and then reached forward to tap her smooth shoulder.

Hair flung out in an arc, she turned on her heel at warp speed, her eyes widening in horror as she pulled on a white cord to release an earbud from her ear.

"Shit."

I smiled. Her eyes widened impossibly further.

"Mr. Brooks. I'm so sorry." She clamped her eyes shut in shame. "I didn't know anyone else was still here."

Her face was mostly hidden in shadow as she tilted it to the ground, but I was still almost positive I saw her mouth the word 'shit' again.

"It's all right," I offered, and her head snapped up in question. I grinned slightly. "The singing and the shits. In fact, if you really need to, you can say it again."

Her face froze in shock.

"I can tell you want to," I prodded. "Maybe even three or four more times."

"Three. Four." She shrugged helplessly. "Forty, maybe."

"Forty shits?" I questioned, raising a brow in amusement.

"Depends on how much you actually heard, I guess."

I craned my neck to one side and back again.

"I'm not sure. I'm feeling particularly attuned to your neck and back, and, well, the rest I'm not sure I can say in an office environment."

"Oh my God," she cried and sank her face into her hands, embarrassment renewed.

"Definitely forty shits. Maybe even fifty."

I coughed on a chuckle before tucking it away, knowing it was the perfect time to get on with what I needed.

"It's okay. I know how you can redeem yourself."

Her gaze jerked up from the floor and her eyes widened with hope. "Yeah?"

"Tomorrow night. Go to the benefit for the Children's Hospital with me."

Horror contorted her face into a scrunched-up version of itself. Not *exactly* what I was going for.

"What? Go to the...with you... No." She shook her head frantically, desperately even, her bright red hair swinging to and fro before settling helplessly on the white fabric at her shoulders.

"No."

I had to admit, the double, *emphatic* nos threw me a little. It wasn't that I thought no one could turn me down. They could, and hell, they probably should. But they hadn't in a long time.

Not in a *very* long time.

"You're busy?" I offered as an excuse, hoping her visible discomfort was more about being caught off guard than anything else.

One slim wrinkle formed between her eyebrows, and the corners of her eyes seemed to pinch together slightly. "No. Not busy."

Ouch.

For the first time in quite a while, I struggled to find my words. "I...uh...well. Okay."

She forced a fake smile in response.

And yet, I couldn't bring myself to give up.

Walking around her desk and into her space enough that she backed up a couple of steps, I leaned my ass into the surface behind me and crossed my arms.

She rubbed goosebumps from her arms in a nervous fidget.

"So, how definite is this 'no'? Is it an 'I'm mildly considering it, but I'm thinking no' or a 'not a snowflake's chance in hell no' or maybe somewhere in the middle where negotiation lives?"

She shook her head as if mystified and tapped the toe of her stiletto twice.

My gaze shot down the length of her legs and back again, only to find her bright cerulean eyes narrowed slightly at the end of my circuit.

"I'm not disgusted with you, if that's what you're asking, but negotiation isn't likely."

Jim Carrey inhabited my body and took over my vocal chords before I could stop him. "So you're telling me there's a chance?"

"What the hell is going on here?" she snapped softly at the ceiling, almost as if to herself. Her eyes jumped to me. "Why are you asking me out? Why now? None of this is making any sense."

The only thing I could do was give it to her straight. Whether it was a good thing or not, I never could stop the honesty. It was just my nature.

"Look. For some godforsaken reason, society has decided to care about my completely uninteresting life because I have money, and because tabloid fodder is way more important than donations or time volunteered, they want me to have a date at every function I attend. Normally, this wouldn't be an issue, as in they can go fuck themselves, but in another slap of fate, my mother has decided she cares. Wants a daughter-in-law and grandbabies and all that crap."

Her previously peachy-tan skin blanched white.

"But she has terrible taste, and though I know next to nothing about you, you're already guaranteed to be better than any of my other options."

"Gee, thanks."

"Trust me, I intended that as an insult to the others, not you."

"Right."

"I'm not trying to marry you, though I'm sure I'll enjoy our time together endlessly—"

"I'm sure."

I couldn't help but smile at her mockery.

"I'm trying to avoid ending up with another chattier, day-spa-loving version of Walter."

"Walter?" she asked with good reason.

"My cat."

Incredulity warred with confusion on her face, pulling her lips out flat to the sides and back again several times.

I knew I was talking her in circles. I just hoped her confusion would lead to grudging acceptance.

Just when I feared she'd chew her lip raw if she kept on at that pace for much longer, she broke the silence with one simple question. "Why me?"

Once again, honesty prevailed.

"Because you're here."

She pursed her lips around the sour of my words, but as I tore my gaze away to look into her bright blue eyes, I knew I wasn't done.

Not with her, not with this conversation, and not with being stupid for the day.

"And you're fucking beautiful."

CHAPTER 7

"Beautiful?!" I shrieked, slamming the door to my apartment behind me. The walls shook from the undeserved abuse. "For fuck's sake, all it takes is one guy—who's never even been on your *let's get naked together* radar—to call you beautiful and you're acting like some desperate hussy! Really? *Really?* That's all it takes?" I dropped my purse to the floor and kicked off my heels. "Where is your pride, you stupid hussy! Where is your *fucking pride*?"

Cassie barreled out of her room like a herd of buffalo with a curling iron in hand and the cord trailing behind her, startling me enough that I slammed my ass into the counter of our island.

"Where's the stupid hussy?" she yelled, eyes manic and searching.

I rolled my own eyes dramatically, too pissed at myself to laugh at her antics. "You're looking at her!" I pointed at myself like a lunatic. "She's here! She's right fucking here!"

"Oh," she sighed, losing her aggressive stance, dropping the unlikely weapon to her side, and standing straight at once. "You don't count. I thought there was *actually* a stupid hussy out here you needed to be saved from. I was ready to throw down and beat some ass."

"Oh, I am a stupid hussy. A pathetic slut who's a disgrace to our gender. Trust me."

"Nooooo, you're not. You're a Wheorgiebag, but even that isn't a *real* whore. Whores have excessively loose vaginas. I'm talking big enough to store all of their whoring money, and yours has never even been open for business. Probably couldn't even fit a nickel."

She had a point. My vagina was sealed tighter than Fort Knox. A proverbial "do not pass go" zone for all cockbandits begging entry. It wasn't because I was a prude or saving myself for marriage. I had just never found the right guy I deemed worthy of thrusting into my goodie bag.

Maybe I was too picky. Maybe my sex therapist mother had driven me to insanity. Or maybe my expectations of waiting to do the deed with a man I had an actual connection with were unrealistic in this day and age. I mean, the plethora of dick and sac pics floating around social media could've been evidence of this.

Don't even get me started on the reaction I received from men when they found out I was a single, twenty-six-year-old woman with an unclaimed V-card. I might as well have told them I was a unicorn who could shoot sparkles out of my ass.

And it wasn't like I was averse to *all* sex. I was a big-time advocate for oral. Well, as long as there was a giving and receiving clause in the agreement. Call me crude, but if I'm going to suck it, you're going to eat it. Period. End of story.

Despite the shocked reactions and stigma revolving around being a woman who had made it through college with her virginity still intact, I stuck to my guns, refusing to just *give it up* to whoever was hard and willing. It wasn't a statement of abstinence or strong religious views. It was just me, being myself, and doing what I thought was right for me.

That's the most important thing when it comes to a woman's sexual prerogative. She should decide what she really wants without being influenced by social norms or penis peer pressure.

"You're doing it again," Cassie interrupted my thoughts.

I tilted my head, confused. "What am I doing?"

"You're doing that 'this is why I'm still a virgin' inner monologue thing. Do I need to turn on the fireplace for a bra-burning ritual? Or should we throw out the razors and let our pit hair run rampant?"

"You're a pain in my ass." I laughed. I couldn't help myself.

"I love you too, my beautiful, virginal best friend."

I ignored Cassie's shit-eating grin and strode for the fridge. Lord knew there was a giant glass of wine with my name on it.

"Let's hear it," she demanded, plopping down at the kitchen table. "Why are you a stupid hussy?"

Grabbing a bottle of moscato from the fridge, I filled a coffee mug to the brim. "I don't want to talk about it. It's too embarrassing."

"Uh-huh. Sure you don't. That explains why you were just talking *to yourself* about it." She eyed me with a pointed look. "Spit it out, Georgia Rose."

I shook my head, taking a giant swig of sugary wine.

Cassie stared.

I shook my head again.

Her eyes did that scary death glare thing where I started to be concerned for my well-being.

"Okay," I relented, holding both hands in the air like I was being held at gunpoint. "Okay. But you have to cool it on the creepy eyes first. You're wigging me out."

She smiled. "Works like a charm. Every. Single. Time."

I groaned.

"So," she encouraged, gesturing with her hand. "What has your panties in such a twist?"

"Kline asked me out."

"*Kline?* Who's Kline?"

"Kline Brooks…Mr. Brooks…" I offered, jogging her memory.

"Holy fucking goat scrotums! *Kline Big-dicked Billionaire*

Brooks? Your crazy-hot, super-rich boss?" she continued before I could utter a response. "Say *whaaaaaaat?* How in the hell did this happen?"

"First of all, what do you mean by 'how in the hell did this happen?' I might be a virgin, but I'm not a two-bagger. I can look pretty when I actually take the time to brush my hair."

"Oh, cool your jets. You're gorgeous and you know it. Kline Brooks would be one lucky son of a bitch to score a date with you."

"And how do you know he has a big dick? You've seen him once. And it was a five-second 'Oh, that's my boss, Kline' conversation while we were walking across the parking lot. You haven't even met him in person."

"Five seconds is all I need." She tapped the side of her head. "You know my cockdar is off the chain. I can sense a giant swinging penis pendulum from at least ten miles away. It's a God-given talent, Georgie."

I choked on my wine. "Let's not bring God into this."

She raised an eyebrow. "God knows the G-spot needs a more than adequate-sized wiener to get the job done."

"I'm pretty sure that comment just got you wait-listed for heaven."

"Probably." She shrugged. "Tell me you said yes to Big-dicked Brooks."

"Stop calling him that!" I shouted, unable to hold back laughter.

"Oh, c'mon, Virgin Mary, you know your boss has that *'Hello, ladies, I'm packing'* swagger." She waggled her eyebrows. "Tell me you said yes to him. For the love of God, tell me you're going on a date with him."

"He's not my type."

"Georgie," she groaned. "He's handsome. He's successful. He's not propositioning you for a five-dollar blow job. What's not to like? I don't get it."

"Five-dollar blow job? What are you even talking about?"

"Obviously, *bad* propositions." She held out both hands, irritated. "Even the worst blow job—with teeth and chapped lips and poor suction—is worth more than five bucks."

I sighed. "Look, he has like eleventy bajillion dollars in his bank account. His suits cost more than our apartment. We are not on the same level. Not even close."

"First off, that's not a number. Secondly, who the fuck cares? Why are you judging him by his money?"

"I'm not judging."

She nodded, eyes wide. "Oh, yes you are. You're totally judging."

"But…he's…"

"Stop it." A stern finger was pointed in my direction. "Stop being judgy."

Was I really judging Kline by his money?

And more importantly, did he really have a big d-i-c-k?

"You're going on a date with him, aren't you?"

I feigned confusion. "I have no idea what you're talking about."

"You little hussy! You're freaking out because you said yes, didn't you?!"

Her evil, victorious laugh pushed me over the edge. "Fine!" I shouted. "He called me 'fucking beautiful' and I folded like a deck of cards. I might as well have lifted my skirt and spread my legs for him. I was pathetic. Like some swooning, teenage girl. I said yes because he tossed a goddamn compliment in my direction!"

"God, I'm sure it's going to be absolutely terrible for you. Having to go on a date with a rich, successful, gorgeous man who also happens to give you compliments." She feigned shock. "Oh, the humanity!"

I stared at Cassie for a good three seconds before her words sank in. And then, I couldn't stop myself from laughing after muttering, "You're such a bitch."

Maybe I was being a tad bit ridiculous over this whole scenario. It was just one compliment. And I only agreed to one date. How bad could it be?

Darth Vader's dark side ringtone filled the room, vibrating my phone across the counter.

Incoming Call Dr. Crazypants

"Ugh," I sighed. "It's my mom. Lord help me, I'm not in the mood for her randomness." I sent her call to voicemail, too tired to keep up with her rambling.

My mom, otherwise known as Dr. Savannah Cummings, was a force to be reckoned with. She spent her days counseling couples and her nights doing God only knows what with my father. Sex therapy was her game and bringing sexy back into the bedroom was her claim to fame.

And yes, I was well aware of the "sex therapist named Cummings" irony. My mother was too. Several years ago, she had made a point to use that satire to her advantage—on a *billboard*, hovering over a *main* interstate that led straight into *New York City*.

Her slogan: "Dr. Cummings wants you to *come*…visit her brand new office."

Needless to say, eighth grade was a pretty hard year for me.

Conversations with Savannah mostly consisted of small talk about my dating and sex life and her usual spiel about the importance of masturbation. *"Make sure you're masturbating at least once a day, Georgia Rose. It's imperative for your sexual health."*

My mother, the sex therapist, was a bit of a weirdo. But she was my weirdo and I loved her dearly. I just couldn't handle her open-ended questions and virginity interrogation at the moment.

I downed the rest of my wine and slammed it on the counter. "I'm calling it a night. I'll see you on the flipside, Casshead."

"Night, Wheorgiebag."

Without wasting time, I did the usual bedtime routine—face washed, teeth brushed, and comfy sleep clothes applied—and happily plopped my tired ass into bed.

But sleep refused to come.

My brain had reached the hamster-on-a-wheel stage of insomnia.

Thoughts raced and unanswered questions refused to leave. I kept replaying Kline asking me out, over and over again. And all I could think was, why me? What made him all of a sudden show interest in me?

"And you're fucking beautiful."

I wasn't dealing with a shortage of self-esteem by any means. I considered myself an intelligent, attractive, confident chick. Now, I wouldn't go as far as saying I was perfect by any stretch of the imagination, but I knew how to highlight my strengths and downplay my weaknesses. Heavy makeup, spandex, and the color yellow were always a hell no. Long hair, red lips, and a pair of well-fitting jeans that accentuated my ass were always a hell yes.

My confusion over Kline asking me out wasn't about my attractiveness.

I'd never had a man like him on my radar.

We were total opposites.

He had a chauffeur. I took the subway. He wore Armani. I shopped at vintage, secondhand shops. He had enough money to invest in things like hedge funds and annuities. I had a fifty-dollar bond from 1996 that my grandmother had gifted me on my birthday. Fingers crossed that baby would gain another two dollars and twenty-five cents this year.

My life and his life were pretty much worlds apart.

Or was Cassie right? Was I judging Kline Brooks by the fact that he had more money than God? Or was I just freaked out over the fact that my boss, the CEO of Brooks Media, had asked me out?

My dating experiences hadn't been the best. They generally ended on epically bad notes. So, what would happen if Kline and I dated a few times and the shitstorm that was my overall luck with men took over?

Fuck.

I had to do something to take my mind off things. It was time to take things into my own hands. Literally. There was no sleep aid better than a climax-induced coma. Just one shot from the orgasm bottle and I'd be out like a light, racing thoughts and restless nights be gone.

Grabbing my vibrator, I lay back, spread wide, and pictured Chris Hemsworth in all of his Thor glory. I'd been on a recent Avengers kick—Captain America, Thor...hell, even Black Widow when I was feeling frisky. Scarlett Johansson in that black leather suit could make a lot of women switch-hit.

A few minutes into my fingerbating session, Thor's hammer was hard and ready. Things were feeling good. Real fucking good. Muscles were tight, fingers were moving at the perfect pace, and Amen for my vibrator, the glorious little clit tickler that he was. I was on the brink, white spots dotting my vision, and then, Thor and his hammer cock slowly morphed into someone else. Someone I had never fantasized about before.

Kline.

He was hovering over me, his hot, naked body mere inches from mine. That body—good God, that body. Lean, tight, toned muscles. So many fucking muscles. Washboard abs and that perfect V pointing right down to his...um...*yeah...Big-dicked Brooks.*

Hot damn, Cassie was right.

He had the kind of cock you could make a five-second GIF out of and never get tired of watching it on loop. I was convinced, somewhere down the line, Kline's dick had a great-great-great-great grandfather dick, and it was that exact shaft that had inspired some woman to pull down a guy's pants and say, "Oh yes, I need to suck on that." This was a history-making, Nobel Prize award-winning cock. The sole reason the blow job was an actual thing.

"I can't wait to taste you," he whispered, *sliding my panties down my legs.*

Yes. Hell. Yes. Taste me.

"God, you're fucking beautiful." He licked across my stomach.

"Your cock is beautiful," I said.

He kneeled between my legs. "Tell me how bad you want my cock, Georgia." Blue eyes scorched my skin as he stroked that perfect dick.

"Bad. So bad," I begged.

"Be patient, sweetheart." He smirked. "I can't wait to fuck you, but right now, I need your taste on my tongue."

Kline gripped my thighs, spreading me wide, while his head was between my legs doing everything a guy should know how to do with his tongue.

"Oh, fuck," I moaned, gripping his hair and following the movements of his mouth with my hips.

"Come for me, Georgia," he demanded.

And like a goddamn romance novel cliché, I came on command...*on my boss's face.*

I was panting. Drained. Sated. My muscles were lax, skin peppered with a sheen of sweat. I had thoroughly worked myself over. When I opened my eyes, I realized I had just gone to a place I could never come back from.

Kline Brooks had just been inaugurated into my spank bank rotation.

And he'd given me the best orgasm I'd had in a long fucking time.

CHAPTER 8

Kline

"So the Sure Romance contract went through as expected. Martin folded like a fitted sheet at the threat of..." Georgia recited as if rehearsed, her attention drifting from the lights overhead to the paperweight on my desk, out the window, and back again.

She'd been trying her damnedest not to look at me since she'd knocked on the door of my office two minutes ago.

"Wait," I interrupted, startling her enough that her eyes found my face. "Aren't fitted sheets hard to fold?" I kicked one corner of my mouth up in a grin, adding, "Mine sure as hell are. Is there some secret I'm missing out on?"

Bewilderment forced her eyebrows together and her plump bottom lip out.

I could see the thoughts race through her eyes one after the other, wondering what we were talking about and why we were talking about it at the same time she questioned the likelihood that *I* was the one who actually folded my sheets, rather than a maid, a butler, or several servants, perhaps.

Once she realized I was teasing her, the lines of her face transformed from confused to punishing.

"Sorry," I apologized, easing from a grin into a full-blown smile. "Continue."

"Right." She huffed adorably. "As I was saying, Martin…"

Her words muffled into a simple rhythm of soothing sounds as my concentration transferred to my thoughts.

Two years of listening to Georgia Cummings talk about product placement and commercial budgets didn't hold a candle to one fucking day of actually talking to her. The flustered, less professional, overtly female version one simple encounter had turned her into, that is.

She was still poised, as always, knowledgeable, and completely on top of her tasks and obligations. But her looks lingered longer—when she forgot to think about being awkward—and her humor lived at the surface, just at the tip of her quick-witted tongue, instead of buried under layers of propriety and boss-employee relations.

Put simply, I looked different to her, and, with her hair swept up off of the smooth, slim column of her neck and her eyes bright with mischief, she sure as fuck looked different to me.

"Mr. Brooks!" she called, fiery and peeved that I wasn't listening to her with full attention.

"Kline," I corrected, thinking about the way she'd sounded singing about her pussy and the faces I thought she'd make while I finger-fucked it, and then waited for her to agree with popped brows.

"Fine," she consented. "*Kline*."

God, I needed to hear her say that while she came.

I smiled again and fought the urge to adjust my tightening pants under my desk.

"Good."

She didn't seem nearly as amused. I forced my mind to the mildly professional side of its coin when she crossed her arms over her chest and tapped a toe on the tile. After years of keeping every exchange with employees above board, I'd never felt such a blatant need for betrayal by my eyes. They wanted to be bad. They wanted to be *really* bad. And my stupid cockblock of a brain wouldn't let them.

"Look, I trust you." Her feathers unruffled slightly. "Do I want to know that the deal went through? Absolutely. Do I need to know the details and question your every move? Not so much."

She unwound her arms from her chest.

"In fact, I'm headed to L.A. tonight, and I need someone to hold down the fort. Can you handle it if I tell everyone to report to you?"

Her spine straightened involuntarily, outrage at having to be asked tensing all of the muscles around it. "Of course I can."

I studiously ignored her irritation.

"I'm not expecting you to solve every issue that comes your way. Just keep the ship afloat and the piratelike crew members from setting her ablaze."

"Done."

She traced a circle on the front edge of my desk, and I could practically *see* her effort to be casual. "So you're, uh—"

She tucked an imaginary strand of hair behind her ear. Not a single one had been out of place.

"You're headed to L.A., huh?"

I bit my lip in victory. She was asking because she wanted to know. She *wanted* to go out with me, she just hadn't accepted it yet.

"Yep."

"Oh…okay. So, um—"

"Quick trip," I said, letting her off the hook. "Just a couple of investor meetings and then right back to the East Coast. I'll be back in plenty of time for Friday night."

"That's cool," she muttered, clasping her hands together like she didn't know what to do with them.

I had a few ideas, but most of them came from the brain downstairs. And I didn't think she'd be extremely welcoming of them at this stage of the game.

"Georgia?"

Her attention jumped from the floor straight to my gaze. The vivid depths of her eyes' blue, swirling with a heady mix of excitement and uncertainty, nearly knocked the wind out of me.

"I'm looking forward to it."

"Looking forward to it?"

"Friday night, with you." Her clasped hands turned white with pressure, and a blush colored the apples of her cheeks. "I wouldn't miss it."

Her face softened briefly, overwhelmed by a powerful look of longing. Fifteen seconds later, when determination replaced it, her sweet jaw flexing under the pressure, I wasn't sure it had ever existed.

In contrast to the harsh hue of her features, her voice was nothing more than a whisper. "Are you sure this is a good idea?"

I considered her question carefully instead of firing out some bullshit answer. I knew the reason she was asking, and it wasn't trivial. I was her *boss*, and for all she knew, I had plans to fuck and forget. There were no guarantees that anything would really bloom between us, and we'd both feel the fallout. She was an asset to my company, and I signed her checks. Everyone would argue she had more to lose, but I wasn't as sure.

Cynthia in HR would ride my ass for a decision like this—because, regardless of the absence of an actual no-fraternization policy, interoffice romance was *always* messy, especially when one of those employees was the boss. She knew it as well as I did, and I might have even known it better. But as I sat there looking at Georgia's face, my big fucking desk in between us, the only thing I could think about was being closer, standing next to her, escorting her as I walked with a hand at the perfect swoop of her lower back—*smelling the sweet curve of her neck and nibbling it with my teeth.*

Maybe I was blind, but as far as I could see, it was the best goddamn idea I'd ever had.

Her gaze followed me as I stood up and pushed my chair back, circling the desk and settling my hips into it a mere foot in front of her. She wanted to move back, I could see it, but she held her ground anyway, ready to listen to whatever I had to say.

I crossed my feet at the ankles and clasped my hands together in front of my thighs.

"I get it."

Her bottom lip rocked as she chewed at the inside of it. My vision locked on to the movement like a heat-seeking missile. With effort, I forced my eyes back to hers.

"I get why you're nervous, and I get the kinds of things a leap of faith could cost you. All I can promise is that I won't be a prick."

Surprised eyebrows ate up half of the distance to her hairline.

"Whatever happens between me and you, Kline and Georgia, is a completely separate entity from what happens under the umbrella of Brooks Media between Mr. Brooks and his Director of Marketing. My employee is efficient, well liked, and boasts a seasoned track record of success. Mr. Brooks has seen it, paid attention to it, and appreciated it for a while now. But Kline..." I laughed. "Well, that guy's been an idiot."

A small hiccuplike laugh bubbled up her throat and right out of her mouth before she could stop it.

"Because Georgia Cummings is a beautiful, smart, intriguing woman, and until yesterday, he hadn't seen her at all."

"Good God," she muttered to herself.

I smiled wholeheartedly, with nothing held back, and felt my heart jump in my chest when her eyes flared like she noticed.

"Kline *is* like Mr. Brooks in some ways, though. He *hates* to be stupid. And now that he knows, he's not too keen to be stupid ever fucking again."

She swung toward me on instinct, the movement excruciatingly slow and too fast to consider all at once. I grabbed her hips, squeezing them too hard, I knew, but I couldn't help it. The thought of leaving my mark on her skin had my hands clenching again.

Heat settled in my palms and shot straight to my crotch as I caught a whiff of all that was her. A mysterious mix of fruit and flowers, her scent stabbed me right in the fucking chest like some kind of olfactory voodoo doll.

I slid my hand up her side with little finesse before cresting her shoulder and forcing it into the tresses of her bright red hair at the back of her head.

Her eyes were open and searching and a whole lot frightened, but her lips moved toward mine with purpose. My fingertips flexed in her hair of their own accord, and a cross between a whimper and a moan caught right at the top of her throat.

"*Kline*," she whispered emphatically. The puff of her hot breath on my lips was enough to push me right over the goddamn edge.

"Knock knock," Leslie called *as* she was pushing open the door.

The two of us shot apart like Leslie's arrival was a hell of a skeet shooter and we were the clay pigeon. At the sudden release of so much sexual tension, I would have sworn shattered pieces of me littered the room.

My heart beat at double its normal speed, and Georgia's cheeks were the color of cherry Kool-Aid. Though, given the fact that *Kline* had been milliseconds away from eating *Georgia* alive, I'd say *Mr. Brooks'* and *Ms. Cummings'* level of faux composure was impressive.

"What do you need, Leslie?" I asked, straining to make my voice sound even, but she was clueless. Most of her attention focused inward, on herself, rather than the things going on around her. I swore it was the first and only time in my life I'd be thankful for that kind of woman.

CHAPTER 9

Georgia

It had been one of those days where staying in bed and calling in sick would have been a better option than actually participating in life. Kline Brooks left his new intern, Leslie, under my watchful eye while he flew out to L.A. for the day to schmooze investors and impress potential advertising clients for TapNext.

I was certain she had been sent straight from Hell. The devil might as well have wrapped a big red bow around her neck and attached a note.

Dear Georgie,
Have fun with this one.
Love,
Satan

I'd seen more of her tits today than I had of my own in the past month. Either she had a severe body temperature control issue or she didn't wear a bra. I didn't care who was setting the dress code policy; nipples would never be considered business casual.

Why Kline had hired her was a goddamn mystery at this point. And I hadn't even brought up her predilection for selfies. Her social media was busier than a Las Vegas escort during March Madness. Which I guess was fine—if only she'd put the same amount of work into her actual job.

Finally at home, I settled into my favorite pastime—sweatpants, a bag of sour cream and cheddar potato chips, and a DVRed episode of *Keeping Up with the Kardashians*. Despite the ridiculousness that this family had made a fortune off reality television, I still found myself recording every damn episode. It was a true mind-suck of valuable time and brain cells, but I couldn't deny my consistent guilty indulgence. What could I say? I was a *true* American—enjoying every trashy reality show produced for my viewing pleasure and shit-talking them the next day.

Kim had just declared that *women wearing the wrong foundation color is, like, the worst thing on the planet* when my phone rang.

Incoming Call Kline Brooks

What in God's name does he need now? He should've been on a plane headed home from L.A. His absence was the exact reason why I would have five pounds worth of potato chips on my hips and ass tomorrow morning. Two days ago, I would have told you he'd put stars in my eyes with swoony almost kisses and confidence in my ability. Now, after a visit to the depths of incompetency hell, the blush on my feelings had more than worn off.

That cocky, demanding bastard damn well knew what he had been doing when he'd asked me if I could handle being in charge.

After five rings' worth of muttered curses, I decided to put him out of his misery. "Good evening, Mr. Brooks. What *else* can I assist you with today?"

His hearty chuckle filled my ears. "I thought we were past the Mr. Brooks bullshit?"

"Yeah, not after today we're not."

"Rough day at work?"

Rough day? Was he serious? I was still trying to scrub my brain free of the moronic comments Leslie had made all day. "Your new intern is a gem. Quite the asset to the company, I might say. It's amazing how many selfies one woman can take in a fifteen-minute stretch, and yet, she can't seem to make a single photocopy in the same amount of time."

"I know she's got some time management issues, but she's a good kid, Georgie." There was a smile in his voice.

"After today, I honestly have no idea how you've gotten anything done for the past two weeks." I strived to be the type of woman who didn't judge other women by their brainpower, but Leslie made the Kardashians look intelligent.

"Are you concerned about my workload, sweetheart?"

Sweetheart? I hated that something as simple as Kline calling me sweetheart made my heart flip-flop inside of my chest. But it did. *Stupid heart.* The damn thing didn't have a clue. I cleared my throat, ignoring my body's reaction to his sweet sentiments. "Of course not. Why would I be concerned when *you're* the one who hired her? Plus, *you're* the one who continues to let *your* intern make a mockery of her job responsibilities."

"Is now the right time to tell you Leslie is a friend of the family? Her dad asked for a favor and I obliged. Plus, I've got Dean keeping an eye on her."

"Oh, so you're making Dean do your dirty work. I see how it is. That explains his bitchy mood today. I was worried Prada went out of business."

Kline laughed.

Good God, that laugh. It was crazy hot and had my body reacting in all sorts of dirty ways. "I'm kind of sad you didn't have Leslie reporting to Meryl."

"Meryl would have had my balls," he teased. "I've seen that woman make grown men cry. Hell, I've had to wipe a few phantom tears of my own. Plus, you asked for it."

I was two seconds away from giving him a telepathic beatdown when his voice turned warm and soft like honey. "Thanks for dealing with Leslie. I really appreciate it."

Did he just thank me? I pinched my arm just to make sure I wasn't dreaming. "Shit, that hurt." I winced.

"Everything okay?"

"Yeah. Just…stubbed my toe," I tossed out. "Sooooo…did you just call to see how truly awful my day was? Or is there something you actually need?"

"For starters, I wanted to make sure we're still on for tomorrow night."

I sighed. "Even though you threw me under the bus and have expressed little to no remorse, I'll be there. But it has nothing to do with you and everything to do with the delicious ten-course meal I know will occur."

"Duly noted." He laughed. "If their food isn't to your standard, I'll make it up to you. Dinner anywhere. Your choice."

"That's easy. BLT Prime."

"The steakhouse in Gramercy Park?"

"You betcha."

"Swanky digs." A low whistle left his lips. "Consider it a deal. I'll take you there Saturday night."

"Slow your roll, buddy. I haven't agreed to a second date yet."

"Yet," he retorted with a flirtatious tone. "Haven't agreed *yet*. And if it makes you feel better, you can think of it as more of a deal than a date. An *I'm sorry for leaving you with Leslie* kind of thing."

When had the tables turned? This wasn't the Kline Brooks I had grown accustomed to. He was the quiet, reserved, yet frequently demanding boss who made a point to keep me on my toes. Our interactions consisted of cursory emails and business meetings to assess my current game plan for Brooks Media's promotions strategy.

This playful, charismatic man requesting my presence at dinner dates and effortlessly turning me on in his office was a complete stranger. I couldn't deny my enjoyment out of seeing this side of him, but dear God, it was completely knocking me off my game. I felt like a fish out of water, floundering for an equally charming response.

And seriously, when had I started wanting to appear enchanting to the enigmatic Kline Brooks?

I cleared my throat. "Mr. Brooks, w-why did you call me?"

"Ms. Cummings, why are we being so formal tonight? I thought we got past the formality bullshit."

He was probably right. *I'd say it happened around the time he pulled my hips into an impressively unprofessional erection in his office two days ago.*

"Okay, *Kline*," I agreed with a mouthful of sass. I didn't really want him referring to me by my middle school joke of a last name anyway. "If you're not calling to chat about work, why are you calling me?"

"I actually need a favor. Are you busy?"

"No, not really. I'm just sitting here…" I paused, reaching for the remote and turning down the volume. Even though we were past "formalities," my boss didn't need to know about my reality show obsession. "Just sitting here reading through emails."

He chuckled into the phone. "I'm sure those emails can wait until tomorrow. I'm in a bit of a bind. Can you turn on ESPN?"

"ESPN?"

"The Western University-New York State game is on. Thatch and I can't get the fucker to stream on the plane. I *need* to know what's happening."

Thatcher Kelly, the ever-mysterious financial consultant of Brooks Media. He worked as a contractor, providing expertise for several companies, or so I'd heard, but no big money decision within Brooks Media happened without him. I'd heard his husky voice and boisterous personality on several conference calls. Even received emails with his signature sarcasm. But I'd never met the man. Hell, I'd yet to successfully locate an actual photo of him. All of his social media accounts were private and most had some random sports-related profile picture.

"This is life or death here, Georgia," Kline interrupted my

thoughts. "Thatch is a big New York State fan, and I've got five on the fact that his Tigers are no match for the Mustangs."

I scrunched my nose up. "So…what exactly do you need me to do?"

"I need you to give me the play-by-play for the next twenty minutes until we land."

"Isn't there anyone else you can bug? I'm probably not the best person for the job." The last football game I'd watched had been the Super Bowl where Janet Jackson's nipple had made its television debut, and I could honestly have told you more about her areola than the game. I literally knew zilch about sports, especially football.

"Please, Georgia." He rasped his words, confusing me by making me think about sex. "I'm begging you."

I held in my answer until I knew I wouldn't stutter. "You owe me. Big time."

"Anything you want, sweetheart."

The promise of his double meaning oozed from his voice, but I ignored him, grabbed the remote, and switched the channel. "Okay, it's on."

CHAPTER 10

Kline

Thatch waved his arms manically, trying to get an update. Our personal flight attendant flashed him a look of distaste, but with one quick wink, her contempt turned into consideration. I didn't have much to my name that said *billionaire*, but the private plane sure did. With the amount that I traveled and the necessary fluctuation in timing, it was just easier.

When his attention came back to me, I flipped him off, putting Georgia on speaker. "What's the score? How much time is left? Who has the ball?" I rambled, desperate to know if Western University was pulling through. Fucking Thatch wouldn't let me live it down if New York State won this thing. It was a nothing game—early season, Thursday night, and unquestionably obscure teams. But Thatch could turn anything into a competition, and he'd created this rivalry out of thin air years ago.

She gave us the rundown in succinct, inaccurate terms, but I got the gist of it.

Fourth quarter. Tigers were winning.

I cursed.

Thatch shouted, "Victory is mine!"

I'd honestly never seen a guy that big Riverdance.

"All of this for five measly bucks?" Georgia asked.

Thatch's loud, boisterous laugh echoed inside the cabin of the plane.

"No, not five *dollars*. A little more than that…"

"Five hundred?" Her voice was incredulous. I pictured Georgia's nose scrunching up in that adorable way of hers.

"Actually…" I cleared my throat. "Five grand."

"Five thousand dollars?" she shouted.

Internally, I cringed. Hell, externally, I cringed.

I probably sounded like a pretentious asshat. Betting exorbitant amounts of money on sports was not my usual M.O. "It's Thatch's fault. He won't take no for an answer and never bets anything less than a grand. He could be the poster child for gambling addicts everywhere. His only redeeming quality is that he actually knows how to invest his profits."

Thatch's smile mocked me. He knew what I was doing, exaggerating his faults to help minimize my own.

"Whatever you say, Mr. Moneybags."

Yeah, she definitely thought I was an ostentatious dick.

"Georgia girl, give me an update. What's going on?" Thatch schmoozed, laying it on thick just to get a rise out of me.

"Uh…" she mumbled, trailing off for a brief second. "Boobear just tackled somebody."

"Boobear? Who the fuck is Boobear?" Thatch mouthed in my direction.

I shrugged. "Who just got a tackle?"

"Boobear. He plays on the orange team," she repeated as though it made sense. "Oh no, I think Boobear is hurt."

It took some serious thinking, but I finally decoded the mystery. "Do you mean *Boudmare?*"

"Yeah, that's him. His nickname is Boobear."

"The commentators are calling him Boobear?" I asked, fighting a smile.

"No, I nicknamed him Boobear. He looks like a giant teddy bear. He's so cute!"

"Oh, dear God," Thatch groaned.

"Oh, thank goodness. Boobear is back up and on his feet. They're lining up again. White team has the ball. The big guy in the middle chucked it to the thrower guy. He threw the ball… really far…" She trailed off, and then the line went silent.

"Georgia?"

Nothing.

"Georgia!" I strived to grab her attention.

"What?" she snapped.

"The ball was thrown…*where?* What happened?"

"Coca-Cola threw it a bunch of yards to Stuart Little. They're lining up again near the touchdown box."

Coca-Cola? Stuart Little? Who in the hell was she talking about?

"Who is she talking about?" Thatch mouthed, arms wide in frustration. "I fucking knew we should've called Wes," he whispered, pacing the aisle.

"Help me out here," I said into the phone. "Who is Coca-Cola?"

"The quarterback on the white team."

"You mean Cokel?"

"Yeah, that's him."

"Is she fucking nicknaming the players?" Thatch boomed in disgrace.

"Uh-huh," she responded over what sounded like a mouthful of chips, not an ounce of shame in her tone.

I couldn't even get pissed at her. She was too fucking adorable. I glanced over at Thatch. He was wearing a figurative hole in the aisle carpet and practically pulling his hair out. I grinned. Even though I hadn't a clue what was happening in the game, watching Thatch's upset come to a crescendo was worth it.

"Touchdown!" she whooped. "Coca-Cola to Howie Mandel!"

Translation: *Cokel to R.J. Howard.*

"Fuck yes!" I cheered.

"Son of a bitch!" Thatch shouted.

"Go Wild Horses!" Georgia put in.

I chuckled. "That's right, sweetheart. The Mustangs are going to pounce on Thatch's pussy Tigers."

While my best friend was cursing up a storm, Georgia commentated the game for the rest of our flight. She added ridiculous nicknames for every player, called running backs' stutter steps *Icky Shuffle* steps, and gave her overall opinions on which player looked the most cuddly (Boobear, of course), the meanest, the nicest, etc. It was an endless list and I damn near forgot there was five grand and a long-standing rivalry between Thatch and me on the line.

Once we landed and were sitting with beers in our hands, watching the final five minutes of the game in the airport bar, I still kept Georgia in my ear.

I couldn't help myself. This woman whom I'd seen handle an entire boardroom full of cocky sons of bitches without batting an eye was crazy adorable. She was tough as nails and hotter than sin. And Christ, she was hilarious. I wanted more of her. A lot fucking more.

"Sorry your flight got delayed on the runway, but I'm glad you guys got home safely."

"Me too," I replied in half-truths, taking a swig of beer. I wasn't even remotely upset about the extra time I'd spent talking to her. "So, is it safe to say that Georgia Cummings is now a Western University fan?"

"Uh-huh." She giggled. "They kick ass."

"Next year, you'll have to come to a game with me. It's insane."

"Kline Brooks, are you still trying to plan a second date before we even go on a first?" she teased.

I laughed. "You'll find I'm a determined kind of guy."

"Ain't that the truth." She yawned. "Well, that's my signal to get my tired ass in bed. I guess I'll see you in the morning."

"Good night, Georgia girl," I said, stealing Thatch's endearment.

"Night," she whispered, ending the call.

I set my phone on the bar and downed the rest of my beer. "Ready to hit it?" I asked Thatch, tossing money down on the bar.

He just shook his head, sighing heavily. "Glad you got time for precious pillow talk during the *fucking game*."

I patted him on the shoulder. "Don't worry, sweetheart. I think Boobear will be healthy and ready to play next season."

"Fucking Boobear." He chuckled with another shake of his head. "Even I can't deny that's hilarious."

CHAPTER 11

Georgia

It was Friday—the big date night with my boss—and I was sitting on the subway, heading home from work a little early. Nerves were starting to get the best of me. My brain ran through a thousand possible scenarios of how the charity event with Kline would go. Most of them were awkward and ended with me doing something outrageous. It was my M.O. I had a serious propensity for word vomit. A certified foot-in-mouth expert.

I needed someone to talk me off the proverbial ledge or else I'd end up faking the flu and backing out last minute.

Cassie was a no-go. She had just boarded a flight to Seattle to photograph an up-and-coming football star who'd signed with the Seahawks. My beautiful, spunky best friend had made a name for herself as a freelance photographer. Her photos had graced the pages of The *Times*, *Cosmopolitan*, and even ESPN. It seemed her lens had a knack for hot men flexing their muscles. Shocker, huh?

My mother was a hell-no. Ever the sex therapist at heart, she'd probably offer her sage advice of rubbing one out pre-date to stave off nerves.

My finger hovering over the TapNext icon, I finally said, "Screw it." Maybe **BAD_Ruck** could make me feel better about this situation. We'd been chatting back and forth over the past few days, and despite the absurdity of our introduction to one another, I was really starting to like the guy. He was funny, laid-back, and could give good flirt. I spent a crazy amount of my day wondering what he was like in person. Did he really look like the guy in his profile? What did he do for a living? Where did he live in New York?

We hadn't shared any intimate details of our personal lives, a la *You've Got Mail*, which I preferred at the present time. We weren't living in the dial-up internet era of Kathleen Kelly, and it was a different world. For me, all of her dangers were magnified by a thousand—and she was worried Tom Hanks was a serial killer! These days, there was a show called *Catfish*. It seemed like people got off on it now more than ever. And, although Ruck was quite charming in our online conversations, I wasn't convinced he wasn't a complete weirdo in real life.

Funny how that didn't stop me from messaging him.

TAPRoseNEXT (2:15PM): Ruck? Come in, Ruck? I need someone to talk me off the ledge.

BAD_Ruck (2:16PM): We're talking proverbial ledge, right?

TAPRoseNEXT (2:16PM): Yes. Don't worry, I'm not literally standing on the ledge of a skyscraper.

BAD_Ruck (2:16PM): That's good news. So, tell me, why are we flirting with proverbial death?

TAPRoseNEXT (2:17PM): I've got a date tonight. I'm nervous. And freaking out. Big time.

BAD_Ruck (2:17PM): And here I thought I was the only man in your life. You wound me, Rose.

TAPRoseNEXT (2:18PM): Get over yourself. I would lay money on the fact that Mr. Charming himself has a date tonight too.

BAD_Ruck (2:18PM): Maybe.

TAPRoseNEXT (2:19PM): My point exactly. Now, help me out here.

BAD_Ruck (2:19PM): Okay. Let's start with the obvious. Why are you nervous?

Why was I nervous? That was the big question. I stared across the aisle, watching an older woman working on a crossword. The tip of her pen ran across the empty blocks as she tried to think of a four-letter word for 15A. "_____ comes trouble!"

Here comes trouble. Apt phrase for my present state. My mind had been shouting this from the second I had agreed to a date with Kline.

God, I was definitely freaking out over a bunch of things, and one thing, in particular, stood out the most.

TAPRoseNEXT (2:20PM): For one, I work with him. If things end up badly, I'm worried it could cost me my job.

BAD_Ruck (2:20PM): Ah, the old coworker conundrum. Did he ask you out? Or did you ask him out? And is it forbidden in your employee contract?

TAPRoseNEXT (2:21PM): He asked me. And I have no earthly clue. Was that something I was supposed to actually read?
BAD_Ruck (2:21PM): Okay. Different tactic. Does he normally date women he works with?

TAPRoseNEXT (2:22PM): No, never. Either that or he's a super sleuth about it. I'm not personally the office gossip, but I know someone with an ear to the ground.

BAD_Ruck (2:23PM): If he asked you out, and you've never seen him date any of your colleagues, he's probably thought this through. How long have you worked with him?

TAPRoseNEXT (2:23PM): A couple of years.

BAD_Ruck (2:24PM): And in that time, has he ever seemed like the kind of man who lets his personal life affect business?

TAPRoseNEXT (2:25PM): Actually, no. Picture of professional. Business always comes first with him.

BAD_Ruck (2:25PM): Then what's different now?

TAPRoseNEXT (2:26PM): I honestly don't know.

BAD_Ruck (2:26PM): Smart money says it's you, Rose.

He had a point. Kline Brooks had never given me any reason to doubt the decisions he made. He wasn't a player. He didn't make a show out of fucking anything in a short skirt and pair of heels that sashayed around the office.

Leslie was a perfect example. The girl was gorgeous and made a job out of flaunting her curves for the world to see. And I'd yet to see Kline act anything but annoyed with her—no salacious glances or devilish intents flashing across his eyes. He was ever the professional when his new intern was around. Most days, he was doing everything he could to push her off on someone else.

But my dating Kline equaled us getting to know each other on a more personal level. If one date turned into more, then eventually, he would know *other* things about me. Things I wouldn't normally want my boss to know.

TAPRoseNEXT (2:27PM): Can I be frank with you?

BAD_Ruck (2:28PM): I guess. I'm surprisingly partial to Rose.

TAPRoseNEXT (2:28PM): I said frank, not Frank, Ruck.

BAD_Ruck (2:29PM): Have you ever not been frank with me?

I laughed, startling the pen out of the crossword woman's hands.

"Sorry." I cringed, leaning forward and picking it up from the aisle.

"No worries, honey." She took the pen from my outstretched hand. "Two words for puppy amuser?" she asked, grinning.

"Chew toy," I answered.

"Aha! You're right! Thank you!" And that was that. She dove right back into her crossword, tuning the rest of the world out.

I replayed past convos with Ruck in my head. I tended to be pretty open and honest with him, maybe a bit too much. The other night I had kept him up until one in the morning discussing why most men thought anal sex was a good idea.

He'd ended the conversation with, "I'm not going to speak on behalf of all men, because let's face it, there are some real morons in my gender. But for me, when I really want a woman, I want to claim every part of her."

See what I mean? He gives damn good convo.

That response made me instantly jealous of the woman Ruck had set his sights on. Even I couldn't ignore the sexiness of Ruck going caveman and wanting to claim every part of her, whoever she was. *Lucky bitch.*

TAPRoseNEXT (2:30PM): There's another reason I'm nervous.

BAD_Ruck (2:31PM): Okay…

BAD_Ruck (2:32PM): Are you going to freely give this reason or is this an invitation to pry?

TAPRoseNEXT (2:33PM): Ugh…

BAD_Ruck (2:34PM): Do you have a foot fetish you're trying to hide?

TAPRoseNEXT (2:34PM): No. I don't even like my own feet, much less anyone else's.

BAD_Ruck (2:35PM): An ex-boyfriend's name tattooed across your lower back?

TAPRoseNEXT (2:35PM): I do not have a tramp stamp!

BAD_Ruck (2:36PM): Hairy back moles?

TAPRoseNEXT (2:36PM): I'm a lady, Ruck. I'm smooth everywhere.

BAD_Ruck (2:37PM): Damn, Rose. Stop talking dirty to me. We're trying to talk you off the ledge, remember? Not push me out onto it.

TAPRoseNEXT (2:40PM): I'm a virgin.

BAD_Ruck (2:41PM): An anal virgin?

TAPRoseNEXT (2:42PM): No. A certified, my-pussy-has-never-been-penetrated virgin.

BAD_Ruck (2:44PM): Jesus.

TAPRoseNEXT (2:45PM): That's sweet, but we don't have time to pray right now.

For what seemed like an hour, I watched the text box bubbles move as he gathered a response.

BAD_Ruck (2:48PM): This scenario deserves a prayer. Hell, it deserves an airplane banner with the words, "Get your shit together, men, because dreams can come true. There are still gorgeous, sexy, intelligent women out there who are saving themselves for the right guy." Christ, I think you might be the last twenty-something virgin in New York.

The last twenty-something virgin in NYC? *Gah.* That did *not* make me feel better. That made me feel a hell of a lot worse. I sounded pathetic.

TAPRoseNEXT (2:50PM): That's one crazy long banner. And thanks for the vote of confidence. I feel even worse about it now. I'm not a total prude, by the way. I've been with men. I know what a penis feels like in my mouth. I've just yet to find the right penis I deem worthy of sex.

BAD_Ruck (2:51PM): You're killing me right now. Do you even realize how rare you are, Rose?

Now, I do. I was the last twenty-something virgin in New York! I might as well have offered up my vagina to the Museum of Natural

History. Surely, it would be shown in the fossils display. I could already picture it, right beside Tyrannosaurus Rex's teeth.

The Last Virginal Vagina in New York.

Georgia Cummings 1990-2080

Died happily in her Chelsea apartment, surrounded by all sixteen of her tabby cats.

TAPRoseNEXT (2:53PM): Yeah, I'm the last single virgin in NYC. I might as well start stocking up on cat food because my future is looking very glum at the moment.

BAD_Ruck (2:54PM): Rose. Listen to me. This is not a bad thing. You're funny, intelligent, and obviously beautiful. And you're confident enough to know what you want and how you want it. Your confidence and self-respect are sexy as hell.

TAPRoseNEXT (2:54PM): Well, when you put it that way, I sound really awesome.

BAD_Ruck (2:55PM): Because you are. So, tell me why your sexual history is even factoring as a problem in your mind?

TAPRoseNEXT (2:57PM): My experiences in telling a guy I'm a virgin have never ended well.

The reactions I received were not usually great. I either became a challenge, where getting into my pants became their sole purpose in life, or treated like some pariah, as if my virginity was a problem that needed a solution. Sometimes, I wondered if it would be easier telling a guy I had crabs.

BAD_Ruck (2:58PM): I can imagine. Most of us are just grunting cavemen.

TAPRoseNEXT (2:59PM): Exactly. And I can't help but wonder what would happen if I told this guy I'm a virgin. He has potential. He could end up being more than just one date. I'm just worried if I tell him, I'll end up being a challenge instead of something more.

Wow. Even I was surprised by that response. Did Kline Brooks really have the potential to be something more?

BAD_Ruck (3:01PM): If he's worth your time, he won't see you as a challenge. Of course, he's going to be silently thanking God you're willing to give him the time of day, but he won't make a one-eighty and just focus on trying to get in your pants. And from what you've told me, he doesn't seem half bad. He apparently knows how to separate his personal life from business. And he doesn't have a reputation of screwing all of the women in your office. This isn't the New York norm.

Everything he said was true. Kline's track record was a good one. He wasn't plastered all over Page Six with a different woman on his arm. He wasn't known as some playboy. He was just Kline—handsome, attractive, and all-business Kline Brooks. Which only made me more curious what he was like outside of the office.

TAPRoseNEXT (3:04PM): So, let's just act like you're him for a second. When would you want the whole "I'm a virgin" bomb to be dropped?

BAD_Ruck (3:05PM): Before it got to the point where our clothes are off and I'm sliding a condom on.

TAPRoseNEXT (3:05PM): LOL. Obviously.

BAD_Ruck (3:07PM): If you're asking me when to bring it up…I don't really have an answer for you. It should come up organically. You know how dates go. Eventually, the whole sex topic does come up. Your being a virgin isn't a fucking crime, so don't feel like you have to confess it the second the date starts.

TAPRoseNEXT (3:07PM): Good point.

BAD_Ruck (3:08PM): Feel better?

TAPRoseNEXT (3:08PM): Consider me officially off the ledge.

BAD_Ruck (3:09PM): Fantastic. Good luck tonight.

TAPRoseNEXT (3:10PM): Thanks, Ruck. Enjoy your date with whomever the lucky woman may be.

BAD_Ruck (3:11PM): Dirty talk and a compliment in one convo? You're too good to me. And listen…

TAPRoseNEXT (3:12PM): LOL. Yeah?

BAD_Ruck (3:12PM): If all this advice turns out to be shit, I might be able to help you out with the cat acquirement. I know a guy.

TAPRoseNEXT (3:13PM): And that's my cue to officially end this convo. Bye, Ruck.

BAD_Ruck (3:12PM): Bye, Rose.

I hopped off the subway way uptown, and instead of heading to my apartment, my legs strode for the one place that always helped take my mind off things. It was a quarter after three. I had four hours to get my hair done, get ready, and meet Kline at the event.

If there was one thing I was good at, it was choosing a kick-ass hair color to suit my mood.

And if there was one thing Betty, my hair stylist, was good at, it was fitting me in last minute. She was a genius when it came to color and cut. If I told her blonde, she'd find the perfect shade to match my skin tone and have me trimmed, dyed, and out the door within two hours.

Hmm… From red to blonde? That might be the best idea I've had all day.

CHAPTER 12

Kline

"**N**ervous." I shook my head. "I can't believe I'm fucking nervous."

I guess Walter *was* having an effect on my life like my mother had predicted. Although, I highly doubted me talking to myself was what she'd had in mind.

That was what this was, though. It had to be. The illusion of someone being there, *listening,* and fooling me into saying all of my rambling thoughts out loud rather than reciting them internally.

Long and unkempt, his whiskers flowed freely from beneath his nose, and in keeping with his old man status, stuck out haphazardly from his kitty eyebrows. His white-rimmed eyes rooted me to the spot with their contempt, and the subtle stripes in his fur did nothing to soften his appearance.

"This is your fault," I told him, his wolflike ears mocking me with every word.

One uninterested lick of his lips is all he gave me in return.

"What? Nothing to say? No support?"

He licked his paw and wiped his face before turning abruptly and sauntering out of the room, holding his tail pointedly straight in the cat version of a middle finger salute.

"Thanks for nothing, asshole," I shouted after him.

Jesus.

I shook my head as I stepped in front of the mirror to adjust my tie. This was a whole new level of low. Not only was I talking to the fucking cat; I was *yelling* at him.

Tonight had my stomach on edge in a way it hadn't been since I'd given Tara Wallowitz my first kiss behind the gym after our seventh-grade dance. She'd had braces and I'd been drowning in all my awkward, barely-a-teenager glory. Two sets of fumbling hands, an overaggressive tongue, and a cut to my lips later, it was over.

I didn't foresee tonight with Georgia being like that at all, but the basis of my feelings was remarkably similar. Out of my element and thrown off by her initial lack of enthusiasm, I'd put in a lot of effort over the last couple of days to turn it around and smooth the way for tonight's date. But now I was invested. I *cared* how tonight went. And that hadn't been the norm in a long time. I felt a little like I was walking into a set-up with no tools to escape the consequences. That wasn't cool. MacGyver was cool, and he always made tools out of whatever he had. I'd have to do the same.

"Mr. Brooks?" my intercom squawked.

I grabbed my phone from the counter and jogged the five steps to press the button.

"Yeah?"

"Your driver's here."

"Thanks."

I snatched my wallet and keys off of the front table and slid out the door without looking at myself in the mirror again. I'd already spent far too much time questioning my tie color.

I was *not* the kind of guy who carefully considered every element of my outfit. Tonight was the closest I would ever get to contradicting that.

"Frank," I greeted as I approached the car, reaching a hand out to shake his. On days like today, I couldn't help but notice how much of his time I monopolized.

"Mr. Brooks." His greeting was warm, and he had a face to match. A smattering of wrinkles at the corners of his eyes pointed to a life filled with laughter, and the gray of his hair hinted at the possibility of a daughter or two.

"I wish you'd call me Kline," I said with a smile, knowing it would never change.

"I'm sorry, sir."

I shook my head and gave him a friendly slap on his shoulder with the hand not clasped in his. "Don't be sorry. I'm the one who should apologize—dragging your ass all over town all day and night."

"No trouble at all, sir."

I chuckled again. "This makes twelve hours in this shift, right?"

"Yes—"

"And you've still got the rest of the night to go?"

"It's no trouble, Mr. Brooks."

A nod was all I could give at the time, so I did. It was a gesture that made it possible to get on our way, to get to the benefit, and to get busy letting Frank off the hook. I'd embellish the not-nearly-enough gesture with a fatter-than-expected tip on the bill later.

I slid into the car and Frank closed the door behind me. I unbuttoned the coat of my tuxedo and pulled at the lapels to make it stop feeling like it was choking me.

As Frank climbed into his seat, he spoke again. "Another stop, sir?"

Forced to give an answer I didn't like, I shook my head. "No. Straight to the benefit."

He nodded and pulled the gearshift into drive. "Yes, sir."

I'd been hell-bent on picking Georgia up like a proper date, but apparently, on this matter, she had a closer relationship with the devil. Refusal was too kind a word to describe her reaction when I had suggested my driver would pick her up. In fact, she'd looked like the suggestion was more revolting than stepping in dog shit.

And I understood to a point. I personally hated taking the car, preferring immeasurably to take the subway and people-watch. I didn't even mind walking fifteen blocks on a nice Manhattan day.

But certain aspects of my life demanded the car. It kept me on schedule during the day, on time to the office, and never late to meetings. Without the motivation of someone like Frank waiting on me, and the desire to respect his time, I'd have been late everywhere I went.

I liked to wander too much, experiment with new spots in the city and observe people as they met and chatted and said goodbye.

Human behavior was fascinating, and I found the more I studied it, the easier it was to manage all of my people-based businesses.

I glanced down at my phone, feeling guilty for checking it on my way to my first date with Georgia, but at the same time, not being able to help myself.

Nothing. All quiet.

My conversation from that afternoon with the mysterious Rose burned in my mind. I hated the fact that any woman would feel like being a virgin was something to be ashamed of or even be embarrassed to talk about it. But I was also a man, and fuck, it wasn't a stretch to understand why. I could feel myself becoming more and more irrational the longer she'd talked about it, even knowing that she'd come to me for honest advice.

I'll be *honest*. I had to *advise* my dick to calm the fuck down.

Very scumbag-like of me, I supposed, but I was convinced hearing or seeing the word 'virgin' or 'anal' or 'sex' fired some kind of hormonal response in the heterosexual male mind.

Maybe it fired it in the homosexual male mind too, but I didn't have any firsthand experience to confirm.

Photographers lined the entrance as we pulled up to 30 Rock, a well-known skyscraper in New York City and home to several entities, including NBC Studios. For me, on this night, it was the Rainbow Room I wanted, an iconic restaurant on the sixty-fifth floor and host to the benefit for Mount Sinai Kravis Children's Hospital. The fundraiser was being held by an outside organization made up of the well-meaning wealthy. I wished they'd spend less money on the event and donate it all to the fucking hospital, but the truth of it was that *this* was what it took to entice people into donations and make it feel worthy of their money. Schmaltzy entertainment, expensive food, and an evening out.

I was here to hand over a check, make my mother happy, and enjoy the evening with Georgia, the level of importance of each not relative to their order.

The dog and pony show passed by in a blur, camera flashes and shouted questions melding and mixing together as I covered my eyes and stepped inside.

Security for the event had taken over two of the elevators, and a small line trickled from the doors of each all the way back to me.

I scanned the crowd for Georgia, hoping to find her sooner rather than later, but, after several sweeps, came up completely empty. It was one of the perils of coming separately, I supposed, but I didn't want her to feel awkward or alone while she waited for me.

A check of my watch confirmed that I was on time, and the line was moving fast. I'd be up there to look for her in no time.

"Macallan on the rocks, half a lime on the side, please."

The bartender confirmed my order with a nod, turning to the glass shelves behind him to grab my scotch. It was fifteen minutes past eight, forty-five minutes later than our agreed upon time, and still no sign of Georgia. I was beginning to think she might have stood me up—hoping that she had, rather than something having happened to her—when Stacey Henderson sauntered up to me and leaned her body into my space with an elbow at the bar.

"Where's your date?"

I grabbed my scotch and the lime as the bartender set it down in front of me, squeezing the juice into my glass before handing the carcass back to him with a smile and a nod. Plucking a napkin from the top of the stack, I wiped the remaining juice off of my palm.

"Well, hello to you too, Stacey." I turned to her in acknowledgment, but my body did it under protest. It feared the effects of cross-contamination if it got too close.

"Your mother told me you already had a date. That's why you couldn't come with me."

"I'm aware. What I wasn't aware of was the fact that she had arranged a date with you in the first place. Don't you think that's the kind of thing you should be asked directly by a man?"

She waved the thought away like a pesky fly.

"If you're not here with someone—"

"I am," I interrupted.

Her eyes narrowed while mine searched the room nearly desperately, and my brain tried to conjure up an excuse. My face and body portrayed an outward calm.

"Where is she, then?"

"The restroom. You know how you ladies are," I patronized in the name of inserting frivolous, vaguely-insulting conversation into a still-civil exchange. As much as Stacey Henderson was asking for a big 'go fuck yourself,' the Mount Sinai Kravis Children's Hospital was not. "Always running to the restroom to touch up something or other or to relieve your peanut-sized bladders."

Stacey scoffed rather indelicately, an effect of too much alcohol too goddamn early in the benefit, and I winced, fearing the turn of events when no one returned from the restroom.

Then, out of the crowd emerged a frazzled—but *stunning*—Georgia.

Red framed her body from breast to foot, the tight material clinging to her in all the right places. Her tan skin peeked out of a cutout just below her chest, and a matching blood red painted her lips and nails. The only thing missing red was her head, her now blonde locks cascading and curling down and around her slim shoulders and damn near robbing me of the ability to think.

Worry from her late arrival ravaged her face as she approached the two of us without pretense or fear.

"Oh my God, Kline, I am so sorry I'm—"

"It's okay," I cut her off, stepping pointedly around Stacey and pulling her into my arms for a hug.

"I'm just glad you're here," I whispered softly into her new hair. Stacey groaned audibly in begrudged response before grabbing her high-priced clutch from the bar and stomping away like a petulant child.

"Who was she?" Georgia asked, leaning back and glancing over my arm as Stacey dragged ass away.

"*That* was a day-spa-loving version of my cat."

Her nose scrunched up adorably as she tried to make sense of my words.

"Would you like something to drink?" I offered, escorting her the few steps back to the bar with a hand at her back. I felt the warmth at my palm all the way in my dick, the need to touch her having been a palpable thing all day long.

She smiled, and it lit up her face and mine. "Can I say 'God yes' without sounding like a lush?"

One side of my mouth hooked up in a grin. My cock said she could say 'God yes' anytime she wanted, but thankfully, my mouth said, "Sure."

I looked away long enough to grab the bartender's attention and then turned back to her.

"You look beautiful."

She started to smile but stopped herself, the skin between her eyebrows pinching slightly.

"I'm an asshole. I can't believe I'm so late. I mean, I *can* believe I'm late," she rambled. "Just not *this* late. This is a new low for me."

"You're always late?" I asked, trying to distract her from the late arrival and learn more about her instead.

"Yes. Every day of my life. Well, to everything other than meetings with you." She winced again. "The work you, at least."

"Don't worry," I promised with a grin. "Kline won't say anything to Mr. Brooks."

"What'll you have?" the bartender asked, tossing a napkin up on the bar for the anticipated glass.

Georgia looked to me in question.

"No." I waved her off and lifted my glass. "I'm good. Just got one. You go ahead."

I glanced down the line of her back as she leaned over the bar. Wide straps criss-crossed to form cut-outs in the fabric of the back as well, and smooth material hugged the curve of her hips and ass. Her body petite but curvy, I wanted to run my hands all over that fabric.

God, she looked gorgeous. It was almost unreal.

She turned to me, holding a glass of wine she had obviously ordered at some point during my ogling.

"Sorry," I apologized through a tight throat. "I was…"

She raised an eyebrow pointedly, a knowing grin on her face. "Staring at my ass."

"Yeah." I nodded. "That's exactly what I was doing."

She laughed.

"It's a really fine ass, though. And your hair…"

She grabbed a strand of it self-consciously, twisting it around her finger. "Oh. Yeah. I have a thing for dyeing my hair. I'm not sure why, but I tend to change it like a hobby. Red or blonde or sometimes—"

"Georgia?"

She finally took a breath. "Yeah?"

"I meant what I said. You look beautiful. Own it."

"Thank you," she whispered, but her face relaxed.

From there on out, she seemed herself: funny, sometimes awkward, but mostly at ease.

We worked the room, schmoozing all of the people who needed it and small-talking with the others. Unable to help myself, I kept a hand on Georgia all night.

Her hand in mine, my palm at the small of her back, a set of my flexing fingers on her perfect hip. Anything to touch her. Anything to keep her in close proximity.

Finally done with my obligations, I asked her something that'd been on my mind all night.

"Would you like to dance?"

She seemed surprised. "You dance?"

"With you, yes."

"I swear," she whispered with a shake of her head. "Do you secretly have one of those things on your wrist that Coca-Cola wears?"

I grinned in confusion.

Her eyes searched mine like I held all the power, a sheen of fear coating them with moisture.

Only then did I realize she meant the quarterback's playbook cheat sheet.

I took her cheek in my palm, smoothing a thumb over the apple of it softly.

Apparently, when it came to Georgia Cummings and tonight, I'd been doing just fine.

"Come on," I coaxed, setting my drink down on a nearby table, pulling her onto the dance floor with me, and pressing her body right to mine.

Hands clasped together, I pulled them into my chest and wrapped my other arm tightly around the curve of her hip.

Her eyes followed mine and mine followed hers, a closed loop of exploration into each other. The moment picked up speed as the band played a sweet and melodic tune, and the rest of the room faded completely away.

My chest felt tight with anticipation of what was to come—right now, in this moment, and beyond, as I gave myself over to getting to know this amazing woman.

Our weight shifted from foot to foot and our hips swayed, very much moving but, at the same time, fighting with everything we had to stay stagnantly lost in that moment.

Without thought or delay, I leaned in, touching my lips to hers for a full second before I felt the tension leave her body and her eyes fluttered closed.

Tentative but bold, her lips began to move under mine, exploring on their own rather than waiting for my invitation.

I abandoned her hand at my chest immediately and sought the solace of her hair instead, entrenching my hand and using its leverage to pull her lips even closer.

A sigh bounced from her mouth to mine as I focused on her bottom lip, pulling it between my own and sucking ever so slightly.

She tasted like the sweet cherry notes of her wine, and my tongue shot out to lick up another drop. When the tip of her tongue touched mine, everything else was lost.

Time.

Space.

All sense of propriety and appropriateness for a crowded dance floor at a Children's Hospital benefit. My hand left her hip, circling around on a path straight for the cheek of her ass.

When the corners of her lips tipped up despite their connection to mine, I knew I'd never experienced *anything* sexier than a woman unable to withhold a smile while we kissed.

"*Kline*," she whispered, pulling away and smiling without inhibition.

Just the way she said my name had me groaning.

"God, I know. Not the time." I pulled her close to me and practically dragged the two of us off the dance floor. The band had started to transition into an old Grand Funk Railroad song, "Some Kind of Wonderful," anyway. In the haze of my peripheral vision, I could see other couples head in the direction we'd just come, and amongst the shuffle and swing of their active bodies, our lip-locked, fully intertwined ones would have been even more obvious.

I grabbed Georgia's wrist lightly, and her pulse thrummed and fluttered under the tips of my fingers. The feeling made my grip tighten minutely as I turned her to face me.

Her hair hung in a veil around her face, but I could actually *feel* our chemistry in the air between us.

When I pulled her body flush with mine, she tipped her chin so that she could look straight into my eyes.

Her signature blue eyes were shining with emotion, but something else wasn't right.

She was still beautiful, but her face—something was different. Her lipstick-smeared lips looked to be twice their normal size.

"Um, Georgia—"

"Georgie," she corrected while looking up at me sweetly. She fluttered her lashes coyly, but I barely even noticed. I couldn't look away from her mouth.

"Right. Georgie." I steeled myself. "Listen, I know this is a weird question, but you wouldn't happen to have had some light work done, would you?"

"Work?" she asked, oblivious.

"Yeah, you know. *Work*."

She shook her head and smiled a little, clearly still in the fog from our kiss. I wished I was. "I don't know what you're asking."

I coughed to clear my throat and wiped the building sweat from my brow. This wasn't a good idea. Asking women questions like this was never a good idea.

Maybe I should just pretend not to notice.

"Kline?"

Shit. Were they getting bigger?

"I don't know," I fumbled. "Some kind of lip filler that has a delayed reaction, maybe?"

"Wip fiwer?" She tried again, her nose scrunching with the effort. "Wip fiwer. Wipppp fiwer."

Concern blanketed my face and hers turned distraught.

"Oh, sit. Sit sit sit."

"Sit?"

"Not sit. Siiit." She dropped her face into her hands. "Sit."

"Ohhh," I said in realization, picking her face up out of her hands to find her lips and the palms that had just touched them swelling at an alarming rate. "Shit, Georgie."

"Exacwy."

"What's happening? What do I need to do?"

I moved to grab some ice out of my forgotten glass, and her eyes followed me and then widened exponentially.

"Sit, Kwine! Is where wime wuice in where?"

"Wime wuice?"

"Wime wuice!"

"Oh! Oh, yeah. Shit. Shit! Yeah, there's lime juice in there."

"I'm awerwic. I nee benedetto. Benedwetto. Sit! Benedwiwww."

"Benadryl!" I shouted, victorious. Like it was some kind of game. She looked disgusted.

"Right. Sorry," I apologized, turning my attention back to surveying her and putting my focus back on her health. "Jesus, it's bad, Georgie. Do we need to go to the emergency room?"

"No." She shook her head, eyes determined.

Her lips looked like cartoons. I panicked at the thought of her throat closing up with the same fervor.

"Please. Let me take you to urgent care or something."

"No, Kwine. Wet's wust wet ouw of hewre. Benedwiwww."

"Right. Benadryl." I grabbed her hand and dragged her toward the elevator without looking back. No way was tonight going to go down in history as the night I fucking killed a woman with one kiss.

I shoved through the crowd that had gathered there without apology, and Georgia shielded her face from their scrutiny. The doors propped open with my foot, I ushered her in and hit the button for the lobby as fast as I could before holding the 'close door' button with excessive force. When they finally shut, I pulled Georgia's gaze from the floor with a gentle finger at her chin.

"I'm so sorry, Georgie."

"Is wit bwad?"

"It isn't good," I answered vaguely. "Please, let me take you to the hospital."

"No," she refused, taking some of the sting out of it by offering a smile. I mean, her mouth didn't smile—it was too swollen—but there was visible happiness in her eyes. "I'm owkay. Pwomise. Wust nee Benedwiw."

The doors opened on the ground floor, and I peeled out of there like a drag car, Georgie in tow.

"Swow down, Kwine," she ordered, tugging on my hand and nearly tripping on her dress.

"I'm sorry," I apologized, knowing I wouldn't be able to beat the panic back enough to slow down to her pace.

She smiled again, but it didn't last long. It turned right into a shout when I swept her off of her feet and into my arms and took off at a jog again, dialing Frank as I did.

Two rings and he answered.

"Mr. Brooks?"

"I need you to meet us at the Rite-Aid on the corner!"

He wasn't used to me shouting, but he sure as hell didn't question it.

"Yes, sir."

One look at Georgie's face, and I started running faster.

For the first time in ten years, I didn't have the first clue what I'd done with my phone after ending the call—and I didn't care one bit.

CHAPTER 13

Georgia

"Here." Kline slid back into the car and handed me a brown paper bag with what I could only assume was Benadryl.

"Tanks," I whispered, offering a small smile.

He furrowed his brow, lips fighting a wince.

Shit. How bad is it?

Seeing as it was my first date with Kline, I knew this wasn't an optimal situation. In a matter of a few minutes and one perfect, sexy kiss, I had gone from smiling and offering up charming, flirty responses to sounding like I was talking around a wiener in my mouth.

Lime juice had sabotaged me. It had been years since I'd come in contact with the allergy-inducing demon. And the last time, it was *way* worse. My throat had started to close up because I had ingested it, whereas this was just contact swelling.

Swallowing a few times, I confirmed my throat was breezy and clear.

But the way Kline was trying *not* to react to my appearance?

Well, that had me rummaging through my purse and getting my compact out. Flipping the clasp, I opened the mirror, coming

face-to-face with something that could nauseate horror movie en-
thusiasts. Bright red blowfish lips consumed my face. The skin was
stretched so tight I feared something might burst.

Bottom line: It was bad. Real fucking bad. Kylie Jenner's mouth
on steroids bad.

"Ah ma gaw," I gasped, tongue still swelling by the second.

I glanced at myself in the mirror again, which was a big, fat mistake of epic proportions. The swelling seemed hell-bent on consuming
my entire face.

"Tis is ba! Tis is so ba!" I grabbed the paper bag off the seat and
pulled it over my head.

On a Britney Spears' scale of embarrassment, I had proverbially
flashed my beaver to millions of people.

*For the love of God, the inflammation is going to my brain. I can
only think in celebrity speak.* My allergic reaction had turned me into
Leslie.

"Georgia, please, don't hide your pretty face." Kline removed the
paper bag, staring back at me with serious concern.

Pfffffft. Pretty? All forms of pretty had fled the building the second I had contracted elephantiasis of the face.

I averted my eyes from his and focused on removing the cello-
phane wrapping from the Benadryl. "Somonabith," I cursed, fumbling
with the childproof cap.

He gently took the bottle out of my hands, detaching the cap with
ease, and handed it back to me. "We need to get you to an emergency
room. St. Luke's is just around the corner."

Oh, hell no. Out of all of the emergency rooms in New York, I was
not going to *that* one.

*Well, unless my reaction gets worse—then I'd reconsider. I'd face the
embarrassment and my brother's incessant teasing for a shot of epine-
phrine over not breathing at all. I'm not a complete moron.*

I shook my head frantically. "Ma brudder. Nob way."

He scrunched his brow up in confusion.

"Nobe. Nob hobitals."

My brother Will was finishing up his ER residency at St. Luke's, and I knew for a fact he was elbow deep in a twenty-four-hour call shift. If I walked into his ER looking like this, I'd never live it down.

"But—"

"Uh-uh. Nob habbenin," I cut him off, resolute.

And to solidify my decision, I tipped the bottle of Benadryl to my goliath lips and knocked back as much as I could.

"Shit! Georgia!" Kline grabbed the bottle from my hands, panicked. "That's too much. Way, way too much."

I shrugged, reaching for the discarded paper bag and pulling a pen from my purse.

No ERs needed, I'll be fine, I wrote, holding it out to him.

He frowned. "I'm really worried."

I promise, I've been through this before. The Benny will do the trick.

I reassured, hating seeing him so anxious.

His mouth offered a wry grin. "Benny?"

I nodded, my neck doing its best impression of a bobblehead doll. It was safe to say, the antihistamine was kicking in.

Yeah, Benny and I go way back. I promise I'll be fine in a few hours.

He assessed my face. "Pretty sure you drank way too much Benny."

I shook my head, hiding my lips with my free hand.

Just stop looking at me until the Benny kicks in. I'm sorry this is the worst first date ever.

He took the pen out of my grip and pulled the bag into his lap. His hand moved in fluid motions as he scribbled something down and then slid it back to me.

~~*Just stop looking at me until the Benny kicks in. I'm sorry this is the worst first date ever.*~~
This is the BEST first date ever.

"Thank you for coming with me tonight." He offered a smile—a real smile, not the *I'm trying to smile, but holy shit, you look bad* kind of smile he was showcasing before. "And, Georgia." Kline touched my cheek. "Even with an allergic reaction, you still have the power to take my breath away. You're gorgeous, sweetheart. Swollen lips and all, you're still gorgeous."

I stared back at him, speechless. There was still so much I didn't know about Kline, but my gut told me, at the root of his soul, he was a good man. A sweet, kind, and undeniably good man.

Despite the lime juice fiasco, I'm glad I'm here too.

My eyelids started to feel heavy, my lashes blinking past the fog. I leaned my head back on the seat.

"You okay?" He wrapped his arm around my shoulder, tucking me into his side.

I wasn't vomiting and I could still breathe, so I muttered, "Uh-huh," as I nuzzled into him. "Jus a lil sweepy."

The pull to go comatose was strong. In the back of my mind, there was a tiny bit of rational thought wondering, *Am I going to overdose on Benadryl?*

Before the urge to sleep snuffed out all the light, I grabbed my phone from my purse. Pulling up my text conversation with Will, I attempted to shoot him a message.

Me: WELLY IM BENNY
Delete.
Me: WELLIUM ODOR
Delete.

Slowly, but surely, my fingers got their shit together and autocorrect stopped trying to make me her bitch.

Me: WILL CAN AN OC GIVE A BENNY!*&

There. Perfect.

If he thinks I'm in trouble, he'll call me. Otherwise, no big dealio, was the last thought before Benny took over and said, "Goodnight, Georgia."

"Georgie. Georgie." A hand nudged my shoulder. "Wake up, Georgie."

"*Fuuuuuuuuuck.*" Someone cursed under their breath.

I opened my eyes, blinking past the blurred vision. Peeling my face off leather, I sat up, finding a concerned Kline staring back at me.

"Thank God. Are you okay?" He touched my cheek.

Mmmmmmmmm. That feels nice. I had the urge to purr into his palm and beg him to scratch my belly. All of a sudden, being a cat sounded like the best idea I'd ever had.

"Meow?" he asked, all four of his eyebrows scrunching together.

"Huh?"

"Did you just say meow?"

"*Meowww... Meowww...*" I tested it on my tongue. My lips felt funny. "Yeah, I think I did." I nuzzled into his palm. "Keep petting me, Kline. I might actually start purring soon."

A deep chuckle vibrated his chest. My head moved of its own accord, leaning forward and resting against his hard pecs. For real,

Kline Brooks had pecs. Hard-as-fuck pecs. Mmm. Nipples. I wondered what his nipples tasted like.

He adjusted in his seat, his hand resting at the nape of my neck.
"Georgie? We need to get you upstairs. I think you might've had too
much Benadryl."

Me thinks so too. Suggested dosage, schmagested mosage.

"Hahaha. Mosage."

My body rocked like he was shaking his head.

"I think I'm high."

He chuckled again, pec-pulsation caressing my cheek.

"Now I remember why I loved Mary Jane so much in high school."

"I'm going to carry you out of the car, okay?"

"We're in a car?" I sat up straight, releasing his perfect chest from
my cheek's assault. "Whose car?"

"This is my regular car, sweetheart. Frank drove us. Are you
ready?"

I glanced at his crotch. "Oh, I had no idea we were already
headed in that direction. I guess this date went pretty good, huh?
We're headed for naked time. That's gotta be a good thing." My hand
stroked his thigh, savoring the feel of muscles sheathed by soft material. "I bet you're fuck-hot naked."

He grinned, grabbing my hand and pulling it to his lips for a soft
kiss. "How about we get out of this car and head up to my apartment?"

I nodded. At least, I thought I was nodding. I decided to nod a
few more times just for good measure. You could never be sure about
a nod. They could be tricky little things.

"Okay, wrap your arms around my neck. I'm going to carry you
upstairs."

"Oh, yeah. Carry me, Kline. Carry me so good."

Big arms wrapped around my body, pulling me out of the car.
Once I was airborne—swaddled up in strong muscles and delicious
male pheromones mixed with sexy cologne—my voice decided to
make its debut. If there was ever a time for a song, it was right now,

while Kline carried me past a doorman and through a lobby I'd never seen.

"Wicky, wicky, wicky, beatbox! K-K-Kline looks like sex and he's so clean, clean!"

I'd always had a talent for freestyling.

"Wicky, wicky, wicky, beatbox! Big-dicked Brooks in da house! Can I get an Amen! Wicky, wicky, wicky, remix!"

"Georgia," Kline whispered through a laugh. "I need to set you down for a second while I get my keys."

My feet touched the ground and the hallway morphed into a dervish's wheel, spinning around in a hypnotic display of plush velvet rugs and cream-colored walls. "Whoa, settle down, hallway! You're outta control!" I reached for the wall, but he was quicker, gripping my waist and stopping my forward momentum.

"Here we go," he instructed, maneuvering me through the door and inside his apartment. "Let's get you settled on the couch and maybe get some non-alcoholic fluids in you."

I threw my body onto the leather sofa, nuzzling my face into the pillows. "Oh yeah, baby. Now, this is the kind of couch I'm talking about."

"Georgia." Kline's face was inches from mine, his long fingers settling below my chin.

"Hey, where'd you come from?" I asked, peeking out from my pillow fort. "I thought you were by the door. Man, you're quick. Are you working out?"

He smiled, blue eyes working their magic on my libido. *Li-bee-dough.* What a weird word. It sounded more courtroom than sex. *"I'd like the record to show he was badgering my key witness for a libido!"* See what I mean?

"Georgia, sweetheart," Kline summoned my gaze. And son of a hooker nut, there were those blue eyes again. Surely, they were trying to hypnotize my vagina. It was working, by the way.

Any minute, my panties would just, *poof!*, disappear into thin air.

"Have mercy," I whispered. "That smile, plus those eyes, it's like a sex cream sundae. I want two scoops."

A small laugh left his lips. "How about we start with a drink first? What sounds good? I've got water, tea, coffee?"

"I'll take the vodka. But on the rocks, please."

He shook his head, amused. "Vodka wasn't an option."

"It wasn't?" I tilted my head and realized things felt so much better with my head resting on the pillows.

"How about you just rest here while I get the drinks?"

"Yes, sir." I saluted him.

"Wait!" I shrieked before he even made it a foot. I had something to tell him, and I had to tell him *now*.

"Yeah, baby?" he asked, concern mixing deliciously with just a hint of a smile.

"You're the best kisser on this side of the Mississippi. NO! The best kisser in the whole entire world!" My voice turned grave. "I'm talking, I've never had better *in my life*."

Any concern disappeared as though it'd never been there.

"Yeah?" His blue eyes twinkled like actual glitter. Like he went to Michael's, got a jar of it, and then poured it in his irises.

"Ohhh, yeah," I agreed before reaching out and yanking him back to me with a fist in his shirt.

A chuckle rumbled his chest as I pushed mine to it tightly and slammed my lips to his without apology. They were just so soft and plump and *mmm, that groan tasted good*. I took what I wanted, exploring and plundering his mouth even though my face wouldn't seem to fucking cooperate. I shoved him away softly, ordering a needy "Thirsty!" in someone else's squeaky voice.

He shook his head and smiled, retreating without a word.

His footsteps moved farther away, toward the land of drinks, I was sure.

My fingers moved to my face, tapping my nose, and then my cheeks, and then my lips. Oh my, these things were bigger than I remembered. I grabbed my boobs just to see if other things had doubled in size.

Damn, no such luck.

If I was Goldilocks and this was the three bears' apartment, this room was too fucking hot.

Relocation was needed. My feet flopped onto the floor. Heels were kicked off across the room, clanking against the wall. Once I got my sea legs in order, I tip-toed into the hallway.

Peeking into the room at the end of the hall, I found a king-size bed summoning me.

"Oh, yes. Come to mama!"

I cannonballed into the bed, fluffy comforter and pillows bouncing around me.

After a few body rolls from one side to the next, I found that it wasn't the room that was stifling my temperate vibe; it was my clothes. Too many clothes.

How'd I get so many clothes on?

I stood at the foot of the bed while my numb fingers worked at the zipper of my dress. It took a bit for me to figure out the zipper was just for show. Someone had superglued me into it. *Geez Louis-a May Alcott, the price we women pay for beauty.*

My hands tore at the front of the dress until the initial rip echoed inside the room.

"Now, that's what I'm talking about."

I got down to my skivvies and decided even those were not up to par for the bed. Call it a superpower, but I could sense when a bed wanted me naked. The king had spoken, and naked was his final offer.

No one could deny the glorious feeling of rolling around naked under a soft sheet. My face met the pillow, and then my nose felt it was the perfect time to sniff the delicious Kline Brooks aroma embedded in the material. God, he smelled good. Like clean laundry and man soap and *I'm going to fuck him.*

Boy, that escalated quickly.

The Benadryl had become my truth serum. I wanted to sex him. I wanted to hand him a valentine that said, "Be my cherry popper," and spread my legs as far as those babies would go. I knew valentines were only meant for a particular holiday, but this felt like an exception to the rule.

"Georgia?" Kline's voice moved down the hallway.

"I'm in here!" I called back.

His tall frame moved through the doorway, finding me luxuriating in the bedding.

"Comfortable?" he asked.

"Oh yeah, baby." I patted the spot beside me. "Come join me. I don't know whose bed this is, but hells bells, it's wonderful."

"It's my bed." He chuckled, setting two glasses on the nightstand and sitting on the edge.

I sat up, holding the comforter to my chest. "This is your bed?"

He nodded, eyes moving to my bare shoulders.

"Well, I'll be damned. I'm a fan of your bed. Big fan. The biggest fan."

His eyes moved around the room, searching for something. His jaw dropped when whatever he was looking for came into view. "Are you naked?" he asked, swallowing hard enough to make his Adam's apple bob.

"The bed made me do it."

"My bed made you get naked?"

"He's a real pervy bastard, but who was I to argue?" I shrugged, the comforter falling to my waist.

Kline's spine stiffened, averting his gaze toward the floor.

I touched his shoulder. "Everything okay?"

"Uh-huh." He coughed out a laugh.

"Is one of those for me?" I nodded at the table.

"Please." He gestured toward the glasses. "Help yourself."

"Only if you stop looking so uncomfortable."

That caught his attention, his curious eyes meeting mine. "Uncomfortable?"

"Yeah. You look really uncomfortable. I insist that you take your shoes off and sit back on the bed."

He ran a hand through his hair. "Georgia, I'm not sure that's such a good idea."

"Of course it is, you silly, gorgeous piece of man meat!" I got to my knees, forcing his body to lie back on the bed. Straddling his hips, I stared down at him. "See what I mean? It's so comfortable down there, isn't it?"

"It sure is something." His gaze raked down my completely bare body, going darker with each second that passed.

While he made himself cozy, I grabbed a glass from the nightstand and took a satisfying drink. "This vodka is delicious. Not very strong, though."

"That's because it's water."

"Hmmmph. Well, look at that."

Kline hesitantly gripped my waist. "I think I should grab you some clothes to wear to bed."

My mouth formed a pout. "Do you not like seeing me naked, Kline? Naked time is fun time."

He shook his head and muttered under his breath, "*Dear fucking Lucifer.*" He cleared his throat. "Shit, Georgie. I don't think I've ever seen anything better than you naked. And *God*, I want naked time to be fun time. I want it really fucking bad."

"Well, then what's the big rush? I'm starting to understand all the fuss about nudist colonies. There's a lot to be said for being naked, Kline. I think you should try it." I moved my hands to his belt, slipping the metal from the prongs.

"This probably isn't a good idea." He stopped my progress before I made my way to his zipper.

I looked up at him, my ass resting against Kline's better half—his bigger, thicker half. The one that seemed to wholeheartedly—or *wholecockedly*—disagree with him. "I think you're wrong. I think you think this is a really good idea." To emphasize my point, I rolled my hips against him.

Jesus. His dick.

Wait, that sounded a little sacrilege.

Kline. His dick.

There, that was better.

"Kline," I moaned, rubbing my clit against him. "This. Feels. So. Good."

"Shit," he groaned, his fingers digging into my hips. "We shouldn't be doing this, but *fuck*. You're gorgeous and naked and *wet*. So fucking wet. I can feel you through my clothes."

"You make me crazy," I half growled like an animal. "I want to kiss you, lick you, suck you, ride you. I want to do *everything*. Right. Now." I leaned forward, pressing one pert nipple to his lips.

He sucked me into his mouth, his tongue flicking my nipple and urging heat to flush across my skin.

"You have the best tits, Georgia. The best fucking tits." He moved to the other breast, kissing and sucking and licking me into a frenzy.

"God, yes. Keep doing that," I begged.

He gripped my chin, pulling my face to his. His lips crashed against mine. We were a delicious mess of tongues and lips and hips grinding and hands groping.

"You're too perfect," he whispered against my skin. "I can't get enough of you."

"I want you to have all of me," I urged. "I want you inside of me, Kline. God, I want it so bad. Christopher Columbus the fuck out of my pussy prideland!"

"What?" he asked as he stilled.

The words ran through my head enough to know I'd screwed some sort of pooch by alluding that my pooch had yet to be screwed.

"What?" I repeated back, attempting, and failing, to be the absolute picture of aloof.

His fingers held my hips still. Blue eyes stared deep into mine before shutting closed.

"Kline? What's wrong?"

His gaze met mine again. "We can't do this, not like this."

"Of course, we can," I disagreed. "I'm naked. You're hard. This seems like the perfect time for screwing. It's like Marvin Gaye himself put us in this moment and whispered, 'Go ahead and let's get it on.'"

A grin kissed his lips. "God, you're adorable," he said, biting back a laugh.

"No." I pouted. "I'm sexy and naked and ready to fornicate."

He quirked a brow. "Fornicate?"

"Penetrate?" I offered, hoping it sounded more enticing.

"Baby, I'm losing my mind over how sexy and beautiful you are, but I'm also trying to be a gentleman here. You're a little under the influence, remember?"

I frowned, mentally counting the amount of drinks I'd had throughout the night.

"I didn't drink that much."

"I'm not talking about alcohol."

My eyes went wide. "Did we do drugs?!"

His grin consumed his face, dimples peeking out and saying hello. "Calm down," he said, humor in his voice. "We didn't do drugs. Not in the illegal sense. But *you* had a crazy amount of Benadryl."

"Oh, I forgot about that."

"So, Benny girl, I think we should press pause on this fantastic moment—because you can bet that sexy ass of yours I want to revisit this—and let's throw some clothes on you and find something a little less tempting to do."

I thought it over for a second. "Do you have any pizza?"

A wry grin creased his mouth. "You want pizza?"

I nodded. "Pizza and Netflix. We'll save the chill part for later."

Kline lifted me off the bed and onto my feet as he sat up. "How about you rummage through my closet and find something you like and I'll order us one?"

I pressed a soft kiss to his lips. "Deal."

As I turned for the closet, his hand met my ass, spanking a high-pitched squeal right from my lips.

"Hey!" I shouted, turning toward him.

He shrugged, smirking like the devil. "Can't expect a man to ignore a perfect ass shimmying around in front of his face."

"I was *not* shimmying."

"Baby, you were shimmying. But don't worry, I was definitely watching and enjoying the show."

I ignored him, striding—*okay, sashaying*—into his walk-in closet, where I enjoyed a few moments to myself to swoon over the whole "Baby" sentiment.

There may have been jumping and silent screaming. Who knows? Maybe I even buried my nose into his dress shirts and put myself in a momentary Kline-induced coma?

But I will tell you this.

The pizza was fucking delicious.

CHAPTER 14

Kline

Confused and sleepy, Georgia stumbled out of my bedroom and into the hall, the light from my sun-beaten bedroom windows backlighting her in the doorway. My shirt hung off of her tiny frame in a bloblike shadow and covered her completely, but the image of her naked body underneath was burned on my brain from having it straddling me last night.

She'd been out of her mind, completely out of control, and most of all, irresistibly fucking adorable. She made the term hot mess look good, and the rambling thoughts of her Benadryl-influenced mind would stick with me forever.

Honestly, I didn't know if I'd ever met someone funnier—and I knew a whole lot of brilliantly funny people.

"I feel like someone buried me alive last night and I spent all twelve hours trying to claw my way out."

I smiled apologetically.

She stopped to lean on the wall at the mouth of the hallway, putting the tips of her fingers of one hand to the skin of her forehead.

"I'm so sorry about last night," I told her.

But I wasn't sorry. Not really anyway. The only thing I regretted was that I should have taken her to the goddamn hospital in spite of her protests. It could have turned out so much worse. My Catholic roots were a little rusty, but I'd dust off the old prayer playbook to thank the big guy for keeping an eye on this one.

Inching her way into the room, she settled on the other end of the couch and pulled her knees carefully into her chest, stretching the cotton of my t-shirt to cover them.

"Fucking lime juice," she muttered into her knees, the skin of her now normal lips teasing the soft knit of the fabric before looking up at me. "Scotch with lime juice, really? Who even drinks that?"

I leaned back into the couch, stretching an arm along the back and propping my feet up on the coffee table in front of me to keep from reaching out and running a finger along those lips.

"Ernest Hemingway drank scotch with lime juice."

She chewed the recently healed skin nervously, and I could imagine what she was thinking. Trying to assess how she felt about waking up here, with me, at the same time she considered what I said. She seemed genuinely intrigued that I'd know something like that, but she warred with herself when it came to concentration on it. "Really?"

I laughed, explaining, "Well, I never witnessed it for myself, but I read it once somewhere, yeah."

A smile crept into the corners of her mouth and brightened the blue of her eyes. And the maroon of my shirt already had them blazing.

Moving her eyes from the couch to the kitchen, down the hall and back again, she asked, "What is this place?"

I pinched one eye in winklike confusion, attempted to survey the scene from her point of view, and then answered the only way I could. "Uh, it's my apartment."

"*Your* apartment?"

"Yeah." I shook my head. "Why did you say 'your apartment' like it's infested with bed bugs?"

"No!" she denied vehemently in surprise. "No, it's nice. It's just…"

Silence lingered where words should have been.

"It's…" I prompted. "What?"

Her cheeks puffed out slightly with the sour taste of her thoughts, and I could see her run the scenario of saying it out loud through her head more than once.

"*Georgie*. It's what?"

"*Normal*."

A laugh slipped out. "Yeah, well. So am I."

And it wasn't *that* normal, I thought a little bitterly. It had a doorman, for fuck's sake. I was a single guy. What the fuck did I need a penthouse with six bedrooms for?

I didn't want Georgia to think I needed some big apartment. I wanted her to *get* it.

"No," she disagreed. "*You're* Kline Brooks."

I just shook my head, trying to find the right words to describe how much nothing my fucking name meant to me—and how very little it should mean to everyone else.

"Trust me, that name doesn't mean nearly the same thing to me, my relatives, or any of my friends as it does to other people."

She untucked her knees from my shirt, stretching her long, tan legs out on the couch toward me and crossing them at the ankles. Unable to resist, I reached down and rested the palm of my hand on her bare shin.

She watched it happen and paused for just a few seconds before looking back up and into my eyes. She forced serenity over her features, but discomfort lived just under the surface. It wasn't that she didn't want it; she just felt awkward because it had been unexpected.

"What's it mean to your family?"

"I don't know." I searched my mind for the best way to put it, ignoring her minor discomfort and running a thumb along the skin of her calf casually. "A guy who eats way more pizza than he should and has sweaty feet and a grumpy cat who hates him."

"Meowwww," Walter said on cue, hopping up onto the arm of the couch and startling her.

"Oh!"

"Speak of the devil."

"Hi?" she prompted.

"Walter."

"Hi, Walter," she cooed, turning her upper body and rubbing his back from head to tail.

He purred and nudged into her. "Meowwwww."

"Sure," I scoffed. "Bond with the pretty girl. How fucking predictable."

"Was he here last night?" she asked haltingly.

I bit my lips to stave off the urge to go into detail. "Uh…yeah. The two of you had quite the lengthy conversation." They had. Georgia and Walter had bonded over pepperoni pizza and reruns of *Friends*. She sang "Smelly Cat" to him no less than fifteen times.

The snooty motherfucker purred for every single one of them.

She nodded as if that made sense. "He seems like the friendly sort."

I scoffed audibly.

"Maybe that's your problem," she suggested simply, scratching behind his ears like they were old lawyer friends there to co-prosecute my trial. "You're being kind of an asshole to Walter. He responds to kind words and soft touches."

"Are you kidding me?!" I nearly yelled, pointing to myself and then back at my grumpy old cat wildly. "I'm not the asshole! *He's* the asshole! I tried to bring that cat around to me for weeks. I'm just treating him how he treats me now."

Walter leaned into her as if scared. That fucking cat con-artist!

"Aw, it's okay, Walter," Georgie swore sweetly, tucking his kitty face between her hands and rubbing their noses together. "I'll protect you from the bad, scary man." Her face turned conspiratorial, an eyebrow arching up menacingly to match the traitor-cat, as she looked me in the eye again. "I know how you feel. He tried to poison me last night!"

"I didn't poison her," I told him calmly, going along with this crazy conversation for some reason. "I ordered the same drink I've been ordering for ten years, and then I gave her the best kiss of her life."

Georgie's playful eyes jumped to mine and turned serious. Panicked even.

"It was not the best kiss of my—"

"Uh-uh-uh." I tsked with a wave of my finger. "Don't lie now, Benny. I know it was the best kiss of your life for a fact."

"And how do you claim to know that?"

"Because last night you told me so yourself."

She gasped. Walter hissed in camaraderie.

"Right before you kissed me again—"

Her cheeks flushed with embarrassment, and everything about her posture said she was two seconds away from sprinting straight out the door.

But I knew there was more, and I gave it to her, sliding a gentle hand from her shin up to her knee as I did. Walter jumped down and trotted off in protest, but we both ignored him.

"And they were both the best kisses of mine." I decided not to focus on the fact that beyond those kisses, she'd given me much more—including a naked lap dance. With the way her skin burned red about the kisses, I thought the trauma of the rest might make her actually combust.

She opened her mouth just to close it again and forced a visible swallow down her throat. I gave her the time she needed, the time to process my words and run them through a cross-check with her emotions.

I'd had all night, listening to her and enjoying her, to prepare for the blow. She hadn't.

Just when I thought she might actually say something in return, her phone started to play the opening beats of "Freek-A-Leek" by Petey Pablo.

It was horrendously endearing.

I had Thatch to thank for that kind of music knowledge myself. It used to be one of his favorite songs in our much wilder post-college days.

She jumped up in a hurry, pink hitting her cheeks with embarrassment.

"Sorry. For the awkward ringtone and the interruption—"

"It's okay," I consoled with a smile and a wink. "It would have been way more awkward had Shonda, Monique, and Christina called you last night at the benefit." Her eyes widened in shock.

"Me, it doesn't bother so much. I'm actually *looking for the good-ies*," I teased, referencing another one of Petey Pablo and Ciara's masterpieces I knew she'd recognize.

And it worked, surprising her so much that she almost didn't make it to the kitchen to answer her phone before it stopped ringing.

I really wasn't much of a mystery, but she was convinced I was.

With the way I craved her company, I planned to enroll her in the accelerated education program and keep her there until she had me mastered.

CHAPTER 15

Georgia

The terrace door clicked shut as I answered Will's call. "Hey, stranger, I'm surprised you're awake right now." Elbows resting on the banister, the sounds of an already popping Upper East Side hustled and bustled below me. "Rough call shift?"

"The ER was hopping last night." Will's raspy, exhausted voice filled my ear. "From the random text I got last night, it appears you had an interesting evening. Night on the town with Cass?"

"Huh?" I tilted my head to the side. How on Earth would my brother know about my night?

"Oh, come on, Gigi." He chuckled softly in my ear. "Have you checked your text messages?"

My face twisted into utter bewilderment. "Text messages?"

"You sent me a text message. To which I did attempt to respond, but honestly, I didn't have a clue what in the hell you were talking about."

I tried to recount last night's events, but my brain still had a residual Benadryl fog.

"Check your messages."

I tapped the screen, putting Will on speaker, while I scrolled through my text conversations.

Me: WILL CAN AN OC GIVE A BENNY!*&

Will: I'd like to buy a vowel, Pat.

Will: Gigi? Hello????

Will: Your Masturbation Camp PTSD is flaring again, isn't it?

Will: You're going to be so fucking sick in the morning.

Will: Seriously, text me if you need anything. I'm pulling an all-nighter in the ER.

Masturbation Camp. My adolescent nightmare that Will won't let me forget about.

Since my mother was a sex therapist, my introduction to sexual health was not the norm. Three days after my thirteenth birthday, I got my period. While most mothers took their daughters to the drug store to buy pads or tampons, my mother signed me up for Camp Love Yourself.

Before your mind wanders to weird and disturbing places, I should explain that we weren't sitting around naked, diddling ourselves to Justin Timberlake music videos.

It was a two-week summer camp focused around teaching teenage girls about sex education, as well as encouraging girls to explore their sexuality in a healthy and safe way. Which explained why my older brother called it "Masturbation Camp."

My empowered and liberated mother was a strong advocate for

Camp Love Yourself and their pro rub-yourself stance. "A few rounds of masturbation a day keeps the babies away, Georgia Rose. It's proven that you're less likely to give in to your teenage hormones if you're exploring your sexuality through healthy, self-love methods."

Needless to say, my experience at "Masturbation Camp" had been about as horrifying and awkward as you'd expect.

It had taken me a good three years to get past the emotional trauma from sitting around a campfire, singing "Kumbaya" with counselor Feather (yes, that was her legal name), while she encouraged us to roast vagina-shaped marshmallows for s'mores. This was one of those life moments where, even ten or fifteen years down the road, I was still wondering if it had really happened.

"Seriously, Wilbur? How many years are you gonna hold on to the Masturbation Camp bit?"

"Forever," he responded, laughing. "That shit will never get old."

I sighed. "You're the world's worst older brother, you know that?"

The insult deflected off of him with ease.

"So, what in the hell were you up to last night?"

Glancing down at the text messages between Will and me, memories from last night hijacked my brain, taking it hostage.

The dance. That kiss. My lips. Benadryl. Kline's bed.

My jaw hit the terrace, my eyes going wide in shock. The details were hazy, but the basics stood out enough to worry me.

Did I really get naked in his bed last night?

"Gigi? You still there?"

Moments and snapshots from twelve or so hours prior flooded my head. *"I'm sexy and naked and ready to fornicate."*

"Oh, no." I covered my mouth with my hand.

"What's wrong?"

"Bye, Will."

"Hey! Wha—"

I ended the call. I didn't have time for his shenanigans or the hour-long physician's lecture that would have occurred had I told him

about my allergic reaction. No doubt, Will would've been furious I
didn't go to the emergency room last night.

This moment required an immediate call to Cassie. The line rang
three times before she answered, her voice drugged with sleep. "It's
kind of early, Wheorgie."

Forgoing pleasantries, I dove right into my current situation,
highlighting the main points. My ramble lasted a good three minutes,
only pausing to take a quick breath between run-on sentences.

"So, what you're telling me is that your date with Kline started off
great, until you had an allergic reaction and your face ballooned up
like a blimp? And then you chugged a bottle of Benadryl, got naked
in his bed, and attempted to hand him your lady flower, but you guys
just ended up eating pizza instead?"

"It sounds even worse when you repeat it back to me," I whined.

"Where are you right now?"

"I'm in his apartment, standing outside on the terrace so he can't
hear me freaking the fuck out."

"And you stayed at his place last night?"

"Yeah, I woke up in his bed this morning."

"Did he try to usher your ass out of his bed the second you woke
up?"

I shook my head. She didn't respond.

"See, the way phone conversations work, is that you actually have
to say the words out loud."

"You're such a pain in the ass," I retorted. "And no, he didn't try
to push me out of bed and send me packing. He was actually pretty
sweet."

"I'm not sure what the problem is, then."

"Are you serious?" I shouted. "I'm mortified, Cass! I pretty much
made a fool out of myself last night! I don't even—"

"Hey," she interrupted my rant.

"What?" I snapped back.

"Take a breath and think this over," she coaxed, her voice cool and calm. "Sure, things didn't go as planned, *but*…you're still at his apartment. He's not acting weird. He didn't try to shove you out the door. Right?"

I nodded.

"I'm assuming you're nodding your head, so I shall continue," she said, amusement highlighting her voice. "You have two options here, Georgie. You can either grab your shit and make a beeline for the door and continue to stew in your mortification back at our apartment. Or you can get some tits and go in there and demand a re-do."

"A re-do?"

"Demand you finish that amazing kiss. Or, you know, turn that sexy lip-lock into something else. Something more *orally* challenging."

I ran through my options. I could either let self-doubt rule my brain or walk back into his apartment and show him what a confident, self-assured woman looks like when she's ready to take what she wants.

"You're right," I agreed, steadfast in my decision. "Embarrassment can go fuck itself. It's time for a re-do."

"That's my girl."

"I love you, Casshead."

"Love you too," she responded, a smile in her voice. "Now, stop wasting time and go in there and kiss the hell out of Big-dicked Brooks."

"Okay, that's my cue to end this call," I teased. "Have fun snapping pics of muscly men."

"Oh, the fun has already been had, my dear. I plan on having even more fun tonight, *without* a lens in front of my face."

I smiled, my nerves finally at ease. "I miss your crazy ass."

"Miss you too, sweet cheeks. Call me later and let me know how things went."

"You got it."

"But make sure it's tomorrow because I'm about to be balls deep in my best impression of a rodeo queen. The Italian Stallion—"

"I'm hanging up now!"

Her laugh was the last thing I heard as I tapped end on the call.

Turning for the door, I stopped mid-step, my eyes meeting my reflection in the glass panes. I did a quick once-over, taking inventory of my current state. My hair was a little askew, pulled up in a messy bun. My legs peeked out from beneath Kline's Harvard cotton tee. My ass was covered by a pair of white cotton boy shorts. It wasn't my sexiest of days, but I didn't look awful. And surprisingly, my lips had gone back to their normal size.

I sniffed the collar of his t-shirt, and despite the clean scent, remnants of his cologne managed to linger on the freshly laundered material. *God, he really did smell good.* Kline just might have been my very own aphrodisiac.

I wanted him. And I was hell-bent on taking what I wanted.

Walking through the doors, I left any inkling of self-doubt on the terrace, finding him shirtless, standing at the sink of his master bathroom. His perfect ass was clad in boxer briefs and nothing else, wide shoulders on display, muscles stretching as he brushed his teeth. His biceps flexed as he finished up, turning off the sink.

His body was perfect. Defined with just enough bulk. Smooth skin sweetened the deal, leading from his muscular shoulders to his defined pectorals. I wanted to trace the lines with my tongue. He didn't shave or wax his chest like guys on magazine covers. No, Kline Brooks was a *man.* A beautiful, sexy man with a natural smattering of dark hair on his chest. His abdomen was defined with ridges and hard lines that led down into a glorious V, and a soft, just barely noticeable trail of hair paved a path from his belly button to territory I'd have had to remove his boxer briefs to see.

I wanted to lick that happy trail, spend some time there, make a fucking day out of it.

My body was getting way too excited over the possibilities.

Cool it, Georgia. Slow your horny roll.

I wanted a re-do of our first kiss, not the beginning of a porno flick.

Cornflower blue eyes, with the tiniest bit of yellow lining the contrasting black pupils, met mine in the mirror. "Everything okay?"

I nodded, moving toward the sink and plucking his just-used toothbrush from the holder. Without hesitation, I made myself at home, putting a glob of toothpaste on the bristles and going to town on cleaning my teeth.

Kline watched with amusement.

"You don't mind, do you?" I asked after two circuits on my top teeth.

"Not at all," he responded, smirking. That perfect ass of his found the edge of the sink as he continued to observe.

"I need a favor," I stated, turning off the sink and wiping my face with the hand towel.

"Favor?"

"Uh-huh. It's a mighty big favor, but there's a possibility it will benefit you greatly."

"I'm all ears, Benny girl." He winked, amused with my new nickname. Though I was less impressed with his creativity than he was, I still felt a tingle.

"Do you have an iPod dock anywhere in the apartment?"

His gaze turned intrigued. "In my bedroom, on the dresser beside the terrace doors."

"Perfect," I said over my shoulder, walking that direction.

He followed me, sitting on the bed, while I set my phone in the dock and found the perfect re-do song.

The Drifters' "Some Kind of Wonderful" filled the room.

"I know this wasn't the song we heard after our dance," I pointed out, shrugging, "but it's my favorite 'Some Kind of Wonderful.'"

"Hmm, I don't know. The first version seemed pretty good to me." He tapped his chin thoughtfully. "I can relate to the lyrics."

I put a hand on my hip. "Is that so?"

He nodded. "I think most men come to a point in their lives

where the concept of one right woman above all other things seems logical—warranted, even."

I swooned. Head, heart, stomach—my entire body was in on it.

"Well, this is *my* show, so this is our some kind of wonderful for right now."

Kline grinned.

My bare feet moved across the soft carpet, stopping once my knees tapped his. "Stand up, please." I gestured with my hand. "I want a re-do. I want to finish what we started, *before* you tried to kill me with lime juice." A teasing smirk crested my lips.

"I did not try to kill you," he said through a chuckle, getting to his feet. "But, I *am* saying yes to the favor."

Blue-tinted tenderness gazed down at me, while strong hands slipped under cotton, finding the curve of my hips.

"I'm sorry I ruined our date last night," I whispered.

"You didn't ruin anything."

I cocked a disagreeing brow.

"Georgie, I had an amazing time." He touched my cheek, warmth spreading across my skin. "And I'd do it all over again. Allergic reaction and Benny high, I'd still do it all over again. You're pretty damn adorable when you're buzzing on antihistamines."

Good Lord, I can only imagine the kind of crazy things that were coming out of my mouth last night...

Self-doubt could be a real tricky bitch. Even when you thought you had her under control, she found a way to creep back in, making you analyze everything. Despite my earlier confidence, I had reached that moment.

"Please, don't remind me of anything I said or did. I have enough embarrassment stocked up to last a lifetime." I groaned, burying my face in his bare chest.

Kline consumed me in a hug. He held me for a long moment, shouldering my mortification. Lips found my ear and whispered, "Do you want to know something?"

"What?" I asked, my voice muffled against his skin.

"I'm glad you're here."

"Really?"

"Yeah, Benny girl, and now, I'm ready for our re-do."

I leaned back, staring up at him. The man I'd come to know as Mr. Brooks, CEO and well-known mogul of the online dating industry, was morphing into someone different. He wasn't just the serious man whose life solely revolved around business. He was funny and sweet and lived in the moment. He wasn't the flashy, ostentatious billionaire I pictured living in a million-dollar apartment. He was practical and humble, so damn humble. He was someone I wanted to spend more time with. He was someone I could see myself *falling* for.

He wasn't Mr. Brooks anymore. He was Kline, the man I wanted to take a *real* chance on. It shocked me how little time it took to recognize the difference.

I slid my hands up his back, savoring the feel of his toned and smooth skin. Gripping the nape of his neck, I rocked my feet forward, standing tippy-toed. Desperate to feel his mouth on mine, I made the first move, slowly, softly, pressing my lips to his and coaxing a kiss from him.

He responded with fervor, sliding his tongue across my bottom lip and then slipping it inside my mouth to dance with mine. In a matter of seconds, our kiss turned heated, hands groping, tongues clashing. Kline gripped the cotton material covering my skin and removed it from my body, tossing it haphazardly across the room.

My breasts pressed against his chest as he pulled me closer. I moaned into his mouth when his hands met the curve of my back, sliding to my ass and slipping under my boy shorts. He gripped my bare skin for a beat before slipping his hands back up the curve of my spine, leaving my underwear back in place in his wake.

It was a crazy-hot move.

"Get on the bed, Georgie," he demanded, turning our bodies and guiding me toward the mattress.

I lay back, staring up at him. Uncertainty started to sneak in. I was worried he might expect more out of this moment than I was prepared to give. But the way he was looking at me—it was enough to make me forget my own name. Light blue eyes took in every inch of my exposed skin, darkening closer to navy by the second.

I couldn't think about anything else besides him touching me.

He rested his hands beside my head, body hovering above mine. His tongue licked a line down my jaw, to my neck, until his lips were sucking a sensual path between my breasts.

"Now, *I* need a favor," he whispered against my skin. "Let me taste you, sweet girl." He sucked a nipple into his mouth, his skilled tongue eliciting panting breaths from my lungs. "Let me taste every inch of this perfect body. Let me hear what you sound like when you come."

"Yes. God, yes," I whimpered.

He grinned against my skin, fingers sliding down my stomach until they found my boy shorts, slipping them down my legs and off my body. Strong hands gripped my thighs, spreading and baring me to his heated gaze.

"You are so beautiful."

He kneeled between my legs, slipping a finger between my lips and sliding through my arousal. "You're soaked and so fucking soft. I want to lick up and down every part of this." His finger traveled the slit and flicked the clit at the top for emphasis. "I'm hard just thinking about how good you'll taste."

Nerves started to fill my stomach with second thoughts. He didn't know I was a virgin. And I knew, even though I was really into him, I wasn't ready to take that kind of step. "Kline," I whispered, my voice too shaky and quiet for him to hear.

"Now this is the kind of pussy a guy can get along with," he said, flashing a wink in my direction.

And just like that, his playfulness washed my worries out to sea.

"Just how good of friends are you?" I asked.

He smiled. The bastard.

"I know *her* really well."

My eyes narrowed, and he smiled harder.

"But it's the kind of friendship built on trust and respect, and I *never* have more than one friend at a time."

God, this man. He didn't even know how good he was for me.

"That's good to hear because this pussy doesn't have more than one friend at a time either. And she demands respect and trust before letting anyone *all the way in*."

"Duly noted." He ran his tongue up the inside of my thigh. "Let the record show, I'm the kind of man who doesn't rush things. I like to take my time and savor every moment, *every single inch*." He moved to the other leg, repeating the same sexy-as-hell move. "And, Georgia?"

"Yeah?"

He slipped a finger inside of me and out again before sliding it into his mouth. He moaned audibly and closed his eyes. "You're going to melt on my tongue."

Holy hell.

"I think I'm already melting," I whimpered, my head falling back on the bed.

"No, baby, you haven't even started to melt yet," he whispered, moving his tongue against me.

God, it felt so good. So fucking good.

I swallowed my moans, gripping the sheet for support. It was intense. My orgasm was building far quicker and stronger than anything I'd experienced. My legs and hips shook as he sucked my clit into his mouth, his tongue working me into a frenzy.

But he didn't let up.

He gripped my thighs, keeping me spread wide for his ministrations.

My fingers found his hair while my hips moved of their own accord, grinding against his mouth, riding his tongue.

This was the hottest round of oral I'd ever received in my life.

He repeatedly built me up, only to slow things down when I got too close.

He wasn't racing to get me off; *no*, he was savoring every second. He told me how good I tasted and how hard he was just from watching me slowly lose control. He told me how sexy I was and how he never wanted to stop.

"Please, Kline. Oh fuck, please," I begged. I didn't even know what I was begging for. I wanted him to get me off—*badly*—yet I never wanted this to end.

"My greedy girl." He sucked harder and my back bowed off the bed.

"Oh, God," I moaned.

"Do me a favor, Georgie. When you come, don't hold back. I *need* to hear your sounds."

"Yes. Yes. Yes," I chanted, too consumed with the orgasm about to pull me under. Hell, he could've asked me to put on a top hat and sing the "Star Spangled Banner" when I came. I would've agreed to anything in that moment. Though, that might have made things a little more awkward.

He grabbed my breasts, caressing the pliant flesh possessively, while his mouth pushed me toward the edge.

My eyes rolled back, gasping breaths escaping my lungs.

"Say it," he demanded.

I moaned, moving my hands to his hair and gripping the strands for leverage. My hips had a mind of their own, grinding into this face with reckless abandon.

"Fucking *say it*, sweet girl." The sexy growl to his voice was enough to push me over.

"Yes! Kline! I'm coming!" My body lost control—legs shaking, lungs gasping for breaths. My pulse roared in my ears.

I didn't just melt. I *dissolved*. And I gave him my sounds. I'm not sure *what* sounds, but I remember shouting, "*This is the best orgasm of my life!*" at some point.

I'm pretty sure I lost consciousness for a moment, only to be stirred when strong hands cradled my body, adjusting me on the bed so my head rested comfortably on the pillows.

My eyelids fluttered opened to find a smirking Kline staring down at me.

He pressed a kiss to my mouth. "Thank you. That was the best orgasm of my life too," he said softly against my lips.

His mouth crested into a wry grin as he stood, adjusting himself in his briefs. He was hard and standing at attention, making his appearance the hottest, most obscene thing I'd ever laid eyes on.

"Now, I think it's time for breakfast. Eggs and bacon sound good to you?"

I glanced down at his crotch, shocked by the nonchalant tone of his voice. His dick was saluting me, yet he didn't seem the least bit affected by his current *situation.*

"But you're, uh, hard." And I mean fucking hard. That soldier was ready for all-out war.

"Seems to be a common occurrence when you're around." He winked and walked toward the doorway, only to shout, "Meet me in the kitchen, Benny girl!" over his shoulder as he strode out of the bedroom.

Did he just…? He did, didn't he?

Orgasms never helped my eloquence with words, but Kline Brooks was a giver.

Like whoa.

This wasn't the norm. We'd all been with the norm. The guys who would only go down on you because they were expecting some sort of oral exchange. Once you'd gotten your rocks off, they were flashing slanty-eyed glances toward their dicks, waiting for you to return the favor. They'd do everything just short of shoving their crotch in your face. They'd rattle off options like an auctioneer: *Blow job? Hand job? Just hold it for a minute? Let me hold your tit while I jerk off?*

They might as well have had flashing neon arrows pointing to their pants or, better yet, taken out a piece of paper and drawn a "here is my dick" treasure map, just in case we might have forgotten where the male member was located.

But Kline hadn't done that.

He'd straight up licked me into an orgasm and then said, "Thank you."

He had thanked *me* for letting him go down on me.

I'd never claimed to be a genius, but I was pretty sure Kline Brooks had just *wham, bam, and you can thank me, ma'am*ed me.

It was the sexiest fucking thing I'd ever experienced.

CHAPTER 16

Kline

Uncomfortable was too cushy a word to describe the kind of hell I was in right now. Hard and engorged, my ax was ready to chop some fucking wood, and because of the redistribution of blood flow, my brain was having a hard time explaining why it couldn't.

It wasn't that I didn't want to, that was for goddamn sure. But Georgie's overall discomfort was easy enough to read. I knew she'd enjoyed my mouth on her—I doubted as much as I had—but she would have reciprocated out of duty or expectation. And honestly, the first time she sucked my cock, I wanted it to be because she *wanted* to. Because she couldn't fucking stand not to.

Gripping the base tight through my underwear, I fought to stop the pulsing and bring it even a little bit of relief.

When the fiery depths of hell felt more like the heat of Death Valley, I rearranged myself into the best position and got to work digging out a skillet to make some omelets.

Eggs, turkey bacon, and cheese, I lined the basic ingredients up on the counter and put some cooking spray in the bottom of the skillet. Poised to crack the first egg directly into the waiting heat, I had a flashing memory of Georgia's swollen face last night and panicked. The egg nearly slipped from my hand, a completely graceless juggle the only thing that saved it.

I needed to do an allergy rundown with her before I even considered preparing any kind of food products.

I rounded the counter to ask her, but stopped abruptly in my tracks when she came sauntering out of my bedroom naked. She was like a new woman, confidence and determination fueling her stride as she ate up the distance between us.

My dick backtracked, immediately swelling with the excitement I'd spent the last several minutes trying to calm.

"Georgie?" I asked as she beared down on me, wondering what was on her mind while my dick prayed whatever it was would end in some form of attention.

She didn't say anything as she planted a hand on my naked chest and pushed me back until the top of my ass hit the edge of the island counter.

The heat of her palm scorched my skin and the look of her body did the same to my eyes. I couldn't focus on one place, my eyes bouncing and bounding from one glorious part of her to the next.

Everything lost focus when she sank to her knees, the room around me blurring so badly I nearly passed out.

"Georgie," I called again, hoping she'd give me something to ease my mind. A look, a comment—anything to put my racing thoughts at ease enough that I could do nothing but enjoy whatever she intended to do. I didn't want to be the guy who said the standard, "You don't have to," at the same time that I was thinking, *Oh yeah, you do* inside—because that was how it worked. But I did want some kind of reassurance that neither of us would regret this.

Finally, her eyes met mine, and she licked her lips as she shoved her hands into the waistband of my boxer briefs, sliding them down with her palms flat against my skin the whole way.

Fuckkkk. Me.

"Mmm," she hummed in anticipation, leaning forward and taking the whole head in her mouth. Just like that. *Right in her fucking mouth.*

Gun to my head, that moment, my cock would have been known as The Grinch. Because that fucker up and swelled to twice its size in the matter of a heartbeat.

"Good God," I breathed, my neck craning back in ecstasy.

She hummed at that, the vibration in her throat coating my skin along with the wet and warmth. I put my hands on the counter to stop from gripping her hair.

This ride was hers, and I was merely a passenger. So many times, women play to what they think a man wants, defaulting to him rather than owning their ability.

I'll let you in on the fucking secret—absolutely nothing *I could ask her to do would be as good as letting her surprise me.*

She slid her mouth down as far as it would go and back, leaving a coat of moisture behind. The chilled air tingled the skin she unsheathed and shot straight to my tightening balls.

Her hand must have sensed it or something, shooting out to cup them at the perfect pressure, just between timid and crushing, rolling each of them between her fingers like a goddamn sac expert.

My legs started to shake, but I fought it, scared she'd stop to ask if I was okay or if I needed to change positions.

A swirl of her tongue at the tip later, she took me inside again, pushing the flat of her tongue against the underside and tapping it in a rapid rhythm. Up and down she worked me, adding her free hand at the base and mesmerizing me with a frenzy-inducing twist.

My mind raced and blanked at once, knowing the cum was coming and working overtime to find the faculties to actually tell her.

"Baby," I groaned, finally letting my hand shoot out to grip her hair. I pulled it up with a jerk, but took care not to be too rough or startle her.

Her eyes fucking destroyed me when they met mine, eating me alive with the same intensity as her mouth. She was swallowing my fucking dick like it was her last meal and she'd had a goddamn choice of the whole menu.

I couldn't hold back anymore.

"Oh shit. Oh *fuck*. I'm gonna come. *Ahhh*, God."

She sucked harder instead of letting go, pushing me to get there faster with a strum of her fingers at my balls.

I didn't think I usually came that fast, but the surprise had everything fucked. My stamina, my mind—my ability to form complete sentences. Gone.

When the last jerk subsided, she soothed me with her tongue, sliding her loose hand up and down the shaft slowly.

"Mmm," she moaned again, nearly knocking me on my ass. "You taste good too."

I would never, *ever* be able to look at this woman without remembering this moment. Not for my entire life. I was fucking sure of it.

I was equally sure, as one of her greatest fears centered around being able to maintain a professional relationship with me in a work environment, she would *not* want to hear that.

She got to her feet slowly, but I sped up the process, grabbing her by the hips and slamming her naked body directly into mine. My slowly softening cock rested between our bellies, and my lips sought hers.

I fought the primal urge to eat her alive, though, teasing her tongue with mine in a sweet dance of thank-you instead.

I wanted her to feel cherished and fucking appreciated. Her bottom lip swelled in my mouth with the pressure of my suction, so I soothed it with my tongue immediately upon its release.

She moaned in my mouth, hard and deep and needy, and I took

it as my completely ass backwards cue to break the kiss. My hands had already found their way to her ass, and I knew if I didn't stop now, I'd end up pushing her into something she really *wasn't* ready for.

"Go put on a shirt, baby," I ordered softly, and then offered, "Take a shower if you want to."

The shy girl was just under the surface, clearing the fog of lust, and I knew she'd much rather succumb to it in the privacy of my room or the shower than have to live through it in front of me.

I pressed a soft peck to the corner of her lips and inhaled the smell of the skin of her cheek with my nose. *Subtly sweet like a rose surrounded by apples.*

"I'll finish making breakfast," I said into her skin before pulling away. "You're not allergic to anything other than lime juice, are you?"

She smiled slightly before shaking her head.

"Good. I'll turn the bacon and eggs into omelets, then."

"Kline?" she asked, ignoring my rundown and sliding her hand up my neck to the juncture of my jaw. My throat tightened and my pulse beat double time as her thumb brushed the line of it.

"Yeah, Benny?"

"Thanks." One soft kiss to my lips later, she turned and retreated to my bedroom and all I could do was watch as she went, my boxer briefs still twisted around my ankles.

I was fucked—really and truly fucked—when it came to Georgia Cummings.

"Omelet's ready," I called through the closed bathroom door after making a quick stop in my closet to put on a pair of jersey shorts until I showered. I was still sticky with the evidence of Georgia's performance, so I opted to go commando underneath them until I could rectify it—this billionaire's apartment only had one bathroom.

I expected her to call something back through the door, but she opened it instead, stepping into the doorway and nearly into me with wet hair, a towel around her body.

With a mind of its own, my hand reached out to wipe away the lingering drop of water on the top swell of her breast. She shivered.

I felt downright needy for more contact. Hugs, hand holding—I didn't give a fuck. I just wanted to touch her, and I wanted to do it all day.

"Spend the day with me," I blurted.

"Kline—"

"No," I interrupted. "Don't say no."

She smiled, a tiny laugh coating my skin as she tilted her head to the side just slightly. "I wasn't going to."

"Good," I breathed in relief.

"But I do need to go home first. I need clothes. Preferably ones that fit and don't smell like you." She held up a hand before I got defensive, admitting softly, "It's distracting."

"Fine," I agreed easily, countering, "But I'm going with you. Last time I let you arrive separately, you were forty-five minutes late."

Her face pinched in annoyance.

I leaned forward and pressed my lips to hers, smoothing it away just as fast. Without moving back, I spoke my parting words right against her lips. "Any other time I'd be patient, baby, but today, when it comes to spending time with you, I find I'm a little less willing to wait."

CHAPTER 17

Georgia

"Cokes from a vending machine? Hot dogs from a vendor? What's next, Mr. Spontaneity?" I nudged him with my shoulder.

He shrugged, taking the last bite of his mustard and relish-covered dog. "I didn't really have a plan. I just wanted to make sure you spent the day with me."

Night was settling over the city, streetlights glittering the pavement with their soft glow. We had spent the day riding the subway and making stops at random. Kline would ask me a question and my answer was what decided our next stop.

Favorite place to relax? A stroll through Central Park.

Favorite childhood memory? Feeding ducks at the Brooklyn zoo.

Dinner was outside of MoMA, after we had spent most of the evening browsing Picasso's sculptures and Jackson Pollock's beautiful landscapes. He had kissed me slow and deep, fogging my brain with memories of this morning. Kline waited until he had me good and turned on, then pulled away, nonchalantly asking what sounded good for dinner.

The horny side of me quickly responded, "Well, I *really* enjoyed breakfast this morning."

"You want bacon and eggs again?"

"No," I answered, standing on my tiptoes and kissing a sensual path along his jaw. Using my teeth to tug at his earlobe, I whispered, "That wasn't my favorite part of breakfast."

And that's how we ended up at a street vendor outside of MoMA, ordering hot dogs. The cheeky bastard had made sure to order us footlongs, adding, "Just trying to get the size right."

He found a bench, pulling me down into his lap. "Let's eat, Benny girl," he said, kissing my forehead and setting dinner in my hands.

I ate my footlong, enjoying every second of being in his company. Pedestrians meandered past us. Taxis sped by in their usual hurry. But the world didn't exist in that moment. I was too busy savoring every soft kiss to my cheek and handsome smile flashed in my direction.

"This might have been better than breakfast." I took my last bite, moaning.

He tickled my ribs with his free hand. "I never pegged you as a liar, Ms. Cummings."

"Who said I was lying?" I winked.

"You got a little something, right here." He wiped a drop of ketchup from the corner of my mouth, sucking it off his finger and waggling his brows. "Always so fucking good."

I laughed, shoving his shoulder playfully. "All right, dirty boy, what's next on the agenda?"

Helping me to my feet, he grinned. "I've got an idea, but I need to know if you're ready to be a little wild."

"How wild?" I questioned, a sassy hand on my hip.

He tossed our empty bottles and napkins in the trash.

"Crazy, insane kind of wild." His eyes turned serious. He grabbed my hips, guiding me toward a vacant alley and gently pushing my back against a brick wall. "Can you handle getting a little crazy with me?"

I nodded, smiling up at him.

He pressed a kiss to mouth. "Are you sure, Benny girl? Because I can't have you chickening out last minute."

"Are you calling me out?"

"Are you too scared to take the challenge?"

I bit his bottom lip, my teeth tugging playfully. "I'll take any challenge you throw my way."

"Is that so?"

"You bet your tight ass it is."

"I've got fifteen dollars *and* a striptease that says you'll chicken out."

"I'll see your bet and raise you an orgasm."

His mouth met mine again, his tongue slipping past my lips. He kissed me passionately, sliding his hands into my hair and taking control. His lips coaxed a moan from my throat, only to leave me disappointed when he pulled away, smirking like the devil.

"Game on, baby." He grabbed my hand, leading me back onto the sidewalk. "Oh, and I want you wearing heels. Sexy fucking heels that'll blow my mind."

I giggled, shaking my head. "You better prepare yourself because I'm demanding Channing Tatum-like dance moves. I'm talking pelvic thrusts and lots of grinding action."

We took the subway until Kline ushered us off at Midtown East. Ten minutes later, we were standing in front of ONE UN—a prestigious hotel in the business of catering to the rich and famous.

"Are we schmoozing with diplomats tonight?"

He chuckled. "No, but we're definitely going to get a little wet."

I raised a curious brow as he led us through the lobby and to a bank of elevators hidden on the eastern side of the facility.

The ride was quick, and once we reached our apparent destination, we hopped off and walked hand in hand past a reception desk. A twenty-something-year-old girl glanced up from her laptop, offering a simple, "Enjoy your workout," and resumed typing. She didn't question our motives, seemingly oblivious to the fact that we were basically breaking in to their facility.

I started to get a little nervous as Kline led me through a locker room. He held open a glass door, ushering me toward an indoor pool. The water was enticing, lights still on and glowing beneath the clear water.

"Uh?" I asked, glancing around.

We were the only ones there, but a white sign with big red letters instructed us why.

No one permitted in the pool area after nine o'clock.

It was half past ten.

The sign also stated, *Members only pool. Police will be contacted in the event this rule is violated.*

Hefty warning for an indoor pool, right? Yeah, but remember, this hotel wasn't just any hotel. It was adjacent to the United Nations Headquarters. When I'd joked about schmoozing with diplomats, I hadn't been kidding.

Kline took off his shoes and socks, setting them on a chair.

"Uh, what are you doing?"

"I'm getting ready to hop in the pool," he responded, unbuckling his belt. "You're joining me, right?"

"Pretty sure I don't have a bathing suit." I glanced down at my attire—jeans, a cotton tank top, a light cotton sweater, and brown leather flats.

"But I thought you said you wanted to be a little wild?" he asked, amusement in his voice.

"Yeah, but…" I paused when he unzipped his jeans and slid them down his legs.

"But…what?" He looked up, his eyes filled with a playful edge.

"We're not even supposed to be in here," I whispered, even though no one outside of the pool could hear me. "And you want me to what? Go for a dip in my bra and panties?"

He shrugged off his shirt. "You could always go without."

My jaw dropped. "You want me to skinny-dip? In a pool that we're not even supposed to be in?"

"Are you getting ready to chicken out?" Kline taunted. His gorgeous body was on full display, only boxers covering his muscular thighs.

"No," I retorted.

He cocked a brow. "Are you sure? Because it kind of looks like you're ready to jet."

I narrowed my eyes.

"Get ready to strip, baby." A grin covered his lips. "And don't forget the heels."

His smug confidence had me changing my tune. I wasn't usually the type of girl to break rules, but I also wasn't the type of girl to back down from a bet.

My stubborn side won the battle for supremacy.

I kicked off my flats and moved toward the pool. My jeans, cardigan, and tank top were removed in quick fashion and discarded onto an empty chair. "Get ready to pay up." I strode to the deep end, staring at his amused expression from across the water. I unclasped my bra and shimmied out of my panties, tossing them in his direction. With a sweet, devious little smile, I said, "Remember, I want lots of pelvic thrusting action," and then dove into the pool.

After savoring the warmth of the water, I broke the surface, resting my arms on the ledge, and grinned back at Kline. "Put your money where your mouth is, Brooks."

He laughed, sliding off his boxer briefs and turning around. He started humming a striptease beat, glancing at me over his shoulder and grinning playfully. Kline proceeded to pelvic thrust, his hands resting behind his head and his grin turning cocky with each punch forward, not an ounce of embarrassment on his face. He was visibly enjoying himself, loving the growing smile on my lips, and he was crazy adorable yet insanely hot at the same time. I watched his tight ass and muscular thighs flex with each circuit. He kept it up until my giggles turned loud and uncontrolled.

He dove into the pool, slicing through the water in succinct maneuvers. He moved toward me, his hands finding my hips and signaling him that he had reached his target.

When he broke the surface, his face hovered mere inches from mine. Water dripped from his eyelashes, down his cheeks, and clung to the very tips of his spiky wet hair. "Are you ready to shove twenty-dollar bills in my g-string?"

"Eh, maybe *one* dollar bills?" I teased.

"One-dollar bills?" he asked. "Baby, I recall a lot of pelvic action back there."

"Yeah, *but...*" I sighed "...I didn't get the full-frontal experience."

He laughed, shaking his head. "I'll make note that you're a fan of full frontal."

I smiled, my cheeks damn near bursting with amusement.

He wrapped his arms around my waist, moving us in the water. It rippled into tiny waves around our bodies. "You know what you're not a fan of?" he asked, brow quirking.

"Small wieners?"

His chest vibrated against my skin, laughter spilling from his lips. "Besides that. I'm well aware you've got an appetite for nothing smaller than a footlong."

I giggled, savoring his teasing smile. "Tell me, Brooks, what am I not a fan of?"

"Emergency rooms."

I tilted my head to the side, perplexed.

"You were really fucking adorable last night, slap-happy and high on Benny, but before you got to that point, I was worried." His forehead touched mine. "I wanted to take you to St. Luke's, but you're pretty damn stubborn."

The look in his eyes warmed my stomach. I couldn't imagine, didn't want to imagine, the kind of shape I had been in last night. I could recall bits and pieces here and there, but for the most part, it seemed like a hazy dream. It had been our first real date. We barely knew each other outside of work, yet Kline hadn't hesitated to take care of me. He hadn't freaked out or gotten embarrassed that his date looked ridiculous. Because, let's face it, I'd looked insane. Like someone had given me botched plastic surgery kind of crazy.

Last night, Kline hadn't been focused on anything but making sure I was okay.

And it was apparent, he really was worried.

Those were not the actions of a man whose intentions were less than genuine.

He was different from anyone I had ever met, in the best way. In the span of forty-eight hours, he had somehow gained a large part of my trust. I wasn't skeptical or scrutinizing his every word; I was merely enjoying feeling safe and cherished in his presence.

"My brother is an ER resident at St. Luke's. He just so happened to be working a twenty-four-hour call shift last night," I explained.

"Oh," he said, understanding in his voice. "Now it makes sense."

"Yeah," I said, shrugging. "He's my older brother. My only sibling. And even though my lips were about to consume my face, no way in hell was I going to give him that kind of ammunition." If I thought Will still bringing up "Masturbation Camp" was bad, my arriving in his ER looking like a blowfish would have made that never-ending joke look easy.

"Do you have any siblings?" I asked, curious to know more about him. The short amount of time we'd spent together outside of the office had me realizing every preconceived notion I'd had about Kline was dead wrong. Hell, his small, quaint apartment was evidence of that. It truly was not the kind of flashy, extravagant place I'd pictured him living in. Sure, it was nice, but it looked more like a place I would live in, not someone who had grossed nearly a billion dollars last year with just TapNext alone.

He shook his head. "Only child."

"What are your parents like?"

"My mom is a meddler, but she means well. She's actually the reason Walter is at my apartment."

"Don't you dare say anything bad about Walter," I teased, pointing my finger at him.

"You try living with that asshole for a few weeks and see how it goes."

"He is *not* an asshole. He's a big, fluffy sweetheart," I defended my feline friend, fighting the urge to grin.

Kline scoffed. "Yeah, he is. He's the world's worst cat."

"Stop talking about my buddy Walter like that!"

"I'll be more than happy to gift him to you. I can have his shit packed up and ready to go tonight," he challenged.

"Tell me more about your parents." I laughed, choosing to change the subject before I ended up with a new roommate.

"My father is an old school Irish Catholic who loves beer and offers a constant supply of dad jokes. Even though they drive me crazy sometimes, Maureen and Bob are pretty wonderful."

There was a soft kindness in his voice that showed how much he adored his folks. "What about your parents?"

"My dad is a sweetheart, but he's a total ballbuster. He has to be to keep my crazy mother on her toes."

"Crazy mother?"

"My mom is a sex therapist. She's just about as quirky as it gets."

"*Sex* therapist?" he asked, smirking. "I did not expect that one."

"It's not really a common profession."

"Wait…your mom's last name is Cummings, right?"

"Yes." I nodded, already knowing where he was going with this. "Dr. Savannah Cummings is my mother, the sex therapist extraordinaire. As if it wasn't hard enough growing up with Cummings as your last name."

"No wonder you're so good at blow jobs," he teased.

I shoved him away, mouthing, *Pervert*.

"Only for you." He chuckled, pulling me close again. Our bare chests were pressed against each other. Water droplets slipped down my skin, and my nipples hardened instantly.

"Do you even know how sexy you are?" His eyes met the curve of my breasts peeking above the waterline. Strong hands slid from my hips to my ribs until they moved around my back and caressed my ass. "Baby, you drive me fucking insane."

My heart tripped. He'd called me *baby*. Sure, he had said it before, but this time, it had just rolled off his tongue with such ease. It was a reflex, *instinctive*. I felt like we were really trying this, trying *us*.

I brushed my lips against his. We weren't kissing at first, just teasing, breathing the same air. I could smell the chlorine on his skin, the hint of sugar on his lips from the soda we'd shared earlier. I saw my reflection in his pupils, eyes wanton and needy.

"I don't think I'll ever get enough of you." He parted his lips, pressing his mouth to mine. "I'll never get enough of these perfect cherry lips." He opened his mouth, sucking on my top lip, my tongue.

Heat pulsed in my lower belly, my heart racing in anticipation.

Kline moved his mouth down my neck to my collarbone and across the curve of my breasts.

I felt the shape of him against my hip, hard and prominent. I reached down to take him into my hand, but he was too quick, gripping my ass and lifting me out of the water and onto the edge of the pool.

He spread my thighs, gazing up at me with wet lashes and hooded eyes. "How many fingers does my wild girl need?" His mouth met my hip, sucking with a force that reddened my sensitive skin.

I had never been so turned on in my life. My body thrummed, blood thundering in my veins, getting off on the illicitness of our location.

And I ached. God, I ached, desperate for more than just his hands. I wanted his mouth on me again.

"Or does she need more? Does she need my lips and tongue to give her what she really wants?"

My head fell back, and I gripped the edge of the pool to hold myself up.

"*Tell me.* Tell me what you need."

"Your mouth," I moaned, sliding my legs over his shoulders. "I need your mouth on me."

He licked a path down my belly. "Hold on tight, baby. This is going to be fast and you're going to fucking *explode.*"

He ate at my pussy until my body was strung tight with the need to come. I tried to hold out, tried to let the intensity build, but Kline's mouth was too talented, too fucking good at seducing a climax out of me.

In the distance, heavy footfalls moved toward us. Keys jingled against a hip. I didn't know where or what or who or how those noises were occurring, my mind stuck somewhere between *suck me harder* and *make me come.*

"Shit," he mumbled, taking that delicious mouth away from where I needed him the most.

"N-N-No," I stuttered out my frustration, but it didn't matter. Kline's hands were wrapped around my waist, yanking me into the water.

My head spun, shocked from the sudden change in position.

"Shh," he quieted me, nodding toward the entrance.

My eyes grew wide in horror, realization setting in. The footsteps, the keys, they were coming from the other side of the door. The very doorknob that was being turned.

Fuck. I was going to get arrested for not only breaking and entering, but for public indecency too. The police were going to be called while my body still throbbed between my legs.

"I got you." He held me tighter. "Hold your breath, baby. We're going under," he instructed, just before sliding us toward a darkened corner and submerging us under the water.

I shut my eyes, held my breath, and prayed to God we wouldn't be seen. Surely, I wasn't going down like *this*, naked in a pool with my boss's cock pressed against my belly.

It really was a fantastic cock, but that was beside the point. Shit was about to hit the fan.

Kline's lips found mine and I felt his smile against my mouth.

Devious bastard.

Trailing his fingers down my belly, he found the spot where I was still slippery and hot. He didn't waste any time, two fingers sliding inside of me while his thumb rubbed my clit.

Seriously? How was he even thinking about getting me off at a time like this?

But did I stop him? *Nope.* My heart pounded in my ears, the needy, orgasm-driven side of me too focused on what he was doing. I wrapped my legs around his hips like the true hussy I was. If we were going to be Bonnie and Clyde tonight, I sure as hell was going to enjoy the ride.

A few seconds later, he floated us to the top, our heads peeking above the waterline, our lungs dragging in much-needed air. The coast was clear, the mystery person no longer in sight. The lights were off, the doors were shut, and Kline was still finger-fucking me, seemingly unfazed by our almost arrest.

"Sweet, dirty, *wild* girl," he whispered in my ear, picking up the pace. "Even when we're thirty seconds away from getting arrested, you still let me slip my fingers inside your pussy. You like this, don't you? You love being bad just for me." He licked the water from the curve of my breasts.

I moaned, my teeth finding his shoulder and biting down.

"Yes, just like that. Christ, baby, when you catch fire, you motherfucking *burn*."

Hot damn, Kline Brooks was a certified, class-A, deserves-the-major-award dirty talker. His words served their purpose, pushing me straight over the edge and spurring my brilliant response.

"Ho-ly fuck."

CHAPTER 18

Kline

Monday night rugby practice was gearing up, but my mind was still on the weekend—laughter and sexiness and a Benadryl-fueled trip through an allergic reaction. The mixture of all three had me smiling to myself.

Georgia Cummings was quickly becoming one of my favorite people. She made me feel high on life and like the world's biggest idiot all at once.

Curiosity about Rose's weekend was the only thing that kept me from thinking about how close I'd come to never experiencing what I had for the last week. Because I wouldn't have traded the last seven days for anything, even if it were to come to an abrupt end tonight. The memories would have been worth it.

Take note, friends. Don't close off any one section of your life from possibility. Fate gives us chances, but we're the ones who have to take them.

A touch of the icon brought the TapNext app to life. Realization swallowed me with an unexpected sense of accomplishment. This thing was my baby. I'd nurtured it, grown with it over the years like a close friend. I'd watched it make mistakes, veer off the path to greatness, but I'd pulled it back and I was proud of what it'd become. A place where people could find almost anything. A place where people who were lucky found something worthwhile like I had.

BAD_Ruck (6:15PM): Hey, Rose. You busy? I'm just curious how the date went. I didn't get to check in with you over the weekend.

I stared at the message window, waiting to see if she would reply. I was just about to give up waiting when the little bubbles popped up on the screen.

TAPRoseNEXT (6:17PM): If avoiding contracting bubonic plague from the passenger next to me can be considered busy, then sure. I'm just on the train on my way back from work.

BAD_Ruck (6:17PM): And the date?

"Put your phone down, K. Everyone is waiting on us," Thatch shouted.

I looked up to find the team captains still in the middle of the rugby field, known as a pitch, chatting, but I tossed my phone down anyway. Any amount of dawdling would only be cause for Thatch to publicly bust my balls. As my best friend of more than a decade, he had too much ammunition and a specially made gun for the job.

I broke into a jog for extra measure, joining the group of no-good assholes I called my teammates. Sponsorship wasn't necessary for obvious reasons, but we played the league on the straight and narrow, using businesses to sponsor the team like everyone else. I'd volunteered Brooks Media, but with a dating site being one of the main focuses of the company, that had resulted in a resounding, "Veto!"

Instead, Wes's restaurant, BAD—a fucking joke of a name for all the success he had—was our sponsor and earned our team as a whole the moniker "BAD Boys." But because everyone thought they were fucking cute, that wasn't enough, and the trio of Thatch, Wes, and I were forever dubbed the *Billionaire Bad Boys*. It was there to stay. Trust me, I'd been trying to shake it for years.

"We're skins," John announced to the informal huddle when he came back from the captains' meeting.

"Fuck," Thatch breathed, rolling his head in distress for some reason.

"What's the matter, Thatch?" Wes asked. "Afraid one of the boys is going to pull out your titty ring?"

"Blow me, Torrence."

"Torrence?" I questioned, feeling a wrinkle form between my eyebrows.

"It's a *Bring It On* reference," John remarked casually as he stretched out his hamstring by pulling his heel to his ass, as though it wasn't weird that he'd know that.

When I turned my curiosity from Thatch to him, he piped up again.

"What? Kirsten Dunst is in the movie, and she's fucking hot." He added, "And I have a younger sister," when the group was slow to buy in.

"How *is* your sister, Johnny?" Thatch asked with a smirk.

John's eyes flashed brightly before turning to stone. "Eighteen, motherfucker."

Thatch turned to me, and I could practically *see* what was coming. He didn't actually want to bone John's little sister. Not even a little.

"What's that he said, Kline?"

He might have been a manwhore, but Thatch fucked *women*— not girls just starting to make the transition. What he wanted was to poke at one of John's pressure points just enough to make him explode.

I trained my face to look serious and held in a laugh. "I think he said she's legal, Thatch."

John lunged and my humor finally broke the surface. I grabbed his shirt with both hands and shoved him away playfully while Thatch busted out in hysterics beside me.

"Relax, John," Wes coaxed. "Thatch doesn't need your sister to fill his pussy punch card. He's got all the tramps he'll ever need right here in Manhattan."

Thatch tsked. "There's no card, Wes. My dick is not a Value Club."

"It sure fucks in bulk," John threw in, eager to even the score because of some running feud between the two of them. We were all well-off, grown-as-fuck men, but you'd be surprised by how similar we were to a group of teenage girls sometimes.

"And how would you know, Johnny? Got a camera in my bedroom?" Thatch snapped back.

"All right," I called, babysitting like usual. "Drama club is over, assholes. Let's go play rugby. Focus all of that energy into your attack, for fuck's sake."

"You're the one who can't manage to make it past halfway without getting tackled and steamrolled into the ground," Wes pointed out. He laughed as he said it, though, continuing the teasing vibe by wrapping his arm around my shoulders and walking out onto the field with me.

"At least I manage to touch the ball every once in a while," I jabbed back, shoving him away and jogging to the other side of the pitch.

At this point in the season, practice consisted mostly of scrimmages, dividing into two teams and trying to outplay each other. I was just glad that when we split up, Thatch was usually on my side. He might have acted like a clown from time to time, but the dude was one big motherfucker and had been known to do some permanent damage when he tackled you. I liked to walk without a limp, and if I was going to be told I couldn't have kids one day, I sure as fuck didn't want testicle mutilation to be the reason.

I shook out of my daydream when the ball slammed into my chest, a smirk ghosting Wes's lips from the success of his unexpected pass.

I took off at a run, dodging a defender and reaching the half-way line. Pain shot through my waist as another defender made hard contact. I tossed the ball underhanded and toward my back, the only direction allowed for a legal pass in rugby, and tucked my arms to my chest to take the impact of the fall without breaking a wrist.

"Jesus," I groaned, shoving Tommy off of me as quickly as I could in order to rejoin play.

"Lay off the cookies, Tom," I shouted as I ran toward the ruck my teammates had going.

"Weights!" he yelled back. "I think when you said cookies, you meant weights!"

And fuck, by the way my spleen throbbed, Tommy just might have been right.

I slammed my body into the linked shoulders of Thatch and Wes, pushing them forward over the loose ball and helping the group gain momentum in the fight upstream against the defenders. Thatch fought for control in front of me, and I nearly took an elbow to the face in the process.

Rugby was a rough game, and when my organs felt like they might fall out or a limb ached like it might fall off, I wondered why I did it.

But then the ball was in my arms again, tossed underhand and over his shoulder by Thatch, and I remembered without question— the adrenaline, the thrill, the all-out expulsion of a week's worth of tension, stress, and aggression.

I was convinced a little extracurricular rugby not only kept me in prime physical shape, but it also kept my mind at peace and on an even keel. I could only hope that as my physical health started to subside with age, my need to vent would dwindle along with it.

The weight of three bodies hit me at once as I was crossing the try line, but Thatch had them off in no time to celebrate the score. I was barely on my feet before the choreography started, Thatch firing off shots from his crotch like a semi-automatic weapon, the men of our team playing into his antics by hitting the ground one by one as he fired off "rounds." As the scorer of the try, I was the only one who'd earned the privilege to stay on my feet.

I laughed and high-fived my teammates before jogging back across the pitch to do it all over again. Practice had just started, and now that I'd scored, my body was ready for more abuse.

I ran for the train just before it was set to depart, sliding through the doors in just the nick of time. Starving and ready to be home, all I could think about was getting there, showering, and ordering a pizza.

As my tired ass met the surface of the seat, I took a moment to be thankful for the lack of pregnant women and elderly. I was worn the hell out, but I wasn't a prick. The rest of these fuckers could fend for themselves.

I wiped some of the lingering sweat and mud from my face with my towel and pulled my phone from my bag.

A message sat waiting from earlier.

TAPRoseNEXT (6:18PM): Gah. The date. The date was amazing. And then it was pretty fucking traumatic.

BAD_Ruck (7:52PM): Traumatic??? Am I going to need to hunt this guy down?

TAPRoseNEXT (7:54PM): No, he's great, I promise. It wasn't traumatic because of him. He's…I don't know, Ruck. I've got this gut feeling that he's some kind of wonderful.

The corners of my lips started to curve, some weird, unconventional but meaningful relationship between us forming and instilling genuine happiness in me. But before the smile cycle could complete, utter disbelief washed over me in a wave of tsunami-like proportions—the conversations we'd had, the things she'd said. Work relationships and awkward yet somehow easy conversation. The way Rose, despite my more than infatuation with Georgie, managed to make me feel.

None of it made sense, not one single piece of it, until all at once, *it did*.

No fucking way.

The doors of the subway opened, and I didn't even hesitate, shoving my way through the throng of people without apology or remorse. I didn't even know what fucking stop we were on, but I ran for the stairs with single-minded abandon, taking them two at a time and reaching the top on a leap.

New Yorkers scoffed and jumped out of the way, burning me with their dirty looks and judging eyes. The yellow of a cab shone like a beacon in front of me.

I ran for it without thought or pause or respect for my surroundings. The heavy leather of a handbag may have even grazed my shoulder in a glancing blow, but I didn't care. Words thrummed in my head in time with the memory of her heartbeat, building and buzzing around my brain until I almost couldn't stand it. The not knowing, the unlikelihood—it was all too much.

"The Winthrop Building. Fast as you can go," I demanded abruptly to the cabbie, but he didn't bat an eye at my brusque delivery—grunts and commands were the nature of more than half of New York City.

I dug in my bag for my wallet and fished out the first bill I came to. With a swift thrust, I dropped it through the plexiglass window and jumped out while the last notes of his screeching tires still rung in the air.

Pigeons panicked and people swerved as I wove my way through them, and a woman strummed a guitar on the corner.

The building was locked after hours, but being the CEO afforded me access to the keyless entry code on the main door. Until today, I could honestly say I'd never broken in to my office building before.

Sixteen smashes of the elevator call button, another code, and a fidgety ride later, I stepped off onto the fifteenth floor in all of my sweaty glory and strode straight for Human Resources.

The lights were dimmed, and once again, the outer door to Cynthia's office door was locked, but nothing could stop me at this point. Not a lock and certainly not my morals.

I ran to my office at a near sprint and around the back of my desk, yanking drawers open one by one in search of my old master key that opened all of the individual office doors. I hadn't had a need for it in years, so it took me several minutes of digging through pounds of junk to find it.

Priority for tomorrow: My desk needed to be fucking reorganized. *Stat.*

Mud under my fingernails from practice, I clutched the key tightly and jogged back down the hall.

With a turn and a click, I was in, moments away from officially violating half a dozen privacy laws.

I breathed a sigh of relief when the drawer of the filing cabinet slid open with ease, laughing maniacally to myself before trailing into words.

"Of course it's not fucking locked. It's not like she was expecting a *fucking psychopath* to break into her office and dig through it."

Like fluttering wings, my fingers shuffled through the labels, knowing Cynthia followed an unbreakable filing system. Nothing was ever out of order or place, and finding it would be easy enough.

Not knowing the actual wording of the label challenged me a little bit, but it wasn't more than five minutes before I was pulling it out of its spot and cracking it open.

Tracing the lines of the employee names, I ran my finger down the page, muttering through last names until the one I wanted stood out in stark relief.

"Cummings, Georgia." I slid it across the page in some kind of slow-motion daydream until the other column sealed my fate in undeniable bold text.

TAPRoseNEXT.

Some Kind of Wonderful.

CHAPTER 19

Georgia

G ary clicked to the next PowerPoint slide, stating something about the cost effectiveness of *blah blah blah...* Who knows what he was talking about by that point? We'd been in the meeting for over two hours, and I was seconds away from losing my cool.

My stomach growled its irritation.

I glanced at my watch and noted it was five minutes past three, which meant it was five minutes past my daily scheduled sugar fix. I had a Greek yogurt and a leftover piece of cherry cheesecake sitting inside the break room fridge with my name on it.

Conclusion: Someone needed to end this or I was going to end Gary.

It was Thursday afternoon, and it'd been five whole days since I'd had any real private interaction with Kline. We'd texted a lot, snuck a few minutes to chat and say hello here and there, and even had lunch together twice, but he'd been unbelievably swamped with work and activities and I was still one hundred percent determined to keep a professional relationship in the office. The combination of all that crap had put the kibosh on substantial alone time. And let me tell you, the memory of last weekend had my anticipation riding at an all-time high.

Gary plodded over to his laptop, tapping around on the keys. The man moved like a turtle. He was a genius when it came to numbers, but a moron when it came to social cues. While everyone in the room was moments away from falling face first into a coma, he appeared to think we had all the time in the world to discuss more goddamn numbers.

I was numbered the fuck out.

"And if you'll just give me a minute here," he mouth-breathed, licking his lips and clicking away. "I'll pull up another spreadsheet that documents how effective we've been in narrowing down our target ratios for the last financial quarter."

Jesus Christ in a peach tree.

My stomach roared its impatience. Hunger pangs. Crazy, loud hunger pangs. It's a mystery no one else heard it over Gary's droning.

The flash of a text notification caught my eye.

Kline: *Was that your stomach, Cummings?*

Okay. Obviously, *someone* heard them.

The handsome bastard was sitting beside me. Honestly, I had no idea why he was subjecting himself to this meeting. It was solely for my marketing team. I glanced at Kline out of the corner of my eye, scratching the side of my face with my middle finger. His body jerked noticeably with the effort to conceal his laugh.

Me: *It's 3:05pm, Brooks.*

Kline: *Ah, right. Georgie's snack time. What was I thinking?*

Me: *I don't know, but if you don't end this soon, I will murder Gary with my pen.*

Fighting a smile, he subtly nodded his head in understanding as he set his phone down on the table. My eyes trailed to his forearms—sleeves rolled up, hard muscles and thick veins on display. To quote Uncle Jesse, *Have mercy*. If I hadn't been so damn hungry, I'd have happily sat through this tedious meeting just to gawk at those glorious arms. They were a beacon of muscly man delight.

Gary chuckled, seemingly entertained by himself. His monotone voice penetrated my daydreams about Kline's forearms, officially popping my Big-dicked Brooks fantasy bubble.

I tapped my pen against my notepad. *Shut Gary up. Now.*

Kline knew it was a warning. He flashed a secret grin, eyes crinkling at the corners. God, his eyes, they were this flawless shade of blue—so bright, so vibrant. Montana-sky blue.

I'd started to make a game out of nicknaming Kline's eyes. Those ever-changing blue retinas could be Montana-sky blue one day or, like today, M&M's blue. But that probably had more to do with the starvation setting in than anything else.

Mmmmmmmm, M&M's. I'd have devoured a bag of that candy-coated chocolate goodness.

"Fantastic work, Gary," Kline interrupted moments later. "I think we can all agree we've gained valuable information on Brooks Media's projections for the fiscal year."

Everyone in the room nodded, agreeing far too enthusiastically.

I *knew* I wasn't the only one dying a slow death with each PowerPoint GoodTime Gary put on the projection screen.

Gary started to respond, but Kline stood up from his chair. "Go ahead and send the materials out to the rest of the team. That way all departments within Brooks Media can see how they've contributed to another fruitful quarter."

"Oh, okay, but—"

"Really great work, Gary." Kline patted him on the back, not giving him an inch. "I think we can officially say, successful meeting adjourned."

My coworkers scattered faster than roaches when light flooded the room. I followed their lead when I realized Kline would be tied up with Gary for a few more minutes. My stomach couldn't wait. I damn near sprinted to the break room, all kinds of ready to dig into my snacks. Would I start with my yogurt and then move on to the cheesecake? Or would I just go for it and dig into the cherry cheese-cake first?

The world was my oyster, baby.

"Uh oh," Dean announced, walking out of the break room. "It's a quarter after three and Georgia isn't eating?" he teased, making a show of glancing between my face and his watch.

"Yeah, GoodTime Gary gave a go at murder by numbers in our quarterly marketing meeting. If Kline hadn't cut it short, I think I would've staged a riot."

"Well, I'm sorry to tell ya, cupcake, but inside there isn't any better. Ivanna Swallow is on her selfie break and she has *blowregard* for anyone but the spoon she's currently sucking yogurt off of for Instagram's sake."

I groaned.

"Head down, don't make eye contact, and you should be fine." He grinned, slapping my ass as he walked past me and down the hall.

Leslie was sitting at one of the break room tables, doing exactly what Dean said she was doing—taking a selfie of a spoon in her mouth. She could probably describe her life in a series of hashtags.

Hashtag, my spoon is so sexy.

Hashtag, my lips bring all the boys to the yard.

Hashtag, my life's goal is to be a walking bonertime.

"Hey, Leslie," I tossed over my shoulder as I headed for the most important thing in the room. The fridge.

"O-M-G. You're, like, never going to believe how adorable peo-ple are."

My phone buzzed in my hand. Thinking it might be Kline

begging for a rescue, I let my heart overpower my stomach and paused to look. No message from Kline, but the TapNext icon was aglow with a message from Ruck. He'd been messaging me in a steady stream ever since Monday night, and I had to admit, he never failed to amuse me.

BAD_Ruck (3:11PM): Lizards or Birds?

Lizards or fucking birds? Jesus.

The sadistic bastard had talked me into this little game by starting it with normal choices. Pillows or blankets, candy or pizza—he'd been getting a real kick out of asking me which thing I'd rather have in bed with me. *You can only have one,* he'd say. With this kind of choice, the decision was a struggle for a different reason.

TAPRoseNEXT (3:11PM): Neither, you lunatic.

My stomach growled, reminding me that I didn't have time for Ruck and his random get-to-know-you choices right now.

Opening the fridge, I started searching for my snack-time loot. I didn't respond to Leslie, knowing full well she'd just prattle on. If Gary was the prime example of not understanding social cues, Leslie was the girl who didn't care about those cues. In her hashtag and selfie-driven mind, *everyone* wanted to know what she had to say.

For fuck's sake, where is my food?

"Seriously," she called, completely oblivious that I'd left a two-minute pause for a reason. "People are, like, so cute. I just ate a turkey sandwich named Gary, and now I'm eating a yogurt named Georgia."

I stopped mid-rummage and slowly stood, glowering at Leslie over the fridge door.

Her answering grin told me that my eyes weren't *actually* shooting out death rays.

"How cute is that?" She held up the half-eaten cup of yogurt. *My half-eaten cup of yogurt.*

"People are naming the food in the break room. I just *can't even.* It's totes adorbs." She went back to wrapping her crazy-huge lips around the spoon that was feeding her *my fucking yogurt.*

It had to be severely unhealthy to want to kill two of your co-workers in the same day.

I took a deep breath, counting to ten in my head.

One-Don't-Kill-Leslie

Two-Don't-Kill-Leslie

Three-Don't-Kill-Leslie...

By the time I reached ten, my hands felt less stabby.

"Hey, Leslie?" I asked through gritted teeth.

"Uh-huh?" she responded, mouth full of yogurt.

"So, that turkey sandwich named Gary was actually just Gary's turkey sandwich. He wrote his name on it so no one else would eat it."

She cocked her head to the side like a confused puppy. "But what about the yogurt named Georgia?"

I fought the urge to shout, inhaling and exhaling another cleansing breath. "The yogurt wasn't named Georgia. I wrote my name on that yogurt because I brought it in. It's *my* yogurt and I planned on eating it today."

She stared back at me, her pea-sized brain visibly processing my words.

The wheels were turning; slowly but surely, they were turning.

"*Ohhh,* my bad." She held out the half-eaten yogurt container. "Here, you can have the rest of it. I'm already so full from eating that turkey sandwich and piece of cherry cheesecake."

Wait a minute...

Piece of cherry cheesecake?

I glared the fuck out of the food-snatching idiot for a good minute before turning for the door.

"So, like, I'm just going to eat the rest of it, okay, Georgia?" was the last thing I heard as I stormed out of the break room and straight for Kline's office. Since he had hired her, I figured it would be a nice gesture to let him know housekeeping was going to need to branch out into crime scene remediation.

His door bounced off the wall with a bang. Kline raised an eyebrow, his expression confused yet curious behind the large mahogany desk. "Everything okay?"

"Nope." The door slammed shut, courtesy of my stiletto-adorned foot. "Everything is not fucking okay."

I strode around his desk and planted my ass on the edge, forcing him to push his chair back to allow room for me and all of my bristling glory.

"I need housekeeping's number. They're going to need to bring a body bag tonight. Figured it'd be nice to give them a heads-up."

"A body bag?"

I nodded. "For Leslie."

He crinkled his forehead, but I guess apprehension did that to a person. "Come again?"

"She's fine," I reassured. "Well, right now. She won't be fine later."

He tilted his head. "What's happening later?"

"I'm going to kill her."

"Any particular reason you're plotting her murder?"

"She's eating everyone's food, including *mine*! She ate my cheesecake and my goddamn yogurt!" I gestured wildly, flinging my hands into the air. "Do you know why she's doing this?"

Kline shook his head. The hint of a smile kissed the corners of his lips.

I pointed my finger at him. "Don't even think about smiling right now."

He held up both hands. "I wouldn't dream of it. I'm taking this very seriously." He forced his mouth to the side, trying to hide another smirk, and his voice turned almost offensively diplomatic. "Why is Leslie eating everyone's food?"

"She thought people were being *totes adorbs* and naming the food."

Blue eyes lit up with amusement. "Leslie didn't realize the names on food meant it belonged to someone?"

"Today, she enjoyed a turkey sandwich named Gary. And a yo-gurt and piece of motherfucking cheesecake named Georgia. She thought it was *like, the cutest thing ever* how her coworkers were nam-ing food. She's too dumb to live. Literally."

I saw the second he couldn't hold back laughter. A grin had cracked the secret code and covered his entire face—his eyes, lips, and cheeks were all lit up with hilarity.

Like a boiling pot, it worked its way up his throat and spilled right over, coating me with its vibration. If I hadn't been so pissed, I might have acknowledged its ability to turn me on.

"This isn't funny! Your intern is a dumbass! All she does is take selfies and eat my food! Why haven't you fired her?"

"Baby," he cooed condescendingly. "She's just an intern. How picky can I be? She's not costing the company anything."

"Not costing anything!" I very nearly shrieked. "She just cost me my goddamn cheesecake!"

Kline shook his head with a smile and started to turn his leather chair in the other direction, away from my glaring eyes, but I was too quick, damn near jumping on top of him. "Don't even think about it!"

His strong hands gripped my hips and finished the job.

In an instant, his laughter was gone, a look of pure, unadulter-ated longing taking its place. For two days, we'd practically crawled all the way inside each other, we'd had so much physical contact, but it'd been a long time since then.

For a few moments, all we did was stare at each other. I was strad-dling Kline's lap, his muscular thighs forcing my legs to spread that perfect amount. Only a few measly inches kept me from finding out if he was as turned on as I was. And judging by the look on his face, if I pressed my hips to his, I'd hit the cock landmine.

"Dessert named Georgia?" He caressed the sliver of skin that was exposed above the waistline of my skirt. His lips were near my ear. "I'm certain this is something I wouldn't be able to stop myself from *devouring.*"

Oh, my…

His hands disappeared under my flowy skirt and gripped my ass, pulling at the cheeks to open me farther to him. Only a minuscule piece of lace was separating his fingers from touching my bare skin. Kline's hips ground into mine, and I had to swallow the moan threatening to spill from my lips. He wanted this as much as I did. The evidence was hard and ready between my thighs.

My breathing turned ragged, heart pounding inside my chest.

I loved seeing this side of him. The all-business, Armani-suited CEO getting messy and wild, *with me.* His reserved side morphing into a man possessed by passion and desire. I felt possessive, wanting to be the only woman who could affect him this way.

I should've been freaked out over the idea that someone could walk into his office and find us in this precarious position, but all I could think about was wanting him to push himself against me, harder, rougher. Good God, I wanted more. So much more.

His lips moved from my ear to my jaw to the sensitive, toe-curling spot on my neck. His teeth just barely scraped at the pulsing vein, and a shiver rolled down my spine. If he kept this up, I'd end up doing something I shouldn't. Like unzip his pants and offer up my V-card as tribute.

Get it together, Georgia.

"Kline?"

"Don't worry," he whispered against my skin. "I won't let this get out of hand."

But he didn't disentangle us. *No.* He did the complete opposite.

He kissed me hard, delving deep enough to brand me, while our tongues tangled in an inferno of want and need and crazy desire.

Sliding a hand up my blouse and underneath my bra, Kline brushed his thumb across my nipple.

I moaned into his mouth, biting at his bottom lip.

"Fuck," he breathed, still cupping my breast.

I sucked at his tongue as my hips circled his, savoring the feel of his cock pressed against my pussy. Even though we were both fully clothed, I could practically feel every inch of him. And hot damn, there were a lot of inches.

He pulsed upward and my pussy clenched in empty agony.

"Oh, yes, yes, Kline, yes," I whispered, my head falling back.

Our ragged, wanton breaths were the only sounds filling the four walls of his office.

"You're driving me wild." His hand covered mine, moving it down to cup him through his slacks. "I want you so fucking bad."

Self-control was nowhere in sight as I went for his belt, fingers sliding against the cold metal of his buckle. The only thing that mattered was touching him. More of him. *All* of him. I wanted Kline hard and ready and bared in my needy hands.

"Mr. Brooks, your four o'clock is here. Should I send him back?" Pam's voice echoed from the intercom.

We froze, startled by the interruption.

"Christ," Kline muttered, his eyes clenched and forehead pressing against mine.

My cheeks turned a terrifying shade of red once realization set in. "I-I should probably leave," I stuttered, attempting to un-plaster myself from him.

"Hold on." He gripped my hips, stopping my momentum. He leaned forward, one finger pressing the intercom to respond. "Just give me a minute, Pam. I'm just finishing up signing some contracts for Georgia."

I was thankful he still had enough brainpower to think of an excuse for me to be in here. Telling Pam that he needed a minute to remove his Director of Marketing from his dick wasn't the best scenario for either of us.

"Hey," he whispered, cupping my cheeks. "Don't freak out."

"I'm not freaking out."

"Are you sure?" He smirked. "Because that deer-in-headlights look you've got going on says otherwise."

I glared. "That's not the look I'm giving you."

He mimicked my wide-eyed stare before his face morphed into a teasing grin.

"Excuse me for being a little freaked out that someone could have walked in and found us going at each other like a couple of horny teenagers. Speaking of which, you should probably let me up."

He massaged my ass. "Only if you promise to let me finish dessert later."

Dear God, what was he trying to do to me?

I couldn't hide my smile. "You're trouble. Big fat fucking trouble." I shoved at his chest and proceeded to remove myself from his lap. Straightening my clothes, I glanced down at his disheveled attire. "And you look ridiculous. Like some woman was in here mauling you with red lipstick." My crimson lips were branded across his face and neck.

It was absurd, but mostly just fuck-hot.

He stood, flashing that sexy smirk of his while I removed my lipstick smudges with my fingers. I adjusted his tie and patted him on the chest. "Don't work too hard, Mr. Brooks."

As I turned for the door, he spanked my ass, earning a small squeal of approval from my traitorous lips.

"Don't worry, I'll save up my energy for later, Ms. Cummings."

Outrageously sexy bastard. I was certain he'd be the death of me.

"Wait." He grabbed me before I could take another step, pulling me toward him, my back against his chest. His breath was warm on my neck. "I'm not letting you out of this office until you agree to another date. A weekend date."

"Like a whole weekend?"

"In the Hamptons, with me."

"You have a place in the Hamptons?" I asked, then realized what a stupid question that was. Kline wasn't a flashy kind of man, but he had made more money from one business deal than most people make in a lifetime. Hell, he could quit working today and would be set for the rest of his life.

"Yeah, baby." He kissed my neck, teasing the sensitive skin with his lips. "So, you'll go?"

I turned in his arms, gazing up at him. He was business Kline laced with a little messy wildness from our earlier tryst behind his desk. The adorable grin cresting his mouth had me smiling in return. "What do I get out of it?" I teased.

His grin grew wider. "You want terms and conditions for a weekend getaway I'm asking you to join me on?"

I nodded. "Sounds about right."

"You're like a little shark when it comes to business." He pressed a kiss to my forehead, chuckling against my skin. "I'll make sure you have a good time. So good you'll be doing a reenactment of my bedroom…and the pool. Who knows, maybe it'll be like both combined."

"Draft the contract, Brooks, but remember, I'm holding you to these terms."

"Wonderful doing business with you, Cummings."

CHAPTER 20

Kline

When the GPS told me I was two blocks away from Georgia's apartment on Friday night, I pulled over and put the car in park. My phone had just buzzed in the cupholder with a message, and I knew I wouldn't be able to answer it once I picked her up. Ignoring the blinding red light on my mail icon, I swung my thumb directly over it before landing on the TapNext app.

TAPRoseNEXT (7:04PM): HE'S GOING TO BE HERE ANY MINUTE, FOR CHRIST'S SAKE. CALM ME DOWN BEFORE HE TAKES ONE LOOK AT ME AND RUNS IN THE OTHER DIRECTION.

A smile overwhelmed me as my chuckles bounced around the echoey interior of an otherwise empty car. She was so fucking cute, I could hardly stand it.

BAD_Ruck (7:06PM): Calm down, sweetheart. Let's start slowly by eliminating the shouty capitals.

TAPRoseNEXT (7:07PM): FUCKING FUCK FUCKERS. Okay. FUCK. Okay, I think I'm good now. Move on to step 2 (the coddling).

I bit my lip and shook my head, smiling like a crazy person.

BAD_Ruck (7:08PM): Good job. Also, creative swearing.

TAPRoseNEXT (7:08PM): The calm is wearing off, Ruck.

BAD_Ruck (7:09PM): Okay, okay. Coddling. Got it. This guy is still talking to you after spending all that time with you last weekend and invited you on a weekend away, right? He sounds smart enough to appreciate a little nervous energy. Everything is going to be fine.

Okay, guys. I know. I can feel you judging me. But let's talk this over.

I knew not telling her that I knew she was Rose, and that I was Ruck, was bad form.

I did, really.

It'd been a few days since I found out, and I should have told her *immediately*.

But God, as twisted as it was, I was having too much fun. Georgia was different with me online, no pretense or fear of saying something to her boss that he couldn't unhear, the safety net of ano-nymity weaving the protective web that it did for a lot of people.

As easy as it was to be someone else online, it was equally easy to be yourself, no expectations or trepidation blinding the true artwork underneath. Knowing Georgia in both places, without her knowing that I knew, was one of the most remarkable experiences of my life. She was the same yet different—honest and open and unafraid of re-crimination. She wasn't afraid to send me messages about freaking the fuck out. She was just her, and I liked getting to be on the receiving end of twice the interaction. She was still scared to wear out her welcome with Kline Brooks. I couldn't fucking welcome her enough. This gave us the best of both worlds.

I even found myself sending her more goddamn messages as Ruck, just to be able to enjoy what she might say. I pushed the envelope, trying to get her even more comfortable with me, even knowing that, in her mind, she was splitting her affection between two men.

It was fucked, but I knew if *she* could forgive *me*, her actions wouldn't be an issue in the slightest. Love, lust, and attraction were base instincts. They were simple and finite and somehow still infinitely complicated. She liked Ruck because *he* was another dimension of *me*.

So as much as it didn't make sense rationally, it made heart-sense. Call me a hopeless romantic, or maybe a fool, but to me, that was all that mattered.

Stowing my phone in the console, I put the car back into drive and pulled away from the curb. Cute brick-front brownstone buildings with iron-railed stairs lined the sides of each street, mature trees casting their shadows every fifty feet. Dusk threatened as the sun made its descent, already hiding behind buildings despite its place just above the horizon.

And my heart? Well, it just about beat right out of my chest.

Georgia sat on the stoop of her building with her arms crossed on her knees and her suitcase at her feet as I pulled up.

Her hair was wild and unkempt, curling just enough that I knew she'd probably showered and left it to dry on its own. Clothed in jeans and a simple sweatshirt with just barely a trace of makeup on her face, she was still the most beautiful thing I'd seen in just about forever.

Eager to put her racing mind at ease, I pushed the gearshift into park, turned the key to off, and jumped out to round the car before she even made it to her feet.

Adorable and wondering at my hurry, her teeth dug into the skin of her lip and her head tilted just slightly to the side.

I watched her as she watched me, a fire lighting her gorgeous blue eyes just as I pulled her directly into my arms and sealed my lips to hers.

"Mmm," she moaned, melting into my frame and wrapping hers around my shoulders. I licked at her tongue and her lips, sucking the taste of her into me as I slowly released.

"Kline," she whispered, overwhelmed.

My eyes shut on their own and my forehead met hers, and I breathed her in until my lungs burned only a little.

"I missed you."

She smiled and pushed her nose deeper along the side of mine. Her voice was barely audible.

"You saw me today at work."

I shook our heads together, lips and noses and foreheads touching the whole time.

"Not like this."

"No," she agreed softly, placing one simple kiss to the corner of my mouth before pulling away. "You're right. It wasn't like this."

I took a step down to grab her suitcase but kept a squeezing hand on her hip.

"You ready?"

Her face was alive and at ease, excitement lining the corners of every angle as she nodded. I couldn't help but return the sentiment.

"Mount up."

She raised a brow, but I just winked, moving to the back of the SUV and lifting the hatch to load her bag.

Looking it over from back to front, she seemed to notice the car for the very first time.

"This is your car?"

I looked at her in question.

She rolled her eyes at my implication, since I was very much accessing said car and the likelihood that I had stolen it was remarkably low.

"This is my *rental* car. I don't own a car."

"You don't own a car?" She was incredulous.

"Baby." I laughed, biting my lip to summon my patience. "I live in Manhattan. For business, I have a driver because you're not the only one with the ability to be late. For everything else, I walk, take a taxi, or ride the subway. If I need to go anywhere outside of the city, I rent one. Simple as that."

"But this is a Ford Edge," she pushed stubbornly, still not getting it.

"I know," I joked. "I sprung for the SUV since I've yet to get a handle on your luggage habits." I jerked my head to the back and slammed the hatch. "Just the one bag. I'll stick to midsize from now on."

"*Kline.*"

Rounding the rear, I walked back to her, leaned my back into the car, grabbed her hips, and pulled her body into mine.

"Baby. I can see you're struggling to get this, but I swear it'd make sense if you met Bob."

"Bob? Of Bob and Maureen?"

I nodded. "The one and only. Bob Brooks, my dad and the biggest influence on my life."

Wrinkles formed on her nose as she grinned, so I kissed it.

Pushing the wild blonde hair back from her face, I trailed one finger along her jaw and then dropped it.

"Let go of who you thought I was...who you think I'm supposed to be. Be here with me now." I grabbed her hand and pushed it to my chest. "*Feel* me."

Her free hand shot to my jaw and stroked it, eyes bright in reaction to my so-obviously-messy emotion.

"I promise, this is who I am, and if you let go of what you thought you knew, you'll get it. You'll get me. I *know* it."

I sounded desperate because I was. Desperate for her to be the woman I thought she could be. Desperate for her to let go of the *billionaire* experience and just be with *Kline*.

"Okay." She sealed her lips to mine and the tip of her tongue ventured into my mouth briefly. An answering tingle ran down the length of my spine. "I'll let go of it all." She pecked me on the mouth once more. "Promise."

"Good," I said before slamming my mouth to hers again. A slow groan rumbled in my chest a second later at the feel of her soft tongue. With effort, I forced myself to extract my mouth from hers. "Plus, nothing humbles a man more than cleaning Walter's litter box. I swear the little fuck flicks shit outside of it on purpose."

She shook her head with a dreamy smile and bit her lip to stop herself from making fun of me. It didn't matter what I did. She'd forever be on Walter's side of this war.

"Now get your ass in the *Ford Edge*, and let's get out of here. I'm ready to have you all to myself for the weekend."

"Yes, sir!" she joked with a salute before reaching for the door. I wrapped an arm around her waist at the last second, swooping her off her feet and swinging her around to put me between her and the car.

She bristled, but the icy edges of her attitude melted as soon as I winked and popped open the handle myself. "What kind of a man would I be if I didn't open the door for you?"

"The kind that fill the streets of Manhattan."

I just shook my head and smiled, waiting patiently for her to climb in.

"Right. You're not those guys."

"Ahh," I teased. "Now she's getting it."

She grabbed the inside handle of the door and pulled it closed as she spoke. "Get in the car, Kline."

The door slammed in my face and I laughed. "Yes, ma'am," I mouthed through the window, rounding the hood and climbing in.

"To the Hamptons!" she shouted.

I shook my head, fired up the engine, and pulled away from the curb with an enormous smile on my face.

An hour and a half or so into the drive, she started to fidget. And I don't mean a little movement here or there. I'm talking, for a few seconds, I feared she was having a seizure.

"What's up, Benny?"

"What?" Her gaze jerked toward me in surprise.

I glanced from the road to her and back again. "You literally look like your skin is in the process of *attacking* you. What's up?"

"I just… I have to tell you something."

Her tone was serious, and her nerves were beginning to eat her alive. I didn't want to be presumptuous, but I had a feeling I knew what was coming. Our intimacy had been on a steady advance from the moment we'd collided, melding together and racing for the finish line like one entity. We were on our way to a weekend alone, and the relevance of her sexual inexperience had to be beating her over the head with a bat at this point.

"So tell me, baby," I coaxed gently, trying to walk the line of someone who didn't know what was coming and someone who absolutely did, having heard it *twice* already, and was prepared to answer in a calm, respectful manner. If it hadn't been for the blunt conversation *Ruck* had had with *Rose*, *Kline* would have never realized that *Georgie* had already told him in a Benadryl-fueled rant.

Christopher Columbus her pussy prideland.

God, I'd laughed so hard about that when I realized how brilliant it had been.

"I'm…like…a…" *incoherent mumbling* "…virgin!"

I bit my lip and considered her words. I knew what she was trying to say, but a little *figurative* ice breaking never hurt anyone. *Literal* ice breaking—well, that hurt a lot of people.

"You want to listen to Madonna?"

I reached for my phone like I was going to search for the song.

"No," she huffed, adorably frustrated at having to gather the nerve to say it *again*. I didn't blame her. This was the fourth time in about twice as many days that she was admitting it to *someone*. That I knew of, anyway.

Turning in her seat, she forced herself to face me head-on. Her eyes sought mine, and I hated that because I was driving, I couldn't fully give them to her. I had no right to it, but that didn't stop me from being proud of her confidence.

When I found a straight stretch of road and glanced her way for more than a quick, passing beat, she spoke. "I'm a virgin." Crisp and calm, her voice managed to be matter-of-fact and silky all at once.

Did I mention I was proud of her?

Was that fucked up? I didn't mean for it to be. I was just happy to see her owning it—being proud of herself and her own choices instead of feeling like she had to answer for them. I wanted to yell out some kind of cry for all of the empowered females, but I thought that might seem suspicious.

So, I went with the only other thing I could think of.

"Okay. Cool."

Eloquent, right?

"Okayyyy," she repeated, adorably confused by my non-response. "Cool."

I'm sure she'd been expecting the usual questions.

How'd you manage that?

or

Are you, like, super religious?

or

What the hell are you waiting for?

As her lover, I had a right to know she'd never taken a sexual encounter to that level before, a warning of sorts to make sure I didn't make an assumption that affected both of us. But really, the rest of it was her business and hers alone. Sharing was a staple of every healthy relationship, but she got to be the creator of the terms and conditions under which said sharing happened.

"Kline?" she called, pulling out of my thoughts.

"Yeah, baby?"

"You don't have any questions? Or…I don't know. You're so quiet."

I *was* being quiet. Obviously, it was doing nothing but torturing her.

"I'm sorry, sweetheart, but it's not what you think."

"What do I think?" She raised a brow and I laughed.

"Okay, fair enough. I don't know what you're thinking. But I'm thinking you're a fucking brilliant, beautiful woman with the most delicious pussy I've ever tasted. I'll be lucky as fuck if you decide you wanna share more of it with me. But I don't fucking expect it, and I've done nothing to earn it. I'm guessing none of the other fuckers in New York ever did, and I don't mind one fucking bit."

"That was a lot of 'fucks,' Mr. Brooks."

I laughed and forced the tension in my shoulders to release. "I know. You got me all worked up. Thatch is usually the only one that can get me to utilize that many fucks in one thought process."

Her laughter rolled through me like a wave.

"God, Thatch. I hear all sorts of lore about that guy, but the only actual interaction I've had with him was when you called me on the plane."

"There's Thatch lore?" I asked, mystified and horrified all at once.

"Oh yeahhh." She laughed. "But most of it is from Dean, so I've taken any and all information with a very large grain of salt."

I laughed.

"Like, rock salt."

I shook my head, knowing Dean usually had a pretty good bead on the reality of things despite his juicy delivery.

"Ehhh. You can probably stick to the regular iodized kind. Thatch is a crazy asshole. Fun, though. And, occasionally, a good friend."

"Is he really that crazy?" she asked, insistent in the belief that he couldn't be as rowdy as people described.

As always with Thatch, examples of his depravity were plentiful, but one stood out above the rest.

"You know the scar on my abdomen?" I asked. "Lower right side?"

I glanced over in time to see her nod, eyes brimming with biblical knowledge. "It's completely plausible I've noticed it."

A smile arrested my features.

"Well, I owe its existence to Thatch and one of his half-baked ideas."

Waiting for an explanation, she settled farther into her seat.

"One night during our freshman year of college, he got this idea that stair surfing on our mattresses on the icy courtyard steps could be the next big campus activity. Three broken fingers, one bloody nose, and a tree-branch-impaled abdominal muscle later, I decided I didn't want to be a part of the sales pitch."

"You could have said no from the beginning," she suggested and I shrugged.

"What fun would that have been?"

I flipped on my blinker and turned into the long gravel drive of the Hamptons house. This had been the quickest drive of my life with Georgia keeping me company, and the salty sea air clung to my skin as I rolled my window down to put in the code for the gate. The stars were brighter now that we'd left the city behind, and when I turned to look at Georgie, I found her head hanging out of her window with her face to the sky like she'd noticed.

"Georgie?" I called, fighting back a grin.

"This place is outrageous!" she all but shouted. "Have you seen the fucking sky? And the length of this driveway?"

I shook my head and laughed some more, pulling forward cautiously so she could stay in her happy place half in, half out of the car.

"I might have noticed it a time or two."

She sank back into the seat and shook her hair out of her smil-ing face.

"You should notice more. Like, a lot more. You know, every weekend or so. Andddd, if you just happen to want some com-pany," she said, feigning nonchalance, "I could *probably* fit it into my schedule. I mean, I'd be willing to check."

"I'll make note."

"Holy hell! Look at that house! It's adorable!"

I followed her eyes through the windshield, smiling so much my cheeks started to ache. The little bungalow wasn't ostentatious, but it didn't lack space either, and the wood-shank shingle siding had seen better days. The inside pretty much matched, but I was working on fixing it. Slowly but surely.

"I'm glad you like it."

She bounced in her seat.

"But you probably shouldn't like it too much. I'm fixing it up to give it to my parents, and I'll start to feel bad if you get too attached."

"Really? You're doing the work yourself?" If she had been a dog, I imagined her ears would have perked up.

I smiled and nodded. "Really. I had an electrician work on the wiring and Thatch and Wes have helped me a couple of times with the heavy lifting, but I've done most of it myself."

She slammed an open hand down on my thigh and squeezed, her expression deadpan.

"I think I just orgasmed."

I shoved the gearshift into park and reached for her neck at the same time. I rubbed my nose with hers and smiled before touching my lips to hers just once. "Please, Benny. For the love of all that's holy, hold on to that thought—and the easy trigger."

Bags inside the house, a quick dinner of sandwiches I'd picked up from Tony's deli and packed to bring along consumed, and wine in hand, Georgia demanded a tour of the house.

"I want to know every detail. What it looked like when you started, what you're in the middle of now, and what you see it being like when you're done. Don't cut corners, Brooks," she'd said.

"I intend to travel each and every curve in its entirety," I'd teased back salaciously.

She'd just laughed and shoved me down the hall we were currently walking.

She'd seen the completely redone kitchen, the room I'd tackled first. I'd known it would be an outrageously extensive job, as well as the heart of the house. Crisp white cabinets, light stone counters, and dark wood floors, I'd kept the character of the house but added a ton of modern twists and convenience.

"God, Kline. I still can't get over that island! It's freaking enormous."

"I know."

Twelve feet by twelve feet, it was nearly enough room to use as an elevated dance floor. Part of me worried that it was too much, but my reasoning was sound. Maureen and Bob Brooks lived their lives in the kitchen, hip to hip or one or the other relaxing at the counter while the other one cooked. I swore ninety-five percent of my childhood memories happened in that room.

"It's perfect, though. Like the epicenter of the house."

My chest tightened with an unexpected surge of pride and accomplishment. The fact that she understood made me feel validated in a way I hadn't even known I'd needed. I turned quickly, grabbing her hips and slamming her surprised and open lips to mine.

"Thank you," I said. "That's exactly what I was going for."

I almost couldn't handle the feeling of her answering smile.

"Watch your step," I advised as we stepped into one of the completely unrenovated bedrooms. The original wainscoting was the only thing I really wanted to keep, and it was acting more like a temporary storage room for supplies than a bedroom at the moment.

"This place is amazing," Georgie remarked in wonder. "It's almost like a time capsule."

"I know. It's nearly a hundred years old. Which was really fucking intimidating when I first started doing the work."

"I bet."

"Come on. Let me show you upstairs real quick and then we can watch a movie. I'm ready to cuddle."

"Kline Brooks, a cuddler?"

"Born, bred, and proud of it, baby."

She pursed her lips, scrunched her nose, and shook her head— Georgia's look of trying to figure something out.

"You almost never say what I'm expecting you to, you know that?"

I shrugged and nuzzled my face into her neck before touching my lips to the shell of her ear.

"Fine by me. As long as what I *actually* say is better."

She shivered and then touched her lips to my cheek. Sauntering toward the door, she looked over her shoulder as soon as her small body lined up with the frame. "You haven't failed me yet."

CHAPTER 21

Georgia

I slowly opened my eyes as Kline lifted me off the couch, cradling me close to his chest. I must've fallen asleep halfway through the movie. Only two glasses of wine deep, I hadn't been drunk, just a delicious mix of relaxed and sleepy—sated from resting by the fire and cozy from being wrapped up in his arms.

His eyes met mine as we moved down the hall, toward the bedroom. "I figured you'd want to be somewhere a little more comfortable than the couch." He gently set me on the mattress, pulling the covers back and tucking me in. After a soft kiss to my forehead, he whispered, "Go back to sleep, baby."

I watched him move around the bedroom—charging his phone, sliding off his jeans, shrugging out of his shirt, and turning off the lights. I wasn't sure I'd ever get used to how amazing Kline looked in just his boxer briefs. It should have been an offense to let a man who looked like *that* walk around without clothes. But I wasn't complaining.

If he is a crime, then by God, get the handcuffs ready, because there is no way I can resist him.

He slid into the bed beside me, oblivious to my awakened state and ogling thoughts.

Tonight had been so perfect. He was perfect—sexy, kind, funny, and so very sweet. He made me want things I'd spent a lot of time wondering if I'd ever have.

Under the covers, I slid toward him, moving my body on top of his.

His eyes popped open.

"Hi," I whispered.

"Hi." He smiled softly, wrapping his arms around my back and holding me close.

"I didn't really feel like sleeping." I brushed my nose against his.

"And what is it you feel like doing?"

I shrugged my shoulders as my lips nibbled along his neck. Kissing a path back to his mouth, I bit his bottom lip and then licked across the plump skin to soothe it better.

He groaned, gripping my hips and flipping me to my back. His mouth locked with mine as he kissed me, long and slow and deep—so deliciously deep. I gripped the strands of hair resting at the nape of his neck. I swallowed his breaths and savored the taste of him.

My body was getting more riled, almost restless, with each heady second that passed.

He pushed my tank top up and over my chest, grabbing my breasts. He sucked a hardened nipple into his mouth, teasing the peak with his tongue, until switching to the other and repeating the same delectable torture.

The pulsing ache between my legs was proof of how badly I wanted Kline.

And God, I wanted to *feel* him, *all* of him.

His mouth found mine again. "Tell me what you want." Our tongues danced. "I'll give you anything."

"I want you inside of me," I moaned against his lips. "I want it so badly." The need burned in a way it never had before—in a way I knew couldn't be otherwise extinguished.

His eyes met mine, searching. "You know I'll wait, right? I'll wait until you know you're really ready. There's no rush."

A tiny, self-doubting voice crept in. "You don't want to have sex with me?"

"Are you kidding?" A soft laugh escaped his lips. "Baby, I'm losing my mind over the idea of feeling you come on my cock. I'd say that's quite obvious." He playfully rubbed the proof against my thigh, spurring a giggle from my lips.

"But I'm not rushing you." He cupped my cheek, eyes tender. "You hold the power. You decide when it's right."

My hands found their way into his hair again, grasping the strands and pulling his face to mine. I kissed him like I'd never kissed him before. My mouth plundered his lips and tongue, taking what they wanted. I was out of my mind with feelings for this man. I had just told him I wanted to have sex, and he'd done the opposite of what I'd expected. He slowed us down, trying to make sure I was making the right decision for myself.

I didn't need time to think, because Kline *was* right. He was all of the rights.

And I wanted to give him another part of myself.

"I want this. I want this more than I've ever wanted anything in my life." I wrapped my legs around his hips, pulling him closer to where I was desperate for him. He settled between my thighs, his hardened cock pressing against me.

My body shook in anticipation. This moment was why I had waited so long to take this step. I wasn't naïve, expecting my first time to be beside a fire or surrounded by rose petals on a bed. I wasn't expecting cheesy lines of undying devotion or an engagement ring. I just wanted to make sure it was meaningful, that it was with someone I trusted, someone I cared about. And most importantly, I needed it to be someone who cared about me too, who wouldn't intentionally hurt me—not just physically, but emotionally as well.

Everyone had their own views on sex. Some people could have

sex for the pure act itself. They could savor spending the night with a gorgeous stranger and have no lingering doubts or feelings nagging them the next day.

I had always been able to leave my emotions at the door when it came to an oral exchange. But when it came to full-on penis penetration, home run sex, I knew I couldn't approach it with that same mindset.

To me, intercourse was more intimate than oral. There was something about looking directly into a person's eyes while your bodies became one. I knew *that* type of sex had to be something more than just physical for me.

I trusted Kline so much, and I'd come to do it quickly. But I felt the way he cared about me with every kiss, every smile, every lingering touch. With him, it wouldn't just be sex. He was more than that to me. I truly cared about him. My feelings for him ran deeper than I was ready to admit. The intensity and depth of those feelings had awareness hitting me like a wrecking ball.

My heart was on the line here, and I had just realized how much I could lose.

Fear drowned my mind, spilling into my eyes.

"What's wrong?" he asked, assessing the uncertainty on my face, acutely in tune with my wavering thoughts.

"I'm scared," I admitted.

He stared deep into my eyes. "There's nothing to be scared of, Georgie. I'd never pressure you into doing something you're not ready for."

I wiped the worry from his brow. "I know that. Believe me, I know that."

"Tell me what you're scared of." His eyes were so earnest. "I'll do everything I can to fix it."

This guy. I swallowed around my heart in my throat.

"I'm scared because…it's so intense." I fumbled to find the right words. "I just…I feel like I'm falling too fast with you. It's scary as hell.

I can't ignore the fear that, one day, I'll wake up and things will have ended badly between us. I don't want to associate you with hurt in the end."

He cupped my face, gazing down at me. "No matter what happens, baby, it will always be a good hurt for me. You make me feel alive. And I'll do everything I can to make sure it's the same goddamn experience for you."

That look. There was a gentleness in his eyes that let me know I wasn't the only one falling.

This wasn't going to be just about sex for him either. This was more. He and I were going places, and his look said, "I'm falling too."

And that look was why I reached for the nightstand to pull a condom from the drawer. The *empty* drawer.

His eyes followed me the whole way; I could feel them, but when I turned back to him, they were slightly pinched together.

"I thought there'd be condoms."

He laughed a little, just enough to ease the tension and make me start to smile.

"There aren't any condoms in the drawer."

"Obviously," I replied.

He smirked and rubbed at the skin of my waist. "I've never brought a woman here."

A comforting statement to all, but somehow I managed to turn it on its head, panicking slightly, thinking that things were going to come to a very abrupt stop. I didn't want them to. I was ready *now*.

"Please tell me you have condoms somewhere."

He smiled fully at that. "In my bag."

I shoved him off and jumped off the bed before running to his bag and rummaging through it without remorse. When the foil of the package met my fingertips, I took off in reverse, shoving him aside, resuming my position, and pulling him back on top of me.

He shook with silent amusement as he grabbed the condom out of my hand, setting it on the bed beside my hip. But his mirth transformed quickly to heat as he moved his hands to my panties, slowly sliding them down my legs, pressing kisses down my body in their wake.

He removed his briefs, his thick erection popping free.

My eyes went wide for a beat, distressed by the size of him. It was one thing to take a cock of that magnitude in my mouth, but it was a whole other ballgame when that cock was going to be the first to slide into home. "Not gonna lie, I wish you were smaller," I blurted out before I could take it back.

Kline stopped mid-kiss, and his forehead fell to my abdomen as a few chuckles escaped his lips. I could feel his smile against my flesh. "No can do, Benny girl. I'm Big-dicked Brooks."

I stilled. "What did you just say?"

"Nothing." He laughed softly into my skin, his tongue sneaking out and licking around my belly button.

"Did you just say *Big-dicked Brooks?*"

"Huh?" He peeked up at me, amusement on his lips and his eyes feigning confusion.

My nose scrunched up. "Where did you hear that?"

"I can't recall the exact moment." He shrugged, playfully biting my hip. "But I really did appreciate the sentiment." Goosebumps dotted my skin as he slid his hand up my thigh, slipping his finger inside of me. "God, you're wet and I haven't even started with you yet."

A hot flush crawled up my neck, my lips parting on a sweet sigh when his thumb circled my clit.

God, if he promised to keep doing that, I'd call him Big-dicked Brooks any time he wanted.

"Remember when I had my mouth on you? How good it felt? How *hard* you came?" He licked my inner thigh while his fingers continued working me over. "In my bed, when I sucked on your pussy until you were begging me to let you come. At the pool when I had you spread so wide and my mouth devoured you even though anyone could have walked in and seen us. They could have seen my face between your legs while your tits bounced with each gasping breath that fell from your pretty lips. Remember that, Georgia?" He moved to the other thigh, sucking a soft bruise into my skin. "God, I can't stop thinking about how perfect you taste. How sexy you look, sound, *feel* when I make you come. I'm dying to know what you feel like wrapped around me."

I was getting so hot, so wet, just from his words alone. As he kissed a slow trail across my pubic bone, my body relaxed—legs opening up and arms falling to the sides.

"I'm going to make it so good, baby." His mouth moved to my clit, sucking and licking and caressing me into an orgasm. He didn't stop until my body quaked and my limbs turned lax and sated.

"Hey," he rasped, moving up my body and kissing me.

I moaned when I tasted my sex on his tongue.

This enormous sense of relief took hold, wringing the air from my lungs. I was thankful, so very thankful, that I had found him. Thankful that he was taking his time with me, making sure my first time was what I wanted it to be. I hoped he could feel it in my kiss, my touch, that this was more, so much more than I'd ever experienced. He was spinning my world out of its orbit, taking me to places I had never been.

I watched in rapt attention as he kneeled between my thighs and slid the condom on. He pulled back, pushing his hips forward and pressing the tip of his cock against my clit.

My eyes found his as he hovered over my body, his hands resting beside my head. His blue eyes glowed in the moonlight, tender and soft.

"You're beautiful," he whispered against my lips, deepening our kiss.

Hips pressed into mine, he started to slip inside of me. The pressure built to the point of pain as he slowly, so very slowly, slid deeper. He didn't rush, didn't hurry to claim me, just took his time. He pushed himself a little farther, then stopped to kiss me until my body let go of the tension and relaxed into him.

My eyes glazed over, overwhelmed by the intensity—not just of the deed itself, but of the feelings that passed between us. Tiny inward gasps accompanied my every breath.

Once he broke the barrier, pain consumed me and forced an involuntary whimper from my lips. I was sure he could see it on my face.

His eyes turned remorseful as he caressed my cheek.

I wanted to remove that look from his face.

"More, Kline. Don't stop." I wanted this. Of course, there was discomfort, but there was also a perfect ache starting to build inside of my core with each small thrust of his hips.

"God, you're so tight. So wet. So perfect. I'm losing my fucking mind." His lips found my neck, sucking and licking and placing little bites across my skin. Every word eased an ounce of discomfort. Every kiss, suck, and lick eased two.

"Baby, move with me," he encouraged.

My muscles relaxed and I lifted my legs higher to my sides, allowing him to slide in farther.

He groaned.

A hiccupping breath escaped my lungs.

I needed more. I wanted Kline as deep as he could go. I rolled my hips, pulling him all the way inside of me. We both cried out. The sensations were overwhelming—his cock fully sheathed by my heat, my thighs pressing against his hips.

I let out a raspy moan, whispering, "God, this feels so good."

"Fuck yes it does." He kissed my jaw, my cheek, the corners of my lips.

My hips pushed up of their own accord, unconsciously telling him I still needed more. This is what it felt like to want to crawl inside a person—to be a part of them. It made me greedy; every inch he gave just made me want another one even more.

Kline moved in an easy rhythm, careful of my sensitivity but not lacking in intensity. He started to pick up the pace when I begged him to go deeper, harder, faster. He sucked savagely on my neck, growing uninhibited and frenzied, only to slow down again, finding my mouth and giving me soft, drugging kisses.

My hands explored his body, moving down his arms, his back, his ass, savoring the flex and strain of his muscles as he thrust.

"You okay, baby?" he asked, sweeping a few damp strands of hair from my forehead.

"I'm more than okay."

"Fuck, Georgia, you look so perfect like this. Here. Under me." His eyes turned fierce and determined, like he wanted to make me lose control, completely turn my world on its head.

My body started to shake as he sped up, only to whimper in taut frustration when he slowed down again.

"Do you trust me, baby?"

I didn't even have to think about the answer.

"Yes. God, yes. I trust you."

"I want to show you how good it can be when there's no rush." He kissed me, sucked on my lips, my tongue, stealing every one of my sounds into his mouth and swallowing them greedily.

And God, I loved his hoarse noises, how he kept telling me how beautiful I was, how good this felt, how hard he was. I loved how he took control and knew the exact way to drive me wild.

"I want to do this for hours and hours, but fuck, you're too much. It's too much." He shifted his pace—lazy morphing into quick and hungry. "Tell me how good it feels," he ground out, pressing his face into my neck. His voice was demanding, but he wasn't chasing my climax so hard for himself. He was doing it for me.

All I could do was nod, too consumed with desire to answer. I gripped his ass, my nails digging into the toned flesh.

"Good, because I'm going to make you feel even better," he swore. "I'm going to make you lose your fucking mind."

He slid out of me, spurring a distraught moan to slip past my lips.

He gripped my thighs and moved his face between my legs

before I could stop him. His mouth consumed me—sucking and licking and tonguing at my pussy until my orgasm started to build at an explosive pace beneath my skin. Warmth spread across my body, a thin sheen of sweat following its lead. Unintelligible words escaped my lips as I started to come.

"That's my wild girl. Let me watch you catch fire," he said, continuing to take me over the edge.

I squeezed my eyes closed, mouth falling open, body bowing off the bed. I didn't just come. I screamed, exploded, burst into flames.

Time. Location. *My name.* Those things didn't exist, my senses too consumed by what Kline was doing to me.

He moved back up the bed, gripping my thigh and pushing my knee to my shoulder, spreading me wide open for his straining cock. He pushed inside of me with ease and started fucking me deep, dragging in and out at the most mind-blowing pace.

He propped himself up on his hands, staring down at where he moved in me. "Fuck, it's so good."

Moving one hand between us, he rubbed my clit. "I need to feel you come around my cock."

"I don't think I can. It's too much already."

He didn't let up, determined. "Yeah, baby, you can. Come on my cock."

I whimpered.

"Let go."

I was his instrument and he had mastered the skill of making me sing. My body arched into his touch, my hips rocking faster with his. "Kline… I… Oh… God…"

"Fuck yes, give me one more." His eyes focused on his hand moving over me, his cock sliding in and out.

I closed my eyes, my mind drowning in pure sensation.

My thighs quivered, my pussy tightening rhythmically around him, and my hips threatened to cramp up from the strain. A surprised cry escaped my lungs as I came hard and fast. My head was thrown back into the pillow, and I gripped his ass, pulling him forward while he rocked into me.

His eyes squeezed shut, lips parted as he chased his own release. His hair was mussed up, sweat wetting his brow. And God, his eyes, they were fierce and hooded with his impending climax.

"I want to feel you come." I gasped, dragging my nails down his back. I needed to see him lose control, needed to feel his body when he came.

He stared down at my breasts that were moving with the force of his thrusts. His skin was sweaty and perfect, and I wanted to lick it off with my tongue. And when he looked up and met my eyes, I watched him lose control.

The moment felt like a dream—everything slowing down so I could imprint every second on my brain. His mouth moved in slow motion with each soft grunt, each guttural moan. And his movements echoed that I was seeing the real thing.

This was real. *We* were real. My feelings, his feelings, even though they hadn't been said out loud, they were real. Deep down, I knew— he was it. My person. My soul's infinitely interesting counterpart.

"Let's stay here, wrapped up in one another until the sun burns out," I whispered into his ear, once his body had stilled and my burning lungs had cooled enough to fill with breath.

He lifted my chin, staring into my eyes. My heart latched on to billowing blue and refused to let go. "I know you're not ready to hear what I'm feeling, but just know, for me, tonight was *more*. It was *everything.*"

I closed my eyes, letting his words wash over me.

This moment would last forever. No matter what happened, I'd never forget the look in his eyes, the sound of his voice, and the feel of him claiming every part of me.

CHAPTER 22

Kline

I woke with a start, the brief confusion of my surroundings passing quickly enough that my hands slid across the sheets in search of Georgia's warm, sweet skin within seconds. The hunt for heated skin turned up nothing but cold cotton.

I lifted my head and opened my eyes to continue the search, and the mid-morning sun filtering in through the glass windows highlighted her clothes from last night, strewn across the bench beneath the bay window. Sitting up to get a better visual perspective, I blinked the sleep from my eyes and scanned the room thoroughly, but still came up empty.

With my sense of sight foiled, the others engaged, and the sound of her voice echoing from down the hall turned my short bout of panic into pride. Beautiful and brilliant, the unpredictably vivacious woman down the hall had chosen me to share last night with.

Her voice wasn't as pretty as the rest of her, though, the familiar, high-pitched, nails-on-a-chalkboard tune of her unrecognized song bringing a smile to my face. And it was *loud*. So loud—and unexpectedly inviting—that I got out of bed and threw on a pair of boxers to find out what she was up to.

Striding down the hall, I found her in one of the bathrooms. The door open and her body in motion, her back was to me as she slid a paint-covered roller across the wall and danced at the same time. Her voice boomed inside the small, confined room, and a Mary Poppins-like accent emphasized her tone. I'd never heard the song before, but I couldn't tell if that was because I didn't know the band or that she was only singing every third word.

In disbelief that I'd found her making her own episode of something on HGTV so early in the morning and without cause, I leaned against the doorframe and just watched her, drinking her in. Blonde hair sat on top of her head, curls cascading from a messy bun. She was a mess, earbuds in with her phone tucked into the side of my boxer briefs, and her black lace bra was the only other article of clothing covering her petite and curvy frame.

Her perfect little ass shook back and forth as she danced in place, painting the wall to the rhythm of whatever offbeat music filled her ears.

I crossed my arms across my chest, smiling at her obliviousness to my presence. She was painting the room the wrong color, smearing the light shade of blue I had decided I hated weeks ago all over the unfinished walls, but I didn't care. She could paint the entire house this godawful blue—as long as she did it in her current uniform, and I got to watch. Bob and Maureen would have to learn to love it, because every time I saw it, I'd think of this—of her, of last night, and of this perfect, simple moment.

I couldn't help but think, if I only made bad decisions for the rest of my life, at least I had made one really good decision with her.

Asking Georgia out was the smartest thing I had ever done. Period.

She turned to soak more paint onto the roller, and her hands flew to her chest, droplets of blue streaming across the room and staining everything in their path.

"Christ, Kline! You scared the bejeezus out of me!" she shouted, the accent of the band still hijacking the normal lilt of her voice. She removed her earbuds, letting the cords fall past her hips.

"My apologies, love," I said, mimicking her English brogue.

Her cheeks turned pink, an embarrassed smile cresting her full lips. "Sorry, I've been listening to English rock bands all morning."

I grinned. "You sound like a young Julie Andrews. It's pretty fucking adorable."

Georgia giggled, setting the roller down. She bounced around the room like a pinball, pouring more paint into the tray. Her excessive energy level piqued my interest.

"Did I wake you? God, I really hope I didn't wake you up. I was up by five, and I couldn't fall back asleep so I put on a pot of coffee. I watched Home Shopping Network for about twenty minutes and walked through the house, and then I saw the room and I figured why not make myself useful, right? So, yeah, I saw you had already painted one of the walls this color blue, so I decided to finish the job. Are you still tired? Hungry? I can make some more coffee if you want some?" Her words were strewn together in one giant, fast-paced, run-on sentence.

I tried to recall the last time I'd seen her take a breath.

She fiddled with bright blue painter's tape while tapping a persistent foot against the squeaky hardwood floor.

I cocked my head to the side. "How much coffee have you had, sweetheart?"

She shrugged. "A few cups. I guess I lost count after three…or maybe it was four?"

My eyebrows popped in understanding.

"Anyway, what do you think? Are you happy with the color? I think I like it. It's cheerful. Serene. Hopefully, your mom will like it. I guess her opinion would be the most important one, huh?"

I nodded. "I think she'll love it," I lied. "Have—"

"Fantastic!" she exclaimed, before I could ask her if she'd eaten anything. Her mind was like a damn hummingbird's wing, flitting around from one thought to the next faster than the naked eye, or in this case, ear, could process.

She grabbed the roller again, sliding it into the tray, and resumed her painting with more-than-necessary focus.

"So, last night…it was…did you…" She glanced over her shoulder, eyes uncertain, and before I could offer a reassuring smile, her gaze was back on the wall, her arm sweeping up and down in quick succession. Her feet fidgeted a few times until she just blurted out, "I had a really good time last night!"

And the light bulb went on.

Normally, I could get a pretty quick read on someone's headspace, more quickly than this, but after waking up to find her painting my house, her beautiful mouth moving a mile a minute, I was a little off my game.

Georgia was nervous. And about a pot of coffee deep into the caffeine jitters.

She seemed uncertain if I'd enjoyed last night, which was insane. First time or not, Georgia Cummings knew just how to sexually woo a man.

A tight, hot pussy was just the beginning because the rest of it was what I would remember. The shake of her body, the gravel in her voice. The way her words turned into moans, and those, in the fiery inferno of her orgasm, gave way to nothing but enraptured silence. Her eyes held mine, and her heartbeat was my second favorite part of her chest.

Nirvana was the only way to describe it.

I knew she felt it along with me then, and I knew, deep down, she knew it now, too. I just needed to remind her.

I moved to the shower, turning the nozzle and letting the water warm up.

She glanced over her shoulder at the squeal of the pipes. "What are you doing?"

"Just want to make sure the plumbing is still good in here," I lied. The only plumbing I cared about was hers.

I smiled in reassurance. She kept the suspicious face but turned back to her task.

Once the water hit a good temperature, I moved toward her, wrapping my arms around her waist, and whispered into her ear, kissing the soft skin of her neck.

"Hey, guess what?"

"What?" She shivered but didn't stop painting.

I kissed her jaw and stepped back, holding my hand out. "Let me borrow that roller for a second. I have a little trick that makes it easier," I lied again.

She shrugged, handing it to me. I set it down in the tray, glancing at the shower and noting the steam rising from the floor.

Perfect.

It was time to take this situation into my own hands. I grabbed her hips and tossed her over my shoulder before she could stop me.

"Kline!" she squeaked as I strode toward the shower, the top fragments of her bun tickling the skin of my thighs. She smacked my ass and back as I stepped under the showerhead, water drenching us both.

"Holy shit!" she shrieked as the water soaked into her skin and very few clothes. "What the hell!"

Chuckling, I set Georgia on her feet and ignored her glare. I reached around her back with a flourish, popping the clasp on her bra and dragging it off her arms and down until it landed at our feet. She was a vision, wet, waiting, and wearing nothing but my briefs.

"I enjoyed last night." Her uncertain eyes warmed just slightly. "So much that I feel compelled to thank you—" I paused and licked my lips with a wink. "And this perfect fucking pussy." Her eyes widened, but I didn't wait, sliding down her body, kissing between her swinging breasts, her belly, until I reached the waistband of my underwear.

"Kline?"

"Shh," I said into her skin, pulling a tiny section between my teeth. "I'm a little busy right now."

She shook as I slipped the briefs down her legs and pressed my mouth against her pubic bone, licking the water from her skin. "God, Benny girl, last night, you blew my fucking mind. It's safe to say I want to do that with you for the next one hundred years. It was the best goddamn sex of my entire life."

"Really?" she whimpered.

"You. Were. Perfect." My lips trailed down her inner thigh.

Her legs were trembling, her hands sliding into my hair and tugging desperately.

"Did you enjoy last night?" I prompted, putting the ball back in her court. "Was it as good for you as it was for me?"

"God, yes. Last night was perfect," she moaned, her head falling back thanks to my suction on her pussy.

Sweet like candy, I feasted on the taste of her until her inner muscles tried to take possession of my tongue.

Goddamn, I wanted that pussy to milk another part of me.

"How sore are you, sweetheart?"

She shook her head 'no,' but her eyes said 'God, yes.'

"I need to feel what it's like to be inside you again. I want to feel that pretty pussy squeeze the cum out of my cock."

"Yes," she moaned. "Please. Now."

I picked her up and wrapped her legs around me tight, moving us down the hall and into my bedroom before tossing her wet body onto the mattress. My sheets would be soaked, but fuck if I cared. I grabbed a condom out of my bag, tearing the package with my teeth as she watched from the bed.

"So, I guess this means there really weren't any painting tips?" she teased, biting her bottom lip.

"It's all about the strokes, baby," I said, flashing a devilish grin as I slid the condom on, stroking up and down my length to punctuate that statement.

I crawled onto the bed, moving between her legs. She gripped my ass as I held her thighs, my fingertips branding her skin, and spreading them wider until the tip of my cock nestled against the one place I *needed* to be.

"Now, Kline. God, I can't wait any longer," she begged. Her hips pushed up, urging me closer.

The second I pushed inside of her, we both cried out, losing ourselves in each other and chasing *each other's* pleasure.

I spent the next two hours using my cock and mouth and hands to reassure Georgia that sex with her was the single best thing I'd ever experienced, and she gave every second of that time to confirming it.

Hands down, motherfucking *nirvana*.

CHAPTER 23

Georgia

"Windows up or down?" he asked, cranking the engine and putting the gearshift into drive.

Reality started to set in. We were headed back to the city, and I knew I'd miss being wrapped up in my perfect Kline bubble. No responsibilities, no plans, just us, lazily enjoying the entire weekend together.

"Down, please." I wanted to smell the ocean one last time. The day was beautiful, sun shining brightly and only filtered by the occasional fluffy white cloud strolling past its glow.

He rolled down the windows then leaned over the console, grabbing two pairs of aviators from his glove box and handing one to me.

"Such a gentleman." I smiled, slipping them on and tossing my hair into a messy bun.

"For you—" he rested his hand on my thigh, squeezing gently "—always, baby."

As we drove onto the main road, the Hamptons house slowly diminished in the passenger mirror and an unexpected surge of melancholy consumed me. I was going to miss that beautiful, rustic house.

If I could've made a Pinterest board of my perfect home, that place would be pretty damn close. Once finished, I bet it would exceed my wildest dreams.

I was still in awe that Kline had bought a home for his mom and dad. And it wasn't a brand new house, which he could obviously afford. It was a home he was filling with love and care and thoughtfulness by fixing it up himself.

Everything I had assumed about him had been dead wrong.

He'd rented a Ford Edge, for goodness' sake. Nothing against that vehicle—I'd have been more than happy to drive one around—but it wasn't the type of car you'd see a man with his kind of money drive.

A Range Rover? Definitely.

But an economy, mid-size SUV that he'd *rented*? Hell no.

He was so damn humble and endearing and *practical*. Every new facet of his personality I discovered, I adored. Kline was one of the most intriguing people I'd ever met.

"I'll drive. You handle the music. Sound good?" He handed me his phone, iTunes already pulled up.

I nodded, scrolling through his playlists and choosing Young the Giant's "12 Fingers." It was the perfect song for this kind of day. I hung my hand out the window and savored the unseasonably warm wind that caressed my skin. After slipping off my flats, I moved my feet up to the seat, knees finding their way under my chin. Catching sight of each mile marker we passed, I felt a twinge of sadness as the distance grew between us and that gorgeous beach view.

I glanced at Kline out of the corner of my eye. He was softly singing the words, tapping out a beat on the steering wheel. He looked delicious—aviators, two days' worth of scruff, handsome mouth set in a soft grin. I wanted to eat him with a spoon.

A swell of emotions tightened my chest as our weekend replayed in my mind.

It had been perfect. *He* had been perfect. Kline hadn't rushed. He'd been attentive and careful and made sure my first time was good for me. And it had been. That night had been more than good. It had been *amazing*.

He made me feel crazy, in the greatest, most overwhelming way. It was hard to describe. Hell, it was hard to even put it into words without saying things I wasn't quite ready to say.

Just… God, this man… He was *everything*.

I felt like I was on the best roller coaster ride of my life. In the beginning, when everything started with us, I had hesitantly hopped in, mind racing: *What the hell am I thinking? Is this a good idea?*

The guy I'd known at work was a fair, honest, friendly guy but not one I'd ever considered. But then, it had been too late to back out because I'd been moving—*we'd* been moving.

We'd been climbing and whirling and twisting all crazy, and my thoughts had immediately shifted. *I'm pretty sure I'll survive, because how many people fall out of roller coasters, right?*

But I didn't really know because I'd never really paid attention to theme park statistics.

Shit, I had never really been into riding roller coasters.

Until Kline.

Every corkscrew and curve was exciting. I was enjoying every nerve-wracking minute, and I started to just let go and trust. I started to truly believe that as scary as it was, I was right where I needed to be.

Then, there was that "holy shit" turn when the bottom would drop out and my stomach would fall to my feet, but I was soaring again and screaming and laughing because I had made it. I was *alive*, and this—Kline and me together—was the most real, amazing thing in my life. And the ride slowed just a little bit, and the turns and twists were more like reverberations of the really crazy ones from before, but I was fine with that.

I was happy with everything.

And when I pulled into the place where I had started, I felt changed—overjoyed, enlightened, and knowing, without a doubt, I was right where I'd always wanted and needed to be.

In the craziest explanation, that was what he made me feel.

Complete. Alive. Amazing. The same but somehow very, very different.

The song switched to The Used's "Smother Me." The lyrics and the slow, silky beat had me looking at Kline again, drinking him in.

He sensed my eyes, glancing in my direction and smiling. One hand left the wheel, reaching for mine and entwining our fingers.

I laid my head back on the seat and just enjoyed, savored, greedily soaked up this little moment. I memorized every second, locking it up tight with the rest of my Kline memories.

We'd made a lot in a short time, but they were good ones. Every single one.

Before I knew it, Kline was hopping out of the driver's side and opening my door. The drive had been nice and we'd made good time. He'd held my hand the entire way, his thumb caressing my fingers. We didn't talk much, just silently enjoyed each other's company.

Sometimes, words don't need to be said. Sometimes, simply enjoying someone's company, just having them beside you, just being in their presence was enough. Plus, my inner monologue had said enough for the both of us.

Since we had spent the majority of the day packing and driving, I was going to stay the night at his place. We'd take the rental car back on our way to work and get into the office a little later than usual.

That was definitely one positive for dating your boss. If he wanted to take you away on a long weekend in the Hamptons and demanded you go into work a few hours later than normal, who were you to argue?

"Let's leave the bags," he said, taking my hand. "I'll grab them later."

He handed his key off to the valet and led me into the lobby and onto the elevator.

"Did you have a good weekend, Benny?" he asked, pushing the button for his floor.

"Eh." I shrugged. "It was okay."

"Just okay?"

I nodded.

He stalked toward me like he was a predator and I was his prey, and he caged me against the wall. "Are you sure about that, baby?"

"It was *pretty good?*" I stared up at him, fighting the urge to smile.

"I have a feeling you're trying to get me riled up." His kissed the corner of my mouth. "Is that what you're doing?"

"Is it working?"

His hand slid into my hair, gripping the strands. "That depends. What kind of reaction were you hoping for?"

"One that includes taking off your pants."

"I think that can be arranged."

His mouth was on me, kissing me hard, making my moan echo in the small confines of the cart.

My hands were all over him, touching his chest and stomach and then sliding up his back. I was about two seconds away from mounting him inside the elevator when the bell dinged, signaling we'd reached his floor.

He didn't waste any time, picking me up and wrapping my legs around his waist as he carried me out, grabbing my ass.

We were a mess of kissing and groping as we reached his door. It took him three tries to fit the key into the lock and open it. We tumbled into his apartment. He kicked the door shut. My back was pressed against the wall as he continued to kiss the hell out of me.

"Kline? Is that you?"

We stopped, glancing toward the female voice coming from the living room.

"Shit," he cursed, untangling us.

My feet hit the floor and Kline discreetly adjusted my shirt.

I looked at him, confused. What the hell?

"My mom," he mouthed just as she rounded the corner.

Panic hit me. I was about to meet his mom. Kline's mom. She was here, in his apartment. And two seconds ago, I'd been about to hump him in the elevator.

I mean, what were the odds? Friday night, Kline had popped my cherry, and today, I was meeting his fucking mother. I felt like I was in the Twilight Zone.

Deep breaths, Georgia. You can do this. You can get through this without looking like a moron.

"Kline, darling! We didn't know you'd be home so early," she greeted, moving toward her son and giving him a hug. His mother was beautiful—dark hair that was cut into a bob, bright blue eyes, blinding smile. I was starting to see where Kline got his looks.

"Uh, hi, Mom." He cleared his throat. Scratched his cheek. "Just out of curiosity, how did you get in my apartment?"

"The spare key you gave us."

"You mean my *emergency* key? The one I gave you just in case I lost mine or managed to lock myself out of my apartment?"

"Yeah, that one." She nodded and smiled, not catching his drift in the slightest.

Kline sighed, scrubbing a hand down his face.

"Kline, my boy!" A tall, handsome man walked toward us. He was a distinguished kind of handsome, with salt and pepper hair and glasses covering his brown eyes.

Oh, shit! His dad is here too?

"Hey, Dad," Kline greeted.

The two men hugged, clapping one another on the back.

His dad's focus turned to me. "And who is this gorgeous woman?"

"Bob, I was just about to ask that," his mother added, almost insulted that he'd gotten to it first. It caused a hint of a smile to spread across my face.

"This is my girlfriend." Kline wrapped his arm around my shoulder, tucking me into his side. If it hadn't been for the panic over his parents, I might have focused a little harder on the use of the label 'girlfriend,' jumped up and down a couple of times—that sort of thing.

"Georgia, these are my parents, Bob and Maureen," he begrudgingly introduced us. I had a feeling he was peeved their unexpected visit had put a damper on our little moment in the elevator.

I fought my normal urges to shout something awkward and completely inappropriate.

"Oh, hi! I'm Georgia! Your son took my virginity this weekend! You really did a great job with him! He sure knows how to please a woman!"

Yeah, don't worry. I managed to keep my foot-in-mouth syndrome under control.

"It's a pleasure to meet you both." I shook their hands. "Kline has told me so much about you."

"Oh, she's very pretty, Kline," Maureen murmured, winking at her son.

"Can't deny that," Bob added. "Looks like you're finally slowing down and enjoying yourself."

"Thank goodness!" his mother agreed. "It's about time our baby boy took some time for himself. He works too hard." She looked at Kline. "You really do, honey. You work way too hard."

Kline started to say something, but his father was already chiming in. "Definitely works too hard. You look good, son. And I have a feeling it has a lot to do with this pretty lady here." Bob nodded in my direction.

I felt like I was in the middle of a tennis match, moving my head back and forth, back and forth, just to keep up with their constant chatter. They were pretty adorable, to be honest.

"So, what brings you guys here, to *my* apartment, on a *Sunday*?"

"Your father still hasn't fixed my washer. And I needed to throw a few loads in," Maureen explained, giving Bob the side-eye. "But don't worry, I went ahead and did all of your laundry while I was at it. And I cleaned your bathroom. It was a mess, Kline Matthew," she scolded.

He chuckled, shaking his head. "Thanks, Mom. I really appreciate it."

"Well, it was the least I could do. But really, Kline, between that and the litter box, I nearly fainted. You should think about getting a maid or something. Georgia shouldn't have to see that."

Pretty sure the last time I was here, what his bathroom looked like was the very last thing on my mind. The bedroom? Yes. Kline naked? Hell yes. But the cleanliness of his toilet? Yeah, not so much.

"Only one of those things is even remotely my fault," Kline grumbled under his breath. It was one of those moves where you want to stick it to a person by saying what you're feeling, but you don't *actually* want them to hear you.

I tried really hard not to laugh.

"How was the Hamptons?" Bob asked as we made our way into the living room.

"Fantastic." Kline encouraged me to sit down on the couch before settling beside me. "We had great weather."

"Had you ever been to the Hamptons, Georgia?" Maureen asked.

"A few times, but not since I was a teenager. It was nice being by the coast. Honestly, it makes me want to live there permanently."

Kline grinned at me, gently squeezing my thigh.

"What'd you rent for the drive, son?" Bob asked.

"Ford Edge."

"Sensible vehicle. Not my first choice, but I guess you didn't want to pick Georgia up in a Focus, huh?" He chuckled, smiling at Kline. "How was the gas mileage?"

"Pretty good," Kline answered. "Twenty-eight miles to the gallon."

"Not too shabby." His dad scrunched his lips together, nodding his head.

The whole practicality thing was really starting to make sense.

"Darling, have you offered Georgia anything to drink?" his mother whispered, but loud enough for me to hear. "I'm sure she's parched from the drive."

Before I could decline, Kline was pulling me to my feet.

"Come on, let's get you something to drink."

"I'll take a beer, son!" his dad called out to us as we walked into the kitchen.

"She's so pretty, Bob," Maureen whispered to her husband, giddy. "Do you think they're having s-e-x?"

"Christ, Maureen, I hope to God our son is having sex by now. He's thirty-four years old. If he isn't, I've screwed up somewhere along the way."

"Shh," she quieted him. "Keep your voice down. And stop talking like that."

"Pretty sure they can hear everything you're saying, Maur. You've never been too good with the inside voice." His father didn't even attempt to keep his volume down.

"Do you think they are, Bob?"

"By the way they looked when they walked in the door, I'd say they were about two seconds away from s-e-x-ing."

If they hadn't already shown me approval, I'd have been burrowing myself into the floor.

The second we got into the kitchen, Kline was lifting me onto the counter and standing between my legs. He gripped my thighs.

"Sorry for the ambush," he said, his eyes apologetic.

"It's not like you planned it. Anyway, I really like Bob and Maureen."

A relieved grin covered his lips. "They really do mean well. My mom can be a bit of a meddler, though. I'm sure that was apparent the second we walked into my apartment and found them making themselves at home."

I laughed, nodding. "It's okay. Once you meet my parents, you'll realize you have nothing to worry about."

He pressed a soft kiss to my lips. "I look forward to it, baby."

"Do you think we'll have s-e-x tonight?" I teased, waggling my brows.

"God, I was praying you hadn't heard them," he groaned, dropping his head to my chest.

I laughed, lifting his chin up to meet my eyes.

"I'm glad you're finding this hilarious."

"I can't wait until we have s-e-x again," I whispered.

Kline's face cracked, a smile consuming his perfect mouth.

"I hope you put your mouth on my p-u-s-s-y, too."

"If I put my c-o-c-k in your mouth, will you stop spelling shit?"

I nodded, my mouth twisting into a devious smile.

He tickled my ribs, urging giggles from my lips.

"Stop it!" I whisper-yelled, squirming away from him. "Now, stop being so damn ornery and get me something to drink. I'm parched."

He rolled his eyes, turning for the fridge.

I stayed on the counter, swinging my legs and watching him rummage around for refreshments.

"Hey…psst…" I tried to get his attention.

Curious blue eyes peeked over the fridge door.

I cupped my mouth with my hands, whispering, "You have the best c-o-c-k."

CHAPTER 24

Kline

"I just realized maybe I should have chosen a more professional meal. Something delicate." Georgia rolled her eyes with a self-deprecating smile and took a sip of wine.

Professional. *Ha.* These days, professional felt like nothing more than a fancy name for a distant memory. I was so wrapped up in her, my eyes were practically staring straight down the barrel of my asshole.

It didn't feel remotely natural, but it sure as fuck didn't feel bad either.

"You're not a delicate professional. You're a take-charge, no-bullshit kind of woman. If Glen would rather watch you eat a salad than a steak, he can go fuck himself."

"Kline!"

"Well, he can. Don't worry about anything other than being yourself and the contract. Fuck the rest."

It had been two weeks since our trip to the Hamptons. We were at a dinner meeting with Glen Waters, President and CEO of FlowersFirst, to button up an exclusive contract with them that I hadn't been crazy about—until Georgia had outlined all of the guaranteed cross-advertising they were contracted to do.

Full disclosure, I still wasn't one hundred percent sold. But Georgia Cummings was a smart, efficient employee, and that wasn't even my dick talking. He got a vote, I supposed—not worth denying it—but that wasn't the basis of my decision. My confidence in her ability was what had brought us to this meeting.

But the flower market share on TapNext alone was gargantuan, and I didn't like giving any one entity the entire pie. Contracts were airtight for a reason, but swearing yourself to one person professionally was just ripe for a fucking.

Glen better have some real unicorn and rainbow type bullshit planned for ad content or I am going to derail this train before it even gets out of the station.

"Sorry about that," Glen apologized as he approached the table. He'd left to take an "important" phone call. It happened from time to time, so I understood, but he rubbed me as one of those people who *thinks* he's hot shit and irreplaceable. Everyone is replaceable in business.

Some people like me, or Georgia, or maybe even Glen, could be an asset, but we sure as fuck weren't necessities. Businesses needed competence, patience, and drive, and plenty of people had those qualities.

"No problem," Georgia appeased easily, obviously feeling like telling him to go fuck himself a little less than I did.

"Now, we were just starting to dive into the specifics when you got pulled away," she began, steering Glen back to the prize. I sat back to watch.

"We'd be looking at a twelve-month exclusivity in exchange for majority placement in each of your ads: television, radio, and print. In general, our website makes up twenty percent of the online daily flower market alone. Brooks Media would contractually reserve the right to approve any and all ad content that references or deals with us."

God, she was something.

Every word she spoke made it clear—business didn't need specific people, but love and relationships sure did. I was starting to realize my specific person was her.

I checked back into reality just in time to find Georgia looking to me in question. Of course, I'd missed the question.

Glen, the helpful bastard, filled me in, though. "Don't you think she'd look sexy in one of the ads, Brooks?"

"No," I answered simply, hoping he'd drop it. We'd just gotten started, and I wanted to believe he was just trying to get into her good graces by complimenting her—inappropriate in both context and manner, but a compliment all the same.

He laughed and gestured at my girlfriend.

"Sex sells. You know this."

I did. Sex was a huge share of marketing in the U.S. specifically. But there was a whole slew of creative ways to use it, and they didn't include Georgia.

"Your whole market is sex, and this girl would *sell*."

I clenched my hand into a fist under the table but worked to keep my voice and demeanor steady. I even managed a completely unfriendly smile. "No, Glen. Georgia is an executive and an asset within the company. What she *isn't*, is *sex to sell*."

"Kline," Georgia whispered. My anger was building and she wasn't oblivious to it.

"Oh, I see," Glen said with a nod. "Her sex isn't for sale because she's already sexing the boss." He reached out to brush the loose hair off of her shoulder. "Good move, sweetheart."

My mind raced with a thousand scenarios of how I could strangle this motherfucker from across the table. *Shit.* I shoved back my chair and fished in my pocket for money at the same time. Rage bubbled and boiled under the surface, singeing the lining of my veins, but I didn't give in to the scene. He wanted that. He'd pushed the last straw to try to get a rise out of me and draw attention to himself because he knew the contract was already swirling the drain.

Guys like Glen were snakes, slithering around until they found the perfect opportunity to pounce. He wanted a physical reaction, one that would land me in handcuffs and balls deep in lawyer's fees. But I wouldn't be a party to it.

He was the coward, not me. Instead of facing his poor, pathetic, unintelligible business decisions head-on, *like a man*, he'd sexually harassed my girlfriend.

"The deal's dead, Glen," I declared, throwing the money down on the white linen tablecloth. "Contract's destroyed. Any future opportunity to do business with Brooks Media and any of its subsidiaries extinguished. And you've lost a powerful business ally, and instead, gained an enemy."

I pulled out Georgia's chair and forced her to stand.

"Kline—"

"Georgia, let's go."

She nodded, grabbed her clutch, and followed, but I could tell she wasn't happy.

And that made fucking two of us.

Frank sat at the curb waiting, and I opened the door and ushered Georgia in without delay.

"Mr. Brooks," Frank said as he jumped to attention in the driver seat.

"My apartment, Frank."

"Yes, sir."

Georgia tried several times to meet my eyes, but I couldn't return the favor. I was too goddamn angry. At Glen, at myself, and a little at her. I hated the last most of all.

I expected her to call to me. Tell me to look at her. Something.

But the more my anger stewed, the more her own built. When I glanced her way, she was staring out the window and grinding her teeth, the curves of her nails cutting into the skin of her palms every few seconds.

The ride remained silent and tense and didn't break until the door to my apartment slammed shut behind us.

I tossed my wallet and keys onto the counter and pulled the tails of my shirt out of my pants. As I loosened my tie, Georgia geared up for battle, turning to face me and slamming her tiny purse down on the kitchen table with force.

"I can't believe you!" she seethed.

"Me?" I asked in disbelief, four fingers pointing to the outside of my chest and raging heart pumping under the surface.

"Yes, you! That was a multi-million dollar deal. Access to ads we don't have to pay for for twelve months!" She shook her head. "I've been working on it for the better part of six months! And you threw in the towel because you were a jealous boyfriend."

"Fuck that, Georgia!" I yelled, and she jumped. It was the first time I'd ever raised my voice at her, and it felt just awful enough that I hoped it was the last. But she needed to hear this. "I didn't screw shit. That deal was menial at best from the beginning, signing away our lives to *him* for an entire year. And the way Glen conducts business is bullshit."

"I'm a woman, Kline! Sometimes I have to play the game a little differently than you."

"That's horseshit."

She jerked back, and her face flushed red with anger.

"The moment you lower yourself to playing into fuckwits like Glen is the moment you've already shot yourself in the goddamn foot *and* leg."

"I had it under control."

"You didn't have shit," I spat. "He was *touching* you. There is nowhere, not one single place, where that's appropriate in business, man or woman."

"Kline—"

It would be bad enough that I'd interrupted her, so I forced my voice to calm. "You are a brilliant woman. When someone notices your beauty and belittles it like that, you tell them to fuck off, and you do it immediately."

TAPPING *the* BILLIONAIRE

"I was trying to—"

"No," I interrupted again, pulling my tie from my neck and tossing it next to my keys, softening my voice even further. "You're right about a lot of things, a lot of the time, baby, but about this, you. Are. Wrong."

Anger lined every angle of her body, the way she stood, and the expression on her face. But she didn't say anything. She knew I was right. She knew she hadn't been on her A-game, and she was fucking pissed about it.

Pissed that women had to be in that position in the first place.

Infuriated that she hadn't held her ground when he'd pushed.

She could carry that anger for the whole night for all I cared. In fact, I hoped she did. Stewed on it. Learned from it.

I didn't mind one fucking bit as long as she got the hell into my arms.

"Be angry," I told her. "But, please, for the love of God, do it while you're touching me."

Two fuming steps ate half the distance between us, and I closed the rest, pulling her face to mine with a clutch of her jaw.

Buttons scattered as she ripped my shirt wide open and pushed the destroyed fabric from my shoulders. Heat ran down my spine like a bullet out of a gun, burning a track all the way down and gripping my balls at the bottom.

I could feel them tighten in excitement, and an aggressiveness I didn't know I possessed surged through my veins in accompaniment.

As soon as the tattered fabric cleared my fingertips, my hands went straight for her ass and around, down the backs of her thighs and back up the inside, bringing her skirt with them. Scratching lightly, my fingernails tested her skin before the urge to grab overwhelmed me. Skin bunched and moved with the pressure before forming a perfect shelf below her ass where my hands could live.

I lifted her with ease, forcing her legs up and around my hips with pressure at my pinkies, and strode for the bedroom. She wrapped her arms around my shoulders to ease the pressure on my own and redistribute it perfectly to my hard-as-fuck cock.

Uninhibited, she ate at my lips, sucking one and then the other between her own and running her tongue along the seam of them.

A groan rumbled in my chest and her breath came out in pants, but that didn't slow either of us. Time versus pleasure was a race, the culmination of both right on the edge with no chance of stopping. I wanted her more than I wanted to breathe, and when she threw her head back, let go of my shoulders, and ripped her shirt over her head, she confirmed I wasn't the only one.

"Suck on them," she ordered, thrusting her tits in my face and reaching behind her back to unhook her bra.

With my hands at her lower back to hold her steady, I didn't delay or disappoint, pulling one cup down with my teeth before she could find the clasp.

Little nibbles and sucking kisses, I tortured every inch of skin, burrowing my face in the bottom swell and biting it enough to make a mark.

She yelped slightly, but it morphed into a moan as she pulled the scrap of fabric down her arms in between us and threw it to the floor of my bedroom.

With my back to the bed, I fell to my ass, unwilling to abandon our current position or circumstances. Her knees sank naturally into the mattress at my sides, and the newfound freedom of my hands made me test the weight of her perfect tits in each one.

"God, Kline," she whimpered. "They ache." She let out two short pants as my tongue swirled the tip and sucked it deep into the warmth of my mouth. "*I ache.*"

"Make it better, Georgie," I dared after releasing her pink nipple with a pop.

Always up for a challenge, she didn't hesitate, backing off of my lap in an instant and unbuckling the belt at my waist. Her tongue flashed out and tasted her own lips as she did, heady arousal running so hot in her blood that she couldn't stop. I nearly lost my fucking mind.

Belt undone, she made quick work of the button and zipper and shoved her hands inside before I could make a move to reciprocate with her skirt.

Jesus Christ.

The feel of her hand diving in to grab my dick without remorse or hesitation nearly made me come in my pants.

"Georgia," I whispered, and her bright, fiery eyes jumped to mine with desperation.

She'd been pouring all of her angst and uncertainty from the meeting into this—*into us*—and I didn't mind. But at the same time, I wanted her to feel what was coming from me. My jealousy, my rage—*sure*—but mostly my fucking disgust at listening to someone treat her like anything less than the smart, beautiful, goddamn goddess of a woman she was.

"Come on, baby. Climb on. Fuck me until it only hurts good."

She finally shucked her skirt and I did the same with my pants, toeing off my shoes in the process. She didn't bother, keeping her heels on her feet and climbing on top of me again.

I reached to grab a condom from my pants, but she slid down on my dick before my fingers even met the fabric.

"*Fuuuuuck.*"

"Oh yeah," she agreed, emphatic. "I'm going to."

"Condom," I reminded her, grabbing her hips to slow her already building speed.

She just shook her head with a smile, a halfway distant look in her eyes suggesting she didn't even understand what the fuck she was doing.

If I thought for even a second there was a chance I'd hurt her in some way or give her some kind of a disease by taking her without a condom, I would have stopped her.

But I knew for a fact I wouldn't, and if there were other consequences, like an unplanned pregnancy, I'd literally run myself ragged to make it worth it for all of us.

Because *good God*, I did not want to interrupt or ruin this show.

I eased my grip on her hips just enough that she could move freely and she took advantage.

She found her rhythm quickly, her tits swinging deliciously and the plump cheeks of her ass cradling my thighs and balls with every stroke down.

Her hair fell down and around her face, and her breath came out in staccato pants. I'd never seen a woman take hold of her pleasure so thoroughly. She squeezed me internally with every stroke, touched the skin on my chest like she couldn't get enough—*connected*—and yet, she worked me with the focus of someone doing nothing but chasing their own pleasure.

A smile swallowed my face as her pussy did the same to my cock. Up and down she went, her thighs shaking more and more with each stroke.

"That's it, sweetheart."

She was getting close now, and her fingernails were digging half-moons into the skin at my chest. I grabbed a handful of flesh at the sides of her hips and held on, saddling up and getting ready for what was to come.

When a moan exploded from her chest, I lost any pretense of control. A clap of sound cracked the heavy, sex-filled air as I reddened the skin of her ass with one hand and plucked at one of her perfect nipples with the other.

"Ride that cock, Georgia."

Her pussy clenched.

Fuck yes.

"Make it yours," I demanded, pushing her to take it to the next level. With an ab curl, my mouth lunged for her untortured nipple and sucked it with a pop. Her pussy grabbed me again, and this time was slow to let go. "Fuckkkkk. God, this cunt. It's gonna make *me* yours for fucking ever."

And it was. That and her mind and her single-minded determination to redefine herself—to redefine her evening's decisions—in one dominating ride on my cock.

If this was how we fought, I'd fight with her forever.

CHAPTER 25

Georgia

"Honey, I'm home!" Cassie yelled. A familiar echoing thud filled my ears as she dropped her bags to the floor. "Where in the hell are you?"

"In here!" I called from the bathroom. My lashes fluttered as I tried to apply mascara without poking my eye out. I liked makeup, loved when someone helped me apply my makeup, but I wasn't very good at doing it myself. Which was why if Cassie—the makeup guru—wasn't around to help me get ready, I stuck with the basics.

"Aw, isn't this sweet," she said, resting her shoulder on the doorframe. "My little baby is all grown up, applying her own makeup and shit."

"I even got my period last week, Mom," I tossed back, my voice monotone. "I think I'm officially a woman."

"What in the hell are you doing?" she scoffed, watching my reflection in the mirror. "Are you trying to remove your eyelid with that brush?"

See what I mean? Makeup and I weren't all that great of friends.

Lipstick? Sure.

Blush? Yeah, okay.

Even mascara I could manage.

But anything else, I was pretty much incompetent.

"Give me that before you detach a retina." She snatched the eye shadow brush from my hand.

I scrunched my nose. "What do you know about detached retinas?"

"I dated an optometrist like a million years ago and there was—" She stopped midsentence, taking in my narrow-eyed expression.

"*Okay*, if you want to be specific about it," she amended. "I *banged* an optometrist a few times."

"That's better. Keep going," I urged her.

"Well, there was an incident, and he freaked the hell out about my eye. Mumbling something about a detached retina."

"Do I even want to know details?"

"If you don't want to hear about how Wally's giant penis poked me in the eye while he was com—"

"Yep." I held up my hand, laughing. "I'm much better without."

"I'll tell ya one thing." She smirked, resting her hip on the sink. "Wally was my first uncircumcised penis."

I stared at her.

"What?" she asked, shrugging. "I felt like I was playing with one of those toys from the '90s. You know, the ones filled with water that would slip through your hands. I wasn't prepared for the foreskin." She looked off into space, thinking about God only knew what. "But once I got the hang—" She stopped, taking in my wordless expression.

Of course, internally, I was cracking up, but I knew Cass. Believe me, I had to disengage before she went any further. Because if she continued, we'd all know far too much about Wally.

"Geez, tough crowd," she muttered, fiddling with my makeup and finding her choice in eye shadow color before gesturing to my eyes. "This color is all wrong, by the way. You have gorgeous blue eyes. You need something that'll make 'em pop."

She motioned for me to sit down.

I plopped my robe-covered butt on the closed toilet seat and waited patiently for her to work her magic.

"I was trying to do a smoky eye," I admitted.

"Yeah, but these dark tones are all wrong," she said, moving toward me with a color palette in hand. "You can do a smoky eye, but you need neutral tones. Otherwise, you're just going to hide that spectacular blue."

"Close 'em," she instructed, brush held up close to my face.

I shut my eyes, sighing in relief. My best friend was home. Sure, we'd still managed to chat nearly every day through texts and short phone calls, but it wasn't the same. Four weeks was a long fucking time.

"I missed you."

"I missed you too," she responded, a smile in her voice. "I'm happy you were actually going out and having fun while I was gone."

"What's that supposed to mean?" I peeked at her out of my left eye.

She flashed an *are you serious?* look.

"I go out," I disagreed. "I go out all the time. I party like a freakin' rockstar!"

"Yeah." She snorted. "A very poor rockstar, who isn't in a band anymore, and starts yawning by nine and just wants to be home drinking wine."

"I'm not like that *all* the time," I denied, laughing despite myself. "But seriously, you're never allowed to leave me again."

The brush swiped over my left eyelid in smooth, sure movements.

"I wasn't even gone for a month, and I'm here for tonight. Anyway, you were a busy little bee with your new boyfriend."

Boyfriend. It felt weird to hear someone else call him that. In private, we'd exchanged the boyfriend/girlfriend sentiment frequently, but we were still keeping our relationship very much on the down low at work. My choice, of course. Kline was more than ready to make us public to everyone, but I just wasn't in that place yet.

We had fallen into this relationship so quickly and I didn't want to be rash about letting my coworkers know I was dating the boss. I couldn't ignore that nagging thought in the back of mind that wanted to find a way to protect myself as much as possible if we didn't work out—and protect myself from the shrieks of Dean if we did.

There was no denying we were together, but in a way, boyfriend didn't feel like the right word for what Kline was to me. It was too small, too casual. In such a short amount of time, he'd become a huge part of my life.

The brush moved to my other lid, working a little quicker once Cassie had found her makeup-applying stride.

As I thought about Kline and me and everything we had together, a smile crept its way across my lips, until happiness consumed my entire mouth.

"Well, look at you, all smiley and smitten. By the looks of it, I'd say someone has got it bad."

My cheeks flushed hot.

"Are you blushing, Wheorgie?"

"No." My hands went straight to my cheeks. "I am most certainly not blushing."

"Of course you're not." She laughed. "Tilt your head back." She gripped my chin. "So, give me the scoop. What's the boss really like?"

"He's just… I don't know even where to begin." That smile was back, taking over my entire face—mouth, cheeks, even my eyes were crinkling at the corners.

"Dude, tone down the cheesy grin or else I'll screw up your makeup."

I laughed, despite myself. "Sorry, I can't help it. I really like him, Cass."

She paused for a second and my eyes opened, meeting her intrigued stare.

"What?" I asked, starting to feel self-conscious. "Does the smoky eye look stupid on me?"

She shook her head.

"Then what? Why are you looking at me like that?"

"Nothing. Close your eyes again so I can finish up. Other people need to get ready around here, you know," she teased, her hip bumping my side.

I did as I was told and enjoyed the luxury of having someone else do the tedious task of applying eye shadow and liner.

"You know," she whispered, "I think you're holding back on me. I think—actually, I know—this thing between you and Kline, it's a whole lot more than just like."

"I said I really like him," I retorted, my mouth staying in a flat line as she slid lipstick across my lips.

"I'm aware," she said, her voice tickled with amusement. "But I think there's another four-letter word rolling around in your brain."

"Fuck?" I deadpanned.

"No, but how is the fucking? Is it everything you dreamed of when you were holding on to your coveted virginity?" she teased.

"Eh." I feigned indifference. "I could take it or leave it." I pulled the corners of my lips down into a pout, hiding another cheesy grin.

She snorted, taking in my absurd expression—smiling eyes, frowning mouth, and cheeks about to burst at the seams. "So, what I think you're telling me is that he's better than you could have ever imagined? Your Big-dicked Brooks billionaire can bring it."

I shrugged, biting back a laugh. "Something like that."

"I knew it!" She fist pumped the blush brush. "I'm not one to say 'I told you so,' but yeah, I told you so!" Cassie danced around the bathroom, shaking her ass and laughing maniacally.

"All right, crazy. Less gloating, more fixing my makeup," I demanded, giggling at her antics.

"I feel like we need a kitchen dance party to commemorate this momentous occasion," she announced, still dancing around in the silent room.

Kitchen dance parties were our thing. We had been doing them since college. They were used for happy times, horrible times, and everything in between.

When Cass told her nasty professor to suck it? Kitchen dance party.

When I got the coveted internship I was striving for? Kitchen dance party.

A hot barista asked Cass out? Kitchen dance party.

The time I managed to do all of our laundry with four quarters? *Epic* kitchen dance party.

There were only three rules: Rotate who got dibs on the music selection. No boys allowed. And always bring your A-dancing-game.

Some of my fondest memories of college were with Cass, dancing around in our shitty apartment, singing our hearts out. God, this girl, she was my rock. My favorite person to vent to, cry with, and most importantly, laugh my ass off with. I wouldn't have traded her for anything.

"All right, sweet cheeks, you're all set," she announced, smirking down at me. "And your makeup is looking pretty damn fabulous if I do say so myself."

I stood, taking in my appearance in the mirror. I touched my cheeks as I examined the gorgeous shades highlighting my eyes. She was right; neutral was better.

"Now, I didn't go crazy, just went with subtle and your signature bright red lips. I still wanted you to look like my Wheorgie." She winked. "You're gorgeous, friend. Absolutely stunning."

Without hesitation, I wrapped my arms around her, hugging her tightly. "Thank you. I love you so much, Cass."

"Love you too." She hugged me back.

We rocked back and forth a few seconds, until I whispered, "You really dated an optometrist named Wally?"

"Banged." She laughed, shoving me away. "There was no dating. His name was Wally, for fuck's sake."

I pointed at her, grinning. "You're a troll."

She was completely unfazed by this. "I'm fully aware. I will not make apologies for my need to judge men by their names."

"That is so weird. You know that, right?"

While some women judge men by their looks or clothes or money, Cass judged them by their names. It was one of her little quirks and it was off-the-wall bizarre, but downright hilarious. I'd seen her in action far too many times, a man asking her out or offering to buy her a drink, and her response always depended on one thing: his name.

The name was always the make it or break it in Cass's dating life scenarios.

"I know, but I can't help it. I can't bring myself to date, much less marry, someone named Wally or Toby or Cliff. Just—" She shudders. "Nope, no way. I'll never do it."

"I need to know how staunch you are on this mindset." My hand went to my hip. "Let's talk hypotheticals. What if Jude Law asked you to marry him, but his name was actually Morty Law?"

She grimaced. "Nope. Sorry, Morty. Take your adorable accent somewhere else."

"What about Angus Efron?"

A look of disgust crossed her face. "I don't care how much cheese he can grate on his abs. Not happening."

I stared at her for a few seconds, deciding if I really wanted to do it.

Cassie eyed me with skepticism. "Don't you dare." She pointed in my direction. "Don't even think about it."

I nodded, a mischievous grin spreading across my lips.

"Georgia," she warned.

"What if..." I smiled, tapping my chin. "Eugene Tatum—" she gasped "—was naked, asking you to marry him while grinding against you to 'Pony'?"

Channing Tatum was Cass's guy. He would always be at the top of her list. When *Magic Mike* had come out, we'd seen the movie not one, but two times on opening night because she was a total hornbag for him.

"I hate you." A hand towel was tossed into my face. "I'm going to forget you ever said that," she grumbled, striding into the hallway.

Of course, I followed her. This was too good of an opportunity to pass up.

"You know? I think Eugene looked hotter in *Magic Mike XXL*."

"Georgia!" Cassie threw her hands up in the air.

I leaned against the doorway as she rummaged through her closet. "What? I really think his stripteases were way sexier. Eugene can bring it. That's for damn sure."

"I will not let you ruin Tatum for me."

"I'd never—" I raised both hands in the air "—ruin the appeal of Eugene Fillmore Tatum."

"Oh my gawd!" She placed her hands tightly over her ears, la-la-la-ing to tune me out.

I laughed the entire way to my bedroom.

Standing in front of my closet, I was wavering between about fifty different options. I wanted to look cute—no, I wanted to look sexy. I wanted Kline to be eating…out of the palm of my hand. I swear that was where I was headed with that.

I needed a guy's opinion.

TAPRoseNEXT (5:30PM): Psst…Ruck…Come in, Ruck.

BAD_Ruck (5:32PM): Need something, Rose?

TAPRoseNEXT (5:33PM): Little black dress (open back) and red heels OR black leather pants and lace top?

BAD_Ruck (5:34PM): Neither. Clothes aren't needed in bed. Anyway, lace isn't really my style.

TAPRoseNEXT (5:34PM): This isn't the bed game. I need a guy's opinion on outfit choices.

BAD_Ruck (5:36PM): You meeting your Some Kind of Wonderful tonight?

TAPRoseNEXT (5:37PM): You bet ya.

BAD_Ruck (5:37PM): You're really into this guy.

TAPRoseNEXT (5:38PM): Are you asking or telling?

BAD_Ruck (5:39PM): Both.

TAPRoseNEXT (5:41PM): For your information, Mr. Nosy, yes, I'm really into this guy. I'm meeting him for drinks later. And I want a guy's opinion on women's attire for date nights.

BAD_Ruck (5:42PM): Which shows the least amount of skin?

TAPRoseNEXT (5:43PM): Leather and lace.

BAD_Ruck (5:44PM): That's the one.

TAPRoseNEXT (5:45PM): Really?

BAD_Ruck (5:47PM): Less is more when it comes to showing skin. There are certain parts of you he wants to be the only one to see.

TAPRoseNEXT (5:48PM): I said the dress had an "open back" not open crotch.

BAD_Ruck (5:51PM): Just trust me, Rose. This is sound advice. I promise.

TAPRoseNEXT (5:52PM): Okay, okay. Leather and lace it is. Big plans tonight?

BAD_Ruck (5:53PM): Maybe…

TAPRoseNEXT (5:54PM): Your own version of Some Kind of Wonderful?

BAD_Ruck (5:55PM): Something like that. Be good tonight, Rose.

TAPRoseNEXT (5:56PM): You too, Ruck.

A part of me felt bad for still messaging Ruck, but we'd fallen into this odd sort of friendship, mostly chatting about one another's dating lives. We never attempted to take things to another level, never tried to meet in person. It had become a sort of unspoken rule since we were both involved with someone else.

I tossed my phone on the bed and grabbed my favorite leather pants and lace blouse. It was black with three-quarter-length sleeves, and the top revealed just enough skin to show off a bit of cleavage.

The only other things I needed were the Dolce & Gabbana leather booties I'd found a week and a half ago in SoHo. They had been a secondhand purchase, and a splurge at that, but I loved them.

"Georgia?" Cassie called from the hall.

"Yeah?"

"What time are we meeting Kline?"

"Not until eight-ish. I figured we could have a little girl time beforehand."

"Harry Potter shots at Barcelona?"

"I'm in." The bar in question specialized in shots. One in particular came with fire and was famously known as the Harry Potter.

If you've never been to Barcelona Bar, add it to your bucket list. It's not the bar you hang out in all night, but it's definitely the place you stop by to get your night started off right.

My screen flashed with a text message notification.

Kline: 8pm at The Raines Law Room?

Holy hell. It was one of those bars that had a secret door, and if you don't know somebody, no way you're getting in. It was a very unlike Kline place to go.

Me: Uh…pretty sure I don't have VIP access there.

Kline: Well, don't worry, because I do.

Me: Kline flaunting his money around? Are you feeling okay?

Kline: Not flaunting. Just using it to our advantage. Anyway, Will was pretty persistent since he's never been.

I should've known my brother was behind it. If Will had Kline's money, he wouldn't have any damn money left. Good thing Will would earn a nice salary as a physician and be too busy taking care of patients to spend it all. Where I was more frugal like our father, he was impulsive like our mother—a true American consumer who could easily be talked into buying a new car or plasma screen TV on a whim.

And I mean all of this in the most loving way.

Me: Okay. Count me in. Cass will be with me.

Kline: Perfect. Meet me there at 8. I'll leave your names at the door.

Me: Okay, I'll let Will know.

Kline: No need. He's with me now.

Me: WHAT? Are you having a bromance with my brother?

Kline and Will had finally met over lunch last week in Gramercy Park. It had taken about one minute of introductions and they were quickly bonding over rugby, scotch, and awkward stories about yours truly. By the end of the meal, they had exchanged numbers and my brother had enthusiastically agreed to guest play for Kline's rugby team the following weekend.

Kline: I had to find one somewhere. Walter certainly isn't filling the position.

I smiled at his ongoing battle with his cat. Every day I witnessed or heard about something else.

Me: What are you accusing my best friend of now?

Kline: I'm not accusing him of anything. I recount the facts. I went to all the trouble of fixing him a fresh bowl of milk, in the dish he likes, mind you, and the grumpy bastard took one drink and spit it out in front of me.

Me: That's probably because you should really be giving him water, not milk. He's probably dehydrated.

Kline: You always take his side.

Another message came before I could send a sarcastic response.

Kline: Are you standing around in your bedroom naked?

Me: Don't try to change the subject.

Kline: I'm not. I'm merely moving on to more important subjects.

I glanced at myself in the full-length mirror on my armoire, fully dressed and about five minutes away from being ready to walk out the door.

Me: Yes, dirty boy. I am very naked.

Kline: Liar.

Me: I'll never tell.

Kline: I'll tell you one thing, I'm going to take your panties off with my teeth tonight. I promise you that.

Well, shit. That had me wishing the night out was just a night in…in Kline's bed, to be specific.

Kline: We're still going out, Benny. Finish getting ready. We'll revisit this conversation later.

Did he suddenly become a mind reader?

Me: In your bed, later?

Kline: My bed. My couch. The floor. Against the wall. Shower. When it comes to my version of later, the sky's the limit.

Me: See you at 8. I'll be the girl with red lips and sexy heels.

Kline: Tease.

Me: You know it, baby ;)

"Okay, you've got about thirty minutes to get ready. We're supposed to meet Kline and Will at eight. That leaves us with about an hour to grab a drink at Barcelona," I shouted from my room as I sat on the edge of the bed, slipping on my new shoes.

"Wait…Will is going to be there?" Her amused voice echoed down the hall.

Internally, I groaned, knowing full well where this was headed. "Yes, my brother will be there."

"I'm definitely going with the dress, then! And sky-high stilettos!"

"I hope you break an ankle!"

"Me too! That way Will and I can play doctor and naughty patient!"

"You are not banging my brother, Cass! He is off-limits!"

"When you say bang…what exactly do you mean?"

"No touching my brother!"

This was an ongoing joke between us. Cassie loved telling me how hot my older brother was. She adored him, and he mostly treated her like his little sister, but every once in a while, she could get him to play along and tease me about the two of them hooking up.

The mere idea of them together had me cringing. They'd be like oil and water. Both were far too opinionated and outspoken. If they got together, my life would implode from their bickering.

Grabbing my silver-studded clutch, I walked out into the kitchen and got my purse in order. Phone, wallet, lipstick, and keys—that's all I'd need for the night. When it came to New York, you learned quickly that the less crap you had to carry around, the better.

Cass came strutting out a few minutes later, legs on full display beneath a form-fitting gray dress and black stilettos. She did a little twirl, grinning at me. "How do I look?"

"Tell me you have underwear on underneath that."

"Of course I do." She feigned offense. "I have a thong on, Georgie."

"Go back in there—" I pointed toward the hall "—and put on another pair. Something that covers your entire ass. When you're around my brother and dressed like that, you'd best be double bagging that shit."

She laughed.

"I'm serious!"

"I know you are. I'm serious too. I'm real serious about getting Will naked. I guarantee his body is—"

"All right, that's enough." I held up my hand. "You made your point. Are we even?"

She nodded, visibly proud of herself for one-upping me. "Yes, I will forget about the Tatum incident."

"Good." I grabbed my clutch and headed for the door. "Eugene would be proud of you."

She groaned behind me. "You're an asshole."

"Let's go get drinks!" I shouted, fist pumping my clutch in the air.

Cass and I caught the train and made it to Barcelona in record time. We hung out for an hour, chatting and laughing and dancing for a few songs to the house band. We were one flaming Harry Potter shot and a beer deep by the time we left to meet the guys.

The Raines Law Room was located in Chelsea, fairly close to my apartment. I had a feeling Kline had had that fact in mind when he'd given in to Will's demands, always trying to make things easy and convenient for me. I'd heard all kinds of cool things about the speak-easy bar, but it was my first time making an appearance.

Hesitantly, I rang the doorbell outside of the discreetly marked door.

"I feel like we're going into a top secret sex club," Cass whispered even though no one was around us. "Shit, now my hopes are up. I'm going to be so disappointed if we're at the right place."

I gaped at her. "Of all the places your mind could go, you're sticking with sex club?"

She shrugged. "I've never been to one."

"I'm pretty sure most people have never been to one."

"Guess we need to add it to our bucket list, Georgie."

"No," I responded through a quiet laugh. "That's not going on my bucket list."

"Speak for yourself."

The door was opened and an attractive guy dressed in a vest and tie answered.

I gave him Kline's name and, just like that, access granted.

In an instant, we were surrounded by silky music, velvety curtains, plush sofas, and dimmed lights. I felt like I had been transported back into the 1920s. Any second a girl in a flapper dress with a glass of gin was going to stroll past me.

Will had already spotted us, walking toward the entrance.

"Well, hello, Cassie Phillips," he greeted, a devilish grin on his face. He picked her up in a bear hug. The second her feet were off the ground, she squealed.

"Just so we're clear, I'm hating both of you right now," I teased, feigning annoyance.

He set Cass down and pulled me in for a tight squeeze. "Aw, don't get mad, Gigi. You know I love you the most."

"Why aren't you with Kline?" I asked, scanning the room.

"I had to make a pit stop in the bathroom. He's at the bar with one of his buddies."

"Buddies?"

Will nodded. "Have you met Thatch?"

I shook my head, more than ready to meet the notorious Thatch. I'd heard enough stories to understand he was an infamous jokester and a ton of fun to hang out with, but Kline and I had yet to get around to hanging out with him.

"Well, follow me, ladies." Will gestured toward the bar. "Your boyfriend's been wondering where you were. I told him you guys probably stopped for shots and dancing at Barcelona before heading this way."

"That sounds like nothing we would do," Cass disagreed, hiding her smile.

"Uh-huh," Will said, grinning. "I'm sure you didn't get Harry Potter shots and request the house band to play Britney Spears either."

I shook my head, biting my cheek. "Nope. Definitely didn't do that."

We totally did.

It had taken a round of beers for the band to play Cass's request, "I'm A Slave 4 U," but they'd done it, and we'd danced like fools. It was an ongoing inside joke when we went out together. If we were going to request songs, it had to be a cheesy pop song. We loved seeing the reactions of the patrons in the establishment when our ridiculous request started to play—annoyed, groaning, cursing our names—but like clockwork, by the end of the song, everyone would be singing and dancing along with us.

"Yeah, no way we did that," Cass agreed, laughing quietly.

As we walked toward the bar, I caught Kline's reflection in the giant mirror accented by liquor bottles. My gaze moved to the attractive guy sitting beside him and déjà vu hit me full force, damn near knocking me to the ground.

Holy shit.

I stopped dead in my tracks, holding on to Cass's arm in a viselike grip.

"What the hell?" She turned toward me, confused.

My hands shook as I realized why I knew the guy next to Kline.

It was Ruck.

Oh, *no.*

Ruck was here and he was sitting beside Kline, chatting like they were the best of friends.

Oh. Fuck.

I pulled Cassie away from the bar.

Will turned toward us, hands pushed out in a *what the fuck?* gesture.

"I forgot I need to go to the bathroom!" I called over my shoulder, damn near dragging Cassie across the floor.

"Holy hell, what is going on?" she questioned as I pushed through the crowd.

I didn't answer her until we were safely tucked inside the ladies' restroom.

"Oh my God, Cass!" I groaned, my voice echoing in the dimly lit room.

"I'm so confused," she muttered. "What is going on?"

"I know that guy next to Kline."

"Because he's Kline's friend Thatch, right?"

I shook my head, pacing the confined room like a caged animal.

"Are you going to give me a hint here or do I need to keep guessing?"

"He's Ruck."

"Huh?"

"Ruck! TapNext Ruck!" I stopped, my arms flying out in front of me.

She tilted her head. "The guy who sent the Hunchcock?"

I nodded maniacally. "Well, it wasn't really his Hunchcock," I started to explain, but realized we really didn't have time for that.

"I think I'm still missing something? I'm not really understanding your panic here…" She paused, waiting for me to give an explanation.

"Well, I never really stopped talking to him," I muttered, feeling ashamed to admit it out loud.

"Excuse me?" she asked, her eyes popping out in shock. "You've been talking to him this whole time?"

I nodded.

Cassie shook her head like she couldn't process it.

"Listen, I'll tell you all of the details later, but you need to act like you're familiar with him."

"With who?" She was still not catching on.

"Ruck!"

"Wait…who's Ruck again?"

I was about three seconds away from pulling my hair out.

"Kline's friend, Thatch! That's Ruck!" I whisper-yelled.

"Okay, okay." She gripped my shoulders. "Just take some breaths, G. Everything will be fine."

I took a few cleansing breaths, calming my racing heart down.

"Just tell me one thing. Why do I need to act like I know him?"

I sighed, staring down at my feet.

"Georgia?"

"Because you're still my profile picture," I whispered in a rush, hoping she wouldn't understand.

She started laughing and shaking her head in disbelief. "Remember this moment." She pointed a finger in my direction. "Because you owe me. Big time."

I nodded. "Anything you want."

"When we get home, you're going to explain why you're still talking to other guys when you're very happy with Kline."

"I swear to you, it's not like that."

She quirked a brow.

"I promise. I really like Kline. I wouldn't do anything to jeopardize that. Ruck is dating someone. I'm dating someone. And we never make plans to meet in person."

"Okay, I believe you." Cass pulled me in for a hug. "Who knows? Maybe he won't even know it's you…well, me…fuck, this is confusing."

I groaned. "How do I get myself into these situations?"

"Don't worry, sweetheart. I've got your back. I'll distract what's-his-face while you and Kline enjoy a night out."

"Thank you."

She handed me my clutch off the sink and moved toward the door.

I glanced at myself in the mirror, making sure I didn't look as crazy as I felt. My makeup was still intact, not a hair out of place. All I needed was another drink, or five, to calm my nerves and I'd be good to go.

Maybe.

As I walked past Cassie, she whispered, "Just so you know, this is really screwing with my big plan of seducing your brother tonight."

I rolled my eyes.

She held the door open for me. "Don't worry, I'll save it for another night," she added, a smirk on her face.

"Good plan, you slutty turncoat."

"Heyyy," she slurred, hinting at less sobriety than I'd hoped for going into a situation like this. "I'm no fucking traitor and you know it. I'm getting ready to eye-fuck the shit out of this guy for an entire evening just for you."

"No," I corrected. "No fucking, eye or otherwise. Just talking. We're friends."

She smirked as we rounded the corner and the guys came into view.

"What's his name again?" she asked, her eyes glowing like the last embers of a dying fire.

"Thatch," I answered by rote, minutely horrified that another member of my work world knew I was a virgin—or that I used to be—even though he didn't know I was me...I was Rose. Whatever. "Thatcher Kelly."

"Mmm," she moaned, fluffing her breasts into an even higher elevation in the cups of her bra and licking her lips.

"I'd thatch that."

Fuckkk. I should have known. For Cass, it was all in the name. This was going to be one long-ass night.

CHAPTER 26

Kline

"This place is unreal. You come here all the time?" Will asked as we walked into The Raines Law Room, dim lights and old-style sofas filled to the brim surrounding us.

"Not really," I answered honestly, knowing it wasn't really the place but the actual *going* that was the problem. "This is really more Thatch's style." The vibe was chill, but the allure was the drama. "The cloak and dagger, the limited access."

Will laughed and nodded in understanding.

I turned from him to the room to finish what I'd already started. My eyes had scanned the crowded bar immediately upon our arrival regardless of my knowledge that such an exercise was foolish and futile. My Georgie would be late to our wedding, the birth of our kids, and her own funeral.

Wait. *What?*

I glanced at her brother, panicked that he could read my mind, but he must have seen something other than outright terror in my eyes.

"Don't worry, man. George'll be here eventually." He laughed.

"But if Cass is with her, they probably stopped at Barcelona Bar before even thinking about coming this way. That girl *actually* gives *no* fucks."

I nodded along as though I understood, but I was barely even listening.

I mean, I could almost understand the wedding thing. I was crazy about her, no ifs, ands, or buts about it. But the kids?

Jesus.

My thoughts were in a tailspin, headed straight for the harsh reality of a quickly approaching ground when my pinballing eyes caught on something unexpected and unwelcome. Loud, boisterous, and impossible to ignore, it was quite possibly the only thing that could have superseded my line of thinking at that point.

Shoving through the crowd as gently as possible, checking to see that Will was trailing along behind me, I sought confirmation of my new, much more immediate fears.

Bodies moved with ease, and flirty smiles bombarded me from several female angles. I didn't have eyes for any of them, though, and for the first time in weeks, it wasn't because of Georgia.

Thatch turned as I approached, a shit-eating grin topping his redwoodlike frame at the sight of me. "K-man! Fuck yes! Out on the town! I thought I'd seen the last of this," he spewed out in quick succession, the effect of being several drinks deep slightly loosening his already slack tongue.

Will smiled at his greeting, and I tried not to cringe.

I really didn't need Thatch to be there tonight. I'd stupidly believed I could keep being Ruck and myself without the gun going off in my face. I was wrong. This was what happened when people played with things they weren't responsible enough to handle.

The walls collapsed, or at least, they felt like they did, and my tie set out to strangle me. Will smiled and greeted Thatch happily.

I ran through the consequences of his presence and tried not to puke.

God, if I couldn't get him the fuck out of here quickly, I was in trouble. His picture was on my profile. *His* face was the one Georgia had been associating with Ruck.

What was already a goatfuck of dishonesty was setting up to turn into an all-out cluster.

I leaned forward and right to Thatch's ear, using the crowd noise as an excuse to keep Will out of the loop.

"You need to leave," I told him succinctly, knowing that if ever there was a time my girl would be less than forty-five minutes late, this was it.

He laughed and slapped me on the back.

"It's good to see you too, man. I miss you. I only get to see you at practice these days."

I shook my head in frustration.

He laughed some more.

"I'm gonna run to the restroom, guys," Will excused himself, fading into the crowd fairly quickly.

Thatch nodded and smiled, taking Will's leave as an opportunity to shit talk.

"But, really, I guess that's the same as always. It's just the reason that's changed, right? Instead of work, it's the mystic pussy."

"Thatch."

"I get it, man. Sometimes your dick just gets caught in the snare of a good snatch. Like a vise grip, am I right?"

"Thatch, listen."

"How is Miss Georgia? Almost done with your ass and looking—"

Eyes to the door, I only heard the first half of his sentence—thank God—because, just as I knew she would, the object of my affection walked in looking like sex on legs right then. Leather and lace and enough beauty to make me think my earlier panic about kids was actually the best idea I'd ever had. Her blonde hair was styled wild, just how I liked it, and I could see the blue topaz of her eyes shining from across the room despite their failure to meet mine.

And arm in arm with her? The face of *her* profile, a woman I could only surmise was the infamous Cassie Phillips. I'd heard a laundry list of antics and anecdotes featuring Georgia's best girl, but I had yet to have the privilege of meeting her.

Fuck.

The web of lies was starting to look more like a convoluted clusterfuck of *what are the goddamn odds?* We'd each put our friends as our profile pictures—a scenario I should have predicted but absolutely *had not*—and now, I had to sit through an evening where any second this mess could brilliantly blow up in my face.

Out of time and patience, I turned to Thatch in a flash, and when I did, I led with my fist.

"Ouch," he said through a smile, rubbing his shoulder teasingly.

"Fuck, Thatch, fucking listen to me."

He mocked me with wide eyes and cupped his hands around his ears.

I considered hitting him again, this time for real, but with a glance in the girls' direction, I knew I didn't have time.

"The girl in the picture from the TapNext profile, the one you took it upon yourself to—"

"Traumatize."

I nodded. "Right. Well, I've been talking to her."

"Behind the lovely Georgie's back?" he asked in faux outrage. Regardless of his mocking, I could tell he was curious. Talking to two women at once wasn't like me, and when it came to these "two," he didn't know the half of it. And I didn't have the fucking time or means to explain.

One quick glance showed the women and Will together, hugging and laughing and all too close to heading this way.

I closed my eyes briefly to gain patience. He'd have to wait to hear how twisted my truth had become because that talk required more than fifteen seconds and several glasses of scotch.

"I've been talking to her ever since, and she's here. She's getting ready to come over here, right now, and she's gonna be doing it with Georgie."

With her? Ha! Fuck! More like, it is her.

"Well, fuck me," he said with a smile, his eyes searching mine in an effort to figure me out.

"Your picture is on that profile. You need to pretend to know her," I urged.

He paused for a beat, but he couldn't miss how important this was to me. Whether he agreed or understood or wanted to play along, or not, Thatch would always have my back. When you pulled back all of the prank-pulling, shit-talking layers, he was unmistakably one of the best kinds of people. "Got it."

I took air all the way into my lungs for the first time in the last two minutes and turned to greet my girl.

But she wasn't there. She and her friend had disappeared, leaving only her brother Will in their wake.

As Will made it to us, shaking his head, Thatch leaned over and added with a whisper, "And all this after I gargoyle-dicked her?" He whistled low. "You must have more game than I thought."

"What's up?" I asked Will, pointedly ignoring Thatch and hoping my face managed to do the same.

"Who knows, man? Hell if I can understand women."

When he provided no further information, I was sure my eyes tried to crawl all the way inside his head.

"Oh," he said, turning from the bar to find my inappropriately intense gaze. "They're in the bathroom."

I nodded woodenly in understanding, and Thatch nudged me as a result.

"You gotta lighten up," he whispered, turning me to the bar and flagging down the bartender. "Order a drink, for fuck's sake, and calm down."

I nodded again because I knew he was right, and it seemed to be the only action I could successfully complete at the time.

"Macallan," I muttered, knowing he'd make sure my order got to someone who actually *made* the drinks. Ordering directly was too complicated for me right now.

"Yeah, man," he said, smirking. "I know you drink Macallan. Macallan and lime, every day, every night for years now."

The cords of my throat tightened in frightened reflex. "No lime."

"No lime?"

I shook my head, feeling the tension drain from my shoulders a little at the memory of my sweet, doped up girl. "Georgie's allergic."

"Well, shit. That's problematic."

I laughed. "Not really," I said, then clarified, "Not now that I know, anyway."

"Make sure to leave out the lime," Will interjected, coming up on my other side to join the conversation.

"I guess she told you?" I asked with a laugh.

"Eventually. I still don't think she told me everything, but now that Cass is here, I'll find out the rest."

"Cass?" Thatch asked.

"Yep. Cassie Phillips. I'd say she's like another little sister to me, but I'm not sure she's the kind of girl who *can* be a little sister."

Thatch's eyes flared with excitement, and my panic came back tenfold. "Wild?"

Will just laughed and jerked his head toward the approaching women. "You'll see."

I forgot about everything else as soon as I saw her again. Long legs, a sliver of tan stomach, and a nervous smile, she was so fucking beautiful, I literally couldn't take my eyes off of her.

I pulled her straight into my arms, put my lips to her ear, and breathed. "Benny."

Out with the words and in with her smell, I held her body to mine and kept it there until she started to giggle.

"*Kline.*" I struggled to remove my face from her hair and my hands from her hips, but she helped it along, turning her body to include her friend in the conversation and making my hand slide along the skin at her back. "This is crazy Cassie."

"Crazy Cassie?" Cass squawked. "Is that my given name now?"

"Yes," Georgia challenged adorably.

"Ohhh, okay then," Cass conceded with a gleam in her eye. "I see. I'm a little slow, but I get it now."

Her hand reached for mine and I took it without question, giving it two quick shakes. "Hi, nice to meet you," she said.

I smiled.

"I'm Crazy Cassie. You must be Big-dicked Brooks."

Thatch spewed his whiskey everywhere, coating us all with a layer of spit to complement the shock courtesy of Cass.

Georgie squealed and Cassie just laughed, and through the chaos my eyes met those of an amused Will. He raised his glass in a gesture of confirmation.

Wild.

And unpredictable and funny and completely apathetic.

Good God, the people in this party were going to make this one interesting night.

I hoped we all survived.

I grabbed some napkins from the bar and handed them to Georgie, watching closely as she wiped Thatch's half-drunk whiskey from her cleavage. She shook her head slightly to let me know she'd noticed, and I felt my face dissolve into an outright smile before I turned back to Cass.

"That's me," I told her. "It's a wonder your friend is still alive."

Thatch and Cassie burst out in hysterics as Georgie slapped at my chest and Will covered his ears playfully.

"Kline!" Georgie screamed.

"Come on, baby. Let's go sit down," I told her, scooping her into my arms before whispering in her ear, "My legs are tired from carrying this thing around."

"Kline!"

"It's a real problem, Benny."

"Kli—" she started to chastise again, but I didn't give her the chance. Sealing my lips over hers, I licked and sucked and nibbled out a real hello. The night had just started and the implications of my lies hadn't even begun to be realized.

But *God*, I'd missed her.

And right then, in my mind, that was all that mattered.

"Where've you been all my life?" I asked against her lips as our kiss pulled to a close.

She smiled just for me, lust and like and maybe a little bit of love lighting her eyes and reflecting into mine. She rubbed the bridge of my nose with her own as I settled her into my lap, finding a space on a couch by sheer miracle. Hell, for all I knew, someone had moved at the last second to avoid having me on their lap. I wouldn't have noticed.

"I've been—eeeep!" she squeaked as she was ripped from my arms.

For a full second and a half, I feared for every single patron, a hulklike rage overwhelming my emotions and tensing the seams of my clothes.

"Relax, K," Thatch teased, cooling my rage but stoking the fire of my aggravation. "Just rearranging the seating chart."

My eyes narrowed as he set Georgie down on the sofa across from me and pushed me back to sitting next to him.

My thoughts were nearly murderous.

"Sheathe your claws, buddy," he cooed in my ear. "You're gonna have to get over your tantrum because old Ruck here needs some information and there's no one else to give it to him."

Goddamn, I hated when Thatch was right. And I hated it even more when it meant Georgia's ass couldn't be in my lap.

I looked at her, across from me, and found startled eyes bouncing back and forth between Thatch and me. To her, we were both a significant part of her life. It felt weird and I felt jealous, but mostly, I just felt *bad*. Bad for lying to her and bad for putting her through the confusion she felt now.

The responsibility for all of it sat squarely on my shoulders, and believe me, I could feel the weight. The sooner tonight was over with, the better.

"Cassie, right?" I heard Thatch ask above the ringing in my ears.

"Yeah."

"You know," he pushed, clearing his throat. "You look familiar."

"You too, actually. You look very Ruckish or Rucklike or something."

I shook my head and glanced at my panic-ridden girlfriend. She couldn't see it like I could—she was too nervous. This was like watching a bad spoof film of Ruck's and Rose's lives where the blind were leading the blind. We would never have reacted like this to seeing one another. Not in a million years.

Thatch's laugh was boisterous, his body nearly falling into my lap with the action. Turning his face to mine, he mouthed "name" quickly. I had to fight the urge to sigh. If it wouldn't have been a spectacular failure and an embarrassment for Georgia, I would have told everyone to give it up right then.

Instead, I typed out Rose on my phone and showed it to him quickly.

"Rose!" Thatch practically shouted. Cassie nodded along while Georgie's eyebrows pulled unconsciously together. She was rightfully confused. "I thought that was you, Rose! I can't believe how beautiful you are in person, Rose!"

I discreetly elbowed Thatch in the ribs. "Say her name one more time and I'll kill you," I whispered through gritted teeth.

He grimaced and shut his mouth.

"What's going on?" Will asked, the spectacle apparently just as confusing from the outside looking in.

"I was wondering the same thing," I said, playing along.

"It, um," Georgia mumbled. "It seems like they know one another or something."

"Thatch and Cass?" Will asked, confused.

"Yeah," Cassie confirmed. "We've been talking online ever since he sent me a picture of his big, ugly dick."

Will jerked in surprise. "What?"

"It wasn't his," I interjected at the same time Thatch taunted through a smile, "Well, you've got the big part right."

Georgie's eyes came to me.

"Or so I've heard," I added.

She looked upset. "He talks to you about it? What…" She paused and swallowed. "About what they say?"

God, this was horrible. I hated this and myself and every-fuck-ing-body right now.

"No, baby. That's the only thing he told me," I assured her, digging my fucking grave a couple of feet deeper.

The urge to flee was strong, but we'd literally just fucking gotten there. To hell.

The Raines Law Room was definitely what hell looked like. The devil and fire and the roaring fucking twenties.

She'd confided in Ruck, and she felt badly about what that meant to her relationship with me. I could see it written in cursive, scribbled and scrawled all over her beautiful face as she warred with herself about not wanting me to know the things she'd told him and feeling like a liar and a cheat for having hidden something behind my back in the first place.

It made me sick inside, twisted the lining of my stomach and my intestines alike, and I just barely managed to stop myself from jetting to the bathroom for reprieve.

But my face was her lifeline in this situation, for as much as she feared being outed, every smile I gave her was a comfort. I refused to leave her on her own in this stormy sea to float and flounder.

Bottom line, Rose would have ditched Ruck ages ago if I hadn't twisted every conversation to my advantage. I was the guilty party here.

As Thatch started to flirt, I pulled my attention from Georgia long enough to tell him to pump the fucking brakes. One comment about her tits and the ruse would be roasted.

"Ruck and Rose are *friends*. Ruck's dating someone else, and Rose is a virgin for fuck's sake," I informed him. "Lay the hell off."

Wild eyes jumped to mine. I wanted to shove the words back in as soon as they escaped.

"Excuse us for a second," Thatch said with a smile, dragging me from the couch and over to the bar in a way no one else could.

My ass hit the stool in front of him and he leaned in menacingly.

"You better start talking, dude. I'm fucking dying over there in the name of *your* two-timing ass, and you can't take your eyes off of your girlfriend long enough to save me."

I shook my head.

"What the fuck is up? If that woman is a virgin, I'll freeze my fucking nuts off with one of those wart removers."

I grimaced.

"Yeah." He nodded. "Not a pretty fucking picture. So tell me, what's the real deal here?"

I considered it for a second, what it would hurt if I told him versus what he would hurt if I didn't. I decided I liked all of my bones like they were. And anything I told him to keep to himself, I knew he would.

"Georgie is Rose, not Cassie. But she doesn't know I know that, and she doesn't know I'm Ruck."

"Jesus." He put his face in his hands and rubbed at his temples. "You don't pay me enough for this level of complication."

"Yeah, well, you're not here as an employee. You're here as a friend. And I didn't invite you, if you'll remember. I tried to get you the fuck out of here *before* they got here."

"All right, all right, I get it. You and Georgie need to leave or something. I can't keep this shit up, but I can't abandon you either."

"Noble of you."

"Duh, dude. My character is top of the pyramid."

I shook my head and scrubbed a hand over my face.

Realization flooded him in a surge, like the swelling of a tide. "Wait a minute. Does this mean Georgia girl is a virgin?"

I tried not to give him anything, but my face must have conveyed some kind of confirmation.

"Oh holy hell, K."

"Thatch—"

"But she's not anymore, is she, you dirty dog?"

"Thatch—"

"Kline?" Georgia asked from behind Thatch timidly. My tongue made a valiant attempt to choke me. The conversation, the circumstances. All of it was fucked, and a timid Georgia was the last fucking straw.

My girl was a fucking shark, and I was completely over anything that made her feel any different.

"Hey, baby," I greeted her from around Thatch, leaning out to make sure my eyes met hers.

"Is everything okay?"

With one last look to Thatch that conveyed *just* how important his eternal silence was, I was up, moving toward my woman to the slow beat of the house band.

I was done with the secrets, done with the space, done with the whole scenario of the night, and nothing made me happier than dragging this woman out onto the dance floor when she least expected it.

"How about a dance, Benny?"

Her eyes cruised the room, but I made her walk as she did, a warm palm at the small of her back allowing her to lead but still guiding the way.

"But no one else is dancing."

"I like being the first," I teased as I pulled her around to face me and planted her square in my arms. She blushed furiously.

"*Kline.*"

"I'm selfish," I admitted through a smile. "I don't want to share you anymore."

The color in her face drained to white, the transition from blush to blanched one of the fastest I'd ever witnessed. Immediately, I regretted the words despite their validity. She didn't need any more evidence to build a case against herself in the court of Georgia's opinion.

Lips to hers, I apologized the only way I could, loving her on an endless loop of licks and swoops and tongue to tongue connection.

She hummed right into my mouth, the rightness too powerful to be contained in silence.

My fingers in her hair, I rubbed at her jaw with my thumbs and sank every ounce of myself into her. I didn't worry about Thatch or Cass or Will or anyone else, and for a couple of minutes, neither did she.

I'd never been this consumed. Not in my entire life, not by anything or anyone.

Wrinkles formed in her little button nose as she pulled back, her delicate hands loosening my tie just enough that I could breathe again.

Relaxed by the music or me, Georgia finally felt comfortable enough to address the night.

"It really is a small world, huh? People crossing paths and never realizing that they already had…or maybe they should have sooner."

Complicated and twisted, she spoke of herself and me and Rose and Ruck and everyone else all at once. But the answer was simple to me.

"The world is small, baby. But love is large. Big enough that coincidence occasionally rubs elbows with opportunity."

"Where'd you get that?" she asked. "Ernest Hemingway again?"

I shook my head and pressed my lips lightly to hers briefly.

"That one's all me."

I lived in her eyes as she searched the depths of mine, swimming in the pools of blue and fighting to stay there. I was so deep in her, deep in this, entrenched in the muck and lies, and I still felt high.

High on her, high on us, and high on everything I wanted us to be. The wedding, the kids, the happily ever after. I thought it because I wanted it. Every minute, every hour, every day, I wanted her to be mine.

I was in fucking love with her.

And I needed to show her.

"Let's get out of here," I pleaded softly, rubbing the tip of my thumb along her perfect bottom lip.

She could feel my desperation, a tremble running through her from the crown of her head to the tips of her toes. Her gaze jumped to our seats, and I followed to find Thatch and Cass deep in flirtatious conversation and Will missing.

I scanned the room ahead of her, finding him at the bar in conversation with a woman and pointing him out.

"They're all busy, Benny," I coaxed. "Come home with me."

I expected her to survey them again, but instead, her eyes just found mine.

"Okay, Kline."

Okay.

All it took was a little love making to turn that okay into a repeated *yes*.

CHAPTER 27

Georgia

I was straddling the line between asleep and awake. My eyes were still shut, but the morning sun rested against my face. Kline's arms were wrapped around me, holding my back to his chest. Big spoon, little spoon, we fit perfectly.

My mind replayed last night. The bar. Finding out Kline's best friend Thatch was actually my TapNext friend, Ruck.

Talk about a twisted kind of irony.

When I'd seen Thatch's reflection in the mirror, a million emotions had steamrolled through me, but the biggest, most palpable one had been disappointment. That in itself had my gut clenching from guilt. That emotion made me feel like I had done wrong by Kline.

I couldn't deny chatting with Ruck had become one of the highlights of my day. He was funny and sweet and charming.

And the more I thought about it, the more it didn't really make sense.

Thatch was a nice guy, but he was also very different from the man I pictured as Ruck. He was boisterous and seemed to have a propensity for using the word fuck...*a lot*. In all actuality, he was Kline's version of Cassie. They were both crazy opinionated, a bit impulsive, and often tossed out humor in otherwise serious conversations.

Nothing like the Ruck I had come to know. But then again, it was the Internet, and just because we chatted often didn't mean I *really* knew him.

But I knew Kline. Despite the awkwardness of last night, it had still been a good night because of him. It was becoming a theme. If he was there, I was happy.

My own little Kline and Georgia movie played behind my lids. I curled into him more, keeping my eyes closed, and watched.

I saw us dancing on our first date, and the way I couldn't stop smiling when he kissed me. His eyes, worried and concerned, when I was having an allergic reaction to lime juice. The way he looked that morning, sleepy and handsome and *mine*.

I saw us walking through New York, holding hands, and taking it all in together. I saw him at the pool, playfully taking off his boxers and turning around, dancing for my entertainment.

I saw us in the Hamptons and the way he'd looked when he'd been inside of me, moving and kissing and loving me. And then, him laughing the next morning when I tried to feed him burnt toast and told him it was supposed to be that way.

The way he'd often sneak into my office, shut the door, and pull me into his arms.

All of the inside jokes and secret smiles that we shared.

We weren't just boyfriend and girlfriend, we weren't just lovers, we weren't just *one* thing.

We were *all the things*.

I was back in the present, blinking sleep from my eyes. I turned in his arms and took him in. The way his chest moved with each soft breath. The way his eyelashes separated into tiny points near the corners of his eyes. I brushed his cheek, fingers sliding past the tiny freckle near his ear.

My mind raced while my heart sped up, pounding in an erratic rhythm. And then, heart and brain collided, becoming one in the way I felt for him.

The bedroom was silent, only the faint sounds of the city filtering past us, but in the stillness, I could still hear it in the way my breath quickened. I could see it lying beside me—jaw slack and eyelashes resting against his cheeks.

And I could *feel* it. God, I could feel it.

I was in love.

I was in love with Kline.

Leaning forward, I pressed my lips to the corner of his mouth, silently saying, "I love you," against his skin.

He mumbled something, but otherwise, barely budged.

Looking at his handsome face, blissfully content in sleep, I knew what I had to do.

Scratch that—I knew what I *wanted* to do.

I didn't want this whole "Ruck" situation hanging over my head. I wanted to move past it, and most importantly, I wanted to move forward with Kline.

Sliding out of the bed as quietly and smoothly as possible, I threw on one of his t-shirts and headed into the kitchen to grab my phone out of my purse. I dialed Cass's number as I stepped onto the terrace and shut the door behind me.

She answered on the fourth ring. "What in the fuck time is it?"

"I need you to take over my TapNext account."

"Georgia?" she asked, her voice scratchy with sleep.

"Of course it's Georgia. Who in the hell did you think it was?"

"An asshole who decided to call me at..." She paused, and the sounds of sheets rustling filled my ears. "Eight in the morning. Jesus, Georgie, couldn't you have postponed this conversation for about four more hours?"

"I couldn't wait. I have to fix this, Cass. I feel like the worst person in the world."

"What? Why?"

"God, I'm such an asshole. Why did I do that? Why did I keep talking to Ruck when I knew the possibilities I had with Kline? I feel like I've been emotionally cheating on him the entire time."

"Georgia—" She started to respond, but I was already chiming in, too damn worked up to stop.

"In some weird way, I think I was invested in Ruck. Not even close to how I feel about Kline, but still, I liked talking to him. I wanted to talk to him. And you know what the worst thing is? When I found out Ruck was Thatch, I was fucking disappointed. It felt like a letdown."

"Shut. Up," she groaned. "You didn't cheat on him. You were just chatting with someone, *as friends*. This is not something you need to feel guilty about."

I stayed quiet, mentally chastising myself for being so stupid.

"Georgia. Did you ever make plans to meet up with Ruck?"

"No," I said, shaking my head. "Never."

"Did you ever tell him you love him or want a relationship with him?"

"Of course not."

"So stop berating yourself over this. It's pointless, and honestly, completely unwarranted. You haven't done anything wrong, sweetheart. You've been completely faithful to your boyfriend."

I took a calming breath. "You're right. I was completely faithful to him."

"Okay, great. I'm so glad we have that settled. I'll call you later."

"Cass," I warned. "Don't you dare hang up on me!"

"I'm so tired, Georgie," she whined. "Why won't you let me sleep?"

"Because I need you to promise you'll take over my TapNext account."

She let out an exasperated sigh. "Why would I want to do that?"

"Because you love me."

"Just unsubscribe from the damn thing," she muttered.

"I don't want to be a complete asshole to Ruck. And I felt like you guys hit if off last night."

"You're talking about Thatch, right?"

"Yes, Thatch. Your face is the one on my profile anyway. And you can just take over and act like it was you the whole time."

"This is a little weird, G."

"I know, but I don't really know what else to do."

She was right. It was bordering on insane to have her take over the conversations, but it felt like the best option. That way, Ruck wasn't left in the dust, and hell, maybe Thatch and Cass would be an interesting little matchup.

I'd just wait to mention all of the random jokes and personal shit I had divulged to Ruck at a later time. Like never. I had a feeling once he started chatting more with my crazy, beautiful, and smart best friend, she'd eventually just be Rose to him, without him knowing there was ever a difference.

It had to work, right?

She was still quiet and I wasn't sure if she actually fell back asleep or was mulling over her options.

"Cass?"

"Yeah, okay," she agreed. "Send me your login shit. I'll message him."

"Really? Oh my God! You're the best!" I squealed.

"I'm not doing this for you, Wheorgie. When I said *I'd Thatch that*, I meant it. I have a feeling that man is a beast in bed."

"Seriously—" I started to say, but the line clicked in my ear.

A word to the wise: never call Cassie before noon. I was lucky I'd managed to keep her on the phone as long as I had.

I don't know how long I stood out on Kline's terrace, elbows resting on the banister, eyes staring off into the distance. I watched the clouds move in, covering the sun and filling the sky with an impending sense of doom. Lightning flashed in the distance.

But the city, it still moved below me, still hustled and bustled and never quit showing off its boisterous personality.

"I missed you in my bed." Warm arms wrapped around my

waist. The smell of his soap and clean laundry and Kline assaulted my senses.

I sighed in contentment, resting my head on his shoulder.

"What are you doing out here?"

"I had to call Cassie," I admitted, omitting the details about the actual conversation. Even though I still felt guilty about the whole Ruck thing, I decided it was best to leave it in the past. No good would've come from me rehashing it with Kline. Because at the end of the day, he was who I wanted. The *only* man I wanted.

"And now you're just standing out here, watching the storm roll in?"

"Something like that."

"God, you smell so good." His nose was buried in my neck, inhaling for a brief moment, until he rested his chin on my shoulder.

I turned in his arms, interlocking my hands high, around his strong neck.

Playful blue eyes stared back at me. He swept my hair off my shoulder, moving his lips to my neck, and then my ear, cheek, before he leaned back, taking in my attire…or lack thereof. A rogue hand slipped down my side, gripping my thigh. "And you're standing out here in nothing but my t-shirt. I think you need to come inside, baby."

My lips found his, placing sweet kisses against his smiling mouth. "Are you trying to have your wicked way with me?"

He slid his fingers up my thigh and brushed across the one place I ached for him. "I'd say I'm not the only one trying in this scenario." He bit my bottom lip, tugging on it until I moaned. His hands moved to my ass, lifting me up and urging my legs to wrap around his waist. Kline was hard beneath his boxer briefs, and the second he was firmly pressed against me, I whimpered against his mouth. And then, he was kissing me deeper, coaxing my lips open and tangling his tongue with mine.

Candles melted when you lit them.

I melted when Kline Brooks kissed me.

Into. A. Puddle. Of. Pliant. Swoony. Mush.

His mouth was my own personal brand of perfection. Every soft caress of his lips against mine only made me crave him more. I doubted I'd ever get tired of this. Him. Us.

My breathing sped up, his touch sparking every tiny nerve ending inside of me. His hands, God, whenever they were touching me, I was losing my mind.

I shuddered against him.

He felt it, smiling as he kissed me.

Thunder filled the air as the sky opened up and started to pour over the city. The wind caused drops of rain to slide into the terrace and onto us.

He didn't break our kiss, whispering against my mouth all of the dirty things he wanted to do to me as he did. My hair was wet and his t-shirt stuck to me like a second skin, but I barely noticed, too consumed by him. My hips moved of their own accord, desperate for the hardness he was so graciously offering against me.

"Fuck, you're perfect," he growled. Yes, he actually growled. I always thought the growl was bullshit, a mythical unicorn put into romance novels, but the guttural noise that came from his lungs proved me wrong.

He moved us back inside the apartment, kicking the door shut with his foot. We were walking across his bedroom one second and then tangled on his bed the next, our mouths never leaving one another.

I giggled against his lips as my ass bounced on the mattress.

Kline pulled back, staring down at me as he moved the wet strands of hair plastered to my cheeks.

I shivered against him. I couldn't help it. Having him this close, wrapped around me, completed me in some odd way. I'd never felt this before, for anyone. And it scared me to think I could have messed this up by never agreeing to that first date or meeting Ruck in person. I could have lived an entire life without getting to feel *this*.

His eyes turned concerned. "What's wrong, baby?"

"Nothing." I swallowed down my emotion and distracted him with my lips. "I want you," I whispered against his mouth.

He grinned, purposefully taking in my soaked attire. "Is that why you're doing your best impression of a wet t-shirt contest?"

I bit my lip. "Am I being too obvious?"

His large hands caressed my breasts through wet cotton, thumbs brushing across my nipples.

"I've never been to a wet t-shirt contest, but is it normal to grope the contestants?"

He waggled his eyebrows. "This judge does."

"What else does this judge do?"

He leaned forward, sucking my nipple into his mouth and licking around the sensitive peak. I felt the warmth of his tongue and the cool wetness from his t-shirt all the way down my body and between my legs.

My fingers found his hair, gripping the strands tightly as he moved to my other breast.

"I think I need to enter these contests more often," I said, moaning.

He glanced up, shaking his head. "No one else is ever going to lay eyes on this perfect fucking body." He held my hips and pushed his pelvis against me, spurring another moan from my lips. "No one else will get to hear your sounds or watch your lips part when you're losing control." He nipped at my bottom lip and then trailed his mouth across my jaw to my neck, until his breath was hot and seductive by my ear. "But, if you promise to be in my bedroom, you can do it any goddamn time you want."

"Deal," I whispered. "Now, less talking and more getting me naked and fucking me until I forget my name."

"Fucking you until you forget your name?" His eyes turned heated, mouth curving into a devilish grin. "I think I can work with this."

And believe me, he did. I had praised Mother Teresa, Jesus, Buddha, and was calling myself Oprah by the time he was finished blowing my mind.

CHAPTER 28

Kline

"I'm sorry," Georgia apologized for the twenty-ninth time as she knocked on the door to her parents' suburban New Jersey home.

"Baby, it's fine. I want to meet them. Didn't I tell you I wanted to meet them?"

"Yes, you did. But I don't think you meant *this afternoon*."

I had to laugh at that. It was true, when I'd had Georgia wrapped around me in bed this morning, I hadn't envisioned meeting her parents only five hours later. But when her mom had called on FaceTime that morning and Georgia had run away to take the call in private, I hadn't been able to resist popping in for a hello.

"It's my own fault. You told me not to show my face on the call," I reminded her.

"I know. It is your fault. Maybe I'm mad at you."

"You're not," I disagreed.

"Okay," she conceded. "I'm not. Honestly, I'm just sorry that when Savannah makes demands, I can't turn her down."

"The power of a mother's guilt trip is compelling. Trust me, I'm familiar. I'd love to bottle it and use it at the office," I consoled just as the door swung open to a man with slightly wild hair that grayed around the edges.

"Georgie!" he called, engulfing her in a hug and pulling her through the door. He nuzzled her hair and breathed her in for a good five seconds before his eyes met mine and turned hard.

"Who's this clown?"

"Dad!" Georgia chastised, her cheeks going cherry with mortification.

I couldn't help but smile. In his most laid-back tone, her dad had thrown the ultimate insult my way. No warm-up or pretense or gestures of fond small talk. This was a man who cared about one thing in this scenario—his daughter. I liked him immediately.

"Kline Brooks," I introduced myself, offering my hand.

"Dick. Dick Cummings." He shook my hand with fervor, purposely trying his damnedest to crush my fingers.

Dick Cummings? Thank God Thatch wasn't here. He would have had a field day with that one.

"His full name is Richard," Georgia's mother interrupted, forcing her way into the open doorway. "I'm Savannah, by the way. It really is a pleasure, Kline."

"Stop with the formality shit, Savannah. If the man can't handle that I'm Dick Cummings, then he's not the right man for our Georgie," he retorted, eyeing me with slanty eyes. "Does it bother you, Kline?"

"No, sir," I answered, fighting the urge to laugh. I literally hadn't even set foot inside of the door to their house yet, and a full-length daytime drama was rounding its way into the second arc of the storyline.

"Son." He patted me on the shoulder, nudging the girls out of the way and pulling me inside.

"When you've got a last name like Cummings, you can either be a chickenshit, or you can grow some balls and roll with it. That's why I go by Dick and I had my son go by Willy for most of his life. Hell, Georgia's lucky we didn't name her vagina," he said through a laugh.

"Plus, it's pretty fucking enjoyable to watch someone squirm when they meet me." He grinned, big and wide, his eyes turning jovial. "You handled yourself well. Much better than the other idiots Georgie's brought home. I like you already."

"Jesus, Dad." Georgie sighed. "Think you can tone done the F-bombs for now? It's not even five p.m."

"No siree, Bob. You're in my home and I'll do anything I damn well please. If I want to walk around in my underwear all night, I'll fucking do it," he responded, unfazed. "Anyway, like you should talk. Last phone conversation I had with you, you were ranting about 'the *fucking* subway.'"

"And five o'clock is an antiquated schedule associated with alcohol, Georgia. The fucks have always been given free rein," Savannah put in.

Georgia's parents were a trip. I was having a hard time keeping my smile in check.

"Come here and give me another hug," her dad ordered. "I've missed you, baby girl."

She flashed a pointed look. "Only if you promise not to bust my boyfriend's balls all night."

"Deal." He grinned.

She hugged her dad, a genuine smile on her face, and then moved to her mom. Hugs and smiles overflowed the small space of the foyer. It was apparent she was close with her folks. I loved we had that in common.

"And Richard." Savannah tsked. "You know the no-pants rule doesn't start until after dinner."

He growled under his breath, wrapping his arm around his wife and whispering something I could only assume was full-on dirty into her ear.

"Later." Savannah giggled, a perfect incarnation of what I knew as her daughter's laugh, and slapped him on the chest.

He chuckled, waggling his brows at her, visibly amused with himself.

"Why don't you two make yourselves comfortable and freshen up from the drive. There's fresh sheets on Georgia's bed and clean towels in the bathroom."

Dick abruptly turned for the hallway, striding toward the kitchen, muttering something about "the fucking grill."

Her mother still remained, smiling at both of us in a way that made me a little concerned about what would come next. "There's also a box of condoms on the nightstand," she whispered. "Feel free to put them to good use."

"Gee, thanks, Mom." Georgia sighed, tipping her red face to the ceiling in an effort not to meet my eyes.

"Anytime, baby girl." Savannah patted her cheek, smiling. "I'm just thrilled you're finally being adventurous with your sexuality."

This meet the parents visit was getting more interesting by the minute.

"Dinner will be ready in about fifteen minutes," she called over her shoulder, following her husband's lead.

The second they were out of eyesight, Georgia sagged against the door.

"I told you they were a little offbeat. Please don't hold it against me."

I grinned, pulling her into my arms, and avoided the urge to tell her that her definition of a little felt more like a lot. "I love everything about your parents."

Her eyes showed she was skeptical, but I spoke only the truth. I'd take a free spirit and a ballbuster over two sticks in the mud any day.

"They're *your* parents, baby. Believe me, I like them. Dick and Savannah are great."

"Yeah, they're *real* awesome. I mean, how great is it that my mother thought to put condoms in my bedroom, you know, just in case we decide to bang it out when they're two doors down."

"Very practical." I fought my smile, rubbing her shoulders to ease the tension in her muscles.

"Come on." She took my hand. "Let me show you my childhood bedroom. Who knows? Maybe my mother left a complimentary bottle of lube on the nightstand."

I stopped her before she could head up the stairs, pulling her tight against me, her back to my chest. "Like you'd even need lube when I've got my hands on you," I growled into her ear, then kissed along her neck.

"Okay." She let out a soft sigh, head falling to my shoulder. "Maybe we can follow the no-pants rule after dinner too."

"Wouldn't want to go against house rules," I added, smirking against her soft skin.

"We *are* guests," she said, lifting her chin and urging my lips to continue down her neck.

"Definitely wouldn't want to come across as rude." I nibbled along her neck a bit more, until I pinched her ass, earning an adorable squeal. "Show me your bedroom, baby."

The stairs creaked as we climbed, and pictures of Georgia and Will lined the wall. One of a toddler Georgia stood out in particular.

"Aw, look at your cute little—"

"Don't even say it!"

"What?" I asked innocently.

"I know you! I know where you were going, and we're *not* going to talk about the fact that my mother keeps a naked picture of me on the wall."

"I was just going to point out that your tushy then was nearly as cute as it is now."

"Kline!" she snapped with a finger in my face.

I threw her over my shoulder in a fireman's hold and slapped at said ass.

"Don't worry, baby. I'll pay special attention to it tonight. Especially if there's lube."

She shrieked and kicked as I ran up the rest and paused, throwing her to the hallway carpet at the top of the stairs and tickling her sensitive sides.

"Kline! Stop!" Her breath heaved. "Stooooop!"

When I removed my hands, she scurried up and out from underneath me, slapping at my shoulder lightly.

"What is it about being in a childhood home that makes a man act like a child?"

"Fun. Freedom." I smiled. "Memories."

"I just bet. Were you a bad boy in your youth, Kline?"

"Nope," I answered honestly. "As a boy, I didn't know enough to be bad." I waggled my eyebrows. "I'm much more convincing now that I'm a man."

She ran again at that, shrieking the whole way and trying to close her bedroom door between us. I played tug of war with the handle convincingly enough, reserving my full strength in an effort not to hurt her, before finally busting through and tackling her cackling form to the bed.

She turned her head to the left and sighed. "Ah. The condoms."

I pulled her eyes to mine and touched our lips together softly before rubbing my nose along the line of hers. "We didn't use one the night that we fought," I whispered. I hadn't even thought about it until now, too consumed by lies and love and the complicated mix of the two, but the box on the nightstand brought my oversight into stark relief.

She nodded.

"I'm okay with that in all the ways I can be. Are you?"

She nodded again, and a shiver ran through her body. I pulled her closer.

"I'm on the pill, and I trust you."

"I'll do every single thing I can to deserve that, baby," I promised.

She looked back over to the nightstand.

"I feel like we have to use a condom tonight because my mom put them there."

"Do you even know what you just said?"

"Kline!"

"Okay." I laughed. "Just tell her we used our own because she failed to get magnum."

Her body shook with laughter despite her stern face.

"Get cleaned up for dinner!"

"Yes, ma'am," I agreed with a wink, sliding my body all the way down hers and pushing my face to the front of her pants.

"Mmm." I inhaled. "I think I should help you clean up here. I'll lick up all of my mess," I promised, pledging my truth with a hand at my chest.

She just shook her head and smiled, sliding a hand into my hair and yanking up on my head. "Go get changed and throw some cold water on your face, you bad *man*, you."

I reached into my pants with a grin and adjusted my dick to a more comfortable position.

"I can't help it, baby," I teased. "It's the house's fault."

She shook her head again, climbing to her knees and pushing her lips softly to mine. She spoke softly right there. "What am I gonna do with you?"

"Keep me."

"What am I gonna do with me?" she whispered. "So lost in you."

I squeezed her tight and answered with a prayer.

"Stay there." *Forever.*

CHAPTER 29

Georgia

"Let me show you one of my favorite places in the house," my father instructed, leading Kline toward the garage. This was another one of his tests.

Hell, he'd been testing my boyfriend all weekend.

There had been the beer test. Dick had offered Miller Lite and Guinness. Kline had chosen Guinness, and my father had patted him on the shoulder, adding, "I'm happy Georgie didn't bring a light-beer, piss-drinking pussy into my home."

There had been the liquor test. Dick had offered him a martini. Kline had politely declined and asked if there was any bourbon or whiskey in the house. Dick's response: another pat on the back.

There had also been the pizza test. Last night, my mother hadn't felt like cooking, so Dick had handed Kline a menu from Pappadoro's—a mom and pop pizza shop up the street—and told him to order a bunch of pies for everyone. Kline had gotten another pat on the back when he ordered three large meat lover's supremes and cheesy garlic bread.

Sports. Cars. Politics. You name it, and Dick tested. Surprisingly enough, Kline had passed every one with flying colors. How'd I know this? The pat on the back, of course.

We stepped out into the three-car garage, and Kline immediately removed his arm from my shoulder, walking over toward one of my dad's cars.

"A 428 Cobra Jet Mustang. Wow." He let out a low whistle, eyeing my father's car with an appreciative gleam in his eyes. "She's a beaut."

"Probably my favorite person in the house." My father patted him on the back, chuckling.

"Bought her in sixty-eight. She's in prime condition. Engine was restored a few years ago."

"Tell me you kept the Low Riser cylinder heads," Kline added, moving around the car with his hands on his hips, his eyes plastered to the red paint of my father's most prized possession.

Sometimes, I wondered if he loved this car more than he loved his own kids.

"Of course I did."

"Thank God." Kline skimmed his fingers across the paint, light enough that he wouldn't leave a mark, and a giant smile consumed his face. "This, right here, was the game changer for Ford."

Dick stared at my boyfriend like he was falling in love. "She redeemed the Ford name in the factory of horsepower."

Kline nodded and glanced up at me, a boyish smile still etched on his handsome face. "Why didn't you tell me your father had this in his garage?"

I shrugged. "I had no idea you'd get such a hard-on for a car."

"Are you kidding me?" Kline laughed. "This is one of my favorite cars. Ever. My father's a Ford man, through and through. He'd lose it if he got his hands on this car."

"I think your dad and I would get along just fine," Dick said with a smile.

Jesus. I'd never seen my dad smile so much in my life. The

pulsating vein in the center of his forehead, yeah, I'd definitely seen my fair share of that, especially when I'd missed curfew in high school. But this giant smile that had taken up residence on my father's face? It was so rare that it was almost creepy.

Dick Cummings was a pretty happy guy, but he didn't usually pass out smiles and giddy looks on a daily basis. Honestly, I think the last time I'd seen him smile like this, my mother had brought home three bags from Victoria's Secret.

"I'd let you take her for a spin, but I've gotta take her into the shop come tomorrow morning. She's having issues when I try to crank her."

"Mind if I take a look?" Kline asked.

By the sounds of their conversation, you'd think my dad's car was an actual person, a female, at that. Men were so weird.

"By all means." My dad gestured toward the car. He grabbed the keys from the hook and tossed them to him.

Kline hopped in the driver's seat and attempted to turn the engine. It didn't start, and I'd never claimed to know car sounds, but whatever abnormal sound was coming from the car couldn't have been good.

"See what I mean, son?" Dick asked, elbows resting on the driver's side window.

Son? One bonding moment over his car and my dad was calling him son. I was sure any minute he'd give Kline his blessing and tell my mother to start planning my bachelorette party. No doubt, Dr. Savannah Cummings would prefer picking out penis straws to floral arrangements.

If anyone bought me dicks for my bachelorette party, it would be my mother. Cassie would provide the liquor and gift bag filled with crotchless panties. Now that I thought about it, it was a wonder I'd stayed a virgin for as long as I did. I was surrounded by a bunch of horny floozies.

"Dick, I think it's the starter motor relay."

"Really?"

Kline nodded. "I can hear the high-load relay engaging. Mind if I pop the hood and take a look at the engine?"

"Of course." My father stood back from the car as Kline hopped out and busied himself under the hood.

After a few minutes, my boyfriend was convinced he knew the issue and could fix it. And by the look on Dick's face, I was starting to wonder if *he* would be the one to marry Kline.

"I'm grabbing something to drink. You guys want anything?" I offered.

"I'm good, babe," Kline declined, while my father merely mumbled, "No," too damn entranced by what was going on underneath the hood of his car.

I walked out of the garage and into the kitchen, leaving them to their man time. Popping the tab on a can of Coke, I leaned my hip against the counter and took a gulp from the sugary soda.

To say I was shocked by the open-armed, constant-back-patting greeting my father had been giving Kline, would be the understatement of the century. My dad was never this nice to any guy I brought home. Growing up, it had been a common occurrence for Dick to clean his guns in the living room if he knew a boy was picking me up.

Sheesh. No wonder I'd fallen so fast for Kline's charms. He practically had my dad, the boyfriend ballbuster, eating out of the palm of his hand.

I walked past my mother's office, finding her typing away on her laptop. She paused, sliding her glasses to the brim of her nose. "What are you up to?"

"Nothing much. Dad and Kline are in the garage talking car shit." I shrugged, leaning against the doorframe.

"Seems like they're hitting it off."

"Pretty sure Dad's going to propose to my boyfriend before we head home."

"I hope he lets me plan his bachelor party," she joked.

See what I mean?

She smiled a wistful smile. "It's always been a dream of mine to jump out of a cake and do a sexy striptease for your father. The closest we ever got to that was when I—"

I held my hand up. "For the love of God, I do not want to hear about you and Dick doing the nasty."

"Georgia, sex is a normal human urge. It doesn't matter how old you are or how many kids you have, you'll still want to do it."

"Are you finished psychoanalyzing my views on human sexuality, Dr. Cummings?" I asked, raising a skeptical brow.

Her smile turned curious and I braced myself for the next question that would come out of her mouth.

"Speaking of sex, how are things with you and Kline?"

"I'm not talking about my sex life with you."

She pouted. "Oh, come on, sweetie."

"Nope." I raised both hands. "Not happening."

My mother cupped her mouth, whispering, "Last night, it sounded like things were going *really* good."

I groaned. "I get that you're a sex therapist and you're extremely open when it comes to talking about sex, but it's a little creepy you were eavesdropping."

"Actually, I wasn't eavesdropping. You were just *that* loud."

I gaped.

"I can't tell you how happy this makes me."

"You realize this isn't a normal mother-daughter conversation, right?"

"It's not the normal conversation society thinks we should be having, but I know it's the conversation we should be having. Just know, I'm beyond thrilled you've found someone who makes you happy in every facet of your life. Not just in bed, which I have to say, from the sounds of it, Kline knows what he's doing." She winked. "But it's obvious he makes you really happy. And anyone who can make my daughter walk around with a constant glow and a gorgeous smile is someone I hope she keeps around." She paused as I smiled, and she considered me closely. "He seems like a really good man, Georgia. And he's extremely lucky he found you."

Although my mom was her own type of crazy, she was still my mom and I loved her. I'd always want her acceptance. And I'd definitely want her to like the man in my life.

I walked toward her, leaning down and wrapping her in a tight hug.

"I love you, Mom."

"I love you too, sweetie. I've missed having you home. I hope you'll start visiting more often."

"Consider it a done deal." I squeezed her tighter. "As long as you promise not to eavesdrop."

"Deal," she agreed, laughing.

As I walked out of her office, she added, "But seriously, sweetie. I was a little jealous. That orgasm must have lasted a good two minutes."

"Three minutes," I called over my shoulder. "It was three minutes and it might have been more, but I'm pretty sure I lost consciousness."

I heard her laugh the entire way to my bedroom.

The second I stepped into my room, I threw my body onto the bed, my back hitting the mattress, causing pillows to fall onto the floor. My eyes took in the many nuances of my childhood stronghold. My parents hadn't changed a thing since I'd left for college. Everything was as I had left it. Old pictures of prom and homecoming littered my desk. My graduation cap hung next to the door. And the pink and yellow flowered wallpaper still lined the walls.

It was hideous by all accounts, but it was still my room. The bedroom I had grown up in. The place I'd had sleepovers and gossiped with friends about our latest crushes. The place I'd had my first kiss with Stevie Jones, even though we were supposed to have been studying for our algebra exam.

Nostalgia was potent, filling my lungs and plastering a reflective smile on my face. So much in my life had changed from the day I'd grabbed my last suitcase and headed to college. I had a great job, amazing friends, and now…Kline. It was funny how two years ago, I'd thought of him only as my boss, refusing to see him as anything else, and now, he had become this fixture in my life, one I was starting to hope would be permanent.

The sound of a phone vibrating across the surface of my nightstand caught my attention. I picked it up, tapping the screen, wondering if Cass was getting ready to harass me about using the last of the coffee creamer and leaving a sink full of dishes before heading to my parents'.

The screen lit up with a TapNext notification.

TAPRoseNEXT: Hey you, how's your day going?

I tilted my head, confused. Why was I getting messages from my account? The one I'd told Cassie to take over?

Turning over the phone, my mind registered the case. Not the glittery sparkle one I'd bought a few weeks ago, but plain, old, simple black.

Kline's phone case.

Not mine.

Kline's.

I dropped the phone like it had caught fire. It hit the hardwood floor with an awful thud and I cringed, wondering for a brief second if I had broken his phone.

But then the shock of the entire situation took over.

If he…

Wait a minute…

Is this?

No way.

NO WAY.

I just stood there, staring down at the screen and the profile name **TAPRoseNEXT** glaring back at me. If he was getting messages from my TapNext account, then that meant...

I gaped, my eyes popping wide. Jesus Christ in a peach tree, did this mean that when I had been messaging Ruck, I had really been messaging Kline?

My heart pounded in my chest, erratically enough that I was a little concerned I might go into cardiac arrest.

Slowly, I bent down and picked up the phone. My mind warred between my options. I could either do the right thing and set the phone back down and act like I had never seen it, or I could swipe the screen, put in his passcode, and see if it was really what I thought it was.

The only reason I knew his passcode was because I'd had to retrieve a few emails for him while we were in the Hamptons. He had remembered he needed to check on a time-sensitive contract and just so happened to be elbow deep in soapy water and dishes. So, he'd told me the passcode, and I just so happened to still remember said passcode.

I scrubbed my left hand down my face while my right white-knuckled his phone. I was sure the correct choice was to act like I had never seen it, set his phone down, and walk away, but I needed to know if what I was seeing was real.

Which was why my fingers slid across the screen and pulled up the TapNext icon. I took one glance at his profile, and when the username **BAD_Ruck** met my confused gaze, I refused to invade any more of his privacy and immediately locked his phone, setting it face-down on the nightstand.

He. Was. Ruck.

My hands went into my hair, resting on top of my head, as I paced my bedroom. I felt like I couldn't breathe, the four walls closing in on me. I had been messaging Kline the entire time, without even knowing it. And he had been messaging me, but he didn't know it was me.

But wait, he *had* met my best friend. He knew her face was Rose's profile picture, but he hadn't known I was the one to put it there.

Irrational jealousy and anger started to build inside of my chest.

Had he still been chatting with Rose *after* meeting Cassie?

Fuck.

I picked his phone back up and quickly unlocked the screen again, pulling up the TapNext app within seconds. My heart threatened to thrash its way out of my body as I found the lone conversation in Ruck's message box.

I felt insane, completely off my rocker, as I found the last few messages and scrutinized the timestamps.

Relief robbed the breath from my lungs as I met the realization that the last message Ruck sent Rose had been *before* we had met up at The Raines Law Room.

Before he had met my best friend.

The edges of my anger, my jealousy, still shook my hands. I couldn't deny I felt betrayed over the fact that he had been chatting with another woman, while dating me.

But I breathed through it, slowly talking myself off the illogical ledge as I set Kline's phone back on the nightstand.

How could I be mad at him when I had been doing the exact same thing?

Of course, I was upset he had been chatting with another woman, not really knowing that woman was me. It hurt. A lot. But I couldn't deny it made sense. It made sense why we would continue to talk, even though we were dating other people. We were drawn to each other, in every possible way.

I was filled with this odd feeling of relief, but it was quickly pushed aside when I started to realize the consequences of my decisions.

My world had officially turned on its axis. I was in the *Twilight Zone* and playing the star role in a weird, modern remake of *You've Got Mail*. The only difference was that I wasn't Kathleen Kelly in this scenario. I was Joe Fox.

Holy. Fox.

And I had gone off script. I hadn't planned a big grand gesture where I would unveil it had been me the whole time.

No.

Not only had I given my best friend free rein to message my boyfriend, I had all but forced her to do it.

Holy. Foxing. Shit.

Finding my phone on my desk, I dialed Cass's number and went into the bathroom, shutting the door and sitting in the bathtub fully clothed.

"Hey, sweet cheeks, how are the parental units?" she answered, her voice too goddamn cheery for the shitstorm that was my life.

"Do not message Ruck ever again."

"Huh?"

I shut my eyes, resting my head on the edge of the tub. "I fucked up, Cass. I fucked up big time."

"Whoa, slow down, Susie. What's going on?"

"Thatch isn't Ruck. Kline is Ruck."

The phone was dead silent.

"Do you hear me?! Kline is Ruck!" I shouted, my voice echoing in the bathroom. I clamped my hand over my mouth, realizing anyone walking by my bedroom would be able to hear me screaming like a lunatic.

I listened closely for any sign I wasn't alone and was relieved when I didn't hear anything but my erratic breathing.

"Okay," Cassie started. "I'm officially confused, so please, spell it out for me in slow, clear sentences."

I rambled on for a good two minutes, giving her the step-by-step details of how I had discovered my boyfriend was Ruck.

"What are the fucking odds?" she asked, sounding just as shocked as I felt.

"I know. I should probably buy a lottery ticket today," I muttered.

"You realize what you've done, don't you?"

"Screwed up big time?"

"No, you catfished your boyfriend." She laughed. "Holy shit, G, he catfished you too."

"This is so messed up," I groaned.

"You're like two fucking catfish, sitting at the bottom of the lake, doing fish shit and stuff."

"Okay, enough with the fish," I snapped. "I'm freaking out here, Cass. What have I done?"

"You haven't done anything wrong," she placated me.

"Oh. M-my. God," I stuttered, panicked and overwhelmed over the entire fucked up situation. "How do I fix this?"

"Jesus, Georgia, relax," she sighed. "Stay calm. Act completely aloof. I'll send him another message and nip this crazy-town shit in the bud."

"What? What are you going to say?"

"For fuck's sake, stop panicking," she chastised. "I'll say something along the lines of 'I'm happily involved with someone else and I can't continue our conversations. Have a nice life.'"

Okay, that would work. It would put an end to the confusion. Rose would message Ruck, they'd stop chatting, and the world would be right again.

Would it work? And is this even the right way to handle this mind-fuck of a situation?

I warred with myself over pretending it never happened versus telling Kline the truth. But then I started remembering the many conversations I'd had with Ruck. My openness. My flirtation. Questions and commentary about *anal.*

Jesus. I cringed in embarrassment. The mere idea of talking to Kline about it had my stomach clenching in discomfort.

I just wanted to leave the whole Ruck and Rose debacle in the past. Truth be told, if I could've paid someone to bury it in a shallow grave somewhere in the depths of the Pinelands along with my stay at Masturbation Camp, I sure as fuck would've done it. Not that I knew anything about that sort of thing.

I sighed. "Could this be any weirder of a situation?"

"Well," she said, deadpan. "Considering he had foreskin, Wally sure put a weird spin on the old phrase 'Taking ol' one-eye to the optometrist.'"

"Old phrase?" I snorted. "I didn't even know that was a phrase."

"Savannah would be so ashamed of you right now," she teased.

That spurred a few giggles from my lips.

"Hey, I hate to do this, but I gotta scoot or I'm going to be late for my shoot," she updated. "Are you going to be okay?"

"Yeah, I'm good. Thanks, Cass. I honestly don't know what I'd do without you."

"Probably live a horribly miserable life trying to find your own way out of your crazy-ass situations."

"So true," I agreed, smiling.

After we hung up, I was so damn exhausted from the roller coaster of emotions that I stayed in the bathtub until I drifted off to sleep.

A throat being cleared startled me awake.

"Fully clothed, bathtub nap?" Kline asked, squatting down beside the tub.

"Would you like to join me?" I grinned and scooted over.

He didn't hesitate, squishing his large frame beside me and wrapping his arm around my shoulders.

"Fix my dad's car?" I asked, resting my head on his chest.

"Yeah. Pretty sure your dad thinks I'm a mechanic now, but honestly, it was an easy fix." His fingers found their way into my hair, running through the strands so softly I nearly purred.

"I think my dad is falling in love with you. He might propose marriage before we leave."

"Don't worry, baby. I won't let your dad steal me from you."

I laughed. "I'm not sure we're going to be able to fit that giant head of yours out of this house."

He wrapped both arms tightly around my body and slid farther into the middle of the tub, forcing me to lie on top of him. "There, that's much better."

"You're too damn big." I nodded toward his feet that were hanging over the edge.

"I thought we already figured this out, Benny. I might be Big-dicked Brooks, but your perfect, tight—"

I clamped my hand over his mouth, laughing.

He licked my palm, waggling his eyebrows.

"Gross," I scoffed, feigning disgust and wiping his spit on his own shirt.

He chuckled a few times and then his eyes turned soft and he brushed a few strands of hair out of my face. "I'm glad you brought me this weekend. I had fun meeting your parents."

I rubbed my nose against his. "Thanks for coming with me and being such a good sport. My mom and dad can be a little overwhelming."

"Your dad is a riot."

"He really likes you." I grinned. "That's huge, by the way. Dick doesn't like anyone."

"After you left the garage, your dad and I had an interesting conversation."

"What was it about?"

"I'll tell you, but you have to promise not to freak out or get embarrassed."

"I'm not sure I like where this is headed." My nose scrunched up in skepticism.

His index finger tapped my nose. "Just promise."

"Fine. I promise."

"Your dad asked me for a few tips."

"Car tips?"

Kline shook his head.

"I don't get it. What kind of tips?"

His eyes creased with amusement.

My jaw dropped to his chest. "Oh God," I whined. "Please tell me what I'm thinking you're about to say is not what happened."

"Apparently, your mother encouraged him to talk to me about sex, particularly two-minute orgasms. I'll be honest, I have no idea why your mom thought I knew anything about that."

I shut my eyes and buried my face in his chest. "She heard us last night."

"What?"

"Well, she heard me last night."

"Oh, shit," he said before quiet laughter started vibrating his body.

I rested my chin on his chest, glaring at him. "Thanks a lot, asshole. You and your Jedi sex tricks had me screaming like a lunatic while my parents were two doors down."

"You didn't seem to be complaining about my Jedi sex tricks last night," he teased, grinding his hips against mine.

"Don't even think about it," I warned, poking him in the belly. "You will not get all frisky with me in this bathtub."

He waggled his brows. "What about in the bed?"

"No," I retorted. "I refuse to go into an orgasm coma again."

He tilted his head, an endearing smirk highlighting his lips.

"Well, not *ever*, just not here." I quickly backtracked because, yeah, no way in hell would I deny myself that kind of orgasm forever. I wasn't a crazy person.

He laughed, kissing my nose. "Whatever you say, Benny girl."

CHAPTER 30

Kline

As the plane throttled forward and took off down the runway, Georgia screamed like we were on a roller coaster, shrieking at every bump, lump, and wind gust.

"Jesus," I shouted over her squeals and rubbed at the meat of her thigh. "If I didn't know any better, I'd think you'd never flown before!"

We'd both been surprised by the trip, a last-minute meeting with a vendor that wanted to go live on our site ASAP. It didn't happen often, but when people jumped up and down and waved money around, we jumped back. This was one of those times and the reason we found ourselves San Diego bound this early in the day on the Tuesday after a weekend with her parents.

"It's different on a private plane," she yelled back, even though there wasn't a need. I'd only had to yell before to be heard over her screeching, but she wasn't concerned. And she didn't seem tired either. I, myself, was exhausted from a weekend filled with Savannah and Dick. And Georgia and my dick. Truly, the D was everywhere.

Gemma, my regular personal flight attendant, smiled happily from her jump seat. Thankfully, she seemed rather amused by it all.

"Baby, it's the same as a normal plane," I argued at a conventional volume. "Just smaller."

"No. Nuh-uh," she disagreed. "This is *not* like regular planes. Regular planes make you feel like a poor, desperate vagabond, willing to subject yourself to any treatment just to make it to your destination."

"What airline are you flying?" I laughed. "Third World Air?"

She shook her head and smiled before looking out the window again. "It's more whoopty or something," she tried to explain.

"Whoopty?"

"Whimsical. Roller-coaster-y."

I smiled and she laughed, throwing her hands up and pointing to her face in confirmation. "Fun!"

I leaned over and kissed the apple of her cheek. "I'm the fun part."

"You are," she agreed with my lie.

She was the fun. Hands down.

"You mind if I take a little nap?" I asked, knowing I'd need my business brain later instead of the current mush.

"Aw, Kline. My old man is tired, huh?"

I had to laugh as I nodded. "He is."

Her body seemed to deflate all at once as she laid her head on my shoulder. "I am too. I feel like I haven't slept in ages."

"We haven't," I pointed out. Weeks of courting and falling and fucking had taken its toll. "Just snuggle into me, baby. We'll both catch some shut-eye. We've got about five hours until we get there."

She didn't say anything out loud, just nuzzled the top of her head farther into my neck and crossed an arm over my body.

I breathed in the smell of her shampoo and rubbed the soft strands of her hair with my fingers. I wanted to stay awake and savor it, talk to her, laugh with her, soak more of her in. But the lull of the plane and the hum of the engine enhanced a pull into sleep that already needed no help.

With my eyes shut and heart full, I was mere moments away from a deep sleep when Georgia called my name.

"Yeah, baby?" I asked, my voice thick and sluggish with the impending doze.

"I've never been happier to miss sleep in my life."

Ditto.

"Just one room," I told the front desk clerk as she handed me our cards. My assistant, Pam, had, of course, made the arrangements, and she'd have had no way of knowing Georgia and I were following a one-room sleeping plan.

Personally, I didn't have even one fuck left to give. But Georgie cared. And I cared about what she cared about. It was a really mushy, complicated web of romance, but in the end, all that mattered was her.

"Yes, sir," the young girl agreed, taking the keys back and tapping away at the computer.

We'd gone straight from the airport to the meeting, and from the meeting to dinner. Thanks to one of the best plane catnaps I'd ever had, we had just enough time to spend another night *not sleeping* before Georgia had to be on a plane back home in the morning.

"Here you go," the desk clerk offered, handing me back a solitary key. "Room 554. The elevators are down the hall behind you and on the right."

"Thanks." I smiled and grabbed my small bag from its spot at my feet.

Georgia was already down the elevator hall, pacing the tile floor in front of them as she talked over the details of things she needed for tomorrow's meeting with Dean. As imperative as the phone call seemed on the surface, I had a suspicion it was more of an excuse to avoid awkwardly standing next to me at the desk than a necessity.

"Ready?" I asked as I came to a stop in front of her.

Her finger shot to my lips and pushed to say 'be quiet'.

"It was just Mr. Brooks," she said into the phone, rolling her eyes. "No, I'm still in the lobby."

I went to speak, but she pushed on my lips harder. "Nope. The meeting ran really late and we still have a couple of things to go over before we call it a night."

I smiled. No one here was going to be calling it a night.

She shook her head in the negative and bit her bottom lip. My balls tightened immediately. Even they knew it was time to play.

"Georgie girl," I whispered mischievously. She shushed me and waved me away, pointing at the phone with wild eyes. She was just too easy.

"Come tuck me in," I teased, grabbing at her hips and backing her toward the elevators.

I pushed the up button to call the car and pulled her hips into mine. Hair loose from its earlier binding, she looked wild and willing and altogether too much like sex to stop.

"Dean, Dean," she called, obviously trying to break into his end of steady conversation. "You know, you've got this covered."

I smiled bigger. Pulled her breasts tighter to my chest.

"It was really just my neuroses calling. You're plenty competent to have everything ready on your own."

"Mm-hmm," I hummed, moving the hair off of her neck and sucking at her skin greedily.

She was dying to give me one of her signature, scolding *Kline!*s, I could feel it in her posture and staccato-timed wording, but with Dean on the line, secrecy won out.

"I know. I'll be sure to give Donatella Versace my recommendation, should I ever run into her on the street." She nodded at the phone, at something Dean said, a gesture he obviously couldn't see, and I swooned.

Hands down, Georgia Cummings was one of the most charmingly fascinating women I'd ever encountered. Dichotomous in nearly everything she did, I never knew which way was up or which version of her I would get. Awkward or easy, bold or shy, endlessly clever or laughably bumbling. Every time, day or night—work or play—I'd take any version I met.

"Hang up the phone, baby," I coaxed, pushing her gently into the open and waiting car.

"I'll see you tomorrow," she said into the line. "Yes, butt-fucking early." We both smiled like lunatics. "I'll see you then."

Finally, blessedly, she cut the call just as the doors of the elevator shut out the people.

I grabbed her hips, groping and squeezing at the top of her ass.

"God. It's about time," I teased, running my tongue along the closed seam of her lips.

"Fuck," she breathed as her head fell back and her hair hung well past her shoulders. I gripped the ends of it and yanked her throat open even farther.

"Ahh," she moaned, shoving her tit right into the palm of my waiting free hand.

"That's it," I cooed, circling her hard nipple with the tip of my thumb.

"Kline," she breathed. She could barely keep up with the rhythm of her pants.

"I can't wait to hear you say that again. On my face, on my cock… I'm gonna strip you down and sit you up on every fucking thing I can think of."

"God," she moaned as the doors opened on our floor. I scooped her up and into my arms, glancing at the sign that would tell me which way to go to our room.

Too fucking far from the elevator, at the end of the hall, I finally came face to face with our door. Georgia clung to me as I set her down to pull the plastic key card from my pocket. I couldn't wait to *make love* to every single inch of her petite body.

As the door clicked open and I slid our intertwined bodies inside, I knew without a doubt that was what this was.

Just lust was gone, like had grown, and love was positioned in Georgia's sumptuous mouth—right at the tip of my tongue.

CHAPTER 31

Georgia

"Just three more questions," Kline demanded, his voice raspy and sleep-filled.

We'd been at this game all night. Asking random questions to one another in between bouts of kissing that always ended in more. Crazy, sexy kind of more.

Best game ever.

But it was half past three in the morning, and I had a six thirty-five flight to catch. A contract meeting was sending me home today, and because he'd tacked on an additional meeting tomorrow morning with one of our regular investors in the name of efficiency, *today* meant *one day earlier* than Kline. *No need to make more than one trip,* he'd said. Now we had to face the consequences of that decision.

I hadn't packed a thing and needed a shower. As badly as I wanted to stay in bed, wrapped up in him, I had to get my ass moving.

I sat up, the sheet pooling around my waist. "You said that three hours and two orgasms ago."

"Two orgasms? I thought it was three…" He was lying on his belly, resting his chin on the pillow, his eyes locked on my bared breasts. "If you can't remember the last one, I'm demanding a re-do."

A re-do. The bastard.

He licked his lips and moved his gaze from my breasts, to my waist, until finally making the slow circuit to my mouth.

Jesus. Kline flashing me smoldering glances during business meetings was dangerous enough, but this? That look. Those heated blue eyes. His sexy, bedhead hair. And that tight ass. It should be illegal.

"Stop smoldering at me!" I smacked his shoulder. "I have to get in the shower. I have a flight to catch, remember?"

He pounced on me, wrapped his arms around my body, and slammed my back into the bed before I could stop him. "Don't leave." His mouth found mine, his teeth tugging on my bottom lip.

"Stay here with me. Let me ask you questions and kiss these lips." He kissed me deeper. "And touch this perfect body." His fingers slid up my sides, resting below the curve of my breasts. "And put my mouth on you." He punctuated that statement by gliding those devious hands down my belly, until his fingers were touching me where I throbbed.

I'd never had marathon sex. Okay, before Kline, I'd never actually had sex. But I'd never experienced this feeling before. I'd never been so attracted, so turned on, so undeniably in love with someone, where the only thing I wanted to do was spend every day for the rest of forever touching him, kissing him, fucking him.

It was overwhelming. And amazing. And should have had me running for the hills. But when it came to Kline, I didn't want to run, unless it was toward his opened arms.

I trusted him. Cared for him. Loved him. I wanted him and only him. He was everything I'd always dreamed of, plus a million things I never even knew I wanted.

"Kiss me, baby," he whispered against my lips.

"I *am* kissing you," I retorted, my mouth still pressed against his.

"No. Fucking kiss me," he growled, his tongue slipping past my lips and making me moan. "I'll never get tired of this. I'll never *not* want this. With you. Only you."

"I'm going to miss my flight and it'll be all your fault," I whimpered.

"Fuck the flight. Fuck the meeting. Stay here and fuck my brains out." That devilish mouth moved to my neck and then my collarbone, sucking softly while his tongue licked along the sensitive skin.

My hands found his ass, tugging him toward me. "You don't play fair." My hips arched up into his, my body begging for him to connect us.

"With you, I'll never play fair." He pressed against me, the tip of his cock moving through my wetness. "I'll do whatever it takes to get you to keep doing this with me. *For-fucking-ever.*"

"We're gonna fuck forever?" I teased.

His laugh vibrated my skin. "Yes. Me and you. Fucking, kissing, groping, making love, *coming*. All the goddamn time. Forever."

"I want this in writing."

He moved away from me, rustling inside the nightstand and finding a complimentary pen clipped to a notepad with the hotel's logo written along the top. He tossed the pad across the room and put the pen in his mouth, removing the cap.

"Pretty sure contracts need paper…"

"Not this contract." He settled between my thighs again, eyes locked on my belly. The tip of the pen touched my skin and I shivered. "This is a different kind of contract, baby." Blue eyes peeked up at me, smirking.

The pen moved across my skin, but I couldn't see what he was writing, his messy hair blocking my view.

"Excuse me, sir, but what are you doing? Are you branding me?"

"Stop calling me sir. I'm trying to focus here and you're making me hard."

"You've been hard for the past eight hours. What's new?"

"You'd think you would have tried to help me with this difficult situation. Honestly, Georgia, I'm disappointed. You really need to work a little harder at this whole girlfriend thing."

I fought my grin. It was stupid that I *still* felt giddy over hearing him say girlfriend. I had officially reverted back to high school. But I didn't care. I loved that he made me giddy and girly and head-over-heels in love.

"Oh, so when I did that thing where I put my mouth on your dick and then didn't remove it until you came, that wasn't what a good girlfriend would do? I'm sorry I did that. I'll make a note to *never* do that again. Don't worry, baby, I'll learn from my mistakes."

"Now, wait a minute. Let's not get too hasty here," he backtracked, still focused on tattooing something on my skin. "I think you need to do that thing a few more times. Like every day, for the next five years or so, before I can really decide if I like it."

I grabbed his hair, pulling his head up so he looked at me. "You didn't like it?" I asked, my eyes narrowed.

"I can't really remember." He shrugged, fighting a smile. "Why don't you do it again and then it might help me give you a proper answer?"

"Oh." I feigned innocent understanding. "So, I should just put my mouth on your cock again? You know, slide it in real deep until it taps the back of my throat, and then suck *hard,* while I run my tongue all over you. Would that help? Or should I do something else?"

"No," he said, swallowing hard enough to make his Adam's apple bob. "You should do those things." He cleared his throat, his body's answer growing hard and straining against my thigh.

"All of those things you just said—yeah, do those."

My face cracked into a smile, amused by the strain in his voice and his, um, *yeah.* That too. I was definitely enjoying that reaction.

"Okay, all set. Per your request, the contract is in writing." He tossed the pen back onto the nightstand. He gripped my thighs as he kneeled on the bed between my legs.

"Now, let's get back to what you were saying before. I believe you said something about putting your mouth on me?" He smirked, waggling his brows playfully. "Or do you want me to just slide inside of you? Because I'm a big fan of this perfect pussy." He ground against me.

"The biggest fan, actually. No one loves this pussy as much as I do. Which is why no one else will ever see it, touch it, taste it. Consider me your orgasm donor for life. Any time, hour, second of any day, you need to come, I'm your guy."

I giggled. "Like my orgasm soul mate?"

I was rewarded with a smile. "Exactly like that."

He brushed his fingers across my belly and hip bone, where the pen's previous ministrations still had my nerve endings tingling. "This is the sexiest thing I've ever seen."

"What did you write?" My eyes followed his, to the place where his hand rested on my skin. "Move your hand," I urged. "I swear to God, if you drew a penis or—" I stopped mid-sentence, my gaze locking onto the straight and narrow lines of his masculine script.

My heart in your hands and you in my arms, that's all I'll ever need.

"I mean it," he whispered. "I mean every word, Georgia."

I looked at him, *really* looked at him, hovering above me, his hands now resting beside my head. His heart was in his eyes—tender, loving, *perfect*.

What simple words for such a profound declaration.

Kline had just laid it all out there. He'd just told me I had him. He was mine. His heart was in my hands. And all he wanted was *me*. And that would be enough for him.

"I love you," I said, my voice choking on emotion. "I love you so much, Kline."

"I love you, too." He kissed me hard, deep, and desperate. His lips, his touch, the way he made love to me, it told me everything I needed to know.

This was real, him and me. This was it. And the best part of that revelation was that we were both certain. Neither of us was in limbo, waiting for the other to catch up or decide if this was right. We were all in, both of us, in love.

Intense, life changing, forever a part of one another kind of love.

I handed my boarding pass off and walked onto the plane. I was beyond exhausted, my arms damn near giving out as I lifted my carry-on up and stowed it away. Kline had switched my seat without my knowing. Yesterday, he had seen my boarding pass on the nightstand and asked if I was in coach because the flight was overbooked. When I responded that I didn't want to take advantage of the company's budget, he told me to *never* book a seat in coach again.

I'd acquiesced with a sassy, "Yes, sir."

Apparently, he'd appreciated that answer because I had been generously rewarded with his talented mouth between my legs.

The second I arrived at the airport and got through security in record time—thank God, considering I was running thirty minutes behind schedule—I was called over to the gate, where an attendant instructed that I had been upgraded to a first class window seat.

He sure was one sneaky, adorable, demanding man when he wanted to be.

I clicked my seatbelt into place and grabbed my phone from my purse as passengers continued to board the plane and find their seats. Even though he was probably sound asleep, I decided to send him a quick text.

Me: *Someone changed my seat. I'm currently relaxing in first class, enjoying the view from the window.*

Kline: *I think you should thank whoever did it with that really awesome thing you do with your mouth.*

And I thought *I* had sex on the brain all the time. *Pervert.*

Me: When I figure it out, I'll keep that idea in mind.

Kline: If I told you it was me, would you make that idea a reality?

Me: I don't know...I'm an in-the-moment kind of gal. I'm not very good with hypotheticals.

Kline: It was me. I'll fit time into my schedule tomorrow night so you can properly thank me.

Me: Now that I'm in the moment, I'm not feeling all that into your idea...

Kline: Did I mention there would be an exchange? You thanking me, me thanking you kind of thing.

Me: Slot me in for tomorrow night at seven.

Kline: Sudden change in feelings?

Me: You presented a very attractive offer, Mr. Brooks.

Kline: Always a pleasure doing business with you, Ms. Cummings.

Me: Likewise...I miss you.

God, I really was a goner. It had only been an hour since I'd kissed him goodbye while he was all sleepy and adorable and begging me to stay, and already, my chest ached over the idea that I wouldn't get to see him again until tomorrow night.

Kline: I haven't stopped thinking about you since you left. I think you should quit your job. You should still be in this bed beside me and not on a goddamn flight back home.

Me: I'll let my boss know ASAP.

Kline: Good idea.

The third round of passengers started to filter down the aisle, heading through the curtains and into coach. I tapped the email icon, drafting a quick message to my "boss."

> From: Georgia Cummings
> To: Kline Brooks
> Subject: My Boyfriend's Requests
>
> Mr. Brooks,
> My boyfriend isn't too happy I'm on a flight instead of in his hotel room fucking his brains out. I'm requesting that this doesn't happen again. He's very upset.
> Sincerely,
> Georgia Cummings
> Director of Marketing, TapNext
> Brooks Media

> From: Kline Brooks
> To: Georgia Cummings
> Re: My Boyfriend's Requests
>
> Ms. Cummings,
> I am taking this concern very seriously. From now on, I guarantee any business trips you are scheduled

to attend, you will be booked in the same room as your boyfriend. I will also make sure there is plenty of time scheduled in throughout your day to allow you to fuck his brains out. And just because I feel terrible about this, I'm requesting you leave work early tomorrow and go to his apartment (his front desk probably knows you need a spare key) so you're there when he gets home. (I bet he'd prefer you to be naked and lying in his bed, too.)

Sincerely,

Kline Brooks

President and CEO Brooks Media

From: Georgia Cummings

To: Kline Brooks

Subject: I think my boyfriend will be very happy…

Mr. Brooks,

Thank you for your utmost concern. I will be sure to leave work early tomorrow and wait for my boyfriend at his apartment. I will also use your suggestion about my attire. Although, I think my boyfriend would prefer me to be wearing the sexiest pair of heels I own while I wait.

Sincerely,

Georgia Cummings

Director of Marketing, TapNext

Brooks Media

P.S. I'm crazy in love with my boyfriend.

From: Kline Brooks
To: Georgia Cummings
Re: I think my boyfriend will be happy…(YES, he will)

Ms. Cummings,
I think your boyfriend would love that. Actually, I bet
he'd insist on that.
Sincerely,
Kline Brooks
President and CEO Brooks Media

P.S. He's crazy in love with you too. For the sake of
everything that's right in the world, don't forget the
fucking heels tomorrow.

Eyes tired, I set my phone in my lap and rested my head on the
seat. My mind replayed last night, highlighting everything from Kline
stealing kisses between asking me my favorite bands, movies, and vacation spots, to him making love to me, over and over again.

My fingers touched my lips, hiding my ridiculous smile.

"I know that look," a woman softly whispered beside me.

My eyes blinked open, finding an older lady with salt and pepper hair and a rounded, smiling face in the seat next to mine. "You're
thinking about someone special, aren't you?"

"Am I that obvious?" I laughed, my cheeks flushing.

"Don't be embarrassed. Love is a beautiful thing when you find
it. It's something to be happy about, something to cherish, something
to wear on your face every single day," she said, genuine happiness in
her voice. "Is he a good man?"

I nodded. Kline's handsome face flashed in my mind. In that moment, I could picture every one of his smiles—happy, teasing, playful,
loving. It was an endless list and one that I wanted to memorize and

keep with me forever. "Yeah, he is. He's definitely one of the good ones."

"Is he your husband?"

"No." I shook my head. "He's my boyfriend."

She grinned, her cheeks puffing out in soft delight. "By the looks of your glow, I'd say you're headed in that direction."

Were we? My rational head wanted me to slow the hell down, but my heart was already picking out invitations and flowers. Even though we had just started exchanging I love yous, there was no denying I'd fallen hard for Kline. I was in so deep I honestly couldn't picture myself without him. *Ever.*

Before I could respond to her statement or ask her something about herself, she was adjusting in her seat, placing a pillow around her neck. "I wish you the best of luck, dear. I hope you and your wonderful man get a very happy ever after. Now, if you don't mind, I'm going to rest my eyes. I can feel my Xanax kicking in." She flashed an apologetic smile. "It's for the best, though," she added. "I'm a very nervous flyer."

She closed her eyes, and within seconds, soft snores fell from her lips.

I made a note to tell my doctor I was a nervous flyer too. The long flights I often took for business trips would have been much more tolerable with the magic that was Xanax. I'd much rather have slept through a four-hour flight than toss and turn without getting any rest.

"Sorry for the delay," a woman's voice filtered through the speakers. "We will be taking off shortly."

My phone buzzed in my lap, catching my attention.

It was a picture message from Cassie, with the words, ***I'm so sorry, Georgia.***

Huh?

I tapped the photo and it filled the screen, zooming in so I could figure out what she was talking about.

It was a screenshot of a TapNext conversation.

TAPRoseNEXT (7:00PM): You're a very nice guy, but I can't continue talking with you anymore. I've gotten more serious with the man I'm seeing and this just doesn't feel right. I'm sorry. Good luck with everything, Ruck.

BAD_Ruck (6:45AM): I get it. I do. But I think we should meet in person, just the two of us. Please, Rose.

I white-knuckled my phone as I stared down at the screen in disbelief.

I don't think I breathed for an entire minute. I felt like someone had reached down my throat and pulled my heart straight out of my body.

My eyes closed of their own accord, my mind in self-preservation mode. My heart roaring in my ears, I took a cavernous breath and found the strength to open my eyes again, hoping—no, *praying*—I had missed something along the line.

But I hadn't. *I fucking hadn't.* The screenshot, Kline's response, it was real. One-hundred percent real.

I scrubbed a hand down my face, pressing into my lids to stop the tears wanting to spill down my cheeks. A shaky sigh escaped my lips as I tried to focus through the blurry mess of emotions.

His message was timestamped from this morning at 3:45 a.m. Pacific.

My throat constricted, cheeks straining in agony to stop myself from losing it.

I won't cry. I will not sob in front of a plane full of strangers.

This morning. He sent that message in between playfully asking me questions and making love to me. Or was it *faking* love to me? Because that was what it felt like now. I'd never felt so betrayed, so utterly devastated in my entire life.

The pain built in my chest, burning like I had swallowed hot coals. I was hanging by a thread, my free hand gripping the armrest in a pathetic attempt to hold myself together.

"Miss, we're about to take off. You need to turn your phone off now."

I pulled my eyes from the screen, finding a flight attendant with long blonde hair and a pink smile standing above me.

All I could do was stare at her. Honestly, I didn't even know what she was saying to me.

"Your phone?" She nodded to my hands.

I followed her eyes and realized what she was asking. "Oh, sorry," I mumbled, and with shaky hands, turned it off.

I felt like I was a passenger in a crash-and-burn landing, going from the highest high, only to be catapulted into the lowest of lows.

Memories flooded my mind.

The night at the Hamptons, when I had given myself to him.

I choked on a sob as a few tears slipped down my cheeks. I swiped at the liquid emotion, telling myself I could do this. I could get through this flight.

A man across the aisle glanced in my direction, his head tilted to the side in concern.

Oh, God, don't look at me like that! I wanted to scream at him. I did not want pity. I couldn't handle someone recognizing that I was falling to pieces. *That* would for sure make it impossible to hold this in until I was somewhere private.

Long, slow breaths were inhaled through my nose and exhaled from my lungs. I stared down at a nonexistent piece of lint on my pants, plucking at the material just because it was something to do, something else to focus on besides my heart falling out of my chest.

More memories drowned me.

Last night, with each kiss, each touch, each soft caress, he had silently been asking me to fall the rest of the way with him. And I had. I had followed his lead, and on the way down, he had made love to me until my heart was beating like he'd wanted it to. Like I'd wanted it to. My world had changed. Inside, my walls had fallen down and he was all around me. All I knew. All I wanted to know.

Kline had gone from being my boss to my best friend, my lover, and my intoxication until he let the needle break off in my skin. This wasn't a little cut that would scab over and flake off. *No.* He had cut me so deep I hadn't even bled.

The pain was so unbearable that all my emotions fled the scene. I switched from distraught—fighting the sob threatening to bubble up from my lungs—to robotic.

I didn't want to talk to him. I didn't want to ask him why, after the night we had shared together, he would still want to meet someone who *wasn't* me. Initially, when I'd found out Kline was Ruck, and he had been chatting with **TAPRoseNEXT** without knowing it was me, it didn't upset me. I looked at the entire situation with a rational, understanding head. Because I had done the same thing.

But the second I had met Thatch, the guy whose picture was on **Bad_Ruck's** TapNext profile, I'd known I needed to stop. I knew I wanted Kline. I knew I was falling in love with him, and I didn't want anything to ruin that. Which was why I had told Cassie to take the reins. Who would've thought that the whole time I was chatting with Ruck, I was actually talking to Kline?

It was the ultimate mindfuck.

Unfortunately for me, that mindfuck had just gotten a whole lot worse.

This was different from a simple response to another woman on an online dating profile. He was requesting to meet someone that wasn't me, someone he *knew* was my best friend.

What on earth did he think he was going to gain from that? Was he planning on being in a relationship with me while screwing Cassie on the side?

God, it didn't add up, didn't seem like the Kline I knew, but the proof was right in front of my face.

I felt so devastated. Knowing what we shared and all of the possibilities of what we could have been, why would Kline have risked
that? In a matter of a few sentences, he had just ruined everything.
Destroyed us. Destroyed me.

I felt sick. Nausea coiled my stomach, constant and unrelenting.

The minute the seatbelt lights went off, I made a beeline for the
lavatory. My breakfast filled the small metal toilet within seconds. It
took a good five minutes before I could stop dry heaving. I held myself up over the sink, staring at a woman I didn't even recognize. I did
my best to clean up, splashing cool water on my face and rinsing my
mouth out, before I made my way back to my seat.

God, I had never felt so cold, so fucking alone.

I didn't want to feel like this. I wanted the pilot to turn the plane
around so I could talk to Kline. I wanted to forget that TapNext conversation had ever happened.

But I wasn't going to be that woman who couldn't step back and
face the facts.

Even though it was going to kill me, I was going to be the woman
who knew when to end things. The woman who could end a relationship with a man—even though she loved him—because she knew she
didn't deserve to be treated like that.

He had told me he loved me, he had touched me and kissed me
in ways a man would only do when he was in love. But while he had
been doing that, he had also found time to request to meet another
woman. These were not the actions of a man I wanted to be in a relationship with.

For the entire five-and-half-hour flight, my mind raced. Every
memory was a picture in my head, his betrayal scratching across the
surface of each photograph and tainting it forever.

I was fucking miserable, stuck on an old airplane with no Wi-Fi
after finding out the man I wanted to spend the rest of my life with
was going behind my back and requesting to meet other women on
the side.

If he did that knowing it was my best friend, what else was he doing behind my back?

I knew it was crazy to go in that direction, but who could blame me?

Trying to talk this out with him was pointless. I could only take so much, and a nasty breakup would push me over the edge. I was afraid of what I might say to him. Hell, I'd have to hold my breath if I was in the same room as him, because breathing the same air meant breathing him in.

And my heart couldn't take any more.

I walked off the plane, my mind fogged with heartbreak and anger. I wanted to scream. I wanted to cry. I wanted to curl up in the fetal position and sleep for forty years.

Pre-life-altering screenshot, I would've sent Kline a text message telling him I had landed, but I didn't even bother turning on my phone. What was the fucking point? I had nothing to say.

Eventually, I found baggage claim and grabbed my suitcase.

I had options. Either I could let this drag me down and turn me into someone I didn't want to be, or I could find a way to get past this.

My decision was made and there was no going back to what we had.

There was no explanation he could give that would fix this, save us.

Steadfast in my choice, I hailed a cab and threw my bags in the back before the driver could even get out of his seat.

"Winthrop Building, Fifth Avenue," I instructed without a second thought.

When he pulled up to the building, I tossed money in the front seat and hopped out, grabbing my suitcases from the trunk. It was afternoon and everyone would be there. My coworkers would be roaming the halls. Dean would be waiting for me to attend the meeting.

Fuck.

No way could I handle sitting through a meeting. I had to go in, do what I needed to do, and get the hell out of there with as little interaction as possible.

I was striding off the elevator within minutes. I offered a few small waves to Meryl and Cynthia as I passed them in the hall before ducking into my office. Leaning against the closed door, I shut my eyes, biting my cheek to hold back the tears.

God, I didn't have time for a breakdown. I had about twenty minutes before Dean would stroll in, ready to escort me to the conference room.

I sat behind my desk and booted up my computer. My hands shook, and my foot tapped against the tile as nervous energy radiated off of me in unpredictable waves.

A letter of resignation was typed out at a quick, efficient pace. I sent a screenshot of the TapNext conversation to my email and printed it out.

And then I was walking down the hall, toward the one place I didn't really want to be.

"Oh, hi, Georgia!" Leslie stopped me as I rounded the corner. "Is Mr. Brooks back? I forgot to give him a few messages last week about some meeting…" She scrunched her eyebrows, her pea-sized brain trying to remember. "I think it was important, but, like, I'm not really sure."

"He won't be back until tomorrow."

"Oh." Her huge mouth jutted out into a pout. "Are you feeling okay? You look, like, really terrible today."

Wow. As if my day wasn't already fantastic.

I didn't even have the energy to form a sarcastic retort. I just nodded, because she was right; I looked like shit.

"Hey, do you mind going into Dean's office and letting him know that I had to go home? Tell him I'm sick and I'll call him later."

He would be crazy pissed at me but would understand. Plus, I was betting on the fact that Leslie would ramble on and on about my haggard appearance. It was the first time I could use her obsession with being the prettiest girl in the room to my advantage.

"Uh...*okay*," she begrudgingly agreed.

You'd think *I* was the intern in this scenario, asking my superior for a favor.

The second I stepped into Kline's office, my heart clenched. I glanced around at the familiar surroundings, taking everything in. Knowing I wouldn't last long, I pulled open a drawer on his desk in search of paper. My eyes got blurry when they caught on a photograph of us in the Hamptons resting on top of everything else. We were sitting on the porch, his arm wrapped around my shoulder. I was looking into the camera, grinning, while he gazed down at me, a soft, smitten smile on his lips.

What should have been a happy memory only made me want to throw up again.

I was starting to wonder if I ever really knew Kline Brooks.

I had to get out of his office and back to my apartment. The impending breakdown was sitting in my throat.

Slamming the drawer closed, I wrote out a simple note on the top edge of the screenshot Cassie had sent me, placing it on top of my resignation letter.

Walking out of his office and getting on the elevator, I was certain I'd never be the same after this. I knew getting myself to a place where I even felt like smiling was going to be the hardest thing I ever did. I knew there was no getting over Kline.

But I also knew I deserved better.

I'd find a new job. I'd find a way to move on.

And I'd be just fine pretending that I was.

CHAPTER 32

Kline

I shook the ice in my glass, watching as the cubes moved from side to side and melted into one another. One water droplet plopped from each surface to the next until it finally disappeared into the shallow amber liquid at the bottom.

I'd taken to drinking scotch on the flight to pass the time, the bouncing of my knee having grown old within the first fifteen minutes. Georgia was still on a plane too, having taken off precisely two hours and seventeen minutes ahead of me—according to the FAA—but every minute felt like a lifetime, and it took real concentration to keep myself from bombarding her turned-off phone with a stream of sappy messages.

Last night—the last few weeks of nights—had been the best of my life. Everything I'd worked for, built for myself, and strived to keep healthy felt like a drop in the life-bucket. Finding someone who made me anticipate each day and crave her company—someone who made me feel even more like me—well, that was what made a man realize the truth, *the importance,* in working to live rather than living to work.

I wanted my days to start and end with her, and I wanted the privilege to have even more of her in the middle.

Put simply, I was in love.

And it was irrevocably clear why I never had been before. *None of them were her.*

"Gemma?" I asked like the pathetic shell of a man I had become. I'd told Georgia I loved her, but it hadn't been enough. I needed some kind of confirmation. Some kind of peace. Some kind of promise of forever.

Gemma had the grace to smile. "She should be landing sometime in the next five minutes, sir."

I could have been the butt of many jokes, the object of numerous men's end-of-world postulation, but I couldn't find it in me to care. And it was clear I'd been feeling that way for the greater part of the morning.

Cutting short a meeting with Wallace Fellers, one of my biggest regular investors, and heading straight for the airport only to chase Georgia's plane across the country was not exactly precedented behavior.

The flight attendant's phone rang, and my head jerked up from my lap at the sound.

Gemma laughed as she hung it up and showed compassion for my pitiful existence by delivering the news from air traffic control immediately. "She should be on the ground, sir."

Phone in hand from the cupholder at my side, I scrolled to her number and dialed.

Two short rings gave way to her voicemail, and I hung up without leaving a message.

I knew it was crazy, dialing someone the moment the wheels of their plane touched the ground, obsessing over their arrival so valiantly in an effort just to hear their voice that I couldn't wait the five-minute security delay a Google search would imply.

But I was a very sick man, the first stages of love overwhelming my cells and multiplying by the minute. It was aggressive like most terminal cases, taking down one organ after the next until I had no choice but to succumb—succumb to the crazy, desperate lengths to make contact and the desire to swaddle myself in her presence and never unwrap.

I typed out a text instead.

Me: After a few bribes and several heinous displays of my money and influence, I got the FAA to give me an exact schedule of your arrival time. Call me as soon as you can.

Several minutes and an intense one-man conversation later, I added the words I should have included in the first place.

Me: PS-I love you.

When she didn't answer immediately, I knew I was one short step away from throwing myself off the proverbial ledge. I couldn't take it anymore. I had to do something else, be something else—if for nothing more than the sake of my poor, overexcited heart.

A nap. That was the only answer.

Determined, I sunk into my seat, reclined the back, and forced my eyes closed.

I pictured her smile and her hair, and as I focused really hard and gave myself over to the dream, I could even smell her perfect Georgia smell.

I woke hours later to the jolt of our wheels meeting the pavement of the runway. Gemma smiled and waved as my eyes met hers, and I jumped to pull my seat back to upright and grab my phone from the cupholder.

No messages showed on the screen, so I unlocked it to be sure, but no amount of hope could make the status change.

Nothing.

No calls. No texts. No messages from Rose. I checked each and every folder rigorously, searching for some phone-cyberspace loophole that'd robbed me of the one thing I desired so much.

But ten minutes and a mild case of carpal tunnel later, I still came up empty.

I prided myself on being a smart man, and something didn't feel right.

But I quieted my thoughts with the power of sheer will and unbuckled my seatbelt as we pulled to a stop.

She'd had a meeting to get to immediately upon landing, and as much as I'd bitched about her waiting for a later plane, she'd already had it scheduled to the very last possible minute.

With New York as her habitat, it probably took every ounce of concentration and a pledge of sainthood to make it there on time, in one piece, and with an inkling of schmooze left in the tank. She wouldn't have much left for me.

I moved to the front of the plane, re-strategizing on the fly and focusing on the element of surprise. I was here, in the same city, free to chase her down until the sun came up if I had to. She didn't know I'd flown home earlier than expected and keeping it that way would only amplify the reunion.

Jesus. *Yeah.* I liked the sound of that.

"Thanks, Gem," I said, giving her a genuine smile as she stepped to the side of the main cabin door to let me by.

"Anytime, Mr. Brooks."

I took two steps down the stairs when she called my name again. I looked back at her over my shoulder.

"She's very lucky, sir."

I shook my head and laughed.

"Me," I corrected, tapping my chest with a wink before scooting down the rest of the stairs to a waiting Frank.

He stood, holding an open door and wearing a smile.

"Mr. Brooks."

"Hey, Frank," I greeted. "Straight to the office, okay?"

I'd start at the beginning and work my way around the city until I found her from there. I couldn't wait to see her face.

"Yes, sir."

The lights of the office were dimmed enough that they rubbed off on my hope, but I headed for the back anyway. As long as I was here, I'd check my desk for messages and change into one of my spare shirts before heading for Georgia and Cassie's apartment.

I kept my pace to a near jog, but considering the strength of my desire to run, I counted it as a victory.

My door was cracked, the lamp at my desk illuminating the immediate surrounding space softly. My eyebrows pulled together at the sight, but I didn't slow my gait, striding for the beckoning light at a canter.

The surface was clear except for two loose sheets of paper. I shuffled them to the side in a hurry, grabbing for the tray at the back where Pam often placed my messages when the photocopy caught my eye.

It looked like a screenshot of a message window on a phone.

At the top, a few short strokes of delicate scrawl demanded my immediate attention.

Ruck,

Of all the people in the world…my best friend?
I hate that I still love you after seeing this,
but I can't be with someone who lies to me.
This <u>doesn't</u> hurt good.

Benny

One word bled into the next as I tried to make sense of the simple sentiment, but a mushrooming cloud of dread jumped and swooped, swallowing me whole.

Bold and cruel, the screen of the messaging page of the TapNext app taunted me.

TAPRoseNEXT (7:00PM): You're a very nice guy, but I can't continue talking with you anymore. I've gotten more serious with the man I'm seeing and this just doesn't feel right. I'm sorry. Good luck with everything, Ruck.

BAD_Ruck (6:45AM): I get it. I do. But I think we should meet in person, just the two of us. Please, Rose.

"No," I muttered, reading the words in a flash and reliving each of the seconds that led up to them and followed. "No, no, no, noooooo!" I screamed into the echoey silence.

So lost in the haze of new and all-encompassing love, I'd foolishly, faithfully believed I'd get the chance to straighten everything out in my time. Practiced, planned, and in a completely unmessy setting. That was what I'd been after, the meeting in person. I figured I could control the situation. She'd have the space to react and I'd have the chance to explain. I'd naïvely thought an in-person revelation could even be a little idyllic. But as I ran through the hours and the days I'd kept it to myself—the time I'd harbored my secret even after learning of our faux foursome with our friends—I knew I'd missed my chance.

Sometimes time is valuable, but it can also be your worst enemy. Because, no matter the root of my intentions, lies never led to romance.

This. This moment, this feeling.

This was hell.

I jumped into action, pulling the phone from the pocket of my pants and considering all the ways I could fix it. I was a fixer, a problem solver. *I could fix this.*

Couldn't I?

I fought the tightness in my throat, but it was potent in a way I wasn't prepared for.

I opened my text messages and typed out several drafts.

Me: Please, let me explain. I know it doesn't look good.

Delete.

I shook my head and scrubbed at my face, willing the right words to come.

Me: I love you. God, let me explain.

Delete.

Me: Georgie. Please talk to me. I've known it was you for a long time now.

Delete.

I opened the TapNext app and drafted a message to Rose.

BAD_Ruck (6:54PM): You've got this all wrong, Rose. I know who you are.

Delete.

Accusing her of *any* wrongdoing in this scenario was probably not a good idea.

BAD_Ruck (6:55PM): Remember the gargoyle dick, Rose. Not everything is what it seems.

Delete.

Goddammit. This was definitely not the time to be a smartass, either.

None of it was good enough. No words powerful enough to convince the inconvincible.

My nose stung and my eyes burned and the screen of my phone blurred before my eyes.

I'd fucked up in a way I didn't know how to fix—didn't know how to *breathe* through the fucking pain.

Jesus. If I couldn't even put together a few fucking words that sounded convincing *to myself*, she was never going to believe me. *Not ever.*

"FUCKKK!" I screamed until fire raged in my throat and chucked my useless phone clear across the room and watched it shatter.

I punched at the top of my desk over and over until my hand developed a throb, pulling the pain and blood away from my pathetic pumping heart. Each thud enhanced the ache, and I prayed that somehow, someway, I'd find a way to make it end before the cycle purged my vital organs of enough blood to end me.

Time.

I needed it. Time to think, time to plan, time to understand what this was going to take.

Taking a deep breath and blowing it out, I pulled the sheet of paper over to expose the one beneath it and immediately lost my footing. I turned just in time, sinking to the floor with my back to the mahogany of my desk and clutched at the paper.

Her resignation letter, effective immediately.

She didn't want my hollow words or pleading looks.

My little shark had bitten the lines of contact clean through.

It was done. Done in a way that I wasn't remotely ready for. Done in a way that I couldn't even conceive.

Done in a way that would never actually be done, *not ever.*

This pain would haunt me for the rest of my life.

CHAPTER 33

Georgia

I gave myself twenty-four hours to wallow and cry and browse Reddit "my boyfriend is a cheating, cock-sucking, piece-of-scum dirtbag" threads. Okay, maybe they weren't really titled that, but I'd always enjoyed nicknaming shit.

And when I wasn't trolling Internet threads, I could've been found doing any of the following:

1. Crying. *A lot.*

2. Turning my phone on and off every five minutes, in hopes that Kline would attempt to contact me. He didn't, by the way. Not a text, a call, nothing but complete radio silence.

3. Re-watching the first four seasons of *Gilmore Girls*. If only we could combine Logan, Jess, and Dean to form the perfect man.

4. Eating all of our food. (Cassie was not happy about this.)

5. Taking one thousand BuzzFeed quizzes. I was a Hufflepuff, who should live in San Francisco and preferred NSYNC over Backstreet Boys. Chris Pratt should have been my celebrity husband, I'd have two kids, and my chocolate IQ was insane. Just in case you were wondering.

When BuzzFeed told me The Notebook was the Nicholas Sparks book that best described my love life, I gave it both middle fingers and shut my laptop.

If I was a bird, Kline Brooks could go fuck himself.

But you know what the hardest part was?

I still loved him. God, I loved him. I loved Kline just as much as I had before I'd seen that screenshot from Cassie. And this voice in the back of my head kept insisting something was off.

That Kline wouldn't have broken my trust like that.

Stupid voice. It was that kind of voice that made people stay in relationships with someone who didn't deserve them. I also gave that voice both middle fingers. Frankly, I was ready to give every-fuck-ing-body the middle finger. Misery loves company and all that jazz.

Day Two, Post-Kline-breaking-my-heart:

I had managed to get myself out of bed, shower, and make some phone calls to a corporate headhunter so I could find a new job. Sure, I'd slept in Kline's t-shirt that night and cried myself to sleep, but at least I was taking a step in the right direction. And it should be noted, I left my cell phone *on* and only checked for missed calls or texts every ten minutes that day.

Baby steps, folks. It was all about the baby steps.

Day three, Post-Kline-breaking-my-heart:

I woke up red-eyed and snotty but had several voicemails with possible job prospects and interview requests. One good thing out of the entire Kline mess, I had a killer résumé and other companies really wanted me on their payroll. I took an interview that day. It was a marketing position for an NFL team, popularly known as the New

York Mavericks. They'd had a recent change in management that had left them in dire straits.

I didn't know anything about football, but I knew marketing. When I sat down for the interview with Frankie Hart, the Maverick's GM, I reminded myself of that very fact. It didn't matter how much I knew about the game; all that mattered was if I could market their franchise in a way that was both profitable and creative.

I showed him slides of the successful campaigns I had done for Brooks Media. I asked questions about their current marketing outlooks and financial profitability. And then I showed Frankie the kind of ingenious skills I had by tossing out a few possible changes that would help build the Maverick name.

He loved my ideas. I left the interview feeling really proud of myself. And I hated that the first person I wanted to call was Kline. I hated that he had become such an important part of my life in such a short amount of time.

After drowning my hate and irritation in three beers and a plate of nachos at the bar up the street from my apartment, my headhunter called with a job offer. The New York Mavericks wanted to hire me and presented their offer with a generous salary and investment plan. I was shocked by their quick trigger. My experiences with getting a response from corporations was *never* this prompt. *But maybe football franchises are different? Who knows?*

I didn't waste time trying figure it out.

Immediately, I accepted the position. Even though football, or any sport for that matter, wasn't my forte, I was excited about the challenge, and honestly, I couldn't afford to sit around for months without a paycheck. Student loans and rent did not accept IOUs.

That night, I slid into bed and checked my phone one last time.

Still no response from Kline.

I clutched my aching stomach and forced my racing mind to sleep.

God, I missed him so much I felt physically ill from it.

Later that week, Cassie surprised me by coming home a few days early from her shoot in San Francisco. This was why she'd always be one of the most important people in my life. I needed her, desperately, and she didn't hesitate to rearrange her schedule to be my shoulder to lean on.

We ordered Chinese, gorged ourselves on chicken fried rice and crab rangoon, and lounged on the couch for a *Friday Night Lights* marathon on Netflix.

If anyone could brighten my mood, it was Tim Riggins, right?

Wrong.

I only got a few episodes deep before I was on the verge of losing it. The second I saw Lyla Garrity smile against Tim Riggins' mouth mid-kiss, the emotional dam was ready to burst.

"Are you okay?" Cass asked as I strode into the bathroom.

All I could do was shake my head. Because I was very far from okay. Probably the furthest I'd ever been from okay.

I stared at myself in the bathroom mirror, my legs trembling and hands gripping the sink like it would somehow give me the strength to fight my pitiful emotions.

Don't cry. He does not deserve your tears.

When that didn't work, I attempted to distract myself by peeing. But I quickly found it didn't serve as any type of distraction, because after about fifteen seconds, I was just peeing *and* crying at the same time. If you'd ever found yourself in that horribly tragic set of circumstances, you'd have understood it was the worst feeling ever. Not only could you not stop peeing, but you couldn't hold back the sobs. Pathetic was the only true way to describe it.

Cass found me in the bathroom that way—pants around my ankles and tears streaming down my cheeks.

"What can I do?" Her face was etched with concern.

"Nothing," I cried, shoving a clump of toilet paper against my nose. My elbows went to my bare knees—yes, I was still on the toilet—and my head was in my hands.

"Have you talked to him since?" She rested her hip against the doorframe.

"Nope. It's been a week and he hasn't tried to contact me. Hasn't called. Texted. Fucking tapped out Morse code. No skywriter or carrier pigeon. Nada. Zip. Zilch." I stared up at her, my chin resting in my hands. "He even knows I was out looking for a new job. How do I know this? Because when the headhunter called with the offer, he also mentioned my prior place of employment provided an amazing recommendation."

"But—" she started to interrupt, but I kept going.

"So, basically, Kline Brooks doesn't give a shit. He saw my letter of resignation. He saw the screenshot with the note I left him. And guess what? He never attempted to contact me. Plus, he was more than happy to give my future job prospect a glowing recommendation. Am I going crazy, Cass? I mean, was I completely deranged and thought Kline and I were way more than what we actually were?"

"No, sweetie," she responded. "I saw you two together and it was more than obvious he adored you."

"Then why did he want to meet up with you? Why did he want to meet up with my best friend?" I stifled a sob, pressing more toilet paper against my eyes. "Obviously, this is nothing against you, Cass," I muttered.

"I know, Georgie. And seriously, you don't have to apologize to me. This entire situation is fucked up, that's for damn sure."

I nodded, blowing my nose.

"How about you get off the toilet and maybe we can find something else to watch? It's safe to say Tim and Lyla are little too much for you at the moment."

"Okay," I agreed through a hiccupping breath.

"I'll give you a minute to get yourself together," she called over her shoulder, moving into the hallway.

I stood by the sink, washing my hands and face. I would not spend another night bawling my eyes out. It was just getting pathetic at that point. Obviously, what I'd thought Kline and I were, and what he'd thought we were, were two very different things.

The voice in my head tried to remind me of the way his blue eyes had looked the night he told me he loved me—tender, vulnerable, his heart resting in their depths.

I told that voice to fuck off. He wouldn't be the first man or woman in the world to profess love to someone they didn't really care about. Believe me, I had seen the threads on Reddit.

People did some horrible shit to one another. Relationships, that were otherwise amazing, could end on the worst of notes. That was not how I had pictured things happening with Kline and me, but that was life, right? Sometimes things didn't go as you planned or hoped they would. Sometimes bad things happened to good people.

Sometimes you just had to suck it up and move on.

I just hated that I missed him as much as I did.

I missed his laugh and his smile and his teasing comments.

I missed my big spoon.

As I wiped my face and hands off with the towel, I glanced down at my pants and noticed a giant grease stain in the crotch region. Normally, I would have just left it, but that night, I needed to *not* feel like the most pitiful person in existence.

I took off the sweats and headed toward my bedroom to grab a new pair of pants.

"Hey, Georgia, what do you think about *The Walking Dead*?" Cass asked from the other end of the hallway.

"Sure, why not?" I shrugged. Zombies seemed like a good, safe choice. How could I think about Kline when I was watching humans turn cannibalistic?

She started to turn back toward the living room but stopped in her tracks. "Hold up…are you wearing boxer briefs?"

Ah, fuck.

"No," I answered, covering my underwear. Well, Kline's underwear.

She flashed a skeptical look.

"Fine!" I threw my hands in the air. "I'm wearing Kline's briefs because I'm pathetic and I miss him and they smell like him!"

"*Smell like him?*" She fought the urge to smile.

"This isn't funny!" I groaned.

She held up both hands. "I never said it was."

I pointed toward her mouth. "Yeah, but you're about two seconds away from laughing your ass off!"

"Honey, you just told me you're wearing your ex-boyfriend's underwear because you miss him and they smell like him. *His underwear.* The material that literally cradles his balls."

"Oh, God," I whined, face scrunching into an agonized expression. "This is definitely a new low point in my life." I leaned against the wall, head falling back. "I'm so desperate for him that I'll take smelling like his sac over not smelling like him at all."

Cass moved toward me and immediately pulled me into a tight hug.

"It'll be okay, Georgie. I promise it'll be okay."

I sniffled back the tears, resting my chin on her shoulder and squeezing her tight.

"Do you want me to try to call him? Maybe it isn't what you think? Maybe he has an explanation?"

"Doubtful," I muttered. "He would have called. If there was an explanation, he would have called." I needed to say the words for myself just as much as I needed to say them for her. Her face reflected my misery perfectly.

"I just want to forget him, Cass. I just want to wake up and not have to go through an entire day of missing him and wishing things were different."

"I know, honey. I know. It'll get easier, but it's just going to take some time." She ran her fingers through my hair. "But you know what?

You're still doing your best to move forward. You went out and got a new job. You're not just sitting around and moping like most people would. I'm really proud of you."

"Thanks for coming home early. I really needed you."

"I will always be here for you. Even when you smell like ball sac," she teased, a smile in her voice, "I'll still be here."

I laughed and groaned at the same time. "God, I know I said they smelled like him but I didn't even really do a sniff check on these. I mean, Kline is usually a clean, well-groomed kind of guy, but for all I know, I'm wearing a post-rugby practice pair."

A quiet laugh escaped her lips. "How about you go take a hot shower while I make those amazing Ghirardelli dark chocolate brownies we have in the pantry? Then we can watch humans turn into zombies and eat one another?"

"I really love you."

"I love you too. Now go rinse the ball sweat off and meet me in the living room."

CHAPTER 34

Kline

A knock at my door picked at my already raging headache with an ice hammer.

"Yeah?" I asked, my voice heavily laden with days' worth of heart-break and aggravation.

The door swung open and closed without delay, Thatch starting on one side and ending on the other.

"Good morning, my old, melancholy friend."

My eyes narrowed in a power-glare. He noticed immediately.

"Right. Not the time, I can see."

Definitely not. I shook my head.

"You're missing out, K. I've got some really fantastic new material I tried out on Gwendolyn last night."

I pinched the bridge of my nose and tilted it toward the ceiling.

Please, God, give me patience right now.

"All right, all right," Thatch conceded. "Not in the mood for Gwendolyn either. I get it."

I sighed.

"I mean, I have a hard time actually *getting* it, you know? I'm pretty much always in the mood for Gwendolyn. Or Amber. Or Yvette."

"Thatch."

"Definitely, Yvette. She does the best work with her tongue."

I had never been less in the mood for his teasing than I was right now. I wasn't sleeping, barely eating. I missed my fucking Benny. I didn't want to hear about any-fucking-body and I didn't want to listen to jokes.

Nonexistent patience tapped out, I scrubbed through the mess on my desk and shoved the bulleted proposal at him. I'd done my best to outline everything I was looking for it to say, but I was no goddamn lawyer. Neither was he, but he'd know what to do.

Wrinkles formed between his eyes as he concentrated and read.

"Are you serious right now?" Thatch asked, shaking the paper in front of him and looking deep into my eyes. He'd never looked at me that seriously. I was obviously scaring him.

"As a fucking heart attack," I confirmed.

"K—"

"Just do it!" I snapped, rolling my neck from side to side and blowing out a deep breath to calm down.

Fuck, I was tense. More so than I'd ever been in my entire goddamn life, and my nerves were shot. If people didn't start doing what I said, right when I said it, I was liable to lose my fucking mind.

He shook his head disdainfully, but either my totally fucked up head was playing tricks on me or the curve of his smile was growing with each pass.

"You are one crazy motherfucker, you know that?" he asked, his lips turned up in a full-on smile. I knew I wasn't making it up now.

I nodded a few times before the intensity of his happiness had me shaking my head. "Why are you smiling like a goddamn lunatic?"

"Because," he said in another uncharacteristic display of seriousness. "I'm fucking thrilled to see you this happy."

Happy? Was he high? I'd never been this fucking heartbroken.

"Dude, I've never been this miserable."

He nearly choked on a laugh. "Yeah, but see, that's the flip side. Crazy in love can only mean one of two things." He ticked each option off on his fingers. "Maniacally happy or butt-fuck desolate. It's one or the other, and it all hangs on the notion of said person loving you back."

He shook the paper in his hands. "I admire you. Fucking up but fucking doing something about it. *This* is what makes a man. Buried to shit in the weeds so he takes out a machete."

I cracked a smile for the first time in two days.

"Just make sure it doesn't take me four fucking years to cut my way out, okay?"

"I'll have the contract ready by Friday at the latest. There's some red tape, but you can thank me again for stopping you from caving to a structure with a board of directors. If you had, you'd have been fucked."

I shook my head.

He turned an ear toward me, cocked a brow, and waved a hand in invitation.

I rolled my eyes but played along. "Thank you, Thatch, for having the foresight to make it possible to make a last-ditch grand gesture in the name of love without being completely fucked."

He bowed slightly, tucking one hand to his stomach and the other to his back. "You're welcome."

My office phone ringing had me rounding the desk and meeting his eyes in question. He waved his permission.

"Brooks," I answered shortly.

"Kline, Kline, Kline." Wes tsked in my ear.

Jesus. I didn't know if I had the energy for both of them.

"This really isn't a good time, Wes."

"It never is—"

True enough.

"But I think you'll want to hear this," he taunted.

Like a starving fish, I took the bait on the line without question. "What?"

"We just interviewed a new employee—"

Goddamn, everyone was making it their fucking mission to annoy me today. New conquests from one and new hires from the next, I had no desire to hear any of it.

"Wes—"

"Pretty little thing. Can't be more than five one, five two, but by God, she's got a body on her."

My stomach jumped with excitement and roiled with sick all at once. He sat silent on the line, just waiting.

"You saw her?"

"Nope, not me. She's in with the GM now. He wanted me to call and look into her references while she's in there, though, seeing as he liked the girl so much and didn't want to waste time getting an offer together."

The words burned my throat as I said them. "You're a fucking moron if you don't hire her."

"No kidding."

I'd never wanted to slit the throat of a friend before, but I guessed there was a time and circumstance for everything.

Thatch looked on as I worked hard to compose myself. Sure, I had a plan, but I had no idea how she'd react. I could very well still be royally screwed.

If that was the case, I still wanted the very best for her.

"Just...look out for her, okay?" My voice didn't even sound like my own, and Thatch looked away. The big fucking ox couldn't stand it either.

"You know I will, dude."

I nodded at the phone, too choked up to speak, and when it made me think of her, a single tear broke through the last goddamn barrier.

CHAPTER 35

Georgia

"Girl, it's pandemonium here! Where in the hell have you been? Do you even know what's going on?!" Dean shouted into my ear, not even offering a simple "Hello" or "How are you?"

I yanked the phone away from my face, my mouth contorting in pain.

Jesus, he was worked up about something. I could picture him pacing, his body vibrating with the need to tell someone whatever gossip he'd grabbed ahold of. If there was one thing Dean was great for when I was at…*yeah, that place I'd rather never speak of again*, it was keeping his ear to the ground and getting the down and dirty scoop on *everything*.

"Give me a minute, Dean. I'm trying to hear you over my ruptured eardrum." I sat down at my new desk, in my new office.

Even though it was a great job with amazing benefits, and the salary alone had me blinking twice when my eyes scanned the contract, it still didn't feel like home. I didn't have that sense of relief I had hoped for. I just felt…numb. I felt like someone had picked me up from my apartment and dropped me off in the middle of nowhere, without a lick of instructions or reassurance.

But I knew I could step up to the challenge and rock this job. I had learned from the best, a man who had started building his multi-billion dollar empire when he was a nineteen-year-old college student at Harvard.

Fuck you very much, Kline Brooks.

"Georgia," he said, ignoring my jab. "Listen. To. Me. Shit is crazy. I think everyone at Brooks Media is losing their ever-loving minds!"

Okay, that definitely caught my attention.

"W-what? Why?"

"Kline's moods revolve around colossally awful and biggest dick around. And *not* in the good way."

I blinked several times, attempting to process that information.

"Georgie? *Hell-o?* Are you still there?"

I swallowed past the shock. "Yeah, I'm here."

"Can you believe it? Kline Brooks, the man who rarely raises his voice and makes a point to be a gentleman, *no matter what,* has turned into the kind of guy his employees want to avoid at all costs. Talk about—"

I couldn't take any more. The last thing I wanted to hear was about Kline and his bad moods.

"Dean, I can't do this," I chimed in before he could continue. The mere thought of Kline had my stomach cursing me for eating a sausage biscuit from McDonald's for breakfast. "I just can't listen to this. I love you. I miss you. But I can't listen to anything related to Kline Brooks."

"Oh. My. Gawd!" he exclaimed. "My spidey sense told me something was off with your rash departure, but I brushed it off, figuring maybe you just wanted to see tight asses in spandex all day. And, girlfriend, I didn't blame you one bit for that. Hell, I would've done a whole lotta things—*emphasis on dirty*—that would've made them football boys blush to snag that job."

"I didn't take the job for the tight asses in spandex, Dean," I muttered.

"Well, I know that now! I can't believe I didn't see this sooner!"

"Didn't see what sooner?"

"You banged the boss." He sighed dramatically. "I am *so* jealous."

"Don't be." I snorted in irritation. "Kline Brooks might be good in bed, but he's even better at tearing your heart to shreds."

"Oh, no he didn't!" I literally heard his fingers give three quick snaps through the receiver. "What happened?"

"One day, when I don't feel like throwing up and crying when I hear his name, I'll give you all of the gory details. I just can't talk about it right now."

"Damn girl. I'm so sorry. It was that bad?"

"Times it by about a thousand and, yeah, it was that bad."

"If I wasn't wearing my new three-piece Gucci suit, I'd strut my ass right into his office and slug him."

That had me laughing. "You've never 'slugged' anyone in your life."

"That's only because I'm a bottom, sweetheart. The men in my life prefer me well-groomed and well-manicured. Slugging would mess up my pretty hands."

"*Wait*...you're a bottom?"

"Well...not *every* time, but yeah, I prefer to be ridden."

I grimaced. "Jesus. That's too much information for nine a.m."

"Pretty sure you asked, doll," he said through a laugh. "I miss having my little diva around. Tell me we can meet up for drinks soon."

"Definitely."

"And if you're curious and want to know what a certain someone—"

I cut him off before he rehashed that argument. "Nope. Not gonna happen. But I will make time for you. Call me this weekend and we'll make some plans."

"Okay, lover. We'll chat later."

After we hung up, I busied myself with the one hundred pages of Excel spreadsheets management had sent my way. I was finding out quickly the asshole who had run this position prior to me didn't give a shit about tracking expenses. The franchise would be lucky if their marketing investments broke even by the end of the fiscal quarter. No wonder he got the boot and they offered me the job at the drop of a hat.

Three soft knocks at the door grabbed my attention.

"Come in," I answered, glancing up from my computer.

A young man in his early twenties, and pretty much too adorable for words, hesitantly walked in. The Breakaway Courier logo was etched on his navy blue polo. His hands gripped a thick envelope.

"Georgia Cummings?" he asked, standing in front of my desk.

"That's me." I got up from my chair. "What can I help you with?"

"I've got an urgent delivery for you." He pulled a small black tablet from his backpack. "Mind giving me a signature?"

"Uh, sure…" I responded, slightly confused. "But are you sure this is for me? I wasn't expecting anything today."

"Definitely for you. I had strict orders to make this my next stop."

My brow rose. "Really?"

He nodded, holding the tablet out for my signature.

"Did they tell you who it's from?" I asked, signing and taking the package from his hands.

He shook his head and shrugged. "No clue, but apparently, it's really important."

"Okay, well, thanks."

I scanned the front of the manila envelope for a clue. Only my name and office address were written across the center, along with the words, *Urgent. Open and read immediately.*

"Have a nice day, Ms. Cummings."

"Thanks. You too," I mumbled.

My fingers slid beneath the lip of the envelope, breaking the seal. Still bewildered, I pulled out a thick stack of legal documents and skimmed the first page.

Business Purchase Agreement

This agreement is made on Monday, October 15th.

Between

1. Kline Matthew Brooks, Brooks Media, (the "Selling Party") and

2. Georgia Rose Cummings, (the "Buying Party")

This Business Purchase Agreement (this "Agreement") is made and entered into on Monday, October 15th, by and between, Kline Matthew Brooks, having its principal office of business at Brooks Media, 15 Fifth Avenue New York, NY ("Seller"), on the one hand, and Georgia Rose Cummings ("Buyer") on the other hand. Buyer and Seller are collectively referred to as (the "Parties") and are sometimes referred individually as a ("Party").

<u>*RECITALS:*</u>

WHEREAS, Seller is the owner of Brooks Media at 15 Fifth Avenue New York, NY, collectively, the ("Business").

NOW, THEREFORE, for and in consideration of the mutual covenants and benefits derived and to be derived from the Agreement by each Party, and for the other good and valuable consideration, the receipt and sufficiency of which are hereby acknowledged. Seller and Buyer hereby agree as follows:

<u>*Agreement to Sell:*</u>

Subject to and in accordance with the terms and conditions of this Agreement. Buyer agrees to purchase the Business from Seller, and Seller agrees to sell the business to Buyer. Seller represents and warrants to Buyer that it has (and Buyer will have) good and marketable title to the Business free and clear of liens and encumbrances.

<u>*Purchase Price and Method of Payment:*</u>

Brooks Media, all stock and investments, and corporations under the Brooks Media name are net worthed at 3.5 billion dollars, along with the ownership of one fluffy cat, Walter Brooks.

Buyer's price will include a 10:00 a.m. appointment at Brooks Media offices on today, October 15th. Buyer will give Seller fifteen minutes

of uninterrupted time to give an explanation to the Buyer. Once the
fifteen-minute time period is up, Buyer may sign the contract and
claim the title, CEO and President of Brooks Media, free and clear.

I stopped reading, staring down at the words in utter dismay.

He was selling—*no*—giving me his company? Just like that? Kline Brooks was just handing over his company and fortune for fifteen minutes of my time?

Oh, and he was tossing in Walter to, what, sweeten the deal?

What in the ever-loving kind of shit was this?

My knees buckled and I was thankful my ass was near the edge of my desk. I gripped the mahogany edge and tried to breathe through the intensifying tightness in my chest.

He had really, truly lost it. What did he think this would solve? Did he think I would just fall into his arms because he was worth over three billion dollars? That he could just buy me back with money?

Fuck. Him.

I would not be bought. *Never.*

He'd messed up. He'd ruined us. Our breakup rested solely on his shoulders, and I was more than ready to throw this stupid, insulting contract back in his face.

In. Person.

I grabbed my purse from my desk and stopped dead in my tracks as I reached the door to my office.

"Well, good morning," Frankie Hart greeted, flanked by a very attractive man who immediately had red flags raising in my mind. I knew his face from somewhere…

"Georgia, I'd like to introduce you to Wes Lancaster, the Mavericks' owner. He's very excited about—"

"*Wes Lancaster?*" I cut in, my jaw practically falling into my purse.

And just like that, the red flags turned to puzzle pieces as everything fell into place. I knew his face because I'd seen his picture, *in Kline's apartment.*

He was the Wes in the Kline, Thatch, and Wes trio. Which, *seriously?* Did they all have to be good looking?

"That's me." He nodded, a handsome smile consuming his stupid, perfect mouth. "Frankie's had nothing but good things to say about you. I'm excited to have you on board with our franchise."

I just stared at him. Speechless. Everything I thought I had earned in the interview went up in flames. I had a feeling I was only here because of Kline. How could I have been so stupid? No one got a call back after an interview that fucking quick, no matter how fast a company wanted to fill the position.

"Tell me, *Wes*, did you consult with Kline before the interview or after?" I snapped.

Obviously, I had lost it. I was standing there calling the owner of the Mavericks out.

My boss. I was calling my boss out on my first day on the job.

"Well..." He cleared his throat, visibly uncomfortable. "He told me I'd be an idiot if we didn't hire you."

I glared. At. My. New. Boss.

"It wasn't just because of him that we offered you the job. Frankie showed me slides from your previous marketing campaigns. He told me your ideas. And I loved them."

For some unknown reason, he seemed more concerned with calming me down than offended by my unprofessional behavior. Because, let's face it, I was being far from professional. So far, I had snapped at him, glared at him, and taken it upon myself to be on a first-name basis with him.

And I knew the reason why he wasn't acting insulted.

Kline motherfucking Brooks.

Wes caught sight of the contract balled up in my hand. "Obviously, we've come at a bad time, and I just remembered I had a nine thirty phone conference." He made a show of looking at his watch. "And it's already nine thirty-two. I better get moving."

Frankie's head tilted in confusion. "But...I thought that wasn't until noon?"

"Nope. It got changed." Wes shook his head. "It was a pleasure meeting you, Georgia," he said, ushering a confused Frankie out of the doorway. He pointedly glanced down at the contract before meeting my eyes again. "I've been friends with him for years because he's one of the good ones. Don't be too hard on him," he added before heading in the other direction.

First, Kline Brooks got me to fall in love with him, before breaking my heart.

Then he called in a favor to his best friend so I'd get a new job, before couriering over a contract to sign his entire business over to me.

Was this real life? Was he fucking joking with this right now?

The shock of meeting Wes was quickly replaced by anger.

I strode out of my office and didn't even bother telling my secretary I would be gone. Hell, with the floor show I had just provided my new boss, I'd have been shocked if they'd let me come back.

But I didn't even care to rehash that horribly awkward meet and greet in my head. I was solely focused on getting to Kline's office and letting him know how I felt about his offer.

Once my feet hit the sidewalk, I hailed a taxi and felt a surge of adrenaline rush through my veins because I was ten minutes away from shoving that ridiculous offer straight up his ass.

CHAPTER 36

Kline

"In all the pining and whining you did over this chick, you failed to ever mention she was scary," Wes said into my ear.

I rolled my eyes. He'd had to listen to me talk about her for a fucking week. That was it.

"Scary?" I asked.

"Fucking *scary*. I wouldn't want to be you right now."

Hope bloomed and blossomed in my chest. "She's on her way?"

"Yep, as we speak. And she. Is. *Pissed*."

I smiled. God, I loved when she was fired up.

"How long ago did she leave?"

"Oh, about twenty minutes or so," he relayed in my ear as bedlam broke out in the office outside my door. I could see Dean running toward the office through the window, a look of pure glee on his face, and Thatch gave me the nod from the other side just as Georgia burst through the door.

She looked like Heaven and Hell and the sole reason for the constant ache in my chest for the last several days.

Hate and love and uncertainty all lined the edges of her face as she warred with herself at the sight of me.

I wanted desperately to pull her into my arms and feel the warmth of her seep into the cold of me, but I knew I had work to do before it was even a remote possibility.

I steeled my features and rounded my desk, leaning into the edge of it with the calm of a man who wasn't mere seconds away from coming out of his skin.

"Good, you're here."

Thatch slammed the door behind her and held it shut. Unable to resist, she ran to it, testing the effectiveness of all of his muscles with three sharp tugs. He didn't budge, one hand on the knob and the other still free to throw her a jaunty wave and a smile through the window.

She growled as she turned to me, stomping her foot in the most adorable way, and then made every effort to kill me with her eyes.

I put everything I had into not smiling and glanced at my watch. It almost worked.

"And for the first time in your life, you're on time."

She pinched her eyebrows together in question and didn't do it lightly. There was real anger there, harnessed between them. She was *raging,* and every single piece of her wanted me to know it.

I nodded to the tattered remnants of the contract, another victim of her wrath, clutched in her hand. "The meeting at ten?" I explained with the lilt of a question. "It was all outlined in the contract."

"Right," she scoffed. "The fucking contract. What kind of a sick fuck does something as mentally unstable as this? Your company?! The whole motherfucking company," she shouted and rambled. "An insane person. You've obviously lost all your marbles. Maybe *Walter* stole them, I don't fucking know."

She shook her head, her wild *brown* hair cascading and swinging and reeling me the fuck in. A handful of days without her, and she'd dyed it again.

She sure was something.

"What I do know is that if the meeting is at ten—" she glanced at her watch "—and it's nine fifty-nine, that makes me *early*."

I bit my lip and pressed my palms into the top of the desk to keep me there.

Her eyes shot to mine at the jagged sound of my whisper. "I'm so sorry, Benny."

Her slender throat jerked with a forced swallow.

"I know I fucked it all up," I admitted, working the edge of my tooth into my bottom lip to keep the pace of my words in check. I wanted to race and ramble like her, but I knew it wouldn't do me any favors.

"But I'm begging you to listen. Watch. Take it all in."

She shook her head and clenched her hands into fists.

"You don't have to change your mind," I offered—a desperate man clinging to whatever scraps he could get. "I want you to." I closed my eyes and prayed as I spoke. "God, Georgie, I want you to." When I opened them again, done with wasting any opportunity to see her, I made sure I didn't even blink. "But all you have to do is this. Be here for a few measly minutes. At least I'll get to fucking look at you. After that, you're free to go."

CHAPTER 37

Georgia

I shook my head, staring at the ground. I needed a reprieve from the havoc that pleading look on his face was doing to me.

"Please, baby, just five minutes of your time."

Immediately, I looked up, glaring at him. "Do *not* call me that."

He lifted both hands in the air. "I'm sorry, Benny."

I cringed. He knew what he was doing, the clever bastard, and that wasn't much better.

"Yeah," I spat. "Me fucking too. I'm sorry about a lot of things."

His face looked pained, but he quickly pushed the emotion down, forcing a soft smile onto his handsome lips instead. "Just fifteen minutes and then you're free to go. I promise."

"Promise?" I scoffed. "I've heard your promises. They're about as empty as my pathetic heart."

He couldn't hide that pain, couldn't push it down like he had before. His eyes creased at the corners, his lips mashed in a tight line. My chest ached as I watched him inhale a shaky breath.

I knew I wasn't being nice and I should have stopped, but I couldn't help myself. Awful words just kept flowing past my lips. Deep down, I wanted to throw knives his way until one of them stuck, cutting him as deep as he cut me.

"I know you're mad and you have every right to be." His voice was calm and composed and it only pissed me off more.

"I don't understand what this is going to help," I spat. "There is nothing you can show me that will change my mind, that will make me trust you again."

He ignored the tight lines of my body language—back stiff, fists clenched at my sides—and guided me to a chair. He gripped my shoulders, urging me to sit down. "Just a few more minutes of your time, Georgia. That's all I'm asking."

I sat, but I didn't want to sit. I wanted to be anywhere else but in that room with him. The simple touch of his fingers on my shoulders, his voice, soft and caressing near my ear, and those blue eyes, fucking slaying me with their pleading intensity—it was too much.

My heart was a rubber band and Kline was pulling too hard. Another glance into his saddened gaze, another tug on my emotions, and it would snap. I would end up doing something I regretted. And I'd be left with nothing.

Screw that. I wasn't going to be convinced. There was no amount of begging and pleading and lines of bullshit that would get me to change my mind. I'd stay strong. I'd watch whatever he wanted me to watch, and then I would leave. We'd both have closure that way.

Once this was over, I was going to be out of that door faster than I'd barged in.

He fiddled with his laptop until the projection screen came to life. I huffed.

Did he really have to make it this dramatic? I could have just watched it, whatever it was, on my laptop—even my phone.

He stood behind me, hands on my shoulders again, and lips near my ear. "I've only lied to you twice. The first time was when I didn't tell you I knew you were Rose."

My head jerked to look at him in surprise and disbelief, a nasty rebuttal on the tip of my tongue, but on the way around, my eyes caught on the video playing on the screen.

Security footage.

It took a minute to recognize the location, but it was Brooks Media's Human Resources. Cynthia's office, to be exact. My brows rose when a crazy person dressed in muddy clothes burst through her doors. He scanned the room until he found what he was searching for. In three quick strides, he was at her filing cabinet, yanking open the drawer and fingers sliding through the files.

The messy hair. The taut, tight muscles of his back, stretching and flexing. And that ass covered in shorts. I knew that body.

My breath caught in my lungs when the camera zoomed in, moving past his face quickly, but not too quick that I didn't recognize the jawline, especially the way it looked before he shaved, covered deliciously with two days' worth of growth.

It was Kline.

My mind tripped into realization that he was filthy and sweaty because he had come from rugby practice. Which also explained why no one else was in the office.

But why was he rummaging through Cynthia's files?

More importantly, why did I need to see this?

I caught sight of the timestamp in the corner. I counted the days in my head. It was a few days after our second date, where he had convinced me to go skinny-dipping at ONE UN. It was nearly eight-thirty in the evening and he was going through one of his employee's offices like a lunatic.

The camera zoomed closer, showing the file in his hands. I couldn't read the label on the edge quick enough before Kline was opening it, his finger tracing down the list of employees names.

The camera zoomed in again, blurry for a second before giving me a clear view. I watched his finger pause on one name.

Cummings, Georgia.

Then it slid across the page and came to a dead stop.

TAPRoseNEXT.

Adrenaline took over. My heart thrashed inside my chest as it furiously pumped the rush through my veins.

He knew.

He knew.

He knew.

It was the only thing my brain could compute.

He was in front of me, squatting down so we were at eye level. "The only other lie I've told you is that I liked you when I knew I was already in love with you."

My vision blurred, an unnamed emotion filling my lids.

Shock? Happiness? Relief? *Love?* I wasn't sure which. I was too overwhelmed.

But my heart, my heart knew what it wanted. It was on an escape mission, frantically trying to pound its way out of my chest, begging to return home.

I blinked, once, twice, three times. The room was clear again, and those blue eyes of his, they were staring at me, intense and pleading and so damn full of love I felt it bursting out of him and into me.

He'd known I was Rose. He had known since a few days after our second date.

Which meant, when he had messaged Cassie, he'd thought he was messaging me.

"W-why didn't you tell me?" I stuttered past the thickness in my throat.

His hand found mine, fingers entwining. "I should've told you. I know I should've told you, but I loved how open you were with me as Rose. I loved how you never held anything back. You were never afraid to tell me what you were thinking or how you felt."

He *would* think that. For the love of Christmas, we'd had a conversation about anal!

"I didn't want to lose that side of you until you were comfortable enough to be that way with me." A heavy sigh left his lips. "When I sent that last message, I thought I was sending it to *you*. I wanted to be open and honest with *you*."

He kissed my hand and then moved it to his chest. "This is yours. It'll always be yours." A frantic, erratic beat vibrated against my palm. "Please, tell me I haven't lost you for good."

I wanted to laugh. I wanted to smile wider than my cheeks would allow. I wanted to jump into his arms and never let go.

But I was scared. The remnants of the past few days had left a scar across my heart. I never wanted to feel like that again. I never wanted to feel so fucking lost.

"I love you," he whispered, his eyes staring into mine, deep and unrelenting. "I love you so much. Please tell me you feel the same."

No longer broken, his words stitched up that last remaining bit of my heart.

"Baby, say something." His voice cracked, desperation highlighting the edges. "Please, say something. Anything. Except for no. Anything but no."

God, he looked broken and defeated. I hated it. I didn't want him to be so sad, so anxious. I wanted him to laugh and smile and be the happy, charming, adorable Kline I had fallen in love with.

"You broke into my company?" I blurted out, trying to take him—take us—back to that place.

He paused, eyes searching mine. "Your company?"

I tilted my head, trying my damnedest to hold back a smile. "You wanted me to sign the contract, right?"

He nodded. "Yeah, I did." His eyes lit up, mouth quirking up at the corner. "But I want you to sign another contract too."

"What?"

He slid a small, black box from his pocket and went down on one knee.

My hand covered my mouth. "W-what are you doing?"

"You know what I'm doing." He gazed up at me, grinning. "Georgia, you are the only person I want to spend the rest of my life with. I knew it from the second you came barreling into my world with your rap lyrics and swollen lips and cute smiles and beautiful laughter. I knew the night of our first date, when you were buzzing on antihistamine and beatboxing about my huge cock, that you were the only woman I wanted. The only person that could make me happy for the rest of my life."

"I *beatboxed?*"

His grin grew wider. "Yeah, baby, you fucking beatboxed. It's one of my fondest memories."

My cheeks heated. There was no doubt in my mind, beatboxing took the cake over Masturbation Camp.

"God, you're so fucking adorable. I can't stand it." He laughed softly, fingers brushing across my cheek. "I can't let you go. I want you, with me, forever. My heart in your hands and you in my arms, that's all I'll ever need." He repeated the words he'd tattooed across my hip. "I said that then because I meant it, and I still mean it now."

Happiness and relief and love, so much love, it bubbled up past my throat and urged tears to spill past my lids. And when I smiled, I tasted the saltiness on my lips.

He brushed the tears from my cheeks with a soft stroke of his thumb. "Georgia Rose Cummings, will you marry me?"

I inhaled a hiccupping breath, smiling down at him.

And then I nodded my head a thousand times.

I was saying, "Yes, yes, yes," over and over again as he slid the ring down my finger and pulled me into his arms.

"I love you," he whispered into my ear.

"I love you too...*so much.*"

He brushed his lips over mine, kissing me soft and sweet, until his tongue slipped past the seam and danced with mine. His fingers slid into my hair, gripping the strands and tilting my head as he kissed me deeper, stronger, pouring everything he was feeling into that perfect kiss.

Kline Brooks had just asked me to marry him.

And I had said yes.

"Baby, will you beatbox your vows at our wedding?" he teased, face pressed against my neck, lips sucking softly.

"I want a prenup," I teased back.

He leaned back, his eyes meeting mine.

"See," I said, unable to stop the smile consuming my face. "I have all of this money now. And I own this awesome business. And I really need to start looking after myself. I don't think you're a gold digger, but—"

He cut me off with another kiss, chuckling against my lips.

"Does this mean you're agreeing to it?" I asked, feigning concern. "Because it's really important to me."

"I'll agree to anything you want as long as I get to keep you forever," he added, a mischievous smirk taking over his mouth. "But first, before we get into all the legalities of your money, we've got some more important things to do."

"Wait…you weren't kidding about signing your business over to me?"

"Fuck no. It's yours."

"Why would you—but that's—" I stuttered, jaw dropping. "Kline, that's ridiculous!"

"The only thing that's ridiculous right now is that we're still standing in this fucking office and not in my bedroom where I can take off that skirt with my mouth."

"Oh," I said, shocked by the sudden change in pace and my body's quick response to that specific pace. My nipples tightened under my blouse, and I was already throbbing in anticipation between my legs.

"Baby, don't get mad, but you're not going to be able to move fast enough in those heels."

"Huh?" I asked two seconds before I was airborne and thrown over Kline's shoulder.

"Kline!" I shouted, gripping his arms for balance.

"Just hold on, Benny," he said, chuckling, as he strode out of his office. One of his hands held tight to my skirt, keeping me covered and safe from flashing the entire office my ass cheeks.

"This is so embarrassing!" I shouted as we passed through the door and into the hallway where most of my former coworkers were gawking at us.

But he didn't care. He was a man on a mission, solely focused on getting us the hell out of there.

"Pam! Hold all of my calls! I'll be busy for the rest of the day!" he called over his shoulder.

"But I thought I owned the company?" I retorted, laughter spilling from my lips.

"I mean, hold all of Georgia's calls! She'll be too busy ri—"

I reached out, covering his mouth.

He laughed against my palm. His finger smashed against the elevator call button, practically breaking the down option.

He didn't waste any time, getting us on and off the elevator in what felt like seconds.

And then we were at his car, Frank opening the door.

Kline tossed me into the back, moving in beside me and telling his driver to get us to his apartment. He was itching with impatience, adding, "And don't worry about the cops. Just gun it. I'll cover the speeding tickets."

I loved that he was that anxious to get me alone in his bed. I loved that he was willing to put everything on the line to prove to me he was the man I had originally thought he was. I loved that he had proposed. I loved that he had carried me out of the office like a man possessed.

I loved him. God, I loved him.

I was so far gone on this man, I felt drunk from it.

I moved over to him, straddling his thighs, gripping his shoulders.

His eyebrows rose, blue eyes twinkling with intrigue.

"I can't wait," I whispered against his lips. "I need you. Right. Now." My finger found the button for the privacy window, shutting it before Kline could refuse.

It was just the two of us in the back seat, Frank's eyes in the rearview mirror no longer visible.

"Fuck, I've missed this." Kline's hands found their way to the hem of my skirt, moving it up my thighs and over my hips. "I was afraid we'd never be here again."

"I've missed this too. I missed you so much."

His heady gaze moved up my body until they found mine again. "You're going to marry me?"

I nodded.

"You're going to move in with me?"

I nodded again, smiling this time.

His cock grew hard and strained beneath me.

"You mean, I get you, every day, for the rest of my life?"

"Yes," I said, a giddy laugh bubbling up from my throat.

"I get live-in Georgia. And beautiful, sleepy Georgia waking up next to me. And singing in the shower Georgia. And dancing around my kitchen Georgia," he rambled, eyes bright with excitement and adoration. "And I get—"

I stopped him with my lips, pressing my mouth urgently against his.

We kissed until we were out of breath, our bodies instinctively moving against one another.

"Baby," he moaned into my mouth. "Not here. Not like this. I want you in our bed." But he didn't stop kissing me, his perfect lips never leaving mine.

Our bed. I smiled, unable to control the love I had for this man.

He chuckled, pulling back to look at me.

"What?" I asked, a crazy, ridiculous smile still consuming my face.

"I love it when you do that."

"Do what?"

"Smile while I'm kissing you. It's like you're too happy to control it."

"I am." My cheeks burned, the goofy grin still intact.

He kissed my nose. "It's like I'm kissing a jack-o'-lantern."

I narrowed my eyes. "You calling me a pumpkin?"

"Yes." His teeth found my bottom lip, tugging gently. "Baby… Georgie…Benny…pumpkin. Mine. All fucking mine."

"Oh, no," I groaned, head falling back in defeat. "Not another nickname."

"Get used to it." He laughed, his tongue soothing the bite. "Remember? I'm Big-dicked Brooks, baby. And I'll call you whatever I want while I'm driving you crazy with my fingers…my mouth…my cock."

And then I was moaning. My eyes rolled back as he kissed down my jaw and sucked at the skin on my neck.

"God, Kline, I ache. I ache so bad right now," I whimpered when his hands slid up my thighs, fingers sliding my underwear to the side.

"Don't worry, soon-to-be Mrs. Brooks." I felt his grin against my skin. "It might hurt, but I'll always make sure it only hurts good."

Cassie

"Wheorgie, we need to go!" I exclaimed, grabbing our bouquets from the table and moving toward the door. We were sitting in the bridal suite, waiting for the ceremony to begin.

"Pretty sure you shouldn't be calling me Wheorgie on my wedding day," she retorted, her eyes still focused on the paper towel her pen was quickly scrawling across.

I stomped my heel, my flower-filled hand going straight to my hip. "Well, you're being a bit of a Wheorgie, considering you're going to be late for your big bridal entrance."

She held up one finger. "Hold on, I have to finish these."

I walked back over to her, glancing down at what she was writing.

"For real? You're writing your vows…like, three minutes before you're supposed to walk down the aisle?"

She shook her head. "No, I'm writing Kline's vows."

"He's too lazy to write his own vows?"

Talk about a broke-ass motherfucker, having his bride write his vows.

"No, we're writing each other's vows."

Oh, never mind.

"God, you guys are so cute that it literally makes me throw up a little in my mouth."

"Ew." She scrunched her nose. "Stop being so gross on my wedding day."

Three hard raps on the door startled us both. "Goddammit, Georgie! Get your ass out here. It's time," her father shouted from the other side.

"Just a minute, Dad!" she called back.

"Ah, shit. You've even got Dick mad," I teased.

"He's just mad because I'm marrying the man of *his* dreams."

We both laughed. It was one hundred percent the truth. Dick Cummings was in love with his soon-to-be son-in-law. He thought Kline walked on water. And after Georgia accepted his proposal, we later found out when Kline had asked her dad for his blessing, Dick had responded,

"Are you sure you want to do that, son? Georgie's a bit of a ballbuster."

Not, "You better protect my baby girl." Or, "If you hurt her, I'll kill you."

Nope. He had basically given him an out, or tried to keep Kline for himself, however you wanted to look at it.

"Finished!" She tossed the pen down and stood up, fluffing her dress. "How do I look?" she asked, taking one last glance at herself in the floor length mirror.

"Like the most beautiful bride I've ever seen." Because she did. Georgia was absolutely stunning.

She turned toward me, pointing an accusing finger in my direction. "Don't start. If you start crying, then I'll start crying."

"I'm not!" My face contorted into that awful expression you get when you're trying to hold back sobs.

"Goddammit, Cass!" Her eyes shimmered with unshed tears.

The processional music started to filter into the bridal room, and we both looked at each other with *Oh, shit!* expressions.

"Georgia! It's time!" her mother sing-songed from the other side of the door.

"Am I really getting married today?" she asked, bewildered, taking the bouquet of white lilies from my outstretched hand.

"Yeah, sweet cheeks, you're really getting married. My little, virginal best friend is all grown up. Marrying the man of her dad's dreams."

She giggled, flipping me the bird in a way only my best friend could pull off in a wedding dress. It was a beautiful dress—elegant mermaid cut with a small train. And it was simple yet blinged out with tiny clear crystals sewn into the bridal-white material.

Georgia had found it at a vintage store—*big surprise*—in Chicago, when we went there for a girls' weekend. It was Vera Wang, which was all Kline's doing. He'd made sure she spent a boatload of money on her dress, refusing to let her come back in the house unless she had drained at least several thousand dollars from their bank account.

Yes, *their* bank account. Even though she refused to sign his ridiculous contract and was adamant on keeping her new job with the Mavericks, he'd made sure to add her to all of his accounts right after she'd said yes. And he'd done this *without* the cushion of a prenup.

If that didn't tell you he was more than sure she was the one, I didn't know what would.

Before we walked out of the bridal suite, I wrapped her up in a tight hug.

"I'm so happy for you. You deserve all of this happiness and then some."

"I love you, Cass."

"I love you too. Now, let's go get you hitched!" I hooted, opening the door.

The wedding party was small, but it was perfect for them. Wes, Thatch, and Will were Kline's groomsmen, while Dean and I were Georgia's bridesmaids.

I walked down the aisle with Dean and took my place on the opposite side of the groomsmen. I couldn't help but notice the intrigued yet slightly salacious smile I received from Thatch. I assumed it was my tits' doing because my cleavage looked pretty damn fantastic in the little black dress Georgia had chosen for me.

And I didn't miss how delicious Thatch looked in his tux. I eye-fucked that Jolly Green Giant for a moment, moving from his brown eyes, to the broad shoulders filling out his jacket *like they fucking owned the joint*, to the noticeable bulge—not, *I'm the weirdo with a boner at a wedding* bulge, but *I'm packing* bulge—in his pants, and then back to his mouth.

Man oh man, those lips looked like they could do *things* (to my puss-ay).

> *Hey, cool your jets. It doesn't count as wedding inappropriate if it's in parentheses.*

Seriously, I'd Thatch that.

The quartet of violins and harps Georgia hired for the ceremony music abruptly stopped. I glanced around, not sure what was happening. This definitely wasn't on her schedule.

Kline looked toward the side of the room and nodded at a woman with a guitar. She smiled, adjusted the microphone near her mouth, and started to strum a song that wasn't the planned "Bridal Chorus."

The crowd stood, turning toward the back doors.

And when they opened, there stood my beautiful best friend, her arm tucked into her father's, her mouth morphed into the biggest smile I'd ever seen.

Every wedding I had ever been to, while everyone was watching the bride, I always snuck a glance at the groom. When my eyes found Kline's face, my heart damn near skipped a beat. Though a sight far more masculine, his smile mimicked Georgia's in all the ways that counted. He looked like a man who had just received everything he'd ever wanted. And it was obvious that everything was Georgia, walking straight toward him without looking back.

I had never seen a man look so in love.

The woman started to sing, softly playing her guitar, and that's when I put the pieces together. It was a slowed down, acoustic version of "Some Kind of Wonderful."

Their song. The song Georgia would always associate with Kline. And he'd done it, knowing how much that song meant to her, to them. Somehow, that sneaky bastard had arranged it on the sly.

It took every ounce of strength for me not to start crying. I was overwhelmed by them. My best friend and the man who'd swept her off her feet. They were happy. They were in love. And God, they were so perfect for each other. The world wouldn't be right if they weren't together.

As Georgia got closer, she was mouthing the words to the song, gazing at Kline.

And when she reached him, Dick hugged them both, and Kline pulled her into his arms. She whispered something into his ear and he nodded, his face pressed against her neck. And then he leaned back, staring down at his bride, and said, "You're so beautiful."

I'm pretty sure every woman in attendance swooned. I sure as hell did.

They stood before the minister, hand in hand, ready to profess their love and the rest of their lives to one another.

The minister greeted the attendants and proceeded to say nice, beautiful things about the happy couple. He was actually one of Dick's closest friends, which was probably a good thing, considering most of the people at this wedding tended to toss out the F-word more often than not.

And when the minister announced it was time for the vows, Dick cheered, "Hell yeah! Let's do this!"

See what I mean? Good thing he knew the kind of room full of morons he was walking into.

Kline pulled a neatly folded piece of white paper from his inside jacket pocket while Georgia slid the balled up paper towel out of her cleavage.

They handed each other their vows.

He glanced down at his tattered version and started laughing. "You finished these about two minutes before you walked down the aisle, didn't you, Benny?"

"I'll never tell," she said through a giggle.

He chuckled again. "God, I love you."

"It's not time for that!" Thatch yelled behind him. "Vows first!"

The crowd laughed.

"Okay, I guess I'll go first," Kline announced, unwrinkling the paper towel.

"Georgia Rose, I promise to trust you even when you deviate from our grocery list and convince me to buy six boxes of Dunkaroos and three bottles of wine I know you'll never drink.

"I promise to give you all of the love and support that I don't give Walter. Also, I promise to be nicer to Walter." He paused, glancing up at her and shaking his head with a giant grin.

"I'm not saying that."

She tapped the towel. "You have to. They're *your* vows, remember?"

He turned toward the attendants, letting everyone else in on the secret. "We wrote each other's vows, if you couldn't already tell."

"I warned you, Kline!" Dick shouted toward him. "Ballbuster."

"Daddy!" Georgia scolded. "There will be no talk of balls during my wedding ceremony."

The room filled with more laughter.

Once everyone settled down, Kline cleared his throat and

continued, "He's a really good cat. The best cat. Man, I sure love Walter." He rolled his eyes, but said it nonetheless.

"I promise I'll never keep anything from you because there are no secrets between us. I vow to love you through the difficult and the easy. I promise to never put you or myself in danger. This includes me never drinking lime juice with my scotch ever again." He winked at her.

"I vow to never change from the amazing man that I already am. I promise to never lose my huge, strong, kind, and determined heart. I will never stop teasing you, making you laugh, or flashing smoldering blue eyes your way. I will always greet you with the smile that's only yours. And when it's just the two of us at home, I vow to only wear boxer briefs around the house. No matter what I'm doing, I'll either be naked or just wearing boxers." His blue eyes found hers, his brows waggling in agreement as a few women in the crowd hooted some catcalls.

"And I vow to listen, for as long as it takes for you to feel heard. I vow to be your unrelenting cheer squad on the days it feels too much. I vow to pick the important fights with you, especially when I know you're selling yourself short or not being treated with respect.

"I vow to spend the rest of our lives laughing, smiling, going on crazy adventures, and most importantly, loving each other through the good times and the bad. And if there are bad times, I promise the kind of makeup sex that has your blouse buttons hitting the floor."

And on the last sentence, he stared deep into her eyes. "I vow that I will love you, Georgia, every day, for the rest of forever."

Georgia sniffled a few times, and I handed her a tissue to wipe her eyes.

"Don't cry, TAPRoseNEXT," Kline whispered, brushing away a few tears. "You may have written those vows, but I'll stand by every last word."

She giggled at his sincerity, but I wasn't used to it, and therefore, found myself completely ill prepared. I dabbed at fresh tears with the back of my hand as she unfolded the paper in her hands.

"Kline Matthew, I stand before you today to become your wife." She paused for a second, looked up at him and then back at the paper. "I think everyone here knows that already, but I've got this feeling that you really wanted to hear me say it."

She turned to the crowd and remarked, "I'm not improvising." She turned the paper toward them. "It really says that."

Everyone laughed and he nodded. "Keep going, Benny."

She looked back to the scrawl of his words.

"From this day forward, I am yours and you are mine. I promise to remind myself of this most important fact every day and smile when you do it for me. I promise not to give up or run away when you make the kinds of mistakes that every man makes, and I promise to use my heart, rather than my ears, to really hear you."

Sweet cookies and dildos, this guy had a knack for saying the right thing.

"I promise to rap my way through our days and beatbox for you each night because it's times like those when I'm so..." She paused and glanced to the crowd. "I'm so...effing...adorable you can't even stand it."

Her amused eyes met his again. "You really wrote the F-word in my vows?"

He shrugged. "Adorable wasn't enough."

She shook her head, smiling, and continued, "I promise to keep you on your toes with my hair and my words and always stand up for myself with the backbone you love and expect."

"And, I promise to be late as often as I want because you'll always be waiting. But when it comes to lovin'—" Georgia stopped midsentence, giggling at her groom. "Kline, I'm not saying that in front of the minister."

"Baby, you have to. They're *your* vows, remember?"

She leaned forward, whispering something into his ear. His mouth twisted into a devilish grin and he whispered back.

Georgia turned toward the attendants. "Please feel free to cover your ears during this part."

She cleared her throat, cheeks pink, and said, "I'll come early and I'll come often because the power of Big-dicked Brooks compels me."

"I knew it!" I shouted. "I told you!"

Pffft. I knew my cockdar wasn't on the fritz.

Everyone in the crowd was a mixture of laughing, clapping, and wolf whistling.

Once we settled down, Georgia gazed at Kline like she would happily crawl inside him and stay there and said the rest of her vows.

"But most of all, I vow to love you with everything that I am, no matter the circumstances, because I know, from the very depths of my tiny, perfect being, that you will be there, doing your best to love me more."

And when the minister told Kline to kiss his bride.

He motherfucking kissed his bride so good it made *my* toes curl.

Thatch

"Congratulate me, boys," Kline toasted with a glass of scotch in the air, the happiest I'd seen the fucking sap in ages.

His body was here with us, but his mind and his eyes were on his boogeying bride on the other side of the dance floor. The space was fairly small. At least, this room known as The Greenhouse was. They'd rented out the entirety of The Foundry out of nothing more than necessity. Kline liked to think his life was boring and normal and that no one cared at all, but the truth was they did. They cared *a lot*. And keeping such an important event completely private was the only way to maintain his happy little bubble of make-believe.

"That," he said with a slightly tipsy gesture, "is *my* wife."

I laughed and slapped him on the shoulder, exchanging smiles with Wes behind his back. I raised my eyebrows in question, and Wes gave me a pursed-lip nod of agreement.

"Go get her," I urged simply, knowing he wanted to be with her a million times more than he wanted to stand here and shoot the shit with us.

And, regardless of what people might have thought they knew about me, that was fine by me. My oldest, closest friend had found it. Found *her*.

Always loyal and loving, I couldn't think of anyone who deserved it more than he did.

"Benny!" he yelled, pulling her attention from the crowd of women around her to him. "Make room on the floor. I'm coming for my dance!" The wattage of her smile was blinding.

I stood next to Wes and watched as Kline danced his way over to her, pulling her into his arms and handing off his drink to the first, unsuspecting free hand he came to so he could hold on to her with both hands. Hands to her jaw and lips to hers, he kissed her in a way that I felt all the way in my stomach.

"Good God, he's a goner," Wes remarked, sinking into the wall and tipping his drink to his lips.

"Yep," I agreed, thinking about the vows they'd exchanged during the ceremony.

"It's nice," I added without thought—because it was.

Wes laughed way harder than I thought was appropriate. "Jesus. Who are you and what have you done with Thatcher Kelly?" He morphed his face into what he thought was a good impression of me and mocked, "It's nice!" with a wobble of his head.

I punched him hard enough in the shoulder that he stopped laughing abruptly.

"Ow! Fuck, Thatch! Christ."

"It *is* nice," I told him again, further delving into the teachings of his lesson. "Take fucking note from your most experienced of friends. Multiple flavors of pussy are great, but what our fucking goner of a friend found is better."

He looked at me like he didn't know what to make of me.

"The two of them stood up in front of God and us and committed to each other forever with enough trust in each other to speak one another's words rather than their own. *That*, motherfucker, is love."

Powerful speech performed, lesson conveyed, I felt content with my message until Wes went and fucking ruined it.

"Jesus, fuck, The Foundry must be some sort of *Twilight Zone*. I don't even know who you guys are anymore," he teased, chuckling into his bourbon.

"One day, Lancaster, when it happens to you, I will remember this moment." I drained the rest of my drink and walked away.

Moving away from the bulk of the crowd, I sat down at a table that was mostly empty. My phone buzzed in my pocket.

I thought it might be the tattoo shop, checking in to see if I'd be there tonight, but instead, I found a number I didn't recognize.

Unknown: She's a lot older than you normally go for, but it looks like you've got a chance.

I looked around, wondering what the fuck whoever this was was talking about. Quickly, I typed out a message.

Me: Who is this?

A reply came almost immediately.

Unknown: Your mom.

I was no less confused, but hell if I didn't fucking laugh.

Me: WTF. Who is this?

Unknown: The hot bitch at the head table.

I looked up across the dance floor as the crowd parted in front of me. Cassie, the craziest bitch I'd ever encountered and Georgia's maid of honor, sat all by her lonesome at the wedding party's table, one leg cocked and her bare foot in the chair beside her. She popped her eyebrows in a mischievous challenge.

This chick had balls, sitting there by herself, just kicked back and relaxed with zero fucks given about it. Fuck, Cassie's balls might have been bigger than mine, and that was saying something.

Me: How'd you get my number?

Unknown: I have my ways.

Cryptic. Another message came right on its heels.

Unknown: But good luck with that pussy tonight.

I looked at her as she raised her glass in cheers and then looked at the area around me. Not even one prospective lay stood out in the nearest twenty-foot radius.

Me: What pussy?

Unknown: The silver-haired cutie beside you.

I looked to my left and then to my right, and what I saw had me smiling like a lunatic. Kline's grandma, Marylynn, sat clapping along to the heavy beat of the music and swaying back and forth. She was cute, but she was no less than eighty-five years old. I looked down to my phone and typed as quickly as my big thumbs would allow.

Me: You should be ashamed of yourself. This is Kline's grandma. But I'll be sure to tell her you find her attractive.

I shifted my gaze from the phone to her table as soon as I was done, but when the dancing crowd finally moved out of the way, she was gone. Gone from sight and gone from my phone, but she'd found a home somewhere else—stuck in my head.

THE END

TAPPING HER

A BILLIONAIRE

Bad Boys

NOVELLA

max monroe

To the extra five pounds we gained while writing this novella: Fuck you.

And to donuts: You're delicious. Don't change.

CHAPTER 1

New York, Thursday, April 20ᵗʰ, Early Morning

Cassie

Georgia: Good Night from Bora Bora!

Ah, Georgia. My beautiful, sweet, funny, newly married, currently annoying as *fuck* best friend.

Her lovely text included a photo of her and her hot husband, lounging in the tropical sun, on a private beach in Bora Bora. They'd been on their honeymoon for no more than three days, and I'd already received fifteen nauseatingly happy messages.

> **Me: You. Are. An. Asshole. Another picture of you and Big Dick at the beach, and I'll drop Walter off at the Humane Society.**

> **Georgia: If you fuck with my cat, I will disown you.**

> **Me: Your cat is Satan. Seriously. I think the devil was reincarnated inside him. He's evil.**

Did I fail to mention that while Georgia and Kline were on their honeymoon, I had been given the responsibility of taking care of Walter? And not in the cool way that a mobster would. Georgie actually wanted me to look out for his *well-being*. Well, Thatch and I had been given that task, but I was the one at their apartment, spending time with their asshole of a cat.

Georgia might've thought he was a big sweetheart, but he was the opposite—a big feline dick. That cat's life mission was to make everyone else's life a living hell. And he did it often. So far, in the span of forty-eight hours, he'd pissed on my favorite pair of Chucks and left a generous gift of his shit—*yes, his actual cat shit*—inside my overnight bag.

Which explained why I was tits out, standing around in only my thong and rummaging through Georgia's closet. Fresh out of the shower, I needed something to wear that didn't smell like feline feces.

"Thanks a lot, douchenozzle," I said out loud, looking directly at Walter—who was currently lounging on their bed, licking himself. "Nice. Real classy, Walnuts."

He just stared back, irritated and completely aloof, all at once. I guess that's the look you get when a good fifteen hours of your day is used up by licking the rim of your own asshole. He eyed me for a solid ten seconds without a single blink and then strode out of the room, kitty paws tip-tapping across the hardwood floor. I couldn't put my finger on the exact reason, but everything about the way he moved screamed *fuck you*.

"Yeah, walk away, buddy! Walk the fuck away!" I shouted toward him as my phone vibrated on top of the dresser next to the closet.

Georgia: He is not evil! He's just a little hesitant with new people. He'll warm up to you.

Me: Ohhhhh…so when he pisses on my shoes, that's just him being "hesitant"? Or is that him "warming up to me"?

Georgia: Another 24 hours and you guys will be buddies. I promise.

Me: He shit inside my overnight bag, Wheorgie. This tells me that your promises mean nothing. I hope you don't mind me going through your closet. Because I already am.

Georgia: You can wear anything but my favorite LuLaRoe leggings.

Damn, she makes it too easy. Looks like hot dog leggings will be worn today.

For all I knew, those leggings were an inside joke about Kline packing a foot-long in his pants, but whatever. I'd make those stretchy pants my bitch. Hell, maybe I'd take a leisurely seventy-mile jog in Central Park just to make sure my twat left her mark.

Gross? Definitely.
But should I remind you her cat has
been using my personal belongings as
his litter box?
Point made.

Georgia: Wait. Why did you bring an overnight bag to my apartment?

Me: Because I'm watching The Asshole.
Georgia: That still doesn't answer my question. We just asked you to check in on Walter and feed him twice a day, not move in.

Me: Yeah, but I can't rummage through your kinky sex box at my apartment.

This was me calling Georgia's bluff. I had no idea if she had a freak-a-leek box of goodies, but I was real curious. She had always been a bit reserved when it came to sex. I mean, she was a virgin up until she let Big Dick inside. Which honestly surprised the shit out of me. It was how I knew, when she gave it up to Kline, he would become a permanent fixture in her life.

To quote Phoebe Buffay, *Kline Brooks was Georgia's motherfucking lobster.*

Okay, so the profanity was all mine. The lobster part was a la *Friends*.

Needless to say, I was the over-sharer in our relationship. Georgia had nailed down the "I don't kiss and tell" role from the very beginning. And I couldn't deny the enjoyment I got from pushing her boundaries and making her blush.

Georgia: Do NOT go through my shit, Casshead.

Me: But this vibrator looks really cool. And a ball gag? Shit, G, I didn't know you had it in you. Color me impressed. Kline's dick looks good on you.

Georgia: Shut. Up. I'm done with this conversation.

Holy mother of awesome. My best friend had a stash full of sex goodies somewhere in her apartment, and I was going to find it.

Me: I was kidding. But now, I'm not kidding. Canceling my "get rid of Walnuts" mission. New mission: Find Georgia's box of freak. I'm so proud of you.

Georgia: Greetings from Bora Bora, asshole!

Attached to that text? A lovely picture of Georgia flipping me off while she stood on a deserted beach, twinkling water and her fucking beaming, handsome husband behind her.

Me: One question before I start my search in your closet. Do you clean your bag o' dildos after each use? Because if you don't, you'll need to pick up a new box of magnums on the ride home. I don't have any latex gloves, and one of these isn't big enough for my whole hand.

Georgia: You've already gone through Kline's nightstand?!

Me: Oh, come on. That's the first place you ALWAYS look. Does Kline really fill the entire magnum? Because if he does, I'm convinced his cock is a mythical unicorn.

Georgia: I'm not discussing my husband's penis with you.

Me: Haha! I could literally hear you say the word penis like a schoolmarm. "Peeee-nis."

Georgia: I'm disowning you when I get back from my honeymoon.

Me: Just remember to pick up milk too on your way home. You're almost out.

Georgia: Since you've made yourself at home. House rules: NO sex in my bed.

Me: Okay, but those rules start right now, right? Yesterday shouldn't count.

Don't worry, I'm not that much of a weirdo. I don't make a point of using my best friend's bed as my own personal brothel. But it's too funny not to make her think that.

Georgia: WASH MY SHEETS.

Me: I love you, Wheorgie. Go back to enjoying your honeymoon and riding Kline's peee-nis with the glow of the sunset behind you. I'll take care of everything here like it's my own.

Georgia: Ugh. I love you too, Casshead. Replace everything you destroy.

I swear, my best friend was far too easy to rile up. I probably shouldn't get that much amusement out of it, but I did. She pulled off adorably embarrassed like no one else. And I wasn't the only one who noticed. Kline used it to his advantage, *frequently*. It was one of the reasons I loved him. He knew Georgia better than she knew herself sometimes, and he also respected her, cherished her, and treated her like a goddamn princess—all the requirements for avoiding genital mutilation, courtesy of me.

Since I was alone and there was absolutely nothing more fun than walking around without a bra on, I stopped my clothes search and placed my phone in their speaker dock. Once my playlist was set, it was time to search this place like I was a key investigator for the FBI.

Rhianna's "Cockiness" was speaking to me, echoing throughout the apartment and getting my exploration mojo off to the right start.

"I love it when you eat it," I sang, shaking my hips to the seductive beat and moving back toward Georgie's closet.

And then, in my peripheral vision, my eyes caught sight of a large, looming figure in the doorway.

"Ahhhhh!" I screamed. "Holy son of a whore tramp!"

CHAPTER 2

Thatch

Fucking fuck.

I mean, fuck me.

No.

Titty-fuck me.

"Helloooo?" Cassie's perfect, heavy tits said while they swung back and forth, free from cover and uninhibited by clothing or bra. "Hey, fuckface!" they yelled. "Are you perverted or just dumb? The normal amount of time to stare at someone uninvited passed like forty-five seconds ago."

God, not only were they the perfect size and shape, they were fucking smart. Speaking in full sentences and shit. This had to be the most talented pair of tits I'd ever encountered. They sounded a little agitated, but I was pretty sure that was just a side effect of the blood roaring in my ears.

"Ow!" I flinched as Cassie grabbed my nipple through the fabric of my dress shirt and twisted. "Jesus! What the fuck?"

"What the fuck? I'll tell you what the fuck. You've been staring at my chest for the last two minutes!"

I watched as her mouth moved, even heard it form the words, but try as I might, I couldn't *not* notice that *they* still hung there, uncovered in all their perfect, creamy, pink-tipped glory. When they swung toward me again with her lunge, I forced my eyes back to her wildly beautiful face.

"Look, I'm sorry. But they're out and they're perfect and they were fucking *talking* to me."

I pressed a hand to the uncontrollably swelling cock in my pants. She raised an eyebrow in response.

On my way to work, I'd decided I should do my bit for the cat, see if I needed to order an exorcist, that kind of thing, but I wasn't expecting tits. And my cock certainly wasn't expecting them to be so perfect. But, first thing in the morning like this, it was no wonder I couldn't control his desire to crow.

"My tits don't talk." She turned her back, and I trained my eyes hard enough that they almost bore their way through to the other side. Voice muffled a little by the still-playing music, she went on. "They bounce and swing and wrap just about perfectly around a worthy cock, but they don't speak."

"I don't believe you," I argued. "They spoke to me, and I'll take that reality to the grave."

"You're fucked in the head, you know that?" she asked as she sauntered brazenly across the room to Kline's closet and pulled it open. The light went on, illuminating the space, and she bent over, her bare ass up and out, and started rummaging around.

"What are you doing?" I asked, giving the base of my cock a healthy squeeze in an attempt to choke the overzealous life out of it.

"Looking for Georgie and Big Dick's box of kink," was the mumbled reply.

I turned away and crossed the room, eager to find some kind of solace.

"Oh. It's under the bed," I said as I closed my eyes tight and flopped back onto it. Hard and hurting, my dick had taken over, and there was absolutely no hope of a resolution until I stopped looking at all of her flawless skin.

"Oh, shit," she squealed. The sound of her running toward me gave me a mental image of her body in motion that would likely be the largest test of willpower my eyes ever had or would receive. I stayed frozen, hand locked on my easily manipulated dick and eyes sealed completely.

"How the hell did you find this before I did?" she complained from below me, the bed shaking slightly from her effort to pull out the box of phallic treasure.

"I found that shit months ago, about two days after they moved in together."

She pulled the box out, dumping it on the bed right beside my head and tossing her body below it, right next to my hip. At the feel of some piece of her skin brushing against my hand, my eyes gave up the fight and popped open faster than a jack-in-the-box.

"Good God," I cried when my vision returned. She was on her hands and knees, digging through the pile of dicks and vibrators beside my head, and her naked tits were no more than ten inches from my lips. "Am I dead?" I whispered, staring at the pink of her nipples and licking my lips.

Is this heaven or hell?

My hand wouldn't be denied, reaching out to test my location. When the soft, full, *fucking perfect* flesh of her breast met my greedy palm, she yelped, smacking me first on the hand and then on the face.

"Ouch!" I groaned before confirming, "Hell."

Definitely hell.

"What?" she snapped. "You can look, but you'll have to do a lot more to earn the right to touch."

My lips pursed in thought. "I could—"

"Not today, asshat!" she yelled. "Come on, help me clean this shit up."

In shock, I couldn't do anything other than what she asked,

touching my best friend's things—things I swear I'd never otherwise touch—and completely abandoning thoughts of being on time for work or accomplishing anything I was supposed to that day.

And yes, I'm sure I wouldn't normally touch them. Look, sure.
Touch, no.

Cassie left me to finish up and crossed the room back to Georgie's dresser, my gaze following her as she did. She was one of the hottest women I'd ever seen and the first ever to stand in front of me naked with the same confidence as she would if clothed. I didn't know where she found that kind of self-esteem, and I wasn't going to ask. The first rule of dealing with a woman without her clothes on is to never ask her anything that could lead to a change of heart.

I slid the box under the bed as she slipped a tight T-shirt over her head, sans bra, and stepped into a pair of what had to be the most ridiculous leggings I'd ever seen.

"Are there fucking hot dogs on those pants?"

"Yeah," she deadpanned, turning to face me and pulling her crazy hair into a sloppy ponytail. As her nipples pushed through the thin cotton, I realized no one would give a goddamn what was on her bottom half.

She turned for the hall, stepping out of the room without a word, and I followed. I'd have followed her into a volcano at this point.

And yes, I am fully aware that this kind of blind arousal
will be my downfall.

"Hey, Walnuts!" she called when we made it to the living room, searching the space with her strikingly blue eyes. They were so vivid they were nearly violent, reaching out and smacking you every time they turned your way.

The contrast between them, her creamy white skin, and the rich chocolate of her hair was arresting. Like God had a sense of humor when he made her, pasting together all the things that shouldn't go well together into a singular messy canvas, but when he was done—her magnificently wild radiance shone *up* to heaven. The joke was on him.

"Yo! Walnuts!" she called again. "I'm talking to you, dick cat! Food's on!"

She turned to me with her eyebrows pinched together, and the simple gesture was enough to break me out of my stupor.

I joined in the search, scanning the room endlessly, and unfortunately, my eyes landed on the open apartment door at the same time Cassie's did.

Shit.

"You idiot!" she yelled, charging for the door and tearing ass out into the hall.

I followed hot on her heels, pulling her to a stop before she got to the stairwell door and spinning her to face me.

When I'd come in and heard the music, I hadn't thought of anything but finding the source. I wasn't used to having a pet, so closing doors wasn't naturally ingrained. It probably would be now.

"You lost Walter!" she screamed immediately.

"You don't know that," I argued. "He could still be in the apartment somewhere."

"He's not! That little ass-licker does a lot of stupid things, but he doesn't skimp on meal times. If you'd helped me feed him at all, you would know that!"

"Cass, calm down."

"I will not calm down!" she screeched.

I reached out to lay a reassuring hand on her arm at the same time another tenant stepped out of the adjacent apartment.

Prim and proper, the conservative woman wrinkled her nose at Cassie's outfit and pinched her eyes at me. "All this yelling. I thought this apartment building had a better handle on class."

Cass turned in a flourish, cocking her head to the side and getting right in the offender's face. "I will go Holly Holm on your ass!"

I jumped into action, wrapping my arms around her and copping a small feel in the process. She burned me with her eyes, and I tried not to smile, but as I turned back to the *still open* apartment door, Walter scurried out like a shot and turned the corner in a flash. Releasing Cass, I traveled the space in as few steps as my giant legs would allow, but when I rounded the bend, not a whisker or a hair remained.

Ah, *fuck*.

The dick cat hadn't been missing, but he sure as fuck was now.

CHAPTER 3

Georgia

Glancing at the clock on the bedside table, I could see 7:00 a.m. glowed red and bright. My internal clock was still on East Coast time, and I had started a bad habit of napping in the midafternoon sun for the past three days. Sounds of the ocean filtered through the open terrace doors, a warm breeze brushing across the room and filling it with aromas of salt water and sand.

Stupidly happy. Thoroughly well-fucked. Blissfully sated.

No doubt, I was all of those things.

The sole reason lay beside me, sprawled out on his back, with soft, white sheets barely covering his deliciously naked form. Kline was sound asleep, hair mussed up and a small grin etched across his full lips. He had passed out that way after round three—*or was it four?*—and that little expression of appreciation had stayed intact for the past hour. Since round four had been an oral experiment in showing him just how much I loved him, I'd say his sexy grin was a direct result of my mouth.

We had been on our honeymoon for three days, and I still

needed to pinch myself to believe it was real. That he—my hand-some, charming, undeniably romantic *husband*—was real. We still had another week and a half to enjoy our privacy in Bora Bora, but I was already feeling grumpy over the idea of returning home and leaving our little slice of tropical heaven.

I grabbed my phone from the nightstand and scrolled through numerous emails. One from my boss, Kline's good friend Wes, urged a quick response.

To: Georgia.Brooks@Mavericks.com
From: Wes.Lancaster@Mavericks.com

Georgia,

I hope you and Kline are enjoying your honeymoon. If you can spare a few minutes away from your husband, I'd be forever in your debt if you could take a glance at this contract. If he gives you grief, just send him my way. I'd really like your opinion on this offer before we pull the trigger.
Wes Lancaster
President and Chief Executive Officer
New York Mavericks
National Football League

The contract in question was for a sports drink campaign. I couldn't deny the drink tasted like gasoline, but the VITAsteel brand had been growing in popularity over the past three years and had made quite the name for itself in the sports industry. Professional athletes across the globe fell over themselves to land an endorsement with this company. And even though the Mavericks were knocked out in the first-round playoffs last year, I had managed to get some raised eyebrows of intrigue over at VITAsteel when I proposed a contract that included our quarterback *and* offensive line.

See? I was starting to understand football lingo. Of course, I still nicknamed all of our players, but no one needed to know that.

I read through the contract and sent a quick email back to Wes, highlighting the things I didn't like. The offer was good, but it could be better. First rule of business, always be prepared to negotiate and *never* take the first offer that's sent your way. My business-savvy husband taught me that.

Considering I was getting emails from my boss during my honeymoon, I'd say it was obvious work was about to get a bit intense for me. The New York Mavericks were in the midst of a marketing overhaul and rebranding, and since I was leading this insane task, my job would require more than a simple, forty-hours-a-week schedule. Late nights, gallons of coffee, and a shitload of frequent flyer miles were about to fill my future.

I had a feeling Kline wasn't going to swallow this pill all that well.

My husband was understanding to a fault, but he had gotten used to me being by his side at the office for the early part of our relationship, and even after I had taken the job with the Mavericks and we had managed to find our way back to one another, my work hours were manageable. He'd been making a real effort to leave work at five o'clock, and I'd done the same. But my workload was about to increase tenfold. Who wants to hear that kind of news from their brand-new wife?

And if I was being honest, I wasn't all that thrilled with the idea of less time with him either. I hated it, actually. But my career was important to me. The drive to pave out my own kind of success ran deep. I wanted, no, *needed,* to accomplish the goals I had set for myself.

Finding the right balance and some serious understanding on my husband's part was going to be key in making it all work without one of us going crazy. We had talked about my soon-to-be demanding schedule and traveling with the team for away games, but with the craziness of the wedding, we never really had a chance to sit down and map it all out.

That conversation would come, but right now, in this perfect little moment, other things would have to *come* first. Big-dicked kind of things.

Before I got down and dirty with Kline, I glanced at the clock again, and knowing that it was six hours later in New York, I sent Cass a quick text message.

Me: How's Walter?

Cassie: He's great! Eating, shitting, pissing, and just doing his normal cat thing around your apartment.

My eyebrows rose at that response. I had expected something more like, "*He's a fucking asshole, but still alive.*" Maybe he had finally warmed up to Cass?

Cassie: And I gotta say, the amount of kinky sex shit you've got stored under your bed is INSANE. My Wheorgie is definitely letting her freak flag fly.

Ugh. I debated telling her the truth about the giant box of kink under our bed. They were all generous and, no doubt, weird gifts from my mother. Since we got engaged, Kline and I had been receiving brand-new toys on the regular from Dr. Savannah Cummings. My crazy mother was convinced we needed to explore our sexuality together, in *every* possible way. Anal beads, ball gags, twelve-inch dildos, you name it, and it was shipped to our apartment.

Thatch found the box while helping us move in, and I swear to God, he wouldn't shut up about it. Hell, he still sent me random text messages asking if I wear Ben Wa balls to work.

The thing my mother didn't understand was that I didn't need thousands of kinky toys when I had Kline. A vibrator was no match for his PhD in Sexual Prowess. I'd actually suggested he teach a course at NYU one night after sex. He'd laughed, but I was serious. The female population of Manhattan *needed* him. I brought it up every so often, but he wasn't going for it. He said he was in charge of keeping exactly one pussy happy, and that position was all filled.

And, yes, I agree. I'm one lucky bitch. Don't worry, I remind myself of this fact at least one hundred times a day.

Kline stirred a little in his sleep, one arm reaching out across the bed and stopping once it met the skin of my hip. For a moment, I just soaked up the sight of him. Hair in disarray and a few days' worth of scruff peppering his jaw, my husband was so goddamn sexy I could hardly stand it. Over the past few days, we'd been doing nothing but climbing inside one another. The sex had been intense, crazy, and incredibly hedonistic. And I would ensure it continued that way for the duration of our honeymoon.

I set my phone down on the nightstand and decided it was time to give my husband a wake-up call. Remembering a conversation Kline and I had yesterday while we were lying under the sun, I decided to return the favor of him giving me a little striptease the night we skinny-dipped at ONE UN.

Gently, so I wouldn't wake him, I slid out from under his arm and crossed the length the spacious bedroom in our bungalow. I put on the only pair of black heels I had brought with me and wrapped my short, silk robe around my body, tying it loosely at my waist.

Once Zayn's "Pillowtalk" was playing from the speakers of the Bose sound system in the bedroom, I turned it *way* up, the beat of the seductive music overpowering the ocean waves.

Facing the bed, I waited for my husband to stir from his precious beauty sleep. His eyelids fluttered, sleepy blue gaze meeting mine, and he rubbed at his face, slowly sitting up and resting against the headboard. The sheet fell away from his hips, revealing an already impressive erection, but he wasn't all the way there, *not yet,* though he would be soon.

"Baby?" he asked, slightly disoriented yet getting harder with each scan his gaze took of my body.

"Good morning," I said, slowly moving my hips to the music.

He tilted his head to the side, eyeing me with equal parts amusement and desire.

"Don't mind me," I teased, turning my back to him and untying my robe. The silk material slid down a bit, revealing the skin of my shoulders. I glanced back at him, winking. "I just felt like dancing a little. You can go back to sleep if you want."

He chuckled, shaking his head. "No, thanks. I think I'll stay awake for this." He fluffed some pillows behind his head and sat up a little, cocking a knee so his erection stood out. "Yeah, I'll just lie here and enjoy my wife taunting me with her luscious ass."

"You want me to keep dancing?" I asked, turning around and holding my robe closed, but still moving to the lust-fueled beat of the music.

"Fuck yeah. Keep doing that." Kline nodded, slowly stroking himself as he watched me. "But lose the robe, Benny."

God, he was hot. It took all of my willpower to continue dancing and not climb on top of him.

"Patience, husband." I shook my head and waggled my index finger at him.

He grinned and scooted forward to sit on the edge of the bed, crooking his finger at me in a "come-hither" motion. "Get that gorgeous body over here."

"You got plans for me, baby?" I asked, raising an eyebrow.

"Oh, sweet Benny. You know you know the answer to that."

The heat in his eyes had a full-body blush overwhelming my skin. I couldn't help it; this man still had the power to turn me on with one sexy glance.

I made my way toward the bed, my movements still mimicking the music. Once I was in front of him, I rested my heel-clad foot on the mattress, beside his knee. The robe glided away from my hips and revealed me bared and wet for him. Only him. *Always* him.

"Fuck, baby." His eyes consumed me. Hands to my hips, he pulled me closer, head leaning toward my waist and devious tongue sneaking out to lick along my inner thighs.

My hips jerked toward him, unable to maintain any sort of rhythm. His mouth on me would always be my undoing.

Kline's hands pushed the robe off my shoulders, the material sliding down my body and falling to the floor in a puddle of silk. His mouth pressed against my pussy and he moaned, his lips vibrating against my wanton skin. "This," he whispered, tongue flicking against my clit. "This is exactly how I want to wake up every fucking morning for the rest of my goddamn life."

My head fell back, and a whimper spilled from my throat as he pushed a finger inside of me.

"Fuck, you're so wet."

"Yes," I moaned, my hips moving with the rhythm of his mouth and hand.

"I think I'll eat this perfect, delicious pussy for breakfast, and then feed you my cock when I'm done. Does that sound good, baby?"

"God, yes."

Within seconds, I was on the bed, lying flat on my back with my legs hanging over his shoulders as Kline made good on his promise.

And boy, oh boy, did he make good on it. The Kline and Georgie honeymoon bubble was officially my favorite place on earth.

CHAPTER 4

Kline

"Benny?" I called as I ran a hand through my damp, fresh-from-a-shower hair and padded across the bungalow's light wood floors.

She didn't answer immediately, but fuck, I wouldn't have either. The place was two stories, ostentatious, and bigger than our Manhattan apartment, so hearing each other wasn't exactly easy. When the hotel had heard my name and that it was our honeymoon, they'd insisted on *making it special.* I was all for that. Georgie deserved the best, and it wasn't like I couldn't afford to give it to her. But I'd honestly thought they'd realize I'd actually want to *see* my bride on our honeymoon. It felt like I spent two hours out of every day just hunting her down.

"Georgie?" I yelled as I came down the staircase to the first floor. I knew I wouldn't find her in the ocean on her own, but the private pool was completely fair game.

We'd had a morning of nothing but fucking and flirting, and I couldn't wait to spend the rest of the day the same way. I'd tried to convince her to shower the stickiness of our lovemaking off with me, but she'd conned me out of it with a flutter of her eyes and a pout of her lips.

That woman fucking owned me.

At the bottom of the steps, I looked from one end of the airy space to the other and then stepped out onto the back deck to look over the pool.

Nothing.

When I turned to head back into the overwater monstrosity, there she sat, her lounge chair tucked into the shady corner with her laptop in her sun-kissed lap.

Busy and buried in a menial task she shouldn't have been doing on our honeymoon, she hadn't even noticed I was there.

"Baby," I greeted softly, stepping under the shade of the porch and directly into her line of sight. Her eyes moved slowly, practically crawling their way off the page, but when they finally landed on me, they nearly bugged all the way out of her head.

"Kline!"

"Yeah, baby," I said with a smile. "That's me."

"And that's your—"

"Big-dicked Brooks. Right again, sweetheart."

"But we're outside! What if someone sees you?" she insisted, looking frantically back and forth around our empty patio and then back to me.

"You mean out in the middle of the ocean?" I asked, turning to point to the only aspect of our bungalow that I truly appreciated— privacy. At the end of a long line of over water huts, the back of our getaway faced no one. So few humans, so much creation. It was our own tropical paradise at the end of the world.

"Well, what if someone comes by in a kayak?"

I waggled my eyebrows and sauntered up close, looking her right in the eyes. "If you're really worried about someone seeing it, I know *just* the place to hide it."

"*Kline.*"

"Yeah. You'll definitely say my name."

"I just have to finish answering this email," she declared, but her eyes strayed to my cock more than one time and lingered on the second. When she rubbed her legs together, I couldn't resist.

One inch, two, I slid my hand up the silky smooth skin of her shin and her knee, and then turned to torture the meat at the inside of her thigh. It was slick with a mix of apple lotion and sweat, and every glossy knead made me want to eat up another sweet spot.

Her eyes glazed over, lost in me and the moment, and it was all I could do to put my free hand to use anywhere other than inside her tiny bikini. But I did, shutting her laptop with a snap and yanking it away just as she came out of her arousal-induced trance.

"I needed to finish that!"

"You need to come play with me," I countered, and her eyes narrowed as I did. I leaned in slowly and licked the line of her jaw before nibbling at the lobe of her ear with my teeth.

She smiled, looking out at the ocean and realizing where we were and exactly what I meant. "Okay. Let's play," she agreed seductively.

I bit my lip just as she reached out and took hold of my hard and waiting dick, and the flimsy string at her hips gave way easily, untying with one simple yank. Flipping her around and letting the scrap of white fabric drop to the deck, I settled my back into the chair and brought her down on me in one full stroke.

"Mmm," she moaned. Her head dropped back, and she shoved her tits closer to my mouth.

God, I loved when she did that. It was one of my favorite things, one of many in a collection of tiny, involuntary indications that she loved me, wanted me—needed me—as much as I did her.

"Do they ache, baby?" I whispered, reaching around behind her to untie the strings of her triangle top.

"Mmhmm, God, yes," she managed, nodding her head and pulling her hair up off her shoulders and into a messy pile on her head. Her cheeks were flushed, and a few flecks of salty moisture from the air dotted the tips of her long eyelashes.

I grabbed her other cheeks and spread them as I lifted. She

gasped, and before she could finish, I slammed her back down until I was seated fully inside. Her pussy spasmed around me. "Yeah, Benny. Just like that. Milk my cock until I come, okay?"

"*Kline.* Please."

She never took long like this, when I caught her by surprise and demanded agreement from her body. My Georgie loved the way I took control—gently teasing her with flattering demands and arousing compliments. But it had been a while since she'd ignited *this* quickly.

"Are you already close, baby?"

One heady moan.

I had a feeling my shy little Benny was enjoying the idea of someone seeing a lot of things they shouldn't.

"Need me to suck on these perfect tits?" I asked, pulling the dangling fabric over her head and tossing it to the side. Her nipples pebbled, and a shiver ran through her body. I closed one in the heat of my mouth and sucked until she started to ride me on her own. Uninhibited. Desperate. She'd passed the point of waiting for me to give her what she needed.

Oh, yeah.

"That's it, baby. Take us both there," I whispered into the skin of her chest. She tightened around me and cried out, throwing her head back until the ends of her hair tickled the sensitive skin of my thighs and pushed me right over the edge with her.

Our breaths came out in a ragged rhythm, one following the other, until the air around us filled the capacity of our lungs.

I kissed the skin of her neck and sucked a sweet spot into the hollow at the center while she breathed out every ounce of hoarded air at once.

"You ready to play now, Benny?"

"Huh?" She laughed, blue eyes blazing through her backlit shadow. "Play now? I thought that was the play."

"Uh-uh," I denied. "*That* was me *making love* to my *wife.*"

A smile belied the shake of her head as she leaned forward and sealed her rosy lips to mine. "I love you," she said before rubbing her nose along the line of mine.

"I know," I whispered. "Now come gallivant in the ocean with me."

Her nose scrunched up in denial. "You had me until *in the ocean*."

I picked her up and set her on her feet before climbing to my own. "Put your bikini back on and wait for me right here. I'm going to grab some trunks, and I don't want to fucking lose you again," I instructed, completely ignoring her aversion to all things sea life. She'd come around once we were in.

"Goddammit," she grumbled under her breath, scooping up the bottom of her bathing suit as she did.

"Don't worry, Benny. It's gonna be fun."

"Yeah, yeah," she agreed, tying the sides closed.

One gentle kiss to the corner of her lips and I pulled her to my chest. "Stay here. I'll be right back."

"Oh, no worries there. I won't be in the ocean without you, that's for sure."

I gave her another kiss and chuckled as I turned to run up the stairs and grab a swimsuit. When I came back, she was standing in the same spot, unfortunately un-naked, and the red-painted toes of her bare foot tapped nervously on the wood planks of the deck.

"Let's go," I said, spinning her around and pushing her forward with a gentle but insistent hand on her back. She paused at the edge, scanning the water for lurking creatures of terror.

"I'll go in first," I offered, stepping to the side and making my way down the ladder next to her. "See?" I asked, when water submerged the lower half of my body. "Nothing to worry about."

Her eyes narrowed, but she moved to the ladder, making her way down it tentatively and tapping a toe on the sandy bottom.

"Baby," I said through a laugh. "You can see the bottom. The water is crystal clear. What are you worried about?"

"It doesn't matter that the water is clear! This is a game of volume,

Kline, and there's a fucking lot of water here. Something could sneak up on me."

"I won't let it," I pledged, crossing an *X* over my heart to seal the promise. She shook her head and worried her lip, but I pulled her off the ladder and into my arms anyway.

She wrapped her legs around my waist easily, and my hands found a comfortable home on her ass. I'd take frightened Georgia any day of the week if it meant she held on this tight.

When I started to rub at the soft flesh, she caught wind of my enjoyment. It probably had something to do with my inability to stop fucking smiling.

"You like that I'm scared, don't you?"

"I wouldn't say I *like* it…" I said in an attempt to avoid ruining my perfectly crafted plan.

Her eyes narrowed, and a hand slapped at the skin of my back. "You're right. You don't like it. You *love* it!" she accused.

"Okay, yeah," I agreed with a telling smirk. "Your body is basically fused to mine, and your ass is in my hands. Of course, I love it."

Her lips met mine actively, aggression and acceptance all at once. My mouth fought back until it won dominance, taking so much that it started to give.

Foreheads together, we stood there, the sound of our breathing and each other the only thing to keep us company in the emptiness of endless ocean.

Or so I thought.

Behind her back, I saw it approach, but I kept a careful watch on the state of my body in order to keep her unaware. A lone stingray swooped and swept its way along the bottom, cruising beautifully straight for us. I watched, glancing at Georgia briefly and waiting for her to notice.

Stepping to the side as the friendly ray drew near, I craned my neck as he circled behind us.

"Oh, sweet fucking Jesus!" Georgie shouted as soon as she saw it, climbing even higher up my body with the agility of a monkey. "Oh, my God!" she yelled. "Kline! Oh, Jesus!"

I started to laugh, but my Benny wasn't laughing at all.

"Help! Help us!"

Shit.

"Georgie, calm down," I cooed softly in an attempt to soothe her. But yeah, I also laughed again, and I knew that didn't help. Limbs flailed, and her eyes grew to twice their original size.

"You calm down, you fucking honeymoon murderer! This is all a ploy, right? I've seen those movies on Lifetime!"

"Oh, my God," I said through my laughter. "Baby, it's just a stingray."

"A fucking death ray!" she screeched from atop my shoulders. I wasn't even sure how she'd gotten there, but I *was* pretty sure it would end in a black eye. My face already throbbed. "You don't use your money for much, but that's because you saved it all up for an untraceable way to kill me, didn't you?"

"Ben—"

"Oh, my God! *Help us!* Call the fucking Coast Guard!"

We were in the middle of nowhere, but not *that* in the middle of nowhere. Fuck. Officials and hotel staff would be descending on us in no time.

"Georgie—"

"Shit! Oh, shit, Kline! He's circling. This is what they do before they strike!" she screamed, and I was reasonably certain my eardrums were bleeding.

"Baby," I said through a grimace. "It's a stingray, not a shark."

Sure, stingrays weren't completely benign, but I'd read all about their frequent tendency to swim among tourists without incident before I'd booked our honeymoon. As long as we were watchful, I didn't see the harm.

"THERE. ARE. SHARKS?!"

So much for calming her down…

"Your plan is fucked! He's going to kill us both!" Her hands were in my hair by that point, yanking the strands with a strength I had no idea she possessed. "Get me the fuck out of here before I end you!"

Unwilling to torture her until both of my eyes were bloodied, I laughed and waded my way to the ladder. I'd thought being close to safety would bring her some comfort, that the idea of an escape route would be enough, but she jumped from my shoulders to the deck without even touching a rung before I could stop her.

"That's it!" she said, pointing at me. "That's the last time I go in the water."

"We're in an over-water bungalow for another week and a half! What do you mean that's the last time?"

"Nope. Nuh-uh. Not gonna happen. If you want me dead, you're just going to have to figure out another way."

CHAPTER 5

Georgia

I pressed my hand against my chest, and my heart pounded against my fingertips, wild and erratic, all thanks to my husband who was still in the water, watching me have a minor—*okay, huge*—freak-out on the deck above him. His eyes were amused, mouth set in a tickled grin.

His crystal-blue gaze turned heated in a flash as it made a circuit of my dripping wet, bikini-clad body.

If I hadn't almost *died,* I might've been turned on.

But I *had* been mere moments from sleeping with the fishes rather than swimming with them, and my otherwise sweet husband found it nothing but comical.

No matter how brutally I stared at him, his smirk never diminished, playful eyes branding me as his and threatening to hump me in broad daylight.

"Don't smolder at me!" I shouted down to him, my feet still firmly planted on our deck.

No way in hell would I ever let him coax me into the sea of death again.

I enjoyed the view of the ocean, but savoring it from the sand or the pool was as far as I preferred to go. Sea creatures of all kinds creeped me the fuck out. Small ones flitted and flaunted, nibbling at your legs when you least expected it, and anything bigger could swallow you whole. No fucking thanks. No man, orgasm expert or not, was going to talk me into seeing it a different way.

"I'm not smoldering, baby." He held up both hands, an irritating display of the exact opposite of innocent. "I'm just enjoying the view that is my beautiful, riled up wife."

How could he smile when I had just been three seconds away from seeing the light?

With annoyance, I watched Kline run a hand through his hair. Droplets of water slipped from those wet locks down his chest, until they disappeared south of his belly and back into the ocean.

Okay, so I wasn't *that* annoyed. But I was doing my best to keep up appearances.

"I'm going inside to make some lunch." I grabbed a towel off one of the lounge chairs on the deck. "*You* can stay out here and risk your life, but *I'm* not going to be a part of it," I huffed over my shoulder as I strode toward the interior of our bungalow. Well, I should say, *sashayed*, because yeah, my ass was a superpower when it came to my husband.

"Bring that sexy ass back here."

"Not a chance!"

"But I love you, Benny! You and your ass. I *really* love your ass."

"Trying to off me is an odd way of showing it!"

"*Baby*, don't be mad," he called from behind me in that tone he knew usually worked like a charm. It was annoyingly sweet yet husky in a way that only Kline could pull off.

Not gonna work this time, buddy.

I flipped him off over my shoulder, and his chuckles followed me inside.

"Save me some food!"

I turned around and peeked out the deck doors. His back was

to me as he stretched his arms for a swim. The muscles in his arms, legs, hell, *everywhere*, were as defined as ever. God bless his aptitude for keeping his body in tip-top shape.

He wasn't the kind of guy who "worked out" at the gym. He liked to *do* things to keep his physique, whether it was rugby or running or fucking his wife into a goddamn coma. His energy was endless, and he'd already spent hours on our honeymoon swimming laps in the pool while I slept myself back to fighting form in the sun. If my ass was my superpower in our relationship, my husband's stamina was its match.

Well, that and his cock. Because, yeah…*Big-dicked Brooks.*

"If I make you lunch, I need at least an hour of you *eating dessert* in return," I demanded while continuing to take in the sight of his ogle-worthy body.

He turned toward my voice, and his mouth curled up at the corners. "Promise?"

I shrugged. "I guess we'll have to see how persuasive that mouth of yours is."

"Mmm, I can't wait. I think I'll just live off your pussy for the rest of our honeymoon."

That comment had me smiling and blushing at once.

"Draft the contract, Brooks. I'll be back in a few," he said with a wink, rapping on the wood of the deck with his knuckles.

I watched as he turned and dove into the sea. His arms sliced through the calm waters in precise movements as he headed for the horizon. Man, he was almost as good at swimming as he was at fucking my brains out. And let's face it, Kline Brooks could *work* it.

I stood there for a good five minutes, stupid smile still intact, until my growling stomach forced my focus to food. Heading into the kitchen, I turned on my laptop and set the mood with a little Bob Marley on my Spotify. And then I got to work, rummaging through the stocked fridge for ingredients. In the mood for something light and savory, I began making a chicken Caesar salad. Sure, we could have had room service delivered on a regular basis, but both me and Kline preferred to keep our honeymoon mostly to ourselves without the threat of even tiny interruptions.

Once the food was ready, and I had changed into a yellow cotton sundress, I stood at the breakfast bar and dug into the crisp salad while going through some emails.

The only one that needed an urgent reply was another one from Wes. I was starting to wonder if he was doing this on purpose, attempting to distract me, his best friend's wife, while on my honeymoon. It wouldn't surprise me if that was his game. The trio, aptly nicknamed Billionaire Bad Boys, tended to give each other shit as often as possible. It was a wonder they had time to do anything else. At least everyone else seemed to be getting the *Leave Georgia Alone* memo.

I promptly read through the newly drafted contract for VITAsteel. It looked a hell of a lot better than the original proposed deal, but I still wasn't thrilled with it. I wanted our players to get as much out of this endorsement as they could, but I didn't want them to have to sign their lives away either.

I didn't care how fantastic the numbers looked on paper. No one should be handcuffed into exclusivity with one sponsor. That type of situation had no way to go but down. Yet another lesson I'd learned from my clever husband. He knew how to see the shit hidden within a field of flowers.

Our players needed and deserved to have the freedom to accept other endorsements while playing in the NFL. Most of them had families to provide for, and let's face it, their careers as professional athletes wouldn't last forever.

The music switched over to one of my favorite Marley songs, "Is This Love." As my hips swayed to the music and my lips hummed the beat, I rested my elbows on the kitchen island and started drafting an email with my suggestions.

To: Wes.Lancaster@Mavericks.com
From: Georgia.Brooks@Mavericks.com

Wes,

Honestly, their offer—numbers-wise—looks great, but I'm not pleased with the exclusivity for two years bit. Our guys deserve better. I dkmlfjiortwu4389

"Eeeeeeep!" I shouted, fingers thumping against the keys.

Large, cool hands already had my dress up to my waist, leaving my bare ass exposed.

"No panties? I approve, Mrs. Brooks," Kline whispered against my skin as his lips peppered kisses down my body. "I swear, your ass is like a gun to my head. There aren't any other possibilities. I *have* to please it for my own survival."

"*Kline,*" I said as I attempted to turn around, but his hands gripped my hips, holding me in place.

"Shh," he admonished, lips still on my skin. "This conversation doesn't involve you." He kneeled behind me, hands gripping my legs and nudging them apart. "It involves my mouth," he murmured, tongue sliding up my inner thigh. "And your delicious pussy." He emphasized the statement by grabbing my ass cheeks and burying his face against me. "And payment for lunch services rendered."

"Oh. *Fuck. Me,*" I moaned, head falling back as Kline ate my pussy from behind. My hips bucked forward once his mouth latched on to my clit, tongue swirling my nerves into a frenzy.

"If you want my cock, baby, you're going to have to wait," he instructed while slipping a finger inside of me. "Because, for the next hour, by your demand, I'm only interested in fucking this perfect cunt with my tongue." I could feel him smile against the skin of my ass. "Or until you come. Which one do you think will happen first?"

"Good God," I whimpered. My body trembled from the intense sensations, tingling and suction and the most delicious burn. And then my hips started rotating with his movements, my climax building at an insanely fast pace. My hands tried to find leverage, fingers banging across the keys of my laptop until I found the edge of the counter to hold on for dear life.

Because holy hell, this was one crazy fucking ride, and my husband wasn't slowing down for anything. Nothing would keep him from getting his fill.

His devious mouth got me off quickly as he knelt on the floor and ate me out from behind.

It wasn't until he was standing, chest pressed against my back, cock hard and already a few inches deep, that I finally remembered I was supposed to be pissed at him.

"I'm mad at you," I breathed, glancing over my shoulder to meet his hooded eyes.

"Still?" he asked, sliding in the rest of the way with one hard, deep thrust.

I moaned.

Fuck, that feels so good. But you're outraged, remember?

You're so mad...ohhhhh...yessssss...

He started to pick up the pace, and my moans grew with each drive of his hips forward.

"Benny?"

"Hmmmm," I mumbled, brain too scrambled to form actual words.

"You still mad at me?"

"Yes," I said in a raspy, damn near porn-y voice. If I wasn't so fucking close to getting off again, I would've been disappointed in my lack of control. But my mind was too focused on reaching that body-shaking moment of perfect horny bliss.

"You mind if we fight about it later, baby?" he asked, slowing his pace to a near stop. "Or did you want to do it now?"

"If you stop fucking me, I'll kill you," I threatened as I drove myself fully onto his cock to emphasize the point.

"Fuck, *yes*," he groaned, picking up speed again. "I love it when you get like this. So fucking greedy to get off."

Kline's hands slid up my sides and pulled down the front of my dress, leaving my breasts bared to his skilled touch. The second his fingers pinched my nipples, tugging them in rhythm with his thrusts, I lost all sense of time, space, *volume.* My moans turned guttural, and I just about screamed the whole place down with each pulsing wave of my orgasm.

"Fuck, fuck, *fuuuuuuuck,*" Kline growled as he fell over the edge. His movements turned wild and uncontrolled as he rode out his climax.

My lips to God's ears, my husband might actually fuck me to death before this honeymoon is over. Oh, and thank you, God. Thank you for sending me this perfect specimen of a man.

Once my breathing slowed and my mind could finally form coherent thoughts, I realized I was supposed to be peeved at my husband. I started to pull away from him, but his arms were locked around my body like a vise-grip.

"No way, Benny. You're staying right here." He leaned forward, kissing a path across my shoulder blades.

My body trembled. "I'm angry with you," I whispered.

"Liar." I felt his lips turn up at the corners against my skin.

"I am not lying," I retorted.

"Yes, you are," he said, punctuating the statement with a few small thrusts of his hips. His cock was still inside of me, and somehow, still gloriously hard. "You know what I think?"

"What?"

His lips brushed the shell of my ear. "I think you're just acting like you're mad at me. I think you're trying to get me to have crazed-wild-angry sex with you because you're insatiable. You want to have my cock inside of you this entire honeymoon."

Bingo.

"That doesn't sound like something I'd do."

"Of course not." He laughed. "Stay there, baby," he instructed as he slipped out of me.

A few minutes later, after he cleaned up his *mess*, my husband placed me on top of the island. His hair was still wet from his swim, but he had thrown on a pair of khakis, top button undone and revealing my favorite happy trail. His hands caressed my thighs as he leaned forward and placed a soft, sweet kiss against my lips. "Are you sure you still want to fight?"

I shrugged.

His teeth latched on to my bottom lip, tugging gently. "Your body might be trying to say yes, but your eyes say otherwise."

"What do my eyes say?"

"'My husband fucks like a god.'"

Giggles spilled from my lips. "Be careful, Mr. Brooks, your ego is showing."

He grinned. "Did I meet the requirements of the contract?"

I nodded. "There's a chicken Caesar salad in the fridge."

"I. Love. You," he said, each word punctuated by playful kisses before he headed for the food.

Pulling my laptop on top of my thighs, I tapped my finger against the mouse, and the screen came to life. A new email from Wes was sitting in my inbox.

To: Georgia.Brooks@Mavericks.com
From: Wes.Lancaster@Mavericks.com
Georgia,

This email started out strong but ended…*oddly*. I have a feeling I don't want to know the details, but I agree with your initial comment about disliking the exclusivity. We'll keep this contract in negotiations until we get our guys the offer they deserve. Tell Kline I said hello.
Wes Lancaster
President and Chief Executive Officer

New York Mavericks
National Football League

I blushed from head to toe. It was one thing for Wes, my boss, to be one of my husband's best friends, but it was another thing for him to *know* I was writing emails while being sexed by my husband.

"Thanks a lot," I muttered as Kline sat down at the breakfast bar, placing his plate beside my thighs.

"Thanks for what?" he asked around a mouthful of salad.

"Your sneak-attack made me send a half-written email to Wes." I held my laptop in front of his eyes, pointing to the message I'd inadvertently sent. "And now he probably thinks I'm just typing up emails while you're fucking me."

"Serves him right," Kline responded with annoyance. "If he doesn't want sexually flawed responses from you, he shouldn't be sending my wife contracts while she's on her honeymoon."

My earlier concerns about my husband not taking my busy work schedule very well had just been confirmed. Sure, his reaction was mild compared to most, but Kline wasn't a lose his temper kind of guy. *That* reaction, albeit, not all that impressive, was him showing his dislike for the situation.

"Oh, I almost forgot to tell you," he said after taking a big gulp of water. "Your mom sent a package. It was sitting on our deck when I got back from my swim."

"Shit," I muttered. "I'm not sure I want to open it."

Kline grinned, knowing full well my mother wasn't known for sending care packages filled with food or gifts from Target.

I hopped off the island and moved toward the deck, where a large cardboard box sat beside the opened doors. The box was made out to Mr. and Mrs. Brooks with the resort's address below it. The sender? *Dr. Crazypants.*

"How in the hell did she manage to get a package to us in Bora Bora? I avoided giving her our hotel information for this very reason."

"She's tenacious."

I huffed out a laugh. "Yeah, she could give you a run for your money in that department."

My fingers removed the tape, and hesitantly, I pried open the cardboard flaps.

"For fuck's sake," I groaned.

"Toys?" Kline asked enthusiastically, standing behind me and peering over my shoulder. He may not have needed the assistance, but my mother's generosity never failed him in entertainment value.

Inside? Three bottles of Anal-Eze—otherwise known as desensitizing lube—four butt plugs in various sizes, and a bunch of other freaky shit I didn't even want to know how to use.

"My mom is a fucking lunatic."

"Well, it's safe to say she's pro-anal," Kline added, amused.

CHAPTER 6

Cassie

"I can't believe you lost their cat!" I shouted, stomping my foot against the pavement of the sidewalk. We'd been walking in circles, covering what felt like every square inch of Central Park and the ten blocks surrounding Georgia and Kline's. And even though Thatch had suggested we comb the apartment building first, I just *knew* with the way that little fucker enjoyed licking himself on a daily basis, he hadn't wasted any time hanging around, and was probably out looking for pussy in the streets.

Thatch stopped in his tracks and turned to face me. God, he was tall. And big. As he moved closer, I realized just how huge he really was—at least six five and every damn inch of him was framed with big, delicious, he-should-be-naked-all-the-time kind of muscles.

His brown eyes shone in the sunlight as one eyebrow quirked up, and a knowing smile curved the line of his lips, highlighting the dark scruff covering his strong jaw. He was about a week's worth of growth from having an actual beard.

"I lost their cat?" he questioned, visibly amused. "The ol' Thatch film roll shows the cat sneaking out when I was holding back a certain someone who was about to go Fight Club on an elderly woman."

"She was not elderly." I rolled my eyes. "She was like fifty, tops."

He laughed, loud and hearty. I kind of hated the way that laugh forced my focus to his lips. They were thick, full, and downright kissable. "Her name is Mrs. Thomas, and she is five years younger than Kline's grandmother, Marylynn."

Well, *shit*. I guess she was a little older than I thought. Whatever. The bitch—*nice, elderly broad*—had asked for it. I mean, she'd stepped out of her apartment and basically said I wasn't classy. *Pffffft.* I was the classiest bitch I knew. And if I wasn't, I was definitely the *Cassiest*, and that was close-e-fucking-nough.

"How do *you* know who that lady was?"

"Because I know everything, honey." He tapped the side of his head and flashed one of his signature winks. "If it can be seen, I'm seeing it, and anything I can get a hand in, I do." His eyes burned with innuendo and confidence. "It's about time you started figuring that out."

"I swear to God, if you wink at me or another horny admirer on the street *one more fucking time,* I will cut your nuts off."

He laughed, *again,* and then his eyes honed in on my chest. "Ah, don't be jealous. I've been a one-girl-at-a-time kind of a guy since last Thursday. And after the conversation I had with your tits, you're the number one girl on my list."

Christ. This guy. He was maybe the biggest flirt I'd ever met. *Besides me.*

I pushed my braless chest out, knowing full well my nipples were nearly poking holes through my T-shirt. "These tits? They do it for you, baby?" I purred.

"Fuck. Yes." He nodded and swayed toward me like a huge tree in the breeze.

I ran my finger between my cleavage and then back up, crooking it toward him.

He followed, *like a fucking puppy*, until we were chest-to-chest. His gaze met mine, and I flashed him a smile that said, "I want you."

Thatch took that as a *hell yes*, his face morphing to something way more serious than I was expecting.

His mouth closed in on mine, and that's when I dropped the seductive act. Both of my hands reached out, and my fingers found his nipples through his shirt. With both index fingers and thumbs working as a team, I pinched and twisted those babies with all of my might. Probably hard enough to leave bruises.

"Ah, hell!" he shouted, jumping away from me while slapping my hands away in the process. "What the fuck was that for?"

I shrugged and bit my bottom lip. "I thought you liked it rough."

"*What?*" His large hands covered his chest while his face turned to a grimace. "You are literally the craziest woman I've ever met."

"It's about time you started figuring that out." I tossed his earlier words back at him. "And maybe you'll think twice the next time you feel like perving out over my fantastic rack."

"Maybe if you'd worn a bra, I wouldn't be so tempted. Your nipples have been saluting me, *and every other motherfucker* in this city, since we left the apartment."

I glanced down and couldn't exactly disagree. The only reason I wasn't wearing a bra was because Walnuts decided to use my bag as a litter box and Georgia's bras were about three sizes too small. My boobs were big, they had always been big, and though I may have been the type to show some skin, I had never set a precedent for trying to poke people's eyes out with my nipples.

"Okay, since you're basically pathetic and can't stop staring at my boobs, we need to run to my apartment so I can change."

"Thank fuck," he mumbled, following my lead toward the street.

Five minutes and one ear-piercing whistle from Thatch's lips later, we were sitting in a cab, heading toward Chelsea.

"Do you make a habit of prancing around with your tits out like that all the time? And if yes, why don't we hang out more?"

"All the time," I lied. "And we don't hang out because I can't do that around you unless I feel like looking at your boner all day."

"Which you obviously do. So no problem there."

"You wish."

"I don't wish, honey. Ever. I do, and I get—always. If you continue to do that around me, I will propose marriage to your tits, and you can bet your sweet pussy they'll accept."

"They accept nothing less than eight inches and a four-carat pink diamond engagement ring."

He winked. "Good thing I'm packing more than eight, then."

More than eight? I tilted my head as my eyes moved to the crotch of his slacks. I wanted to call bullshit, but I wasn't actually sure I *could* call bullshit.

Fuck it. No use wondering. I reached my hand out toward his lap until it met his zipper. My fingers wrapped around his dick in a viselike grip, assessing the size and girth through his pants. "*Is he a show-er or a grower?*" I silently wondered, but I was quickly denied any further exploration when Thatch shrieked the cabbie's and my ears off.

"What the fuck?" he asked, covering his thick, semi-aroused cock with his large hand.

And just FYI, it was most definitely thick, *and he wasn't lying. That man had a lot of inches, and judging by the half-chub state I managed to get him in, he still had* more *inches to go.*

"First off, that was payback for the boob grab from earlier. Secondly, you can't say shit like that and not expect me to ask questions."

"*Ask questions?*" he said through an incredulous laugh. "Cass, you didn't ask shit. You fucking grabbed my dick and—." He stopped mid-sentence and then quickly changed his tune. With both hands held away from his lap, he nodded toward the crotch of his pants. "You know what? Go ahead, honey. Ask all the questions you want."

I laughed at his forwardness. This man could give me a run for my money in the over-sharer department. "You're practically gagging over the possibility of grabbing my tits again."

"You have no fucking idea how much."

"Don't mind me," the cabbie interjected with a thick, New York accent. "I won't even charge extra, dollface," he offered with a smirk in the rearview mirror.

I glanced toward the front of the cab, finding the laminated copy of our driver's New York license displayed on the dashboard, and just barely saw Thatch's eyes narrow in my peripheral vision. "Maybe next time, Paul," I teased before hooking a thumb right in front of my giant companion's face. "I got naked in front of this guy once, and I'll never make that mistake again."

"Take it back," Thatch demanded, his nosiness over my cab-driver relations forgotten.

"Consider my curiosity curbed, Thatcher. You can go ahead and put your boner away."

"I can't wait for the day when you eat those words." His grin was all cocky and self-assured.

"Don't hold your breath," I taunted.

I was so totally full of shit, by the way. My curiosity wasn't curbed; it was at an all-time high after getting my grope on. Thatcher Kelly was packing, and my puss-ay was practically begging for a ride on his baloney pony.

"Oh, yeah?" he asked.

"Yeah!"

"Your words are going to continue to feel hollow until you actually take your hand off my dick, Pinocchio."

I looked down to see he was right. My small hand sat firm and full in the crotch of his pants.

How the fuck did that thing get back there?

"Do you think they have one of those microchips on Walter?" Thatch asked as we got off the elevator and moved toward my apartment door.

"Micro-whats? What are you talking about?" I slid the key in the lock and opened the door.

"Micro*chips*," he answered, following me inside and shutting the door with a quiet click. "You know, when the vet uses a needle to place a little chip under your pet's skin. The chip has a unique number on it, and if your pet gets lost—" He stopped, assessing the confused look on my face. "You have no idea what I'm talking about, do you?"

"Not a clue." I shook my head, walking down the hall and into my bedroom. "I did hear the words *if your pet gets lost*, though, so I'm kind of hoping you're on to something."

"You've never heard of microchips before?" Thatch stayed hot on my heels, seemingly making himself right at home and plopping his fine ass onto my bed.

"Um, no. But that's probably because I don't have any pets that would require one," I muttered, rummaging through my armoire and pulling a white lace bra out of the drawer.

"Have you ever owned a pet?"

I turned to face him, hand on my hip. "What does that have to do with anything?"

"You just don't really seem like the pet-owning type." He shrugged, sliding his giant hands behind his head. His biceps flexed from the movement, making those delicious muscles pop and protrude for my appreciative eyes.

I had always had a thing for biceps. Big, thick, muscular arms were my jam. And for the love of porn GIFs, did this man have some glorious fucking biceps. I wanted to pet them, caress them, rub my tongue, tits, and pussy all over them.

Yeah, I don't understand the whole dynamics of rubbing my vagina on his arms either, but I thought it, so there you have it.

"Cass?" His voice pulled me from my bicep-humping daydream. "Huh?"

He flashed a knowing smirk in my direction. "You never answered my question."

"Obviously, it didn't seem that important to me. Otherwise, I would've answered," I retorted as I Houdini'd my bra on without removing my shirt. I honestly didn't know what Thatch would do if he got another glance at my bare chest.

"You can touch them, you know." He flexed one meaty arm and winked. "You can touch any fucking thing you want."

Obviously, Mr. Ego hadn't missed my admiring perusal of his arms.

I sighed. "Just because I was appreciating your fuck-hot body does *not* mean I want to play hide the salami. I'd need a blood test before I even thought about letting you inside my tight, hot pussy."

"Prove it, honey."

"Prove what?"

He patted the empty spot on the bed beside him. "I need to know exactly how tight and hot before I provide you with a vial of my blood and medical records."

"Get over yourself," I said with a laugh. "And what did you ask me before?"

"Have you ever had a pet?"

Childhood memories flooded my brain. "Like, as a kid?"

"Yeah, did you have a dog or cat or even a goldfish?"

I nodded, picturing Dad running through the backyard. "As a matter of fact, I did have a pet growing up."

He waited a good thirty seconds before saying, "Okay, care to share?"

"When I was eight, I had a mini-pig. He was the coolest motherfucking pet in my neighborhood. I loved that pig. Probably more than my baby brother, Sean."

"What was his name?"

"Dad."

His eyebrows scrunched together. *"Dad?"*

"Yeah, his name was Dad. Dad, the mini-pig. He was white with—" I started to respond, but Thatch held his hand up, laughter spilling from his lips.

"Hold up. Your pig's name was Dad?"

"Uh, yeah." My right eyebrow rose on my forehead, high and annoyed. "How many times do I have to tell you my pig's name?"

"Who named him?"

"Me. I named him. He was my pig." I stared at him, frustrated by his interrogation. "English is your first language, right?"

He chuckled at that. "You realize how fucking absurd and downright hilarious it is that you, little toothless, pigtail-wearing-Cassie, named her pig Dad, right?"

"He looked like a Dad. And I was never innocent enough to pull off pigtails."

"Fuck, you're fantastic." A giant grin consumed his face. "What happened to Dad?"

"My mom got tired of him constantly tearing up the house, so they sent him to a farm."

"A farm, farm? Or like 'a farm'?" he asked, gesturing quotation marks with his fingers.

I squinted. "I don't understand the difference. I thought a farm was a fucking farm."

He slowly tilted his head to the side, assessing my incredulous expression. After a few seconds, he merely smiled and got off my bed, walking around my bedroom and getting all up in my personal shit.

I followed his big-ass feet across the room, yanking a picture frame from his hands. "Not so fast, Thatcher. What other kind of farm are you talking about?"

For a fraction of a second, I watched his eyes go wide before he schooled his expression into one that was irritatingly neutral.

And then, it clicked. The bastard was insinuating that my mom had Dad offed. He hadn't been—I'd checked, and had even made my mother get pictures of Dad with his new farm family. Well, two could play that game. I'd make Thatch rethink opening his big fucking mouth before I was through with him. Good thing I'd always been a *fantastic* actress.

"Oh, my God!" My hand went to my mouth. "You don't think my—"

"No," he backtracked, eyes wide and head shaking adamantly.

I almost wanted to drop the act when I saw the distressed look on his face. *Almost.*

"That's not what I said. I'm sure your parents sent Dad to a real farm. A really nice farm. I bet Dad had the time of his life at that farm. I bet he was a wild man, doing crazy pig shit and frolicking in the fields. Maybe you ate a lot of ham that month, but I'm sure it was a coincidence."

Ham. It took a whole lot of willpower not to burst out into laughter. Even when he was trying to be serious, he couldn't help himself. The man was sarcastic to his core, and it gave me a very odd sense of déjà vu.

"Oh. My. God!" I shoved his shoulder hard, forcing him to take a step back. "You think my mom had Dad killed?!"

His eyes transformed from playful to panicked.

"No. No. That's not what I think. I think he grew old on that happy, beautiful farm. I bet Dad died doing what he loved, rolling around in shit and pulling some serious piggy tail."

"I can't believe this," I said, staring off into space and putting on my best distraught look. "I can't believe my mom killed Dad. I feel like my entire childhood is a lie. My whole life is one big fucking lie. Thanks a lot, Thatch!" I stabbed him in the chest with my index finger. "You have ruined *everything.*"

"Fuck." He ran a hand through his hair. "I'm sure Dad is still alive. I bet that fucker's gonna live to be a hundred!"

"Shut up. Just. Shut. Up." I turned away from him, fighting the smile threatening to cover my entire face, and threw myself onto my mattress. "This whole time I thought Dad was happy with another family on a farm, when in reality, he was dead." My voice was muffled in my pillows. "Dad was dead, and no one even fucking knew about it. My mom fucking had Dad offed because, apparently, he was too much of a hassle."

A soft chuckle hit my ears, and I turned onto my back, finding Thatch vibrating with silent laughter. The expression on his face—a fine mix of hilarity and constipation—almost made me break.

"Are you laughing?" My lips burned as I tried to hide my amusement with feigned disgust.

"Definitely not. That'd be a real asshole thing to do," he muttered, trying like hell to fight a smile. He assessed my face and started to grin. "Wait a minute…" He paused, pointing a finger at my face. "Are you fucking with me?"

"Are you insinuating I'm not upset about Dad?"

He nodded. "That's exactly what I'm saying. And by the look of that smile trying to swallow your face, I'd say I'm right. You look like the fucking Joker." He laughed, shaking his head. "It actually scares me how good you are at acting. I feel bad for every motherfucker that's fallen inside your trap. You should come with a warning label, honey."

Even though he was one-hundred-percent correct, I still grabbed my TV remote from the nightstand and chucked it at him for having the audacity to accuse me of being a lot to handle. I *was*, but only *I* got to say I was high-maintenance.

Unfortunately, Thatch was a lot quicker than he looked, crouching down, and giving the remote nowhere else to go but straight at my window. It cracked and shattered with an impressive screech, glass flying onto the hardwood floor like confetti.

Well, *fuck*.

He straightened from his crouched position and assessed the damage. His fingers running along the broken glass and noting the giant hole in the center.

Thatch turned around, facing me. "I'll take the blame for break-ing the news to you about Dad's death, but this—" he gestured a thumb over his shoulder "—this one's on you, crazy."

I sighed. "Son. Of. A. Bitch."

And that was how I had managed to get Thatcher Kelly shirtless and sweaty, hammering nails into a piece of plywood that covered my broken window.

"Honestly, Cass, if you wanted a striptease, all you had to do was ask. I would've obliged, and you wouldn't have to replace a window." He glanced over his shoulder, smirking.

I was lying on my belly, chin resting in my hands, and enjoying the show from the comfort of my bed. A few rogue droplets of sweat slid down his back, bumping over the beautiful dips and valleys of his muscular form. Damn, this man had to put some serious hours in at the gym to look that good.

"Did you hear me?" he asked, lining up another nail against the wood. "Next time, let's avoid all of the menial labor and focus both of our energies on something more entertaining. Something that in-volves your tits and me in a deep, mouth-to-nipple conversation."

"Why are you still talking?" I took a sip from the straw inside my can of Coke. "You're supposed to be standing there, hammering your wood, and looking pretty. I'm not paying you for small talk."

"Pretty sure you're not paying me at all," he pointed out. "Your crazy ass broke the window, and now I'm stuck putting up a tempo-rary solution until you can get someone in here to replace it."

"Meh, those are just minor details at this point."

"Okay. Here's the deal," he said, lining up another nail. "Wrap those gorgeous lips of yours around my cock, and we'll call it even."

"*Slut,*" I responded through a cough.

"I never said dirty talk was a requirement, but if that's what gets you off, I guess I can roll with it." He glanced over his shoulder and waggled his eyebrows in my direction.

"You know," I responded, tapping my chin. "Considering I'm a fan of sucking cock, I probably would've gone for it. But since you lost Walter, and we've yet to find Satan himself, I'm gonna have to pass."

"Shit. I almost forgot about that goddamn cat," Thatch muttered.

"Yeah, I kind of did too," I said, eyes still fixated on his biceps as he hammered in the last nail. I was starting to think we were terrible friends to Kline and Georgie. I probably should have been out searching for Walnuts rather than lounging around, watching Thatch's big muscles at work.

It was definitely time to resume our search. No way in hell could I let Georgia come home to her cat missing.

I got up from my bed and headed for the hallway. "Move those fucking clown feet into my bathroom and get cleaned up. Time's a wastin' on finding The Asshole." I called over my shoulder.

A few feet into the hallway, I heard Thatch mutter, "Jesus Christ. That little cocksucker. Not even my cat, and he's ruining *everything*."

CHAPTER 7

Thatch

"**D**on't you think we should actually search the *apartment building* in which he vanished *before* the rest of Manhattan?" I asked for the *second* time today.

Crazy Cassie had been convinced immediately after Walter's disappearing act that he'd up and, I don't know, fucking teleported himself to the other side of Central Park. She'd dragged me out onto the sidewalk, and led by the helpful direction of her tits, I'd followed right along on a roller coaster ride straight into hell. Up and down the sidewalks of the park, from one side to the other and back again, a Twilight Zone cab ride, and a little light manual labor at her apartment later, and here I was, about to follow her into the depths of Manhattan fitness and fornication *again*.

I guess that makes me the crazy one.

"Would you stop contradicting every fucking thing I say? Use that beanstalk body of yours and search the surrounding area."

Fed up, I pulled her to a stop with the hand she was dragging me by. "I'm going back to search the building, and if I don't find him, I'm calling Kline."

"Thatcher—"

"No, Cass. Stay out here and search if you want, but you'll never find Walnuts in the bevy of strays combing Central Park. God, for all we know, the little prick has a key to their apartment and is halfway through his afternoon bath in the middle of their goddamn bed."

"*Shit!*" she yelled, her face falling as she started running in the direction we had come, shoving people out of the way as she went.

"What?" I asked, breaking into a jog to keep up.

"The door!" she shrieked. "We left the door to their apartment open!"

Oh, *fuck.*

Yeah, safe bet they weren't going to be asking us to watch their apartment or their cat again.

My legs were twice the length of hers, so I passed her easily, sprinting through the crowded sidewalk. I slammed through the door, nodding at the doorman as I went, and thanking *fuck* their building had one.

Too impatient to wait for the elevator, I took the stairs three at a time. Fourteen stories up with sweat pouring like a fucking faucet from my temples, I finally burst through the stairwell door and out into their hallway.

The door was open just like Cass had said, so I said a silent prayer I hadn't just deprived my best friend and his new bride of all their belongings.

Shoving the door as I went, I slid to a stop just inside and examined the open floor plan with manic eyes. All the furniture seemed to be in place, and nothing of value stood out as missing, but I hadn't kept an actual fucking inventory list either.

I'd just started to take a full breath when a tap on my shoulder sent me into a near seizure.

Cassie spoke as if nothing was amiss. "Stuff's all here, but no devil cat. The door was closed, by the way. Whoops."

I put a hand to my forehead and tried to stop the nearly brain-piercing urge to strangle her.

"What took you so long?" she went on, having beaten me up here by taking the elevator.

White-hot rage consumed every cubic inch of my insides, but I tried my best to tamp it down.

Is this what an aneurysm feels like?

"Hey, Thatcher, you okay?" she asked, her face turning serious as I sank to the floor and rubbed at the tension in my temples. Her bra-covered breasts pushed against the fabric of her T-shirt as she sat down beside me.

How in the fuck did I still find this crazy asshole woman attractive? What was wrong with me?

"Jesus Christ," I mumbled, scrubbing at my eyes and hoping they had some kind of link to my actions. "I want to donate my brain to science."

"Huh?"

"Like the football players are doing for concussions. I think this would be worthwhile research too." As my head fell back to the wall behind me, she nudged me roughly with one of her feet.

"I don't even know what you're talking about right now, but stop it," she demanded. "You're scaring me, and it's pissing me off."

I turned my head and looked into her eyes to find them *actually* angry, spitting blue flames and making the end of her nose pull slightly askew. She straddled the line between angelic and evil too easily. She foiled that boundary with the mystifying mix of her peaches and cream skin and powerful, knowing eyes.

Too wild to be innocent, too authentic to be wicked.

Her light pink lips pursed, and without a thought, mine were on them. They acted on their own, begging for an invitation from her or me, or both of us, to take it further. One moment bled into the next without thought or action until her lips moved under mine. Not far and not open, but not away either.

Stunned, I pulled back. I couldn't understand it, but something in me didn't want to hear her say no—so I said it for her.

"Thank fuck," I said, a rough rasp lingering in the edges of my voice. "I finally found a way to shut you up."

The vivid blue of her eyes clouded by derision, she jumped to standing. Though they were marred, they were still resoundingly powerful, chaining me to them. Even knowing her chest must have bounced with the movement, my gaze never left the confounded lines of her face. It was so out of character; I didn't even recognize myself.

"Don't ever kiss me again without permission," she whispered shakily. The rough edge of her command cut like a knife. All traces of superficial playfulness had disappeared, and the look in her eyes burned through several layers of flesh until it met my soul.

Some kind of nerve had been frayed, and I wasn't sure I was a talented enough surgeon to execute the repair. The only option was to move on, and the only tactic I knew how to employ was avoidance.

I climbed to my feet. "Let's search for Walter one more time. Here, inside the apartment, and around this floor. If we don't find him in the next thirty minutes or so, I'll call Kline."

"That deadbeat isn't going to care! Georgie cares. Fuck, she's gonna be mad."

"Don't worry," I comforted her but didn't move closer. "Kline gives no fucks about Walter, but he gives all kinds of fucks about Georgia. He'll hire a fucking private detective if he has to."

"A cat detective?" she asked as she considered my words, tilting her head to the side and grinning just enough to look normal again.

I shrugged and breathed out a sigh of relief. "Yeah. If there are cat burglars, there must be cat detectives, right?"

"You're an idiot."

"Yeah." We didn't agree on much, but on that, we were on the same fucking page.

I was thinking things I shouldn't be thinking. Things that would probably never happen. Things I wasn't even sure I wanted to happen.

And that made me the goddamn king of royally fucked.

CHAPTER 8

Bora Bora, Thursday, April 20th, Afternoon

Kline

I glanced through the open bathroom door to the steam coming out of the shower and back down to the screen of my phone to confirm the name on the incoming call said what I thought it did.

It fucking did.

With a touch of the green phone icon and a frustrated groan, I answered and didn't mince words. "You, Cassie, Wes, or Walter better be dead or in the process of getting that way."

"What if I told you Wes is fine, Cassie's crazy, I almost died, and the cat is missing?" Thatch said in my ear without pause.

"Shit." The piercing pain of aggravation made me squeeze the bridge of my nose between my thumb and forefinger.

"Yeah," he confirmed.

I turned to face away from the bathroom and paced the space in front of the bed.

"The first three I understand, but how in the fuck did we arrive at the fourth? Walter is the bane of my existence, but other than being sloppy and surly, he's surprisingly easy to watch."

"Well, we thought it happened while I was having a conversation with Cassie's tits—and seriously, we'll have to have another talk about that later—but it actually happened while she was threatening to go all Fight Club with your neighbor."

"It's actually painful to be friends with you right now."

Exasperated laughter pulsed in my ear. "I'm picking up on that. You've got a seriously heavy aura pouring through the phone lines right now."

"You know what comes through right after my aura?" I asked.

"Something tells me I don't wanna know, but at the same time, I have to know."

"My hand. To fucking strangle you."

"Kline—"

"I'm on my honeymoon right now," I pointed out the obvious. "A vacation specifically designed for constant sex with my insanely hot wife. And you and fucking Wes won't stop interrupting it."

I sat down on the edge of the bed and glanced toward the bathroom again.

"I don't know about Wes, but this is my first and final time, dude. I just want to know if the cat's got a tracking chip in it."

I wrapped a hand around my throat, dropped my head back, and closed my eyes. "I'm not completely sure, but my mom would know. She did all of his vet stuff."

"Thank fuck," he muttered. He actually sounded worn-out and weird. But I didn't care. I planned to save all of my energy for exponentially more pleasurable activities, and I refused to let my tendency to *care* get in the way of that.

"She's also likely to make your life a living hell if you speak with her directly about her missing, beloved cat," I advised. "Your best bet is to talk to Bob."

Thatch chuckled. "I don't know why you decided to show leniency toward me by telling me that, but thank you. I can only handle one irrational woman at a time."

"You're welcome. And you owe me." I stood from the bed again and looked out at the turquoise water. If it weren't for the sun, it might have looked like it went on forever.

He sighed. "I'm completely unsure how my watching your cat has ended in me owing you *another* favor, but I don't even care. As long as this day ends without bloodshed or blue balls, I'll count it as a very difficult win."

My eyebrows pinched together, and I turned to the sound of Georgie in the bathroom door. "I don't know, I don't want to know, I don't need to know. Just take care of it," I said in vague dismissal.

Thatch laughed yet again in my ear. "Break it to her easy, K. Probably best if you mumble it while your mouth is otherwise occup—"

"Bye," I interrupted, pulling the phone from my ear and hanging up before he could say anything else.

"Who was that?" Georgie asked, cinching her towel tighter around her body. This definitely wasn't the way I wanted to start the second part of our day. I had a special dinner planned, and I wanted my wife nothing but sated, sassy, and seductive. If she knew about Walter, all of those things would go straight to hell.

"Thatch," I muttered, turning around to set my phone on the nightstand and gathering my thoughts on how to handle this.

"Is everything okay? Is Cass okay? Did Walter kill her?" she asked rapid-fire, immediately on edge. I had to smile about the last question.

"Did he *kill* her?" I asked with a snicker. "You know, Benny, I'm searching my brain, but all I can seem to remember is you defending him. Telling people what a sweetheart he is. Why would you think affable little Walter would do anything other than love and protect your best friend?"

Her eyes narrowed, and a foot rotated out into her fighting stance. I bit my lip to curtail a smile. "This isn't about Walter. This is about Cassie. I love her dearly, but she's really good at instigating and infuriating. It wouldn't take much of her to make our softhearted cat turn."

I shook my head and charged her, scooping her into my arms and smelling the fresh scent of her neck. She squealed but wrapped her arms around my shoulders. I tugged her towel free and spoke at the same time. "God, you're good. Are you sure you can't come back to work with me?"

She pulled back, pushing me off her gently and raising a brow. "Kline—"

"I know, I know. You're happy where you are. I get it," I surrendered, pulling her immediately back into my arms.

"Kline, we should talk about this. It's obviously bothering you."

"I don't want to talk about it," I told her honestly. "I want to ignore it and everything else but you and us and our honeymoon."

She put a hand to my jaw and looked into my eyes.

"Does it bother me?" I went on. "Yeah. Obviously, it does. But not like you're thinking, and not to the point that I can't put on my fucking big-boy pants and get over it. When our honeymoon is over, we'll talk about it more. Make the compromises we need to. But for now, the only aggression I want between the two of us is between the sheets, on the deck, in the pool, in the shower—any-goddamn-where as long as our clothes are off and our bodies are as close as we can get them."

"Baby," she whispered, wrapping her tan, bare legs around my waist and squeezing tight.

"Let's start now, Benny. Argue with me the only way I like it."

"Why are you so good with words?" she replied softly as she pulled her body closer into mine.

"Business," I told her with a wink. She laughed. "And to use as a tool to woo you."

"I'm wooed," she responded with a smirk. "Whatever will you use your mouth for now?"

Reaching around and under her ass, I sank the tips of my fingers right in between her legs and nibbled at her shoulder. "I was going to use it to get your pussy ready for me, but she's already all set."

"Um," she mumbled through a moan. "What *is* ready? I mean, can you ever *really* be ready?"

"You're right," I agreed as I laid her gently on the bed and shoved my boxer briefs down my legs and stepped out of them. I stroked my cock from root to tip and back again before running the fingers of my other hand straight up the middle of her wet pussy. "There's no way she's ready for this," I taunted. "My tongue is gonna tease you until you think you're prepared. That sound good, Rose?"

She always blushed when I called her that, and when she was completely bare, the color didn't stop at her cheeks.

Down to my knees, I scooped her legs up and over my shoulders and buried my face right in the middle. Her hips chased my tongue, and I pushed forward to make sure they didn't have to go far.

"Mmm," I moaned, deeply sucking in all of her sweetness. "My little flower tastes good."

"God, Kline," she hummed.

She was magnificent in all of her pleasure, licking lips and greedy hips moving at a constant pace. She wanted more and less, and I intended to give her everything she wanted, even if it was impossible. The sun-darkened color of her skin made her eyes stand out, and every second I spent looking at her pussy, I could feel them on me. Watching, begging—fucking forcing me to work her harder, faster, slower, softer. Everything she asked for, I felt it, and you couldn't convince me there was any better feeling in the world than being this in tune with another person.

"Come on, baby," I pushed while I teased her ass with my thumb and her clit with my tongue. "Get *ready*. Get fucking soaked."

I pumped two fingers in and out of her and she clenched around me, but she did it silently. Lost in her euphoria, her head fell back and her mouth fell open. I hated not seeing her eyes, but the line of her throat, the spasm in her thighs, and the grip of her hand in my hair told me every goddamn thing I ever wanted or needed to know.

"Ready?" I asked, climbing to my feet and wrapping a hand around the base of my aching dick.

She demanded my arousal with her eyes and my heart with her words. "Always."

Always.

CHAPTER 9

Bora Bora, Friday, April 21ˢᵗ, Afternoon

Georgia

I stirred from my afternoon doze on the quiet beach as strong hands kneaded into my back. Glancing over my shoulder, I found Kline kneeling beside my prone form, holding a bottle of sunscreen in one hand as he squirted more lotion into his open palm.

I took a minute to enjoy the view. His body gloriously bared, only a pair of swim trunks sat low on his trim waist. He was fresh off a swim, dark hair slicked back with several rogue droplets of water slipping down his chest to the muscles of his abdomen, and if his hands kept up this delicious torture, he wouldn't be the only one wet.

"How long have I been asleep?" I asked, voice raspy from yet another nap under the sun.

In my defense, I was tired from last night's exertions that included more than one round of hot honeymoon sex. Before that, we had dinner on the beach, with Kline hand-feeding me through most of it. Yeah, there was no denying my husband was one swoony bastard. He wooed me right out of my panties and onto his orgasm-inducing cock.

"Probably an hour," he said, a smile in his voice. His hands made a slow descent down my back, rubbing soft circles into my skin. "This is becoming a habit, Benny girl. You falling asleep by noon."

"It's all your fault," I muttered, turning my head to the side and resting it on my folded hands.

"My fault?" he asked while his devious fingers slid my bikini bottoms out of the way.

"Uh-huh." I shut my eyes and swallowed a moan.

His large hands gripped my ass and *pretended* to apply sunscreen.

"Pretty sure I don't need sun protection there."

"I'm thorough, Georgie." He was undeterred, still groping my body in the name of preventing sunburn.

"This feels less like you applying sunscreen and more like you trying to get me naked."

He smacked my ass, and I squealed in surprise. When my eyes met his, I wasn't surprised to find them positively glowing.

"Turn over and let me get the rest of you."

I giggled, turning over onto my back, and my eyes squinted as the bright sun shone directly into them.

Kline kneeled between my spread legs, hands sliding up my sides until his fingers stopped to play with the edge of my bikini top. "Damn, you're fucking beautiful." He rested his elbows beside my head and placed soft, sweet kisses against my lips. "I could spend the next fifty years just staring at my gorgeous wife and never have my fill."

"Fifty years from now, I'll be a lot less gorgeous and a lot more wrinkled and gray," I said against his persistent mouth.

He leaned back just enough to meet my gaze. "In my eyes, you'll always be the most stunning, tiny, perfect being."

"Even when I'm old?"

"Especially when you're old." He placed a wet, deep kiss against my lips.

See what I mean? Swoony fucking bastard.

His lips rested against mine as he spoke again. "My standards will have lessened, and I'm pretty sure you'll age well."

Hmm…Okay, so maybe he's just a bastard.

Chuckles bounced off my skin as he lost himself in his humor. "Relax, baby. I'm kidding."

"You better be kidding," I mumbled, huffing and puffing on my chair as I pushed him away.

He resumed his sunscreen application, squirting more into his palm and kneading those strong fingers into my belly. "What do you want to do today?"

Hells bells, his hands were an aphrodisiac.

I thought it over, but I didn't have to think hard. "Stay here and let my husband give me the five-star treatment."

He chuckled, waggling his brows. "All of my massages end with happy endings."

"I thought this was sunscreen application?"

"Okay. All activities that include my hands on you end happily." He winked and moved those greedy hands farther up my stomach until they were resting just below the swell of my breasts.

Oh boy, this man was perfect. If he kept it up, I'd start purring like a fucking cat.

Purring like a cat? For some reason, I felt like I'd been down this line of thinking before.

Oh, shit! Cat! The cat!

I sat up abruptly, forcing Kline's hands to fall from my skin.

"Hey, I wasn't done," he responded, hands moving toward me again. They found my ribs and started tickling me into giggling.

"Stop it!" I playfully slapped him away and grabbed my beach bag, rummaging through it in search of my phone.

"You bring some toys to the beach, Benny?"

"No, you kinky bastard," I said through a laugh. I pulled my phone from the bag and held it up for him to see. "I forgot to call Cass and check on Walter."

His expression changed from devilish smirk to something a lot less excited in the span of a heartbeat.

"What's wrong?" I tilted my head to the side, taken aback by his sudden change in mood.

Silent and brooding, he stared into my eyes and searched for an answer to an unknown question.

"Kline?"

He grimaced before he spoke. "I need to tell you something."

My nose crinkled involuntarily. "Is everything okay?"

"I talked to Thatch and—"

"Oh, my God!" My hand covered my mouth. "Did something happen? Did something happen to Cass?"

He shook his head. "No, baby. Cassie is fine."

I put my hand to my chest, trying to slow my racing heart. "Don't scare me like that. I thought something terrible happened."

"Baby, Thatch called yesterday to tell me that…" He trailed off, watching me with concerned and cautious eyes. He took a deep breath and then finally added, "Walter got out of the apartment, and they're having a hard time locating him."

"*What?*" My eyes bugged out and I shot to my feet, pointing an accusatory finger in Kline's face. "Walter is missing, and you didn't fucking tell me?!"

His face was a mask of shame and *Ah, shit, yes*, and the combination of the two sent me running for our bungalow.

"Georgia!" I heard him call after me.

But I was at a damn near sprint, racing to get inside and pack my shit. Call me a lunatic, I didn't care. My baby was missing, and I'd be damned if he spent another lonely night in some decrepit alley in New York.

Tears filled my eyes as I pictured him walking the streets, cold, wet, and with no goddamn food.

My husband found me in the bedroom, tossing my suitcase onto the mattress.

"Baby," he said, voice hesitant. "What are you doing?"

"What does it look like I'm doing?" I threw my hands out in front of me in a wild, erratic gesture of *isn't it fucking obvious*. "I'm packing my shit. I need to get home! Walter is missing and cold and wet and lonely and just walking the streets of New York looking for me."

I moved toward the closet to get my clothes, but I stopped in my tracks as my brain started conjuring all of the worst scenarios. "Oh, my God!" I covered my mouth with my hand as a shocked gasp escaped my lungs. "What if he becomes desperate, Kline? What if he has no other choice but to start prostituting himself for food? You know he's not good at making new friends! There's no way he's been accepted by the good crowd. He's probably already addicted to heroin!"

"Georgie," Kline cooed in my ear, arms wrapping around my body and pulling my back into his chest. "I'm sure Walter is fine. You know Maureen. She made sure he has one of those GPS tracking chips. I bet Cass and Thatch have already found him by this point."

"You don't know that! They would've called if they found him." I pushed his arms away and moved into the closet, yanking clothes off the hangers.

Kline was standing by my suitcase when I strode back in with both arms full of sundresses and bikinis.

"Call the airline! We have to get on the next flight out." I threw everything into my suitcase and headed for the bathroom to grab my toiletries.

But my husband stopped my momentum, wrapping his arms around me again and pulling me into a tight bear hug.

"We don't have time for this!"

He kept his hold on me, lifting me into his arms and carrying me into the hallway.

"Put me down!" I tried like hell to get out of his hold as he walked down the stairs, but it was pointless. He was too strong, no matter how much adrenaline I had running through my system.

He sat me down on the kitchen island, stood between my knees, and his hands gripped my thighs to hold me in place. "I need you to take a deep breath and calm down for a minute." His voice should have been calming, but it was just pissing me off more.

"I can't calm down!" I shouted. "Everything is all fucked up! Our cat is missing, and *you* didn't tell me. You lied to me, Kline! I feel like you keep lying to me about a lot of shit."

His eyes turned remorseful at my accusations, but they weren't completely complacent either. "I know I should have told you about Walter, but I didn't want you to panic."

"You told me everything was fine and that Walter was good, but in reality, he's sitting in an alley shooting up heroin!"

"Baby, I—"

"Do *not* baby me." I pointed my index finger at him.

His eyes narrowed, and one thing became clear. Sweet, patient Kline was losing a little of both.

I knew I was probably being a little—okay, *a lot*—irrational, but I couldn't help it. Ever since the whole Rose and Ruck debacle, my husband had made it a point always to be open and honest with me, but lately, he had been doing the opposite. I knew he wasn't happy about my job situation, yet he just kept brushing it off and refusing to discuss it.

But it *was* bothering him. *Big. Time.* And, let's be honest, the fact that it was bothering him was *really* bothering me.

And now, he'd lied to me about the cat. It felt like the icing on the dishonesty cake.

"Georgia," he started to say, but I held up my hand.

"I can't go there right now. I need to call Cassie and see if they've found Walter."

I glanced around the kitchen, but I remembered the last time I had my phone was *before* I had hauled ass to our bungalow. "Shit! I think I left my phone on the beach."

Kline grabbed my bag—that he had obviously carried inside for me—from one of the barstools and reached inside. "Here." He handed the phone to me. "Call Cassie and see if they found Walter."

I didn't even hesitate. Three rings in, I hopped off the island and started to pace.

On the fourth ring, she finally answered. "Helloooooo, Wheorgie! How's Bora Bora? Is Kline at least feeding you between—"

"Did you find Walter?" I asked, too worried to let her ramble any further.

"Uh…I guess Kline told you about that, huh?"

"Did you find my cat?" I snapped.

"He has a tracking device, Georgie. We could find him on the moon with the GPS shit your mother-in-law embedded under his skin."

"Oh, thank God." I breathed a sigh of relief. "I was about one minute away from booking a flight home."

"You were going to leave your honeymoon because the dick-head…was missing?"

"Are you kidding me? My baby was missing! Of course, I was going to fly home to find him!"

"Slow your roll, Susie. No need to make me deaf," she muttered into my ear.

"Is he okay?"

"Uh…yeah…I'm sure he's just fine."

"He's not hurt? Was he scared? I can't believe he was lost and roaming the streets of New York all by himself."

"Walter is one tough little asshole. You have nothing to worry about."

"Will you stay at our apartment for the rest of our trip? I think he could really use the companionship."

"Already planned on it. Sorry to cut this short, but I gotta jet. I've got a shoot in about thirty minutes. I'll call you later, okay?"

"Sounds good. Oh, hey, Cass?

"Yeah?"

"If you lose my cat again, I will kill you."

She scoffed. "You can guarantee I won't lose that little bastard a second time."

"Good."

"Georgia, stop sulking and go blow your husband. Lord knows he probably needs the extra attention after watching you lose your shit."

"I did not lose my shit!"

Kline snorted in the background.

"Sure you didn't." She laughed. "My money says you had half your shit packed and were *already* telling Kline to book a flight."

Jesus, she knew me too fucking well.

"Shut up. Go snap pervy photos of naked men."

"Later, Wheorgie!"

I hung up the call and met Kline's gaze. He was still standing by the island, watching me with uncertainty and unhappiness dulling his blue eyes.

"Everything okay?"

I nodded and tried to collect the scattered pieces of myself. "They found him."

"That's good news."

"Yeah, it is," I agreed.

We just stared at one another, lost in my earlier mania and the deeper issues it'd brought to light. A cloud of hurt feelings and harsh accusations hung over our otherwise blissful honeymoon.

"Well…I guess I better go clean up the disaster area. I'll make us some lunch once I finish, okay?" I called over my shoulder as I walked up the stairs toward our bedroom, hoping to have a few moments to find my way back to five on the emotional scale.

To my surprise, Kline followed me.

He sat on the bed as I started to empty my suitcase. "Come here, sweetheart." When I looked to him but didn't move, he gestured for me to come closer.

The second I was within his reach, he pulled me onto his lap and wrapped his arms around my stomach. His face was pressed against my neck, lips brushing the sensitive spot below my ear. The intimate silence healed half the hurt, but some of it stayed, buried deep.

After a few quiet moments, I whispered, "I'm sorry I went a little crazy before."

Hot, relieved air coated my skin. "I'm sorry I lied to you."

I leaned back, gripping his chin and forcing his eyes to look at mine. "Are you really sorry about that?"

"*Yes*. Of course I am, Ben." His remorseful eyes stared deep into mine.

"What about my job?"

He cocked an eyebrow. "What about your job?"

"Are you going to start being honest with me about how you really feel about it?"

He sighed and gave me a squeeze. "I'm not happy about the amount of time it will demand from you, but I'll deal."

"I don't think saying you'll deal is a solution, Kline. What if you start resenting me for traveling so much? For being occupied with work too much? Where will that lead us?"

God, the words stung as soon as I said them.

What if my job started to put a giant wedge between us?

We had gotten together in a rush. Too consumed with one another, too deep in love not to dive headfirst into our relationship. We had known each other for a few years, but we hadn't actually been together, been a couple, for all that long.

What if my job strained my marriage?

The mere thought of that awful scenario caused tears to pool in my eyes.

CHAPTER 10

Kline

Seeing tears in her eyes over the possibility of a disillusioned marriage courtesy of a fucking job was the last straw. I'd wanted to maintain our "eat, fuck, cuddle, sleep, be nauseatingly happy" bubble for these two weeks, but the bubble wasn't any fucking good if it hurt her.

And right now? The compartmentalization on my part was very much hurting my sweet wife.

"All right," I declared, picking her up from my lap and setting her down on the edge of the bed. Standing in front of her, I tipped her chin up until her pretty, sad eyes met mine. "Real talk time." She steeled herself for what she thought might come. "First things first, no more tears, okay?"

"Kline—"

"They break my fucking heart, Benny. I can't think of a scenario where I like to see you cry, but I fucking *loathe* it when I'm the cause."

She did her best to stop, as I moved on. The important point wasn't that she actually stop crying; it was that she knew I *wanted* her to.

"How often am I right while you're wrong?" I asked, catching her off guard. I could see at first that she wasn't sure how to answer, but I prompted her to be honest with gentle eyes and a soft smile.

"Not often."

Bingo.

"So not often," I admitted. "I'm completely prepared for the inevitable. With me being the man and you the woman, the rightness ratio in this relationship will always heavily favor you. It's been the way of the world for centuries, but most guys are too fucking insecure to admit it." She coughed a surprised giggle. "I'm not. When it comes to you and us, I'm gonna fuck up more often than I'd like."

She started to shake her head, but I held up a hand to stop her.

"It's because you make me irrational."

Her chin jerked back, and her tears were completely gone. I was halfway there. "You're one of the most clever-minded, rational people I know."

"In business," I agreed. "With you, I lose all sense of everything but us."

She tilted her head, but I pushed on. "Look at my track record. You know it's true."

"Kline." She reached for me, but I started to pace just outside of her range, before turning to face her again and kneeling on the wood floor in front of her feet.

Her hands reached desperately for mine, and this time I didn't deny them.

"I don't want to hold you back."

"I know you don't," she cut in.

"You're brilliant, and you deserve every facet of success you can get your hands on."

"Baby," she whispered.

I smiled and reached out to brush some stray hair from her face, pulling her other hand flat to the pounding beat in my chest. My voice dropped to an intimate whisper as I admitted, "But I thought I was going to be along for the ride. I thought your success would flourish with me. At my company." I shrugged and finished with the part that bothered me most. "That I'd get to watch."

"Oh, Kline." She pulled my palm to her lips and kissed it.

"I'm so fucking proud of you. You're not where you are out of luck or chance. You're there because you deserve it. You're tenacious and smart, and God, I'd gotten used to sitting in on shit just so I could see it."

"I've been gone for months now, though," she pointed out gently. "If that's really it, why is it just bothering you now?"

I shrugged. "We're on our honeymoon. Thousands of miles away, just you and me. I know the traveling is coming, and baby, I'm going to miss you, but I'm prepared for it. Really."

Her brow creased in confusion.

"But I was fully expecting this to be *our* time. The calm before the storm. You, me, and absolutely nothing else. But it hasn't been that way. It's been you, me, and Wes, and I don't find him nearly as fucking pretty."

She laughed a little, a barely there smile of realization lifting the unbearable weight from her tiny shoulders.

"I feel a little like your aging wife, and your new job feels like your mistress. Unfortunately, it turns out I'm not above showing up naked in a trench coat in an effort to restore your interest."

"You're no aging wife. You run your own multibillion-dollar corporation, for God's sake."

"Not here, I don't. Here, I am nothing but your new husband. And I've selfishly been wishing you were here as only my wife."

"Couldn't this just be an opportunity to *watch me*?" she ventured, and I smiled.

"Ben."

"Ack. Okay. So you're right. I probably shouldn't be doing anything while I'm here."

"Me," I corrected playfully. "You should be doing nothing but me."

"Right, right. Don't worry, I've got you marked down on my to-do list."

"Thank God," I said with a wink.

"I'll call Wes and see if he can spare me for the rest of our time here," she offered.

"Oh, please, let me do it," I said a little too gleefully.

"No. Come on. He's your friend, but he's my boss. At least let me maintain a modicum of professionalism."

"I think that ship sailed, sweetheart. Back around Sexually-Influenced-Email-Island," I teased.

She flushed and slapped superficially at my chest. "That was your fault too!"

I smiled and waggled my eyebrows in triumph. She tried to resist, but in the end, she couldn't contain her smile either.

"Kline!"

"He's your boss, but trust me, this isn't Wes, your boss. This is Wes, my friend, and he's sitting back in New York merrily watching as he fucks with me. Let me call him."

"*Kline.*"

"That means yes. That's the same way you say my name during sex, and I *know* that means yes."

I grabbed her phone from the bed and scrolled through the numbers until I found Wes's office. She struggled to reach, but even on the tips of her toes, my outstretched arm kept her a good foot out of range of my ear.

It rang twice before his assistant answered. "Wes Lancaster's office."

I raised my voice an octave and did my best impression of my wife. "Hey, Gail, it's Georgia. Can you put me through?"

"Kline Brooks!" Georgia shrieked in the background.

I laughed and jogged out of the bedroom and onto the terrace, shutting the all-glass door behind me and holding it closed. My little Benny waved frantically on the other side.

"Georgia?" Gail questioned. She had to have been going through some fucking head trip. I didn't *sound* like Georgia, but it was sure as shit her number on the caller ID.

"That's me," I responded.

"Oh. Okay. I'll put you through," Gail muttered, mystified. I winked at Georgia through the glass and her eyes narrowed.

"Thanks!"

Wes's voice came over the line less than five seconds later. "Georgia?"

"Close," I said in my normal voice.

"Kline. Hey, buddy. How's the honeymoon?"

"Fucking fantastic," I said, telling him the truth but making sure my words had a little extra bite.

"Good, good," he murmured in response.

"Look. I know my wife is fucking essential to your operation," I started, diving right into the heart of it and turning to face the ocean so Georgia couldn't read my lips.

"Kline—"

"I handed her over on a silver fucking platter, so I know." He sighed, and I heard the door burst open behind me.

I kept talking anyway. "I don't know if you really needed her or if you just wanted to mess with me, but she's officially off duty for the rest of our trip."

"Yeah, I get it," he agreed, "and it was both. Messing with you and needing her."

I closed my eyes and forced myself to make an offer I really didn't want to extend. "You need to talk to her before you cut off all communication?"

"Yes!" Georgia demanded behind me. "Give me the phone."

"Yeah," Wes replied. "But it's not for work shit. I owe you, and I have a strong feeling you're in hot water."

I laughed. "Does your *feeling* have anything to do with the fact that you can hear my wife in the background?"

"It might," he said through a chuckle.

"Fine. Fix this, and we're even."

"Done."

Done. Because that was how problems between men got resolved.

Well, it was either that or hit each other in the face, and right now, neither of us was interested in making the trip.

CHAPTER 11

New York, Monday April 24th, Early Afternoon

Thatch

"He's been missing for four nights," Cassie said in my ear through the phone. Unable to avoid the office for more than a day, I'd given her my work number in case of an emergency or breakthrough. Apparently, she took those parameters very lightly. This was her tenth call today.

Yeah, I hear you. Yet again, I am the one answering her calls.
Therefore, I'm still the idiot here.

"I know, honey. But I'm sure he's fine. He's scrappy. A real street cat. His assholishness might actually be coming in handy."

I'd gotten in touch with Kline's dad, and ever efficient, Bob had the vet on the hunt. But four long nights without an actual capture, and even I was starting to miss the little bastard. Or maybe I wasn't, but I was visualizing the pain in sweet Georgie's eyes when she heard the news and listening to near hysteria from her best friend at that very moment. Their pain was feeling very much like my pain.

"You think he's falling in line with the right cats, though?" she asked ridiculously. "Georgie'll be so pissed if she comes home to find him in a gang of runaways."

I rubbed at the tension in my forehead and turned my chair to face the floor-to-ceiling windows in my office.

"Well, if he does, we'll be here to force him into rehabilitation through intervention."

"Right," she scoffed, like *I* was the crazy one. "Like there's a cat rehab. Good one, Thatcher. It must be right next door to the cat detective."

"Cass—"

"I lied to her."

"Who? The cat detective?" I asked, completely lost.

"Wheorgie, numbnuts! I told her about the microchip, but I didn't tell her that we hadn't *actually* found him."

"The vet's been getting a signal," I told her, even though she already knew. I hoped that hearing it again might help to calm her down. "He's just been moving around too much to pinpoint an exact location for pickup."

"Yeah, Thatcher. I know all these things. Jesus."

Closing my eyes, I leaned back into my leather desk chair and sighed. "You called me. What exactly are you after here? Honest to God, I'm trying." *Harder than I would with anyone else*, I thought to myself. "But I can't for the life of me figure out what you want."

"I don't know either," she said, but fuck, the uncertainty, the longing—all of it made her simple words sound an awful lot like, *I just wanted to talk to you.*

"Cass—"

"I gotta go, T-bag. Let me know if you hear anything about Walnuts," she rushed out. And then with a quick click of the line, she was gone.

I spun around to my desk and tossed the phone in the cradle before rubbing a hand down my face in annoyance. Everything between us felt foreign, like I couldn't get a handle on it. The weirdest part was not knowing if I wanted to.

"Mr. Kelly?" my assistant, Madeline, called on the intercom. Reaching forward, I pushed the button on my phone panel to answer.

"Yeah?"

"There's someone on the line for you from Green Gardens in Frogsneck, NY?"

Fuck. That was the venue for my parent's surprise fortieth anniversary party next month. "Put them through, Mad."

"You got it."

Two quick rings confirmed her response before I put the phone to my ear. "Hey, Tom," I greeted. My hometown was the size of a chicken nugget, and only one person would be calling me from Green Gardens.

"Thatcher? It's Tom."

"Yeah, Tom. I got that. That's why I said 'Hey, Tom.'"

"Oh."

"The reason you're calling?" I prompted when silence consumed the line for nearly half a minute. It was times like these that made me really *not* miss home.

"Oh. Yeah. I know you said you wanted an open bar and that you wanted lobster *and* steak, but that's gonna be pretty expensive, bud. I just wanted to double-check before I made the order because once it's in, it's in. I can't do you any favors, even if I like you."

"Thanks, Tom, but I'm good. Open bar, lobster, *and* steak. Don't worry about the order, I won't leave you hanging."

"Oh, right, right," Tom agreed, taking a tone I knew well and absolutely hated. "I guess I forgot you're some hot shot zillionaire whoseewhatsit in the city these days."

My patience was unraveling, but I fought hard to pretend like I had some. "Yeah, that's not it, Tom. It's just my parents' fortieth. They deserve a nice night."

Mad gave a quick knock and peeked her red head in the door. "Someone is here for you," she mouthed.

I nodded and rushed to get Tom off the phone. "Listen, I have to go. But thanks for checking in. I really appreciate it."

"All right. I guess I'll put the order in if you're sure."

Mad peeked in again and raised her brows in question. Waving a big hand, I signaled to let whomever it was in.

"I'm sure. Thanks, Tom."

My eyebrows pulled together as Cassie bounded into my office while Mad held the door. She wore tight jeans and a crop top, and I'll admit, my gaze traveled to the bottom of her shirt—or half of a shirt—in the hopes there was boob swell to be seen more than once.

"You bet. I guess this means you'll be coming home soon, huh?" Tom asked, fucking refusing to get off the fucking phone. And with my new guest, I was obviously getting zero work done today.

"Yep," I said grudgingly. "That's what it means."

"How long's it been?"

Five years. It'd been five years.

"A few years," I murmured as I tried to make out Cassie's charades. Her arms waved and her tits bounced, and she'd just started to get down on the ground and crawl around on all fours.

Is she licking the tops of her hands and purring?

"Gotta go, Tom," I reiterated. "Thanks for checking in. See you soon."

The phone barely met its base before Cassie jumped to her feet.

"Thank fuck. I thought you'd never get off the phone."

"What are you doing here, Cass? How the fuck did you know where my office was? And what in the *fuck* are you doing crawling around on my floor?"

"Well, hello to you too," she said, and it struck me like lightning. We were so similar, so like-minded. So much so, neither of us knew how to handle it. "And it's called Google, Thatcher."

"What's going on?" I asked again. "I thought you had somewhere to be. And how in the hell did you get here so fast? Do you have a teleportation device I need to try out?"

"Bob called me. Said he couldn't get through to you. The vet's got Walnuts." Her eyes fucking gleamed.

"Bob called when? Weren't you just crying to me about that little shit being missing?"

She shrugged. "Yeah, but that was just for fun. I was already on my way here."

"That was an act? An exercise in annoying me?" I asked.

She nodded and smiled.

"You're scary."

Her eyebrows just bounced.

"Well, shit. At least they found him." Air filled my lungs at the relief that I wouldn't have to tell Kline I'd permanently lost his wife's cat. "Thank fuck, right? You look relieved, and I'm sure Georgie will be too."

"Yep," she agreed with a bounce. "Thrilled all around." Too much bounce.

"What am I missing?"

"Let's just say Kline Brooks is going to have fucking hemorrhoids from trying to shit this load of news."

"*Fuck.*"

CHAPTER 12

Cassie

"240 East 80th, please," I instructed the cabbie as Thatch slid in to sit beside me.

The cab driver was midforties, sloppily dressed, and sported a serious fucking scowl. I glanced at his driver's license on the dashboard and saw that Jenk was his name. I'd say it was apparent Ol' Jenkie boy was having a shit day.

"240 East 80th?" He glimpsed at us in the rearview mirror and then huffed out a sigh, death-gripping his steering wheel.

"Yes, please," I responded, trying to be sweet even though I felt like telling him to cool it on the attitude.

"Isn't that a friggin' vet hospital?" he snapped for some unknown reason. I honestly had no idea why driving us to a vet hospital would put him over the edge, but I did know that Jenk the fuckface wasn't just having a shit day, it was more like a shit year…or *life*.

"Well, shit. Who needs Google Maps when the world has men like you running around?" I retorted loud enough for him to hear. I *wanted* him to hear. Hell, he needed to hear it. This dude needed a reality check.

Thatch bumped me with his elbow, hoping I'd get the message and shut up. I turned to him and kept going. "Last time I checked, Jenk the fuckface was the cab driver. Not me or you. Sorry if we're not going to the destination of his liking, but them's the breaks when your job is to drive people around."

"What was that?" Jenk asked, beaming me with the stink-eye in the rearview mirror.

"I *said*—"

Thatch placed his hand over my mouth. "She said, she loves your hat. Go Mavericks!"

That wasn't even close to the content or length of what I'd said, but the cabbie nodded anyway, trying his hand at a stiff smile. It looked like a grimace, but I guess that was what happened to your face when you never smiled.

News flash, kids. Apparently, it will freeze that way.

"Our boys are lookin' good. I think we're gonna have one helluva season this year."

"That's not what I said, asshat," I muttered to Thatch.

"First rule of Fight Club, Cass. Don't start shit with the man behind the wheel. Especially when you're in *his* car and at his mercy."

"Whatever, Thatcher," I huffed out, adjusting myself in the leather seat and accidentally brushing my boob against Thatch's bicep in the process. Honestly, it was an accident. The Jolly Green Giant was practically taking up the whole back seat.

He sighed in response, shutting his eyes and holding the bridge of his nose with his forefinger and thumb. "Tell me your tits are out again. *Please.* I'm at the end of my rope here, but your tits have the ability to make all kinds of things grow."

I glanced down at my chest. *Shit.* "Uh, it's a really thin bra."

Yeah, I didn't have a bra on, and the air conditioning blasting in the cab had my nipples at full attention. It wasn't even on purpose.

I'd been in the shower when Bob had called, and the second he told me the vet found Walter, I hauled ass to Thatch's office.

"Is it made out of fucking air?" he asked, voice hopeful and irritated at once. It seemed Thatcher was losing patience with the whole Walter, Cassie, and Thatch circus.

"What the fuck does it matter to you?" I snapped back. "If I want to walk around without a bra, that's my business, dude."

"Trust me, it's everyone's business when they have the power to save humanity from my mental breakdown."

"My nipples do not talk, and they don't have the power to save lives."

He glanced at me out of the corner of his eye. "Honey, they do. All they're doing right now is waving hello, and I already feel a million times better than I did five minutes ago. I bet Jenk feels better too."

Jenk didn't respond. And frankly, I took offense to that. Thatch noticed the change in me and pulled my attention back to him.

"Actually, right now, your tits are doing a 'we're stuck on a desert island and trying to wave down a plane,' kind of wave. Not just a hello. That means their power is double."

The ridiculousness of this entire conversation had me laughing. "Fuck, for a numbers guy, you're imaginative. I'll give you that."

He smirked. "Your tits put all sorts of creative ideas in my head, honey."

I eye-fucked him for a good ten seconds, honing in on the crotch of his dress slacks before meeting his eyes. "Put your boner away, Thatcher."

He glanced at my tits and then his dark brown eyes held my gaze as he nodded toward them. "Do it for me, Cassie."

We were at a stalemate, just staring at one another, the "let's fuck" tension building with each second, and I wasn't sure if it would end with me smacking the shit out of him or getting his dick out. Hell, maybe both.

The cab's brakes squealed as we came to an abrupt stop, and my face almost hit the back of the driver's seat.

"We're here!" Jenk shouted over his shoulder. "Fifteen bucks and I don't got fucking change."

While Thatch pulled his wallet out of his back pocket and tossed money into the front seat, I hopped out and turned toward the open window on the driver's side, ready to give the cabbie a piece of my mind.

"Wow, you really fucking suck at—" I started to say, but strong arms wrapped around my middle and carried me toward the entrance of the animal hospital.

"Fuck you hard, Thatcher! That guy needs to know he's a fucking *asshole!*" I shouted loud enough for most of Manhattan to hear.

Thatch just laughed in my ear while carrying me toward the doors. Each chuckle fueled my fake rage.

"The second you set me down, I'd protect my balls if I were you."

His lips were near my ear. "I'd love to wrestle you, maybe wind up tangled in your deliciously free tits, but we're about to go in to get Walter, and if you're acting like a lunatic, they probably won't let us take him home. And if we don't get that little asshole home, then you'll be the one who has to break that news to Georgia."

He was so strong and gentle at the same time, and he didn't seem anything but amused by my antics. I ignored the mating call from my puss-ay. If it were up to her, I'd have Thatch'd that in the cab. "*Fine.* Just set me down, motherfucker."

He set me down, and I strode into the office, not wasting any time holding the door for him.

"We've tried to separate them, but Walter isn't really having it," the vet tech stated vaguely, guiding us toward the back room where cages were lined up and stacked on top of one another.

"What do you mean 'Walter isn't really having it'?" Thatch asked, sliding his hands into his pockets as we stood in front of a cage holding one big motherfucker of a dog.

"Well…" She trailed off hesitantly. "He just gets really upset."

I put a hand on my hip. "Upset? You're going to have to explain what Walter getting upset looks like. That cat generally shows two emotions—utter indifference or satisfaction from spending three hours licking his asshole."

Thatch nodded. "Yeah, he's pretty big on the asshole licking. Is that normal?"

"Um, yes. Actually, that's very normal," she responded as she opened a drawer by the dog's cage. "Cats are predators. Their instincts are to clean themselves to avoid being scented by their prey."

Thatch smirked at me while Julie, the vet tech, was busy rummaging through a drawer full of collars and leashes. "Maybe we should start licking your tits to see if it'd help deter horny motherfuckers from staring," he whispered.

I cocked an eyebrow. "*We?*"

He shrugged. "Figured you'd need help. Most chicks can't get their tongues to their nipples without pulling a muscle in the process."

"That's very generous of you, but there's no risk of injury when it comes to sucking on my own tits."

His eyes heated, and he stepped closer. "Prove. It."

I grinned. "Make. Me."

"Here it is!" Julie yelled victoriously, waving a collar and leash in the air.

"This conversation isn't over, honey," Thatch muttered.

"Meh, I'm already over it," I retorted before turning my attention to Julie. "That collar looks a little small for that dog." I nodded toward the cage she was in the process of unlatching.

"It's not for him, it's for Walter," Julie said with a laugh. Before she unhooked the final latch, she stopped abruptly. "I almost forgot the gloves!" she said, grabbing an oversized pair from the counter beside her.

"Gloves?" Thatch questioned, eyebrows raised.

"When Walter gets upset, he tends to scratch a lot."

"Okay…but why are you opening that dog's cage? You know Walter is a cat, right?"

I glanced at Thatch, and it was apparent I wasn't the only one confused.

"Walter is inside this cage," she answered.

"What?" we said at the same time.

Julie nodded and opened the cage door. She nudged the giant dog to the side, and sure enough, there was the little dickhead, curled up against the dog's back.

"This is Walter's new friend?" I asked, eyes wide and shocked.

When Bob had called, he'd said the vet had warned him that The Asshole had a new friend he wasn't too keen on being removed from. I had assumed it was a cat, a female cat, but apparently my assumptions about Georgia's little buddy were dead wrong. And judging by the size of the balls on the dog he was curled up to, this little dickhead was on Team Dean.

"Yep," Julie announced on a whisper as she attempted to pick up Walnuts carefully without waking him. "Walter has really taken a liking to Stan here."

I glanced at Thatch and knew the second he got an eyeful of Stan's gonads.

"Seems there's a bigger reason behind Walter's enjoyment of tossing his own salad."

I snorted in laughter, and Julie just glanced over her shoulder, confusion stamped on her face.

This poor girl. She was so sweet, and yet somehow, she'd managed to pull the short straw and get stuck with Thatch and me. Two assholes who had no filters.

And all at once, it hit me.

Thatch and I were very alike. Almost *too* alike.

I stared at him, taking in his stupid, sexy smirk. *Jesus.* He was the guy version of me.

"You okay, honey?" he asked, his gaze catching on the befuddled expression gracing my face.

"Yep," I answered, averting my eyes and trying like hell to forget that revelation.

But I couldn't.

If opposites attracted, then what in the hell was happening between numbnuts and me?

An ear-piercing shriek grabbed my attention.

"It's okay, Walter," Julie cooed as she tried to disentangle his paws from the cage.

Was he fucking holding on to the cage door?

More shrieking and clawing echoed inside the large room. Other pets started to take notice, standing up in their cages and watching shit hit the fan before their curious eyes.

Stan woke up from his slumber and started barking like a banshee. And within minutes, the entire room was filled with barking and growling and cages rattling.

"Holy fucking shit!" I covered my ears.

"This looks like a bit of a problem, Julie," Thatch shouted over the rising noise.

She just nodded, sweat dripping from her forehead, and resumed wrestling with Walter, who now had the support of his boyfriend. Stan's teeth were wrapped around the leash connected to Walter's collar, and he was tugging the cat back into the cage.

"Hey, Julie, you guys wouldn't happen to offer pet boarding services would you?" Thatch's voice boomed over the barks.

"Yes, sir, we do!"

"Fantastic!" He clapped his hands together. "Let's go ahead and let Walter spend more time with Ol' Stan here, and I'll just cover boarding until my buddy and his wife get back from their honeymoon."

I actually heard her sigh of relief over the barks.

"It's weird. All we've really talked about are my tits and his boner, but there's a strange connection there," I told Georgia over the phone, fiddling with a napkin on the bistro table.

I called her to fess up about my lie of omission and let her know that Walnuts would be staying with his boyfriend until they got back from their honeymoon. I just chose to start the conversation off on a much lighter note. And for some reason, the weirdness between me and Thatch seemed like the best lead-in.

"That's *all* you've talked about?" she asked, shock in her voice.

My eyes caught sight of Thatch standing at the coffee shop counter, ordering our drinks and food. After the shit show at the vet's office, we decided to grab a bite about ten blocks away from my apartment. Well, *I* decided, and he bitched about the distance from his office, but he still came along regardless.

Why we were doing this was a mystery, but here we were.

"Pretty much," I answered. It was the truth. His boner and my tits seemed to be the number one topic of discussion whenever we were together. Yet another mystery that needed to be solved.

"For the love of God, why?"

I shrugged. "Mostly because they're out, I guess. My tits and his boner."

"Jesus. Next time you're around him, make like an evangelical and cover those things up. See if that helps…" She paused, and then added, "*Wait*… What do you mean *they're out*?"

Thatch smirked at the barista, and her cheeks flushed pink. For fuck's sake, he held some kind of magical power over women. One smile and he had the girl making our coffee two seconds away from convulsing into a spontaneous orgasm.

What would he be like in bed?

My mind took that as a green light to conjure up the possibilities—me riding his face, him fucking me with my legs in the air, my tongue sliding up his shaft, my tits wrapped around his cock… Yeah, they were some wickedly dirty fantasies.

My brain and pussy were convinced he'd be a fantastic fuck, and that only made me more intrigued about Thatcher Kelly.

"Cass? Are you still there?" Georgia's voice filled my ear.

"Yep."

"You totally just drifted off into 'I'm gonna Thatch that' fantasyland."

"Yep," I agreed.

"Just promise me you'll wait to screw his brains out until after you leave the restaurant. I'd like to enjoy the rest of my honeymoon without trying to wire you bail money."

"I'm not gonna fuck Thatch," I lied.

Wait…what? Was I already planning on getting in the Jolly Green Giant's pants?

I'd save that question to mull over at a later time. Preferably when he wasn't heading toward me with his arms full of coffee and blueberry muffins.

She snorted in laughter. "Yeah, and I'm not looking forward to riding my husband's cock in about five minutes."

"He's standing there with his giant schlong in front of your face, isn't he?"

Georgia giggled.

"All right, well, before you have your mouthful of pee-nis, I need to give you the rundown on Walnuts."

"Okay," she muttered, already sounding distracted.

Perfect.

I took a deep breath and said everything in a rush. "We actually just found him a few hours ago. He's good. Sorry I lied. He's at the vet. Gonna stay there until you guys get back because I've got a shoot, and obviously, we're really bad babysitters. So it's better that way. Okayloveyoubye."

I hit end on the call as Thatch sat across from me at the table, setting my coffee and muffin before me.

"She take it well?" he asked, his long fingers sliding the wrapper off his muffin with surprising finesse.

Yeah, he could definitely butter my muffin. Any fucking day of the week.

"I don't know." I shrugged.

Thatch chuckled. "You hung up before she even responded, didn't you?"

"Yep," I answered, taking a sip from my coffee. "You use that same tactic with Kline, don't you?"

He nodded. "All the fucking time."

Man, we were so much alike it was creepy.

My phone vibrated across the table with a text notification.

Georgia: You're lucky I'm in a different time zone. Text me the vet's info.

Me: You're a surprisingly good multitasker.

Georgia: Why are we friends?

Me: Less typing. More sucking. P.S. Friends don't let friends blow and text at the same time, Wheorgie. It's dangerous.

Georgia: Put a bra on.

I laughed out loud at that one.

Thatch tilted his head to the side. "What's so funny?"

I held my phone out to him, letting him see the conversation. He chuckled a few times and then took it upon himself to snatch my phone and start scrolling through my shit.

"Oh, so it's like that, is it?" I held out my hand. "If you want to be nosy, it has to be on equal terms."

He didn't bat an eye at my demand, sliding his phone out of his pocket and across the table.

To be honest, I was a little surprised by his openness, but I probably shouldn't have been. I didn't have anything to hide or be embarrassed about. Therefore, the guy version of me probably didn't either.

Shit. The asshat didn't even have a passcode set up on his phone.

My fingers tapped on his pictures first, scrolling through numerous photos of sports games and hilarious candids of his friends. I stopped on one that made me smile. "Are you wearing a 'Single and Ready to Mingle' shirt in this pic?"

"Fuck yeah, I am. Don't knock the shirt, it's my favorite."

"I'm stealing that shirt. I'll fucking wrestle you for it if I have to."

"You don't need to come up with excuses to wrestle me, honey. Name the time and place and lose the crop top, and I'm there."

I laughed. "Keep dreaming."

"All dreams can come true, if we have the courage to pursue them."

"Did you just quote Walt Disney in the context of getting me naked?"

"Sure did," he said, eyes back on my phone.

I moved to his contacts next, finding a slew of female names.

"Who's Tasara?" I asked, clicking on her name and finding a picture of an extremely attractive brunette.

His eyes met mine. "Who's Sean?"

"My brother," I answered honestly.

"Your brother? You know he's black, right?"

My eyes narrowed, and I flipped him the bird. He just smirked.

"Tell me about Tasara," I demanded. "And do you make a point of taking pictures of all of your contacts?"

"Tasara is my sister, and yes, I do. It's one of my favorite things."

"She is not your sister," I said, laughing.

"Nah, but she's a really nice girl."

"How nice?" I asked, wanting some details. I was curious about this man and the way he handled relationships.

"She's a fucking *giver*."

I tapped another name and stumbled upon yet another picture of a different gorgeous face. "What about Rachel?"

"She's a sweetheart. A really down-to-earth cool chick."

Next contact. "And Samantha?"

"She's a doll. Definitely a bit wild."

"You don't like wild?" I asked.

He smirked and raised his eyebrows, sitting back in his chair. "I *love* wild."

Of course he did.

"What about JoAnna?"

"She's a *multiples* kind of girl."

"And Ella, is she a wild sweetheart too?"

"All of those girls are sweethearts," he corrected. "I don't waste my time on anything else. But Ella did have a bit of a wild streak, too. I tend to migrate toward that kind of woman," he answered with a knowing glance.

My chest stung—like an actual stinging, burning feeling—and I found my hand rubbing it seeking relief. So many girls, but he didn't even hesitate to put details to a name. They weren't all faceless screws; that was apparent.

Was I having a heart attack?

This was definitely something I had never felt before. Fuck, I hated it. I knew that much. And the more I scrolled, the worse the pain got. I looked away from the screen, wanting a reprieve from the torturous feeling, or whatever the hell it was.

I guess if I keeled over while stuffing my face, I'd know the root cause was clogged arteries.

"So, these girls, how does it work? Are they actually cool with the fact that you're not a one-chick kind of guy? Or is that something you don't tell them?" I asked, no disdain in my voice. I was honestly just curious.

"Of course, they know the score, honey. I've been open and honest with every woman I've ever been with. I don't feed women bullshit lies to get in their pants. Never have and never will." He set my phone on the table. "And who said I wasn't a monogamous kind of guy?"

I cocked an eyebrow, sliding his phone toward him. Trapping the phone to a stop, his big hand spanned nearly the entire tiny table. "No one said it. I just assumed you're more focused on playing the field than actually looking for The One."

A hard-to-decipher emotion crossed his face, but I knew it wasn't happiness. There was some sort of sadness lying beneath the surface of his brown eyes.

"I'm not judging, Thatch. Honestly. I'm not exactly known for settling down, either."

He spun his phone on the table and glanced up at me. "Do you think you ever will?"

I shrugged. "I'm not sure. I guess if I found the right person, I would. What about you?"

"Same. I don't have my future mapped out, but I'm always open to possibilities."

I glanced at the time on my phone and realize I only had about an hour to get home, pack, and get to the airport. "Shit, I better get out of here," I announced, standing up from my chair.

Thatch glanced around, confused. "You have somewhere to be?"

I picked my purse up off the ground, sliding it over my shoulder. "Yeah, I've got a flight to catch."

"A flight?" He stood up, grabbing our empty cups and discarded wrappers, and tossed them in the trash can across from our table.

"A few last-minute shoots in the Bahamas. Just found out this morning."

He looked surprised. "You're flying to the Bahamas? *Today?* For a photo shoot?"

"Yeah, ESPN asked me to do a couple of pictorials… I'm pretty sure I'm speaking English right now…"

He ignored my sarcastic retort. "Why didn't you say anything about it?"

"It just slipped my mind," I said, walking beside him as we headed out of the coffee shop.

He held open the door. "How long are you going to be gone?"

"Not sure. Three, maybe four, weeks tops."

Thatch stopped abruptly in the middle of the sidewalk. "You're going to be gone an entire month?"

My face scrunched up in confusion. "Yeah, is that okay?"

He ran a hand through his hair. "I guess so, yeah."

"Is your boner going to miss me, Thatcher?" I teased.

He chuckled, but he stepped closer to me. "Your tits? Fuck yes. You? Eh, I think I'll be okay. Maybe I'll even manage to get some work done without you calling my office fifteen times a day."

I grinned, standing on my tiptoes to kiss his cheek. "Don't worry, T-bag, I'll set time aside out of my busy schedule to brighten your day with my beautiful voice."

He smiled back, eyes amused. "At the very least, shoot me a text so I know you made it there safely."

"You got it," I agreed. "Bye, Thatch," I said, turning and heading for my apartment.

A smack to my ass startled a squeal from my lips and stopped my feet dead in their tracks. I turned back around to find him smirking and walking backward in the opposite direction.

"Be good, Cass!"

"I don't know about that, Thatcher! I'm feelin' a bit *wild*!"

"Be. Good," he demanded and then turned on his heels, getting lost in the crowd.

Be good?

What in the fuck did that even mean? And more importantly, why did I care?

He didn't have a say in what I did or didn't do. But fuck, he sure had a say in whether or not he wiggled his way into my head. Like a leech, he had taken up residence in my thoughts, and I wasn't sure how to get rid of him.

Did I even want to?

CHAPTER 13

New York, Monday, May 1ˢᵗ, Late Afternoon

Georgia

I was damn near bouncing in the car as Frank drove us to the vet's office to pick up Walter. In the two weeks since I'd seen him, he'd been forced to spend time with Cassie and Thatch *and* gone missing. I could hardly fathom the thought of him roaming the city streets by himself, but bearing Cassie's disdain probably wasn't much better.

"Little excited, Benny?" Kline asked, placing a soothing hand on my thigh to stop my leg from bouncing.

I held out my thumb and forefinger, adding, "Just a little bit."

He grinned, wrapping his arm around my shoulders and tucking me close to his side.

Instead of going home and catching some shut-eye after a long flight, I had convinced Kline to go straight from the airport to pick up my little buddy. Well, maybe less *convinced*, more told him if he didn't go, I still was. Walter didn't need to stay another night in a cold crate. He needed to be home with his family.

Kline kissed my forehead. "Thanks for a wonderful honeymoon, Mrs. Brooks."

I looked up at him, my heart in my eyes. "Likewise, Mr. Brooks. I'll probably be bow-legged for the next three months, but I had the best time. You're real good at honeymoons."

He smirked, tucking a lone curl behind my ear. "Who says that treatment stops after the honeymoon? Consider yourself thoroughly well-fucked and bow-legged for the next hundred years."

I laughed, grinning back at him. "If you can still fuck me like that when we're ninety years old, you're not real."

"Should I expect a blood test? A surgical examination?"

"Gross."

One perfect eye shut in a wink. "I'm real, Benny. *Really* in fucking love with my wife, and love has the power to do crazy things. I'm just hopeful those things include giving a ninety-year-old man the stamina to keep his pretty little wife *satisfied*."

"Jesus. Cool it on the swoon, you bastard. I might actually pass out from it."

He didn't cool it, though—his blue eyes still smoldered.

"Kline!" I smacked his chest. "I'm being serious."

"No, you're not." He leaned in close, whispering in my ear, "You love the swoon. In fact, you're already thinking about how to get me naked the second we get home."

"Shut up," I said through a giggle. He wasn't too far off base with that one though. My mind was considering the backseat of the car, but I'd keep that to myself.

He laughed and placed a soft kiss on my lips. "You won't have to try very hard." His nose rubbed mine and his voice dropped to a whisper. "With me, you'll never even have to ask."

Like I said, swoony motherfucking bastard.

God, I loved him.

I should've known things weren't going to go smoothly the minute we stepped into the vet's office. Few words were spoken in exchange with the receptionist, but as soon as we mentioned we were there to pick up Walter, utter panic consumed her face. She muttered something about getting Julie and then strode off without another word. *A bad omen.*

Fifteen minutes and a brief video on veterinarian-office safety later, we were standing in front of the crate of a Great Dane named Stan. *I knew that video wasn't standard procedure.*

"We're actually here to pick up Walter," Kline instructed. "Walter is a cat."

Julie pointed to the cage. "Yeah, well, Walter is actually inside there."

We looked at one another, confused.

"What do you mean he's in there?" I asked.

"He's really taken a liking to Stan and quite adamantly refuses to be anywhere but curled up next to Stan's back."

"He's taken a liking to this giant dog? This giant, *male dog*?" Kline questioned, eyes wide.

"Honestly, I've never seen anything like it," Julie admitted. "They seem very attached to one another."

"Christ." Kline ran his hand through his hair, visibly disturbed by the whole scenario.

I leaned toward the cage, peering inside until I saw the fluff of multicolored dark and light fur that was Walter. "Holy moly, he's really in there."

"Yes, he really is," Julie said, exasperated.

"Well, let's get him out so we can take him home." It was obvious Kline was ready to get home and relax. Being on a plane for over thirteen hours tended to do that to a person.

"That's actually easier said than done, Mr. Brooks," Julie replied, turning to look at both of us. "Your friends didn't tell you what happened when they tried to pick him up?"

"No." I shook my head. I had a feeling Cassie left out the important

details for a reason—like making sure we suffered through this without warning.

"What exactly happened?" Kline asked, tone hinting at irritation.

Thatch would definitely be getting an earful later. Kline Brooks
wasn't the kind of guy you sent in blind. The fallout would probably
be entertaining to watch, though.

"Walter gets very...intense whenever we try to remove him
from Stan's cage."

"Intense?" My eyes nearly bugged out of my head.

Julie nodded. "*Violently* intense."

This doesn't sound good.

"With all due respect, Julie, my wife and I have been on a plane
all day. I'd really like to just get Walter and head on home, so what
exactly do we need to do to make that happen?"

"I'll get suited up, and we can give it another shot," she said,
turning on her heels and striding through a door toward a back
room.

"Suited up?" I asked, my concern growing by the minute.

Kline just sighed, shaking his head. "Fuck if I even know what
that means, but I don't fucking like the sound of it."

Yeah, my husband was pretty much done with this entire scenario, and I had a feeling we hadn't even really seen anything yet.
When he started throwing around f-bombs, I knew his ironclad patience was on its last legs.

Julie came out of the back room with a lot more clothing on
than she started with. She looked like she had wrapped herself up in
a mattress and thrown on some type of heavy-duty, protective clothing over top. Her hands were covered in giant gloves, and a hard hat
adorned her head.

"You have *got* to be shitting me," Kline muttered to himself.

"Uh...Julie? You need that much...*gear*? Just to get our cat out
of the cage?"

"Yes." She nodded, face determined. "You'll see."

You'll see? Talk about ominous. This just got worse and worse.

She stood in front of the cage and took a deep breath, mumbling something to herself. She looked like she was preparing to exchange gunfire with terrorists. Her hands shook as they unlatched the door and reached inside to nudge Stan off to the side.

I was starting to think this whole thing was a bit dramatic, but then, as she wrapped her gloves around Walter's body, I realized it wasn't dramatic at all. Not one bit. Hell, she probably should have worn more gear.

Walter screeched and clawed, banshee cries louder than I'd ever heard echoed through the room as he valiantly fought her efforts.

"It's okay, Walter," she cooed, but he wasn't having one bit of it. His claws dug into the padding on her arms, making any question of its necessity vanish.

My hand covered my mouth in shock, and Kline just muttered, "Oh, for fuck's sake."

"Come on, Walter, your mom and dad are here to pick you up," Julie soothed, trying her damnedest to comfort a cat who wanted no fucking comfort.

More screeching and clawing.

Was he holding on to the cage?

Stan woke up at that moment and started barking—loud, deep barks that filled the room and started to wake up the other dogs.

Within minutes, every animal was losing their shit.

Walter's paws lost their grip on the cage, but somehow, he managed to latch himself onto Stan, holding on to him for dear life. Stan's eyes found his, and they weren't the angry eyes of a clawed dog, but those of a companion offering encouragement.

Oh. My. God. My buddy was in love!

That's why he didn't want to leave Stan. Tears filled my eyes as I watched Julie yank Walter out of the cage and slam the door shut. Stan stood on his legs, howling in distress. He'd found The One while Kline and I were on our honeymoon.

"We can't tear them apart, Kline!" I cried. "They're in love!"

Kline looked away from the sight of Julie wrestling Walter into a traveling crate, and his eyes met mine. His brow was scrunched, and he was staring at me like I had truly lost it.

"Kline, I'm being serious. They love each other. We can't tear them apart."

He scrubbed a hand over his face, muttering, "I'm going to fucking *kill* Thatch."

Julie managed to get Walter inside the traveling crate and lock the door, and all I could do was watch as my cat and his new boyfriend cried for each other. Stan howled. Walter screeched. It was the saddest fucking thing I'd ever seen.

"Can we take Stan home?" I asked Julie.

"*No*," my husband interjected. "Baby, I love you, I really do, but we are not taking that dog home with us."

"But Kline," I started to plead, but he wasn't having it.

He shook his head. "He's a Great Dane, Georgia. And he's not even full grown yet. He probably has another fifty pounds to go. There is no way in hell we can bring him back to the apartment."

Even though I knew he was right, I still wasn't happy. I knew our co-op only allowed pets under twenty-five pounds, but I couldn't stop myself from being irrationally angry with Kline for not letting us take Stan.

"We also have a two-week waiting period," Julie offered, trying to smooth things over. When my eyes jumped to hers, she explained. "To see if anyone claims him. He's a suspected lost pet too."

Kline's eyes were relieved. That made one of us.

"Fine," I cried, then grabbed Walter's crate, and stomped off toward the exit.

Kline followed quickly, but I turned to him just as we reached the door and pointed an irrational finger in his face. "You may not want a dog, but you're gonna be needing a fucking dog house."

Mic drop. Georgia out.

New York, Sunday, May 7th, Late Morning

We had been home for about a week since the vet debacle, and I'd managed to stop blaming Kline for the reason Stan wasn't at our apartment, but Walter was still sulking.

Actually, we were both sulking.

For the past six days, if I wasn't working, Walter and I were lying in bed, watching reruns of *Friends* together. He only seemed to perk up when the episode where Phoebe sings "Smelly Cat" was on. We had watched that episode, *The One With The Baby On The Bus*, a good fifteen times.

My husband did his best to cheer me up, but I still couldn't get over the fact that Walter's little kitty heart was breaking. It was his first true love, and it was playing out like an animal version of *Romeo and Juliet*. Well, without the families at war or the poison or the whole guy and girl scenario, but yeah, it was definitely a tragic, star-crossed love story.

When Julie had told us that the second Stan walked into the office, Walter had sidled up to the big dog and started cleaning his fur, I knew, without a doubt, it had been love at first lick.

My poor little buddy.

And now, I was going to have to leave him to mourn by himself.

Wes had asked me to join him on a recruiting trip for the Mavericks, and even though I'd much rather stay home and console my heartbroken cat than go to Phoenix for the next week, I needed to go. I needed to start getting my feet wet and diving headfirst into my job with the Mavericks' organization.

I tossed my toiletries into my suitcase and zipped it shut. Sitting on the bed beside Walter and stroking my fingers behind his ears, I said, "It'll be okay, buddy. I promise, it'll be okay."

He purred, but his eyes were still sad.

Kline walked into the bedroom, leaning against the doorframe. "All set?"

I nodded, stood up from the bed, and kissed the top of Walter's head. "I'll be back in a week, buddy. Be good for Kline while I'm gone."

My husband grabbed my suitcase, and I followed his lead into the hallway.

"Promise me you'll take good care of Walter while I'm gone," I said as we stepped into the elevator.

"I promise, baby."

"My kind of good care," I specified.

"Nothing but the best for the grumpy cat," he assured me.

"And promise me you'll take him places. He needs to get out of the apartment. I think it would be good for him while I'm gone."

He grinned, laughing and groaning softly. "I promise. You have nothing to worry about, sweetheart. Walter and I will bond like fucking hydrogen while you're gone."

I moved closer to him, wrapping my arms around his waist and looking up into his blue eyes. "What about you? Will my husband be okay, too?"

He pressed a soft kiss to my lips. "I'll be missing you for the next week, but there's only one thing I need to hear to make it okay."

I smiled. "I'll be missing you too."

CHAPTER 14

New Jersey/New York, Wednesday, May 10th, Late Morning

Kline

Sunlight streaked through the windshield as I pulled to a stop and put the rental car in park. I'd have to do something more permanent about our lack of vehicle eventually, but I wanted to leave *something* for when Georgie got home. There was a risk she'd be feeling left out or pushed at that point thanks to my unconventionally large surprises, and I wanted at least one thing to be completely of her making. Picking out a couple of cars seemed like a good start.

I'd seen fifteen houses in the last two days, and not one of them had been right. Too big or too small, I was starting to feel a little like Goldilocks—lost and tired and hoping someone would show up with some beds. But my Realtor said she had a feeling about this one, and it was located less than thirty minutes from Georgia's parents, Dick and Savannah, in a pretty little town in New Jersey. I wasn't sure if that was really a pro or a con, but thirty minutes was safe either way—far enough if she didn't want to be close, just a short trip if she did. And the work commute to the city wouldn't be traumatizing either. It often took more than thirty minutes to get from one place in the city to the other anyway.

"Well, what do you think?" I asked, turning to my only companion and helper in the search for the perfect home.

He didn't say much, but then, I didn't really expect him to. We were really just starting to come to terms with one another, and he still felt lingering animosity about our most recent disagreement. But Georgie trusted him, so I knew making an effort to show I did too would go a long way toward making her feel comfortable about our new normal. Even though she was the only one going through a major professional change, we were still very much a *we* now, and I wanted the change to get marked with just enough significance.

"I'm not sure yet either," I told Walter. "Maybe you'll know once you lick yourself in a few rooms."

He meowed in agreement, a huge step in the right direction, and then leaned his head toward me so I could hook the thin leash to his collar.

I hopped out first and helped him to the ground so he wouldn't hurt his paws. The picture of us together was ridiculous—confirmed by the Realtor's face on the first day. *Kline Brooks, the eccentric billionaire who goes nowhere without his cat.*

Far from the truth, but luckily, all I'd had to say was "my wife loves this cat" for the sweet, middle-aged woman to understand.

"Mr. Brooks," she greeted us as Walter and I climbed the small hill of the driveway.

"Hey, Helen," I replied, watching with never-ending fascination as she got down on her knees and greeted Walter with strokes and kisses.

"Hello, Walter," she cooed in his little kitty ear. I swear, this cat was *catnip* for women. But I guess most of them did love a good asshole.

Holding out a hand, I helped Helen to her feet, and we made our way toward the front door. A huge front porch lined the entire front of the house, and a swing hung in the far right corner. Soft tan siding covered the guts, and tasteful black-and-white accents made up the trim, shutters, and door. So far, so good.

"From what you've told me, I think this one is really going to hit on all of Georgia's tastes. Simple, updated, but with a ton of character in the moldings and fixtures," Helen explained as she worked the lockbox to retrieve the key. "It's just gone on the market, and I think it's priced pretty fair, so there's a good chance it's going to move fast."

"And how much property?" I asked as I glanced down at Walter.

"Just over four acres. The backyard is large and well-maintained, but we'll get to that. I think it's got a lot of possibility if you're thinking about more pets." She smirked and shrugged. "Or maybe some kids?"

I just laughed, not about to discuss my family's future plans with Helen before discussing it with my wife, but I appreciated the woman's sentiment. She could tell I wanted to make a home for Georgie that had room for *all* the possibilities.

Nothing made me happier than making Benny happy, and Walter on a fucking leash beside me made that really fucking apparent.

"And you told the seller about the quick close?"

"Yes. They're completely on board. If you're interested and pay a premium," she said, cocking her head and smiling. Almost everyone got motivated when you paid extra. "They'll happily close by the end of this week. But, that does mean we really have to make a quick decision."

I hummed my agreement. I'd know by the end of the tour. Georgie had been laying down plenty of information about what she preferred and what she didn't while she helped me with my parents' Hamptons house, and I'd been storing it all up like a fucking library.

As we stepped through the front door, Walter took off and pulled the leash right out of my hand. Straight through the large, open space, he immediately settled in front of the wall-to-wall glass windows at the back and started licking himself. I took that to mean he liked it.

"Isn't that adorable?" Helen commented, putting a hand to her chest and sighing. Apparently, Walter knew how to lay on the swoon. I, personally, didn't fucking see it, but what did I know?

"So it's five bedrooms, open floor plan, as you can see. The kitchen is huge, maybe a little overdone for the rest of the house, but it's *beautiful*. Antique white cabinets and fresh quartz counters."

She spoke, and I listened as I walked, scanning the space and immediately picturing us living there. Everything reeked of Georgie, from the dark wood floors, to the serene blue-gray on the walls, and when the kitchen came into view, it hit me. She and me and little blue-eyed babies carefully perched on the edge of the counter. I could see spilled milk and lazy Sundays and more goddamn happiness than my chest could contain.

"The floor is—"

"This is it," I cut in, knowing I'd spend some of the best years of my life here.

"Don't you want to see the bedrooms? And the basement? And the backyard?" Helen asked rapid-fire.

"Sure," I said, because I knew I shouldn't buy a house I hadn't even seen in its entirety, but this was it. I knew it on a cellular level.

This. This was the home my wife would love and had never once asked for. All the things I'd ever hoped to find in a woman lived in her. When she looked at me, she didn't see anything other than love and her one true match—and maybe a big dick.

"Why don't you go ahead and call the seller while we walk the rest?"

"But what if you see something you don't like?" Helen asked.

With a gentle hand at her elbow, I tried to convey just how sure I was. "Helen, the only thing that's gonna stop me from buying this house is a body in the basement. And even then, I might overlook it if they can give me a good reason."

"Okay, Walt. You have to stay in the car for this one."

A hiss and swipe of his claw.

"I get it. I know you know where we are. I'm not really sure *how* you know because you're a cat, but I know you know."

He let loose with a suspicious, mewling meow.

"After the way things went when we picked you up, they've forbidden you to come back in there. But I promise, everyone is going to be really happy when I come back out." He seemed somewhat placated. "Well, probably everyone but me," I added, which turned his kitty expression into satisfaction.

"Right," I said to him and myself, and hoped that, one day, I'd either stop talking to my cat or stop feeling so ridiculous about it.

I shut the car door with a slam and walked up to the building, the bell over the door ringing as I stepped inside.

The receptionist looked up from her paperwork with a smile, ready to greet me, but when she saw who it was, the smile melted right off of her face.

"Walter's in the car. With the windows rolled down," I said, not wasting any time setting everyone's mind at ease. The tension in her shoulders relaxed immediately, answering the question of whether she had a neck or not affirmatively. "I called and talked to Julie, and she said there'd been no one looking to claim Stan."

Julie stepped through the door from the back. She smiled freely, but she'd had fair warning of my arrival—and the chance to remind me that Walter was strictly prohibited from entering the building.

"Hey, Mr. Brooks. Come on back. I'm pretty sure Stan is going to be happy to see you."

With a nod to Receptionist Melanie, I stepped through the door as Julie held it open. Barking filled my ears, but it wasn't Stan. The fucking enormous Great Dane puppy lay sleeping in the center of his cage, curled up into the tightest coil he could manage.

"All he's really been doing since you guys left is sleeping," Julie explained. "I think he's been depressed."

He did seem to frown in his sleep, and I was happy Georgie wasn't seeing him like this.

"I can open the cage for you," Julie offered, pulling my eyes to her. "He's really big, but super gentle. Walter seemed to be the violent one of the two."

That much I could believe.

I nodded my agreement, and she pulled up the latch and swung open the door.

"Hey, Stan," I whispered to warn him I was there. He opened his big black eyes just as I reached out to touch him, leaned into my hand, and blew out a big doggie breath. "You ready to come home?"

CHAPTER 15

Phoenix, Friday, May 12th, Very Late Night

Georgia

Five days away from Kline had been five too many. Phone calls, text messages, video chats, emails, none of them lived up to the real thing. Which was why I was sitting on a red-eye flight from Phoenix to New York. My work travel had only just begun, but I could already tell it'd never be the highlight of my job.

When I'd told Wes I wasn't flying home with the team, he had laughed at the hilarity of me missing my husband after only five days. Thankfully, he'd ended his laughter by being surprisingly supportive, even though he let me know how ridiculous he thought it was.

But I didn't care that I was sitting in a cramped coach seat versus the luxury leather recliners on the team's jet. I didn't care that I was dead on my feet and about one blink away from falling into a coma. I just wanted to get home to my husband.

I slid my earbuds in and reclined my chair back the measly two inches it was willing to go. I was ready for the time to pass at full speed so I could be in my bed, all wrapped up in Kline. *Never Been Kissed* was the courtesy movie for my flight home, and I couldn't deny my excitement.

Even though that movie came out forever ago, it will always have one of my favorite endings. Sam Coulson running down the stadium steps. "Don't Worry Baby" by The Beach Boys playing in the background.
The crowd cheering.
Josie Gellar watching him stride toward her.
And then, that kiss. How he just grabs her and kisses the fuck out of her.
Yeah. Talk about cinematic perfection.

I could remember watching that movie when I was young and just wishing, hoping, *fucking praying* I'd get my Josie Gellar, "Don't Worry Baby" moment. I'd truly believed that everyone got to experience one of those epically romantic moments once in their lives.

I had mine with Kline when he stood in his office—proving to me that he was every bit of the man I knew he was—and got down on one knee, asking me to spend the rest of my life with him. He'd lived up to the fantasy and then some. Sure, we'd had other amazing, swoony moments, but that one topped the rest by a landslide.

Damn, I miss my husband.

The flight had been long, and despite my valiant efforts to catch some shut-eye, I stayed wide-eyed and fidgety the whole way. After navigating my way out of baggage claim, I hopped in a cab and headed home.

I was nearly vibrating with excitement over surprising Kline.

The cab ride was short and sweet thanks to the time of morning, and with no rush-hour traffic or random construction delays to stop my progress, I was out of the cab and onto our elevator within 30 minutes.

I slipped in through the door, toeing off my heels and locking the dead bolt with a soft click. Leaving my suitcase and purse in the entry, I tiptoed down the dark hall and stopped at the doorway of our bedroom. It took a second for my eyes to adjust to the lack of light, but when they did, it didn't take long to find myself very, very confused by the number of figures lying in our bed. As I moved farther into the room, my night vision transitioned completely, and what I saw had me stopping dead in my tracks.

Kline lay on his back in his familiar sleeping pose—one leg hanging out from beneath the blankets and an arm strewn across his abdomen. And Walter was in his familiar spot, curled up at the foot of the bed.

But he wasn't alone.

Nope.

Stan was sleeping soundly on my side of the bed, his giant head resting on my pillow. And his little buddy Walter was pressed up against his stretched out legs.

Kline Brooks had officially caved on Stan.

Jesus. Could he be any swoonier?

I needed to thank him. *A lot.* Because hell, I was pretty sure he had just given me another "Don't Worry Baby" moment.

Quietly, so as not to disturb my husband, I roused Walter and Stan awake, encouraging them to slip off the bed and out of our bedroom.

Stan followed my lead with puppy-like movements, his long tail wagging and paws awkwardly tapping against the hardwood floor. Walter was less enthused, but he followed nonetheless. I had a feeling it had more to do with his boyfriend than me, but I'd take what I could get.

Guiding them into the living room, I threw an old comforter on the couch and got them settled. Within a few minutes, my two boys were sawing logs, adorably cuddled up to one another.

When I returned to the bedroom, Kline was still where I had left him, deep in sleep and looking sexy as hell with bedhead and only a pair of boxer briefs and a thin sheet covering his body.

I quickly got undressed and climbed onto the foot of the bed, crawled under the covers and stopped once I reached the waistband of his boxer briefs. When my fingers started to slide them down, Kline stirred in his sleep, his eyes blinking in confusion.

"What the…? Georgie?"

"Hi, baby," I whispered, tugging his briefs down just enough to reveal his…*oh, yeah.*

"What are you doing home so early?" he asked, rubbing at his eyes feverishly.

"I was missing you too much."

"What time is it?" His voice was thick and groggy.

"It's time for me to thank my amazing husband."

His brows lifted. "I like where this is headed, but what exactly are you thanking me for?"

I straddled his hips, leaning forward to brush my mouth against his. "You caved on Stan," I said, tugging on his bottom lip.

He grinned. "Oh, yeah, Stan."

"Oh, yeah, *him.* The giant dog that was just sleeping on my pillow."

Kline laughed as his fingers slid into my hair, tangling with the loose curls. "Walter's boyfriend snores, by the way. *A lot.*"

I giggled, but I needed to ask, "What made you change your mind?"

"Your happiness is my happiness," he said, like it was the most normal thing in the world. "So are you happy?"

I leaned back, staring down at my stupidly romantic husband. "Yes, Mr. Brooks, I am very fucking happy. I'm literally the luckiest woman on the planet, and it's all thanks to my sweet, amazing, perfect husband." I caressed his cheek with my hand. "I love you. I love you so very much."

"Fuck, I missed you, Benny." He tugged my mouth back to his, kissing me hard and deep. He kissed me until moans hijacked my lips and my hips started to move against his instinctively.

"So…about that whole thanking your husband thing?" he asked, smirking like the devil.

"Oh, yeah, about that," I answered as I slid down his body. My lips found his skin and started a slow, seductive path down his stomach. "I'm feeling all sorts of generous this morning."

"I'm loving the sound of this," he said, his voice choppy.

"This morning," I said, wrapping my hand around his cock, "my happiness will be all about *my husband's* happiness."

"That's one hell of a cycle."

The instant my tongue tasted him, he groaned.

"*Fuck*, yeah, this is definitely making me happy."

New York, Saturday, May 14th, Morning

Kline

"Go ahead, Stan," I whispered in the late morning sunlight of our bedroom. "Get closer. Come on, scoot closer. Really crowd her."

Waking up to Georgie earlier was one of the best unexpected treats I'd ever experienced. I'd missed her an awful lot—to the point that I was starting to annoy myself. Long, drawn-out conversations with Walter and Stan weren't my idea of an ideal reality. I'd needed my wife, I'd needed her surprise, and now, I couldn't wait to give her another one of her own.

I turned to look behind me and found Walter looking on from the edge of the area rug, completely unamused. "You too. Get up here!" I whisper-yelled. "I need your help." He narrowed his eyes at me, and I mirrored the gesture right back at him. "Don't you want to show her our other surprise?"

Two more licks to his paw later, he finally moved forward and jumped up on the bed.

"Thank you."

Now I'm thanking cats? Jesus.

"Get close, guys," I instructed again, and for once, they listened.

Stan's nose nudged under the curve of Georgie's neck, and Walter laid his kitty paw on her cheek on the other side. She swiped and swatted and tried to shoo it away, but my boys were relentless.

"Georgie," I whispered, trying to help her along on the trip from Sleepytown to Awakeville.

"Bratwurst," she mumbled.

"Pickles," she went on. I laughed. "Big-dicked—"

Hell yes!

"Thor."

Fuck.

"Benny, wake up."

She moaned and tried to move, but the animals wouldn't let her, and finally, her eyes popped open in frustration. "Fucking space management, you little shits are a bigger problem than I realized," she announced immediately, seeing them and not me.

"I tried to tell you."

"Shit!" she shrieked, a hand rising to her chest as a flimsy shield. "You scared me to death."

I smiled and raised my eyebrows. "Rough wake-up call, baby?"

"No," she denied. "I was just surprised is all."

"You're drowning in paws."

"Okay," she hedged. "Maybe a little, but it's no big deal."

She was afraid I was going to take the dog back. Stan barked like he could sense it.

"I don't know." I pushed on, desperate to get her good and riled up. "I was afraid this would happen. There's no room for me in that bed, and I don't like the sound of that."

"Kline—"

"No, Benny. If there's a bed with you, I want to be in it."

"We'll get a bigger bed," she offered quickly.

"This bedroom really isn't big enough for a king."

I was expecting her to get angry, but she just looked crestfallen. *Shit.*

Tears threatened the corners of her pretty blue eyes, and I knew I'd do anything to stop them. Striding to the bed, I shoved Walter out of the way with a hiss and cupped her cheek.

"Don't cry, baby. I was just messing with you. Stan's here to stay, I swear."

Her waterfall of melancholy dried up faster than a raindrop.

"What the fuck? Were you faking those tears?"

"Maybe," she admitted with a smirk.

Fuck. I would have fucking sworn those tears were real. "I don't like this. I don't like this one bit."

"I'm sorry," she laughed. "I promise to never trap you with fake tears if you promise to always keep Stan."

I had no plans to get rid of Stan. Quite frankly, I kind of liked him. "Deal."

She smiled again and wrapped her arms around my neck, and it took a full thirty seconds before I realized my perfectly crafted plan hadn't been executed even close to the blueprints.

"Shit."

"What?" she asked, pulling back to look at me.

"Nothing. Just…that didn't go according to plan at all. I started that whole mess for a reason."

"A reason?"

"A big one," I clarified with a playful wince.

"Just spit it out!" she yelled through a laugh, smacking me on the chest.

So I did.

"You want to go see our new house?"

"House? As in…a house?!"

"It's the housiest house *I've* ever seen," I joked.

"Oh, my God! I fucking love housey houses!" she shouted and stage dived directly off the bed and even deeper into my heart.

She was perfect in all of her awkward excitement, and I was just the man at her mercy.

"I love you," I told her, just as her mouth met mine.

"Me too," she said. "I can't believe you did this. Why? Why did you do this?"

"Because you want the dog, and Walter wants the dog, and that means I want Stan too. Stan means fucking space. This'll give it to us."

"*Kline.*"

"We'll always miss you when you're gone, but when you come back, you'll always know we're all happy and healthy and waiting completely impatiently at home."

<hr />

New York, Tuesday, May 16th, Very Early Morning

Kline and Georgia had been back from their honeymoon for two weeks, and already, the fucker had gone and gotten her a house *and* a dog. He was sick in the head, but if you asked me, that was the definition of love. I hated that they were moving out of the city, but they still worked here, and Kline never went out anyway. I'd just have to travel a little farther when I felt like crashing on their couch. Otherwise, my life would remain pretty much the same.

My phone chirping over the hum of needles pulled my attention away from my friend Frankie's latest portrait tattoo. Some guy from Detroit had driven all the way here just for Frankie's unique talent. I still got a kick out of that shit.

When I picked up my phone, a text message from a number I didn't recognize read like a fucking novel.

Unknown: The Mingan Island Cetacean Study Group has been using photographic techniques to study humpback whales for the last 16 years. In that time, they began to realize that female

humpback whales not only make friends with one another, but they reunite each year.

Isn't that adorable! Such cuties!

If you've received this message in error, please text Unsubscribe. If you're ready for another complementary fact, text Whale Lover.

What in the ever-loving fuck is this shit?

Me: UNSUBSCRIBE

Unknown: If you would like to unsubscribe from Interesting Whale Facts of the Day, text yes. But we really hope you don't because we'd sure miss you!

Me: YES.

Unknown: YES, PLEASE! You just received a superspecial subscription to Sexy Words of the Day. There's nothing sexier than a man whispering, "You're beautiful," into a woman's ear.

What the fucking fuck? My fingers tapped violently across the screen.

Me: Goddammit. I don't want this.

Unknown: We had an issue with processing your request. If you'd like to unsubscribe from Sexy Words of the Day, text yes.

Me: FUCK YES. UNSUBSCRIBE YOU STUPID MOTHERFUCKERS.

Unknown: You're a dirty, dirty boy who just received a free picture subscription to Spank Me Daddy. Are you ready for your first picture? Text yes, if you are.

Okay. I'd been frustrated, but fuck if I wasn't intrigued by this turn of events.

Me: YES

Unknown: Uh-oh, you just unsubscribed from Spank Me Daddy. We're going to be so sad you're leaving.

Me: I said YES, cocksucker. Fucking hell, you need better IT.

Unknown: Did someone just say the secret password?

Oh, yeah! Now we were speaking the same language.

Me: Cocksucker? That's my secret password?

Unknown: Yes, he did! You've just won 30 days of getting to watch Cassie masturbate without getting to touch her. Congratulations, dickwad.

Unknown: Oh, hey, by the way, I got a new number.

Goddammit, this fucking girl. She was pure evil. I hadn't heard from her since we'd parted ways in front of the coffee shop. I glanced around the crowded tattoo parlor and found no one was paying me or my half chub any attention. It was nearing one a.m., but this was when the place got really busy. Everyone was occupied.

I assigned her name to this number and shot her a reply.

Me: *whispering into your ear* You're beautiful, Cassie.

Cass: I know. You should see me right now. Bent forward at the waist. Legs spread. And…

Jesus Christ.

Me: And what? What are you doing, babe?

Cass: Touching…Lots of touching…

Yes. Hell yes.

Cass: Phones. Touching phones, you perv. Verizon has a strict pants policy.

Verizon? What the hell? I glanced around one more time before stepping out onto the sidewalk and pushing the little phone at the top of her message.

She answered on the first ring.

"Well, hello, Thatcher. You sure are a naughty boy, Daddy."

I chuckled. "I'm only as naughty as you want me to be, honey."

"How are you? Out chasing pussy?" she asked, and my eyebrows pinched together. She sounded like she was fishing.

I looked back inside the shop through the glass door and back down to the sidewalk. "No. At work, actually."

"Work?" she yelled. "It's like middle-of-the-night o'clock there too, isn't it?"

"Ah, but I'm a man of many mysteries. You didn't think I just had the one job, did you?"

"Well, yeah. I fucking did."

I laughed. "I told you. I have my hands in *everything*."

"I just figured that was a euphemism for pussy."

Frankie's gaze jerked toward me through the door at the sound of my booming laughter, and I shook my head at him. "What are you doing with a new number? If you lost your phone, you can just get a new one, you know."

"Fuck that shit. And I didn't lose my phone. I'm fucking responsible."

"Right," I lied.

"I am. That's what the number change is all about, actually. The last four digits spell out 'Cass' now. How fucking great is that?"

My eyebrows pinched together again. "You changed your number so that you'd have a text acronym at the end?"

"Yes! I had a late afternoon shoot, and then went for a couple of drinks with the guys afterward."

"The guys?"

"And we were talking and drinking, and it just hit me. I had to change my number."

I was curious about the guys. Really fucking curious. But now I was curious about other things. "You're drunk right now?"

"Tipsy," she admitted.

Jesus. All that whale shit and subterfuge. "You're probably the most proficient drunk texter I've ever encountered in my life," I said and laughed.

"Baby," drunk Cassie cooed, and my dick swelled from half cocked to fully loaded. "I'm proficient at *all kinds of things.*"

Bahamas, Tuesday, May 16th, Very Early Morning

"I'm all ears, honey." His husky voice vibrated against my cheek.

I ran my finger across the rim of my margarita glass and then slid it into my mouth, sucking the salt off. The jury was still out on why Thatch had been my first text from my new number, but for some odd reason, he was.

I couldn't help myself. I just really liked screwing with him—he took any shit I gave with ease and tossed it right back. And if I was being honest, I really fucking liked it. Not many men could handle my version of sarcasm. But, Thatch? Yeah, he handled it all right, seemingly entertained by whatever came out of my mouth.

Well, that and my tits. Yeah, he found them entertaining too.

"Put your boner away, Thatcher," I teased him with our running joke. An inside fucking joke. With Thatcher Kelly. *What was the world coming to?*

"You started this," he said, and I could picture his sexy smirk. "What are your tits wearing, Cass?"

"None of your business." I laughed. And smiled.

"Oh, but it is my business. Your tits and I are on a first-name basis. We're like Pam and Jim. P, B, and motherfucking J."

I kept smiling. "You watch *The Office?*"

"Would Kline eat dog shit for Georgia? Of course, I watch *The Office.*"

"I take it you heard about Stan."

"Yeah," he said with a chuckle. "I owe Kline a lot of favors thanks to you losing their cat."

"I did not lose their cat!" I exclaimed, and nearly everyone in the bar turned in my direction. "Oh, fuck off! This is a bar, not a goddamn library!" I shouted toward no asshole in particular.

"Starting your UFC career in the Bahamas doesn't sound like a good idea, Cass," Thatch said. "I thought you agreed to be good?" His voice was edged with something my drunken brain couldn't decipher.

"Yeah, but it's your version of good. That leaves room for a lot of possibilities."

He ignored the jab. "Promise me something, honey."

"And what would that be?"

"No Fight Club unless I'm with you."

"Ohhh…Thatcher doesn't think I'm strong enough to take care of myself?" I retorted sarcastically.

"I *know* you are, Cass," he responded immediately.

"Then why would I need you around?"

"Because I *want* to be there. I don't want anything to happen to you."

My chest felt tingly and weird. "Well…that's really kind of sweet of you to say."

"I can be sweet, honey. I can be real fucking sweet when I want to be."

"Cass! We're getting ready to head out. You comin'?" Arnoldo yelled from the bar as he closed out his tab.

"Who was that?" Thatch asked.

"Arnoldo," I answered. "He's one of the models I've been working with down here."

The phone went silent for a few beats, and for some odd reason, I felt the need to add a few more details. "Arnoldo is crazy good-looking…and getting over a harsh breakup with his boyfriend. I told him we could spend the rest of the night in my hotel room, stuffing our faces with room service and trashing stupid men."

He chuckled. "Sounds like a party."

"You know it." I got up from my barstool and grabbed my purse. "I better go. I've got a guy to console, feed, and shove off to bed, before I rub one out and call it a night."

"Tell your tits I miss them."

"I'll be sure to pass along the message."

"Do that while you're spread-eagled on your bed and getting yourself off to thoughts of me."

"I would, but you haven't given me anything to have thoughts about."

Yeah, yeah, I know that was a lie.
Of course, he'd given me things to think about. I had felt his cock.
Believe me, I had a lot of fucking thoughts about that monster.

"I accept that challenge."

God, he was like the king of one-upping.

"Good night, Cass. Be good."

"Be sweet, Thatch," I said and then ended the call.

Be sweet? Did I really just say that?

Hell, Thatcher Kelly hadn't crawled inside my brain and started demanding attention. And I knew, without a doubt, this situation had nowhere else to go but down...and up...and back down again...on the Jolly Green Giant's cock.

THE END

Be My BILLIONAIRE VALENTINE

max monroe

To every girl out there who is looking for their very own swoony valentine.
If we could send Kline Brooks to you in the mail, you bet your sweet ass we'd do it.
XOXO

Intro

It had been two days since we'd arrived at our tropical honeymoon destination, and I was certain, if given the option, I would have stayed right there forever. Just Georgia and me and nothing but an infinite amount of time to relax in the sun and celebrate the smartest, most brilliant thing I had ever done—marrying her.

Graduating Harvard, starting Brooks Media, developing an app called TapNext that skyrocketed my net worth into the billions—none of them even came close to outshining landing Georgia Brooks, née Cummings. In fact, I wasn't a fortune-teller, and I wanted nothing to do with looking into a stranger's crystal ball, but if I were into that sort of thing, I would guarantee, no matter the things life had planned for me, she would *always* be the best thing that had ever happened to me.

My Georgie was *that* kind of woman—the kind you worked to appreciate until it killed you.

My face ached a little from a permasmile as I leaned back into the support of my chair and sighed. The sound of waves gently crashing against the sand filled my ears, while the sun's rays bounced off the water, creating a shimmery glow of aqua blue. But no matter how splendid the view created by nature, I was fixated on an object of even greater beauty—blond hair, tanned, sun-kissed skin, and petite features in the best, fun-loving, smile-inducing package—sprawled out on a giant beach towel the resort concierge kindly set up for us.

I sat up on my elbows to take in the delectable view—my *wife* in a hot-pink bikini—and the smile that consumed my lips was so big, I could feel it throbbing in the back of my head.

Is it obvious that I'm a man who's completely and utterly in love with his wife?
Truthfully, every time I even think about her, my heart skips a fucking beat.

Georgie was laid out on her belly, her head resting to the side and her long eyelashes fawning across her cheeks. Miles upon miles of her gorgeous skin was all I could see.

I had no idea what time of day it was—hell, I didn't even know *what* day it was.

All I knew was that if there were a real-life version of heaven, I'd be fucking living it right now.

I took my time soaking up the tempting view. My gaze started at her cute feet and worked its way up her svelte legs, over her perfect fucking ass that was *sadly* covered up by bright, cheerful fabric, and I didn't stop until I noted the slight hints of pink-tinged skin on her shoulders.

"You're gonna burn, baby," I said softly, reaching out to rub a helpful, possibly unnecessary hand on her bum. She peeked out of one eye to meet my gaze. "Your shoulders," I elucidated, nodding toward them. "They're looking a little red."

Sleepy blue eyes stared back at me, but the owner of said eyes made no move to remedy her sunburn situation. I wasn't sure if she was sun-drunk or obstinate, but I loved when she looked at me like that. "But I put sunscreen on before we came out here this morning."

I smiled. Pig-headed, it was.

"Baby, that was nearly four hours ago." I smirked down at her. "I know you'd like the action of dousing with sunscreen to be an infinite principle, but the laws of physical science *and* chemistry say it's time to reapply."

"I'm too comfortable to be convinced by all your smart-talking logic, Mr. Brooks." She pouted. "Any type of movement, *even just lifting a finger*, sounds like a horrible idea right now."

I chuckled at that. "So, what should we do about it?"

She frowned, turning over just enough to present her breasts to me like a platter of fruity delights. If it weren't for the time I'd spent learning about all the things that made Georgia tick, I might have been sucked into the trap. "I don't know. It seems we're at a stalemate. An impasse. An impossible threshold to the unknown."

"Really?" I challenged as she pursed her cute pink lips. "That little pout isn't your cutesy way of trying to get me to do it for you?"

Her eyebrows bounced with one quick waggle. I wasn't even sure I was supposed to notice it, but when it came to my wife, there wasn't much that passed me by. "That depends."

"On what?"

A little smile creased her lips at the corners, biting into the otherwise flawless elasticity of her complexion. It was one of my favorites of her smiles, so at odds with her do-gooder personality. It made her look like she had a nefarious secret. "Is it working?"

"Don't act so coy, Benny." I winked and reached out to brush a loose strand of her blond hair out of her eyes, tucking it gently behind her ear. "You and I both already know that little pout of yours—*fake or not*—could get me to do anything. Frankly, I'm kind of hoping it's asking me to do more than rub sunscreen. The naughtier, the better."

Her giggle tinkled loudly enough for bystanders to hear, but I only had eyes for her as I lifted an eyebrow, hopeful it put me ahead in my race to get between her thighs by using the power of suggestion.

Having fun with our game now, Georgia let her coquettish smile turn devious. "Does that mean you'll do it?"

I feigned a beleaguered sigh. "It's a tough job, but I guess this is what husbands do for their wives, huh?"

"If they're smart." Georgie asserted with a nod and a grin.

I had been called a lot of things in my nearly thirty-five years of life, but shamelessly dumb wasn't one of them.

"All hail, Queen Georgie. Ruler of the beach and commander of sunscreen application," I teased, and she snorted, waving a hand and sitting up on her towel like Queen Elizabeth on her way to a palace gala. All that bullshit about not wanting to move a muscle disappeared as soon as she got the royal title. I mean, it made sense. Fame, as it were, changed people.

I shook my head, smiled, and grabbed the bottle of sunscreen out of our beach bag despite her duplicity. In the end, I was still being blessed with the chance to rub slick hands over many, many inches of her legs, stomach, breasts, and ass. It would be a cold day in hell before I offered up a complaint that might take that away.

Sliding closer to my beautiful—*and lazy*—wife, I squirted a small amount of lotion into my hands, rubbed them together, and began to gently rub it into the skin of her shoulders.

"Oh yes," she purred. "That feels so amazing that you should just keep doing it for at least another ten or so minutes."

"I swear, Benny," I said on a laugh. "You were a cat in a past life. There is no one on the planet who enjoys back rubs and foot rubs and head massages, and pretty much anything revolving around being petted in some form or another, more than you."

She giggled and shrugged. "Hey, at least I don't lick myself."

"No," I said smartly. "That's my job."

She swatted at me feebly—another sign that she was feline in another life—and I smirked.

"I suppose I shouldn't be surprised that you and that asshole cat get along so well," I added.

"His name is Walter," she interjected, turning her neck into an awkward position just to glare up at me. Dramatic outrage consumed her face. "And he's *not* an asshole. He's a total sweetheart, and I'm already missing him like crazy."

"I miss him too," I agreed sarcastically. Eager to believe me, though, she didn't pick up on my tone.

"Really?" Hope practically bled out of her pores.

"Sure. I miss him in the way a kidnapping victim misses their abductor." Her eyes narrowed. "Very Stockholm-ish."

She was so committed to our cat, she growled. "Be serious."

"Serious?" I questioned, and she nodded.

I returned the gesture. "Okay. Seriously…I am *not* missing that *asshole* at all."

"Kline Matthew!" Georgia shouted and reached behind her back with one hand to awkwardly slap my arm. "He's not an asshole!"

"To you, *no*," I retorted on a chuckle. "But to me? *Yes.* He's an asshole. Always has been, and probably always will be."

She sighed. "He's not that bad."

He *was* that bad. Quite frankly, he was the *worst* and he deserved a hell of a lot crueler nicknames, but I bit my tongue in the name of my marriage. Sometimes, you needed to let your partner be right, even if they weren't.

For the sake of the relationship and maintaining a high level of respect and understanding. And really—*and this one was the most important*—you needed to take some losses sometimes if you wanted to keep having sex.

And, frankly, the sooner I got my ass in agreement, the sooner we could leave Walter out of our honeymoon and back at home where the little bastard belonged.

"You're right, sweetheart. He's not that bad."

Georgia smiled as expected, and I jumped on the opportunity to bring our discussion back around to sexier things. *Honeymoon-worthy things.*

"So, Your Royal Highness, besides applier of sunscreen and giver of massages, what other jobs are included in my husbandly duties?" I asked, lulling all of the tension back out of her body with my hands at her shoulders.

"Oh boy." She turned her head again, but this time, she grinned up at me. "Lots of jobs. *So* many jobs…"

"Is that right?" I retorted, my lips curving up playfully. "Lay 'em on me, baby. What jobs?"

"Well, you are officially the man in charge of taking the trash out."

"Okay." Not exactly what my dick wanted to hear, but it was also easy, so I could handle that one.

"Fixer of all things that need fixing. Basically, anything that requires a hammer or some kind of tool or screwdriver or whatever, it's your job to fix it." Also no problem, and if we were playing a game of Hunt the Thimble, we'd definitely be getting hotter.

Though, I feel strongly that I should note here that if Georgie were hunting my dick, she would not be hunting a thimble. It's just the name of the game, okay? They don't call me Big-dicked Brooks for nothing.

"Okay." I laughed, hinting, "Anything else?"

"Um…" She paused and turned over onto her back, her eyes meeting mine. "Awesome gift giver."

I tilted my head to the side. The conversation had certainly taken a turn I wasn't expecting, but this was important, nonetheless. We were a newly married couple, hopefully poised at the brink of the rest of our lives. The time to get my husband game plan strategized and filed was now. The stakes were too high not to.

"You know," she continued. "You have to give me really awesome, exciting presents for things like my birthday and our anniversary and Christmas."

I nodded. She wanted to be romanced, not taken for granted. I could handle that. "What about Valentine's Day? Does that gift need to be even more special?"

"No way." She scrunched up her nose and shook her head, spinning her shoulders completely out from under my hands, and then declared, "Valentine's doesn't exist. It is a black-hole holiday, and I will not fall down into its trap. No gifts, no nothing. Just pretend it doesn't exist."

"What?" I questioned, surprise in my voice. "Why would we skip Valentine's Day? You're supposed to hate it when you're single, not when you're married. You've got a date locked in for life."

She shook her head vehemently. "It's not about that. Not for me, anyway. February 14th brings me nothing but bad luck," she answered. "I mean, look at what happened on *our* first Valentine's Day together, Kline."

Visions of flames and fire extinguishers and the New York City Fire Department flashed through my mind. Sure, there'd been a failure in candle safety, but I'd put out the flames well before my apartment building burned. In fact, I'd had it completely under control before our neighbors even dialed the fire department. And now that the contractors had fixed the damage, you couldn't even tell anything had happened. "That was a fluke, baby. Not a premonition. The rest of our Valentine's Days are destined to be beautiful memories."

Eyes pinched with skepticism, Georgia rearranged herself on the beach towel to fully face me and started counting off bullet points—proof of reasoning, as it were—with her fingers.

"A fluke? Really?" She shook her head. "Let's take quick stock of Georgia Cummings's Valentine's past. They're messy. And cruel. And twisted. I'm surprised they haven't cast Brittany Snow in a movie to play the role of my ghost, like a Valentine's version of Scrooge." Georgie flipped her hair over her shoulder, licked her lips, and continued. "When I was eight, my parents set their bedroom on fire, and Will and I ended up standing out on the front lawn at eleven o'clock at night while firemen had to put it out. I should mention that ole Dick Cummings was wearing Speedo-style red silk underwear with the words 'Mr. Handsome' written across his ass."

"Oh fuck," I said, and a laugh jumped from my throat. "So, your history with fire departments isn't the best. That could still be a coincidence."

"Dick had on a Speedo, Kline," Georgia emphasized, making me laugh.

"Yes, but that's really not that out of the ordinary, is it? It could happen any day of the week with your parents, not just on Valentine's Day. And as a bonus, you don't live at home anymore. That scenario is very unlikely to repeat."

Georgia snorted. "Don't hold your breath. I wouldn't put it past Dick to show up in a banana hammock on our next momentous occasion, just for the hell of it."

I smiled. "I really do love your parents."

She rolled her eyes. "That's because you grew up with Bob and Maureen. You have no idea the lasting impact these kinds of things have on a young adult."

"You're right, baby. I have no idea what it feels like in the depths of your pain. But none of these things means that Valentine's Day from here until the end of time is going to be a shitshow for us. We can change its course."

"Oh, Kline. You're so sweet and hopeful—and so dang foolish."

"Georgie—"

"You want to know what else has happened to me on February 14th?" she challenged smarmily before pushing on to answer without waiting for a response from me. "Horrible breakups, dinner dates that ended up with my boyfriend-at-the-time choking on a Rally's hot dog and needing the Heimlich, Grandma Cummings getting arrested for illegally selling roses outside a strip club, and much,

much more. The list is endless, Kline—from the time I was born to now, it's been a disaster."

"Good God, baby," I responded and ran a hand through my hair as I tried to wrap my head around everything she just divulged. "Fuck, I don't even know where to begin with all of that."

"That's not even close to *every*thing because I have thirty-plus years of horrible Valentine's Day catastrophes. And Valentine's with the perfect man you thought you had zero freaking chance of meeting and falling in love with shouldn't be a disaster. So, from here on out, I'm not even going to give it a chance. Honestly, we probably need to take steps to ensure our safety. Take off work, spend the whole day in bed. Avoid candles, roses, takeout meals, *other people*. Literally just try to sleep through the entire day."

"Baby, that sounds ridiculous."

"Yeah, well, you've never had to spend the majority of your middle school years hearing your friends talk about how you didn't need a Valentine's date because your mom was pro-masturbation."

"Holy hell." I laughed, but also, I nodded. I knew my Georgie had been through the wringer growing up with Dick and Savannah as her parents, no matter how much I loved their openness about sexuality as an adult.

"So, unless Hallmark decides to change the official day of love, we'll be spending the rest of our February 14ths in a bunker."

On another laugh, I reached out and pulled Georgia into my arms and gently repositioned our bodies so that I lay on my back and her chest was pressed against mine. "Okay, baby, from here on out, every February 14th, we'll be vigilant and prepared. Zombie Apocalypse Doomsday preppers will have nothing on us."

"Perfect." She breathed with a relief so acute, I had to lean forward and press my lips to hers, hard and swift.

Heat and excitement stirred in my blood, and by the dramatic new bloom of rose-colored flesh on Georgia's chest, she felt the same.

Not one to waste an opportunity with my wife, I leaned back in and took another drink from her mouth, this time deeper, sexier, more eager.

By the time I pulled away, Georgia's eyes burned so hot, if I didn't do something about it, I'd need to make another call to the fire department.

Since I didn't know the number for emergency services in Bora Bora, it seemed like a much, much better idea to take her to bed and fuck her until all that remained were a few burning embers and their exhausted smoke.

"Bungalow, baby. Now," I ordered, and a shiver ran all the way from my wife's shoulders to her toes. And then she jumped into action. I didn't need to explain. She was reading me loud and clear.

While Georgia packed up the beach bag, I folded up the towel and made a mental note to, in the very near future, find another way to give my wife a true Valentine's Day experience.

I didn't know when or what or where, but I was certain I'd find a better alternative than dad dicks and special dinners at Rally's restaurant.

Because whether you were the type of person who thought Valentine's Day was some sham bullshit holiday or not, every woman on the planet deserved to get spoiled in the name of love and Cupid's arrow.

And if you're my wife? That chubby old guy in a
diaper needs to be working overtime.

Chapter 1

After a long as hell day at the office, I was more than pleased to pull into the driveway of Georgia's and my new house and shut out the rest of the world with just one tap of my finger to the garage button.

At last, home sweet home.

We had only been out of our Bora Bora bubble and back in the real world for a few weeks. But damn, there had yet to be a day that had gone by when I didn't mentally wish I could go back in time and revisit what it was like to laze around on the beach and witness how glorious my wife's ass looked in a bikini.

For a man who loathed frivolous spending, I still would have paid an obscene amount of money to make that happen.

On a relieved sigh that the rest of my night would be a hell of a lot better than my workday, I stepped inside the house, walking through the mud room and toward the kitchen.

"Benny, I'm home!" I called out as I walked through the cased opening between the two, but when I stopped near the marble kitchen island and dropped my wallet, keys, and cell phone on the counter, I realized I still hadn't heard anything back. Curious, I drew my eyebrows together as I called out again, a little louder this time. "Georgie? Where the hell are you, baby?"

"I'm in here!" she finally responded, her voice a distant nebula in space. To say I knew her exact location in this big house would be an outright lie.

"Where is here, exactly?" I asked, dancing delicately around my confusion.

"The living room!"

Geez. The living room was relatively close. Why did she sound like she was in another galaxy?

Shrugging, I stepped through the kitchen, past the breakfast nook, and into the living room. I glanced left and right and left again like a kid first learning to cross the street. Now, I knew men were normally pretty dense, but not being able to find my own wife in a single room seemed like a bit of a stretch even for the inferior sex. I mean, I did build a billion-dollar company from the ground up. I should be able to find a petite blonde on a canvas of gray décor. "Benny girl, is this some kind of game?" I asked, my voice of a volume that would make me seem crazy if she did turn out to be in this room, but oh well. If she was in here and I was missing her, we'd need to hop in the car and head for the hospital immediately anyway.

"And if it is, does it include me finding you naked?" I added under my breath.

"The living room!" she yelled back again. "I'm in the *living room!*"

Okay, what in the fuck was going on here? I didn't see Thatch today, so it was unlikely that he slipped me a drug. And I'd yet to even crack open a beer. So, I shouldn't be feeling like I was taking a trip on a hallucinogen.

After the day I had at the office, I was starting to get frustrated. It wasn't my wife's fault, and I wasn't going to take it out on her because that would be completely counterproductive to my end goal of getting into her pants, but I was like a real-life John Travolta GIF, glancing around the room with both arms out.

"Oh really? Because I'm in the living room. And I'm at least ninety-nine percent sure you're not here."

Georgia giggled so loud it made me smile, even across the mysterious distance. "You're in the family room, husband! I'm in the *living room*."

I furrowed my brow and walked through the empty dining room—the one we'd yet to furnish—and into what was apparently the *actual* living room. And perched right in the middle of the lush cream sofa—the one Georgie had fallen in love with a few days ago while we were shopping in SoHo and simply *had* to have—sat my beautiful wife.

Flanking her on either side? Our cat—*aka my archnemesis*—Walter, and our Great Dane, Stan.

Stan the man was a new addition to the family, the dog we ended up adopting because Thatch and Cassie lost our freaking cat. And instead of just, you know, letting someone else find him and deal with his asshole-ish behavior, they had located the bastard in a vet clinic *after* he had fallen in love with a dog that could quite literally pass for a horse.

"So, *this* is the living room?" I questioned, a small smile on my lips as I put both hands on my hips and glanced around the half-decorated space.

Truthfully, most of the house was still filled with empty walls, stacks of boxes, and half-arranged furniture. But that was mostly because we had just moved in a little less than a week ago *and* Georgia was a perfectionist when it came to picking out the perfect décor. If it were only the time constraint, I would have paid someone to unpack and organize everything, just so Georgie didn't have to deal with the stress of the mess.

She looked up at me, a book in her lap and a breathtaking smile on her face. "Yes, baby. This is the living room."

"Jesus," I muttered on a laugh. "Family room, living room, mud room…it's hard to keep it all straight. I'm starting to think we bought too big of a house." Oh, man. I could only imagine what my father would say when he got a chance to come see this place. He had been drilling practicality into my head for years, and normally, I had no trouble following his teaching. Obviously, though, the thought of exciting my wife with the house of her dreams did a good job of getting me a little carried away.

Georgie snorted and lifted one knowing index finger to point in my direction. "Well, you only have yourself to blame for that, baby. You're the one who picked it out."

I grinned at that. I would take the blame from her and the scrutiny from my father, because one look from her, and I knew I'd hit my goal right on the head. "Only because I knew it would make you happy."

The instant she had seen this house, it was love at first sight, the attachment damn near as strong as Walter's codependency for his canine lover, Stan.

"Wait…don't *you* like the house?" she asked, tilting her head to the side.

I shrugged. "Baby, you should know by now that the only thing I need in a house is you inside it. The rest? I don't really care about the specifics."

Georgia smiled, and the faintest hint of pink highlighted her cheeks. "Goodness, you're going to have to reel in that swoon of yours, Mr. Brooks."

"And why is that, Mrs. Brooks?"

"Because it's dangerous," she proclaimed, eyes serious. "One day, I swear, it might make me pass out or, hell, make my panties just go *poof* and disappear into thin air. Could you imagine if we were in public when something like that happened?"

"Oh, I can imagine you without panties anywhere, baby. It's my superpower." I waggled my brows and walked toward her. It didn't take long before I was lifting her off the couch and into my arms, gently wrapping her thighs around my waist.

Stan groaned a little at the disruption of his sleep, but when Walter curled up next to his head, he smacked his lips a few times and went back to relaxing.

"I missed you today," I whispered, and her smile only grew.

"You just saw me this morning." She wrapped her arms around my neck, and I didn't hesitate to press a kiss to her smiling lips.

"Exactly. Nine fucking hours ago," I retorted and rubbed my nose against hers. "Which is why you need to quit working for that bastard boss of yours and come back to work for me."

She giggled and rolled her eyes at the same time. "That bastard boss of mine is one of your best friends."

"I don't give a fuck. Tell Wes Lancaster you're done working for his little football team and you're ready to come back to Brooks Media."

"And what would be the benefits of working at Brooks Media?"

"Orgasmic lunch breaks," I returned swiftly and without hesitation, and she rolled her eyes again.

"*That* is exactly why I should stay where I'm at."

"What?" I fake frowned. "You don't like when I give you orgasms, Benny girl?"

"Don't be dramatic," she said with a laugh I could feel in the depths of my chest. "You know I love it. I love it too much, in fact." She bit her lip as she stared at mine, adding softly, "We'd never get any work done."

I gripped her perfect, lush ass in my hands. "We'd get tons done. It might not be related to Brooks Media or any of our subsidiaries, but oh baby, would we *ever* get it done."

"That's exactly what I'm talking about!" She snorted and playfully slapped my chest.

Unfortunately, she didn't stay put and, instead, placed a smacking kiss to my lips and gently disentangled herself from my arms until her feet were firmly back on the ground.

"Where are you going?" I questioned with a whine.

She winked over her shoulder. "Into the kitchen."

"Which kitchen? The room I think is the kitchen?" I questioned. "Or a different kitchen?"

"The *only* kitchen, smartass," she retorted on a laugh. "Where our dinner is currently located in the oven."

"All right, fine. But I'll follow you this time, just so I don't get lost."

She laughed smugly and swayed her hips extra hard as she led the way back to the room I'd come from.

It was truly cute that she thought the show she was putting on for me was some kind of punishment.

If that were the case, I'd be bad a lot more often.

Back in the kitchen, she busied herself with something in the oven, and I hitched a hip against the counter and enjoyed the view that was my wife bent over with her perfect ass perched toward the air.

Damn, I was a lucky son of a bitch.

"Wah, wah wah wah wah wah wah?" Georgia asked, doing her best impression of Charlie Brown's mother. Truly, though, it wasn't her fault. My ears had just redirected their energy to my eyes, hoping that with their powers combined, I'd be gifted with a sexy version of X-ray vision.

"Sorry, babe. What was that?" I asked for clarification, prompting her to roll her eyes and speak slowly.

She shut the oven door and stood back up to face me. "So, how…was…your…day…at…work?"

"Oh," I muttered and ran a hand through my hair. "Considering I had to deal with Leslie for most of it because Meryl had to leave early for an appointment and Dean took a vacation day, it was about as fucking awful as you'd imagine."

Once the glorious distraction that was Georgia had left Brooks Media to take a job as Director of Marketing for the New York

Mavericks, it had become more and more apparent that Leslie—an intern turned lazy-fucking-employee—was a seriously huge thorn in my side.

"You do realize you're the boss, right? You could fire her." Georgia grinned at me as she set a potholder on the counter by the stove. Of course, now that she didn't have to deal with Leslie directly, my pain was no more than a tool for her amusement. She didn't care if I fired Leslie or not because she didn't work with Leslie anymore.

I definitely needed to care more—grow some balls—and send her upriver to a nice temp job at a different company. *Maybe the PerfectMatch—TapNext's direct competition—headquarters was looking for someone.*

Every time I actually got close to pulling the trigger, though, my conscience kicked in. *Manipulative bastard.*

"Yeah." I groaned and laughed at the same time. "Trust me, I've considered it. A lot. But when I imagine her trying to find another job, I'm torn between guilt at making someone else deal with her and fear that she'll end up homeless and on the street."

Georgia cackled.

"What?" I questioned and tilted my head to the side. "Why is that so funny?"

"You do realize that she has far too many sugar daddies to end up on the street, right?"

I furrowed my brow. "What do you mean she has *sugar daddies*?"

"Sugar daddies, Kline," Georgia repeated. "Men who buy her things. Who do you think paid for her huge boobs and lip injections?"

"Baby, I try really hard to forget that she works for me, much less trying to figure out who paid for her plastic surgery."

If I was being honest, while some men might have loved the big, fake tits and huge lips, I was mostly just disturbed by it all. Human skin wasn't supposed to be stretched to the point of translucency.

Not to mention, I liked it when breasts moved when I played with them.

"Kline, you're a real sweetheart, but…" My wife paused and then shook her head with a grin. "Just trust me, Leslie would survive if you fired her."

"So, you're telling me I should fire her?"

"Oh, no. No, no." Georgia laughed, wagging a finger at me like a sword. "You're not putting that decision on *my* shoulders. You, Mr. Big Shot CEO, are going to have to make that decision on your own. If I were her boss, I'd have to make the decision to fire Tits McGee myself, and you do too."

"Baby, I love how you're acting all tough right now, but you and I both know, you're so full of shit, the flies are descending." I eyed her knowingly. "If you were in my shoes, Tits McGee would still be on your payroll, employee of the month, and on the list of staff up for a raise."

"Shut up," she snapped, picking up a dish towel and throwing it at me. "I'm a softy, but not for *her*. Mary in Billing still makes a disgusted face at me every time I come into the office to visit you."

"Mary?"

"I quoted Ren and Stimpy in her condolence card, Kline!"

I chuckled and dodged a plastic cup as it flew at my face. "Oh, right. When her husband died. I forgot about that. I thought Dean caught it before it went to her?"

Georgia turned and pulled something out of the oven, slamming it down with the most adorable fuming nostrils. "He did! But then Leslie told her I'd done it anyway."

"Sorry, baby," I said with a small smirk. It wasn't funny, but it was funny…you know?

I sighed. "Anyway, I think it's possible she's lost a few of her *sugar daddies,* as you call them, because she was crazy fucking busy today with the task of nailing down who she wants to be dating for Valentine's Day. I swear, all damn day, she was on her phone, chatting with God knows who on TapNext."

Georgia's face crinkled in confusion. "It's May."

I shrugged. "I know."

"So, why is she looking for Valentine's Day dates in May?"

I stared at her for a minute until she bugged out her eyes and lifted her arms to her sides.

"Oh. Were you wanting a real answer to that question? Because I don't have a fucking clue."

Georgia shook her head, turned to grab two plates from the cabinet, and set them down on the counter beside the tray of roasted broccoli from the oven. "Well, part of this is your fault. You made TapNext a work-approved app, and now she thinks she's entitled to troll for penis during the day."

"Because it's *our* fucking app," I retorted. "My employees need to know how the app works to be able to promote it, fix it, improve it."

Georgie shrugged on a laugh. "Yeah, but still. Leslie thinks she's doing sugar daddy market research or something."

I groaned. "Fucking hell, I probably should fire her."

Georgia shrugged, clearly determined to avoid the trap of giving me permission.

I cocked my head to the side, unwilling to lose without trying one last time. "So, you agree, you think I should fire her?"

"Nice try, baby." My wife laughed. Outright. And then turned around to open the oven door and bend over to check the chicken marsala in the pan still inside.

I took that opportunity to step forward and place two greedy hands on her ass and squeeze.

She squealed on a giggle. "Kline Brooks!"

"You have only yourself to blame." I waggled my brows and glanced down at where my hands met her backside and squeezed. "Flaunting this perfect ass in my face like that."

"I'm not flaunting, I'm making dinner," she retorted and stood back up to face me.

"Looked like flaunting to me."

"Because you're a horny pervert."

"When it comes to you, Benny girl, I am a total degenerate," I replied and reached out to brush a strand of blond hair out of her face. "You have no idea the things I want to do to you right now."

Georgia leaned forward to press a kiss to my lips. "Hold that thought until later tonight."

"What? Why?" I pouted.

"Because dinner is ready."

"But I want to be your sugar daddy." I wrapped my arms around her waist, pulling her body tight to mine.

She quirked a knowing brow. "And what exactly are you trying to give me?"

"Orgasms, Benny. Lots and lots of orgasms."

She rolled her eyes and started to turn back to the oven, but I made the executive decision that we'd eat dinner later. After I spend a good hour worshiping her perfect ass. Chicken marsala was good, but it didn't even come close to the taste of my wife.

Between one breath and the next, I had her tossed over my shoulder in a fireman's carry and my fingers were tapping the oven off.

"Kline Brooks! Put me down!"

"Oh, don't worry, baby. I'll put you down," I answered and headed for the stairs. "Once we make it to the bedroom."

"But our dinner!" she half shouted, half giggled. "It will get cold!"

"That's what microwaves are for."

Once I reached our bedroom, I kicked the door shut behind me and tossed her onto the bed.

It didn't take long before her panties were on the floor and her skirt was pushed up past her waist, revealing the gorgeous spot between her thighs.

Like a dog on a bone, I fell on her pussy and feasted until her squeals and giggles turned to moans and whimpers.

Fuck yes. This, right here, was my favorite thing in the whole damn world.

Déjà vu of the blissful days of our honeymoon filled my mind while the sweet taste of her arousal coated my tongue, and a plan took shape in my mind.

My first order of business would be making Georgia come.

But the next priority on my agenda? Setting up a fantastic fucking surprise.

Chapter 2

New York, Wednesday, May 24th

Kline

Two days of scheming later, and my week was finally looking up. Thanks to Meryl and Dean putting in a full day at the office, my insane workload was somewhat manageable, and Leslie's always-infuriating presence was presenting itself somewhere far away from my office doors.

In fact, if I'd decoded all the office gossip correctly, Dean had spent the better part of last night coming up with a never-ending scavenger hunt that would keep her away and occupied until the end of the week. Granted, when an employee's greatest strength was being sent away from the office on pointless errands, it was probably time for them to go.

But for now, I could ignore the looming need to fire her.

Though, that didn't stop outside distractions from seeping in. I was deep in the trenches of planning a huge fuck-you to my wife's history with the holiday of love, and apparently, sabotaging the plans of the devil took a good amount of energy and dedication.

An iMessage notification flashed on the screen of my laptop, and I clicked it open to find a text.

Wes: Is this how it's going to be now that you're married? I mean, thank fuck you made Brooks Media so successful before you met her. If you hadn't, TapNext would be swirling around in the shitter by now.

I laughed.

We had spent the better part of this morning in email negotiations that he didn't like, and Wes's mood was deteriorating by the minute. Considering his baseline hovered just outside of *broody bastard* ninety percent of the time, that was really saying something.

The target deal? Ensuring that Georgia would be off work starting tomorrow for the awesome surprise I had planned. All of which, thanks to Meryl's quick work, had been officially booked as of this morning.

Obviously, Wes hadn't technically officially agreed, but I knew if I booked the trip anyway—nonrefundable, of course—even if he got salty, he'd never be able to turn me down.

Me: Come on, Wes. It's four days. And it's important.

Wes: Important? You take trips to the tropics more often than I take shits at this point, dude. Why should your wife's fucked relationship with Valentine's Day be my problem?

Obviously, I'd filled him in on the essential details to pull at his heartstrings. Too bad I'd forgotten he didn't have any organs in his cold, dead chest.

Me: Who hurt you, Mr. Grinch? And why do you have to take it out on poor little Cindy Lou Who?

Wes: You know what? It's a shame I don't have the authority to fire my Director of Marketing's husband. Because he's a pain in my fucking ass.

Me: You act like I'm stealing my wife away for a getaway during the play-offs. It's the OFF-SEASON. Truthfully, you should be thanking me that I had the foresight to celebrate Valentine's Day now. You're welcome, by the way.

His text rebuttal was instant and brutal, as expected.

Wes: HA. Don't play the martyr, Brooks. You'd fuck over your dying grandma if it meant taking your new, hot wife on some sort of fuckfest at the beach. Even if we were in the middle of a championship bid with media and sponsors crawling out my asshole, you'd still be requesting this time off—play-offs be damned.

He was one hundred percent correct about all of it—except the dying grandma thing—but I refused to give him that satisfaction.

So, I did what any good friend would do in that situation—cleverly diverted the conversation to less irritable territories in the hope that it would turn his prickly attitude around.

Me: Speaking of play-offs, how's Quinn Bailey looking in training camp?

Wes: Like a fucking football god. Mark my words, Kline, under QB, the Mavericks will bring home a Championship SOON.

Me: Hell yeah, buddy. That's what I like to hear. I can't wait to see the team thrive with your ownership. We all knew you were the man for the job.

Wes: Goddammit. I've been had, haven't I? You're just sucking up so I'll say yes to the trip.

I grinned and typed out a response.

Me: A man's gotta do what a man's gotta do.

Wes: Enjoy your trip, you bastard.

Me: Thanks, man. Lunch next week?

Wes: Only if you're buying.

Pretty sure me paying for lunch was the least I could do.

I mean, he wasn't exactly wrong that I kept stealing my wife away from work. We'd only been home from our honeymoon for a few weeks at this point.

Still…maybe if I kept pushing back, he'd actually end up firing her. If it were up to me, Georgia would be back at Brooks Media, letting me slide my hand up her skirt during lunch breaks anyway.

Me: Don't you own a restaurant where we can eat for free?

Wes: No. Fuck you and your free food.

I laughed and typed out another message. Even if I'd have preferred to have her around every day, Georgie loved her job with the Mavericks. It was probably best if I didn't push him over the line after all.

Me: You're right, buddy. I owe you. Lunch is on me, and you can even pick the place.

After laughing at the return picture text of Wes's grumpy face in the background of an extended middle finger, I set my cell back down on my desk and returned to the business of emails. There were at least twenty of them in the urgent response folder Meryl controlled for me, and if I wanted to get out of this office by five so I could beat Georgie home and set up for the surprise, I needed to get

through them before my marathon of conference calls that was due
to start in about thirty minutes.

If only I'd been quick enough to get entrenched before my
phone lit up again with **Incoming Call Thatch** flashing on the screen.

I knew I shouldn't answer. Any sane person knew to *never*
answer calls from Thatch when they were trying to get shit
accomplished.

But for the same crazy reasons that have kept me friends with
the lunatic and given that he was in charge of a very large portion of
both my professional and personal finances, I answered by the third
ring. I just never knew when he would have something important to
say, and he didn't hesitate to dangle the carrot that he might several
times a week.

"Yes, Thatcher?"

"Special K!" He bellowed a greeting into the receiver. "My main
man!"

The tone of his voice was immediately suspicious. Thatch Kelly was
a happy guy, sure, but there was a certain douchey quality to his voice I
could discern right away when he was winding up to be truly annoying.

*Think of any guy named Chad still sporting a popped collar and
preppy boat shoes, and that was Thatcher Kelly when he was scheming.*

A sigh escaped my lungs, and I ran a hand through my hair. "What
do you want, T?"

"What do I want?" he tossed back. "You say that like I'm always
bugging you for shit."

"Because you are," I retorted on a raspy laugh. "Or gathering intel
to carry out your next big plot. Or fishing for a way to bury your face
in a set of tits you almost definitely shouldn't be burying your face in.
There's always something with you."

"Ah, c'mon, man." His deep chuckle reverberated in my ear. "That's
not true."

"Oh, really?" I shook my head. "So, you're just calling me to, what…say hi? To check in with me emotionally? Help me out here by cutting to the chase. I've got a whole lot of actually important shit to get done before I can go home."

"You know, it's good that I called, even with your mocking. You sound like you could use a little emotional support. What's troubling you, Kline? Tell Dr. Thatch all about it."

"I really can't stand you sometimes."

"That's cold, brother. Ice Ice Baby."

"Thatch, come on."

He sniffled, the rat bastard, selling his sob story for all it was worth. "Sorry, bro. It's gonna take my heart a minute to recover from the stab wound. I'm not that hot cardiothoracic surgeon Teddy Altman, okay? I just have to emotionally mend and hope that it stops the hemorrhage."

I swear to God, I spent ninety percent of my conversations with him not even knowing what the fuck he was talking about. It was his gift, though—talking you in circles until you were so fucking dizzy, you fell right into his trap.

He sighed heavily, and I scrubbed a frustrated hand down my face before metering my voice like I was talking to a kid.

"Okay, T. I'm going to need you to do me a favor and let me know why you're calling, please."

I could hear the smile in his voice, and I knew he was taking great pleasure in driving me to the point of surrender so quickly. I didn't care. Just as long as I got this over with so I could get home and surprise my wife.

"I was just missing you. I feel like it's been forever since we bro-ed it up."

"You just saw me Monday." We had literally had lunch together. Not exactly by my choice, but I had been enjoying a quiet lunch by myself in my office and the big bastard had just shown up, taken off his goddamn shoes, stretched out on my leather sofa, and eaten half of my fucking sandwich. Regardless, we did, in fact, spend the hour in each other's company.

"I did?" He feigned short-term amnesia. "Well, I think that just proves you're not spending enough time with your best friend, K. Obviously, we need to rectify that *stat*," he said, pausing for a moment and then acting like some random not-premeditated-at-all idea popped into his big-ass head. "Oh, wait a sec! I know exactly what we should do to strengthen our brotherly bond."

"And what's that, T?" I questioned. My voice was so monotone, it could have been used as a sleep aid for insomniacs.

"Meet me at the Raines Law Room after work tomorrow night for some drinks and bro-time. Pretty sure they're having some kind of fun shindig. Should be a good time and the perfect bandage to heal our breach."

And there it was, friends. The whole reason for him calling. Door number three—tits.

He wanted to motorboat, and he needed a co-captain to get him there.

You'd think the fact that I was married now would take me out of the running for wingman, but sadly, it had only made me more of a commodity in his eyes. Something about using me to garner attention and then hoarding it all for himself really seemed to hit his pleasure nail into the headboard.

"I wasn't born fucking yesterday, you bastard." I called him out. "You and I both know every Thursday night is ladies' night at the Law Room."

"No shit?" He acted surprised. "Are you having some sort of postmarital cold feet?"

"What? No. What the fuck are you talking about?"

"Relax, bro. Don't get defensive. Just surprising that you're keeping tabs on when ladies' night is at the watering hole is all. I won't tell Georgia girl or anything. I'm locked up tight like a vault. Dedicated to the bro-code."

"Fuck off, Thatch. I'm not keeping tabs on what night has the best odds for tripping with my dick out and landing in a pussy. I'm *married*. If I play my cards right, the odds are *always* going to be higher at home. Shit just doesn't change often, and Raines Law Room is no different."

"Okay, okay. I get it. You don't have to get so worked up, Klinehole. It's not good for your blood pressure."

"*You're* not good for my blood pressure."

"Ouch, dude. That one stung."

I took a deep breath and let my head fall back on my shoulders. Maybe that was a little too far, considering he was my best friend, but he just knew the exact buttons to push to drive me to my limit.

"Look, I'm sorry. That was a little harsh, but you need to stop trying to foist this off on me. You know you came into this conversation with this plan from the beginning."

"No hard feelings, K. You can make it up to me by coming with me tomorrow night to mend our fence. I know you're married, but I'm sure the two of us can still make it fun, right?" he said, his voice downright jovial now that he'd cornered me where he wanted me.

Unfortunately for him, my Thursday night was already spoken for in a way he couldn't easily subvert. "Sorry to burst your bubble, but I won't be in town tomorrow night. So, I won't be able to aid and abet in your troll for pussy."

"What the fucking fuck are you talking about? Where the hell are you going on such short notice?" he asked like an outraged housewife.

I smiled. Finally. It'd taken way too long, but I finally had the upper hand. "I'm taking Georgie on a surprise getaway."

"Wait…are you serious? You *just* got back from your honeymoon, you fucker. I know because I've still got one more bill to pay for the room and board on your devil cat and his canine fuck buddy."

I guffawed. "Now, I know you don't want to go there, do you?

You're the one who lost Walter, hence you're the reason he was in that vet's office, double-fucking-hence, *you* are the reason I now have a motherfucking horse for a dog."

He grumbled under his breath, lots of colorful words, I was sure, but when he came back on the line to talk to me, he'd changed his tune a little bit. "Where in the hell are you going?"

"On a trip," I answered, pointedly leaving out the details. "We leave tomorrow. Won't be back until Sunday."

"You're going to be gone the whole weekend?!" His outrage made zero sense from a friend with his own apartment, career, and sense of purpose. The thing with Thatch, though, was that things often didn't make much sense. When I wasn't directly involved, it was funny. When I was, it was mostly painful. "And why is this the first time I'm hearing about it? Does Wes know about this?"

"I don't know, Mom," I answered, sarcasm combining with soft chuckles. "I guess it slipped my mind that I should've requested your approval before scheduling it. And, yes, Wes knows about it because he's Georgie's boss and I had to make sure she had the days off work."

"I'm going to be honest, K. I am not happy about this one bit."

"And while your honesty is appreciated, I would like to respectfully counter that I don't give a shit. All I care about is taking my wife to Cabo."

"Wait…you're going to Cabo?"

Ah, *shit*. Telling him where we were going definitely wasn't part of the original plan.

I didn't respond, but I didn't have to. He was happy to inquire again, this time at a yell. "*You're going to Cabo, and you didn't invite me?*"

"Yes, T. I'm taking Georgie to Cabo, and you're not invited."

"By God, I finally know how Caesar felt at Brutus's hand. The betrayal! The conspiracy! You know, *you fucking know*, I love Cabo!"

"Yeah, well, call me crazy, but I felt like you coming along as a third wheel for Georgie's and my Valentine's getaway would've been a little awkward, so knifing you in the back was a necessary consequence."

"Wait…*Valentine's* getaway?" he questioned, confusion in his voice making the anger a little less potent. "It's fucking May, dude. Almost June. That ship sailed months ago."

"It's not for the one that's passed. It's for the next one. An early Valentine's getaway."

"Explain yourself," he demanded hotly.

As much as it was an option to hang up the phone, it also wasn't. The other thing about Thatch was that he took Dylan Thomas's poem "Do not go gentle into that good night" very seriously. And Thatcher's form of *raging* in this situation would be to demon dial me until I picked up again, and if necessary, to show up *in Cabo* just to hear me explain this shit to his face.

The sooner I put it to rest, the better off I'd be.

I sighed. "February 14th has, historically, been a very unlucky day for Georgia. Fires, mishaps, her dad running around the lawn in a Speedo like the fucking Kool-Aid man—it's all very traumatic."

Thatch laughed raucously. "Man, I love Dick Cummings."

"Of course you do. And frankly, I love him too. But Georgia's been through the wringer, and I'm gonna try like hell to turn this holiday's curse around. Even if that means starting by celebrating in May."

"Point taken," Thatch confirmed. "So, I take it you have a whole bunch of romantic fucking plans for Cabo? A bid to maintain your status as the swooniest billionaire to ever live or some shit?"

"Yes. Well, sort of. I wouldn't say I have an actual itinerary. Pretty sure the whole surprise getaway speaks for itself."

"That's it? *Pfft*. What a disappointment."

"What are you talking about?" I retorted. "I'm taking my wife on a surprise getaway to Cabo. The point of vacation is to relax. We'll go to the beach, eat good food, and have lots of sex. Sounds pretty fucking swoony to me."

"Sure, sure. But do you have any fancy dinners reserved?"

I paused, hating that Thatch was climbing inside my brain and starting to plant seeds of doubt. I didn't need to have a plan. We'd make it when we were there, based on what we felt like. There were plenty of options. "The resort has some really nice restaurants to eat at."

"Wow," Thatch boomed, transitioning into a boisterous laugh that made me a little nervous. "What about something awesome? Once-in-a-lifetime type shit."

"Once in a lifetime?"

"Yes, bro. Keep up, okay? Like skydiving. Or a hot air balloon ride. You know, something that will take her fucking breath away."

"Georgie isn't a fan of heights, dude."

"I can't believe this. You have zero plans. Not even a fucking dinner reservation."

"We don't need reservations," I stressed. "We're VIP status at the resort, so they'll squeeze us into whatever restaurant we want." Starting to get stressed, I ran a hand through my hair. I didn't need this fucker getting in my head. Jesus. This was like showing a pro-football player a reel of all the shit he's messed up right before the big game.

"What resort are you staying at?"

"The Diamond," I divulged reluctantly.

He wolf-whistled. "Very nice."

"I know." And it was. Georgie was going to love it, and she was going to love the simple relaxing lack of schedule I had planned. I knew it because I knew her. I just needed to get this fucker off the phone and out of my head for good.

"But still, your plans suck, dude. Downright pathetic."

"My plans are just fine." I rolled my eyes. "And, if you don't mind, now that you've wasted about twenty minutes of my time with nonsense, I really have to go."

"But—" He started to say more, but I shut that possibility down quick as a whip.

"Bye, Thatch!"

Thirty seconds later, two text message notifications flashed across the screen of my phone, but I ignored them. I knew who they would be from. In fact, thinking on it more, I scrolled into the options on my contact for Thatch and set him to *Do Not Disturb*. I could deal with anything else he had to say when I got back—after I'd successfully broken the Valentine's Day curse.

Hell yes. I couldn't wait.

Chapter 3

Georgia

Goodness gracious, today had been a long day at work.

If only it were Friday and I were headed home with the weekend serving as the light at the end of my work-stress tunnel. Sadly, though, seeing as it was only Wednesday, I still had two more days to get through before this busy week came to a close. *Ugh.*

Don't get me wrong, I *loved* my job. There was no doubt that working for the New York Mavericks was a *dream* job, but damn, handling marketing for a group of big, burly professional football players wasn't the easiest of tasks. And today's team photos were a prime example of that reality.

The photographer had been twenty minutes late.

The players had been annoyed. Trust me, I'd heard enough expletives to make my own rap album like the ones the store used to label as *explicit* when I was a kid to warn parents.

And Wes Lancaster—my boss and owner of the New York Mavericks—had been on a bit of a warpath when his team was forty minutes late to training because of said delay.

Thankfully, he had pointed that frustration toward the

photography team and not me. But when a dragon breathed fire any-where in your vicinity, there was still a high percentage chance that at least your eyebrows would get singed.

Even though he was one of Kline's best friends, Wes could give off some seriously broody-and-grumpy-as-hell vibes.

My phone chimed with a notification from the cupholder of my SUV, but I waited until I came to a stop at a red light about two miles from home before I picked it up and checked the screen. My hus-band was pretty specific about requesting I didn't text and drive now that we lived outside the city and didn't always commute together, which made it highly ironic to find a message from him waiting in my inbox.

Kline: Baby, it's past 7. Where the hell are you?

Ironic or not, one measly message from my husband and I was smiling like a loon.

It was dumb, I knew, to get all smiley from a simple *"Where are you?"* text from my spouse, but I couldn't help it. Call it love. Call it the honeymoon phase. Call it whatever you wanted. Kline Brooks and his big organs made me giddy—big heart, big penis; it was truly the perfect combination for a man.

I glanced up to see that the light was still red and tapped out a quick response.

Me: Running a little late tonight. But I'll be there in about 5 minutes.

Most days, I was usually home by six with dinner in the oven because Kline's cooking was one of his *only* flaws and I was a bit of a control freak about my meal selections, but today's chaotic photo shoot had me running *way* behind schedule. My husband, being the kind of guy he was, didn't even balk at the change. Truth was, if I'd have let him, he'd have gladly taken more of the meal responsibility off my shoulders on a regular basis.

Kline: I'll order takeout.

Me: Yay! My vote is for pizza, but I'd also go for burgers or tacos. Whatever you want.

Kline: Okay. Drive safe and stop texting. I'll see you soon. Love you.

The light turned green, and I quickly sent a heart emoji before setting my phone back in the cupholder to finish the drive to our house. Suddenly, a nagging thought popped into my head, so I grabbed my phone, scrolled to the number I wanted, and hit call to pull up the connection on my hands-free speaker through the stereo.

I'd been meaning to make this call for a couple of days now, but knowing his tendency to ramble, I'd put it off. Still, I had a quick moment now that would hopefully aid in my ability to end the call swiftly, and as it wasn't technically texting, I figured it'd be a lesser evil in the world of distractions.

Three rings later, and Thatch came on the line, booming over the speakers so forcefully, I swerved a little before reaching forward to turn the volume knob down. "Well, well, Georgia girl. How are you, sweetheart?"

I smiled and shook my head. Thatch was a character, and I found it unbelievably hard not to love him, even when I hated him. He was my best friend Cassie in male form come to life, and I didn't know how the world survived having two of them.

"Hey, Thatch," I greeted much more softly. "Sorry to bother you, but I've been wanting to touch base about a favor, if you wouldn't mind."

"A favor for you?"

"Yes," I confirmed.

"You got it. Lay it on me, sister."

See? That right there. That's why I always found myself loving him.

"Okay, great. I'm sure you know, but Kline's thirty-fifth birthday is coming up at the end of next month, and I'm planning on surprising him with a party."

"Righteous!"

I laughed. "Well, I was hoping you might be willing to help. Maybe with some of the planning, but mostly—"

"Oh, you bet your sweet ass, babe. I'm in. I'm a *great* planner. Terrific planner. Much better than your husband, as it turns out, but that's a topic for another time."

My eyes widened at the huge, running stream of word vomit coming out of his mouth, so I waded back in to try to get control of the situation.

"Well, that's great. Really. I appreciate your willingness. I just probably more need you for distracting Kline, getting him there. That sort of thing."

"Are you sure you don't want me to handle some of the arrangements? Honestly, I'm pretty damn good at it," he urged again, the confidence in his voice making me imagine him cocked back in his desk chair with his feet up on his desk. Still, I didn't need a co-planner. Not really anyway. Cassie had already volunteered for the job, and she was more than enough crazy to handle.

"I'm good. If you can just stand by for instruction from me on the specifics of distraction and escorting him to the party, I'll be forever grateful."

"Well, then, you got it, doll. I'm at your service."

I took one last right turn onto our quaint, suburban street and a left turn into my driveway, and I was finally *home sweet home*.

Thank goodness. Now I had an excuse to end the call before it got out of hand.

"Okay, then. Thanks again. I'll talk to you soon."

"You bet. Oh, and Georgia girl?"

"Yeah?"

"Have a *great* weekend."

My eyes narrowed at his weirdness, but I didn't focus on it for too long. The thing with Thatcher Kelly was that there was always at least a little weirdness.

"Thanks. I will. Bye."

Finally, I shut off the engine, grabbed my purse from the passenger seat, and headed for the door.

Honestly, two years ago, I never would've guessed that I'd find myself married, moved out of the vibrant city that is New York, and happily living in the suburbs, but here I was.

Married.

Happy.

And, as of a little over a week ago, officially moved out of the city and into the quiet suburbs.

No doubt, it was the one thing my best friend, Cassie—*a self-proclaimed "I'm never fucking leaving the city" New Yorker*—would probably never let me live down. But fingers crossed, one day soon, she would find the kind of man who made her eat those I-will-never-live-in-suburbia words.

As for me, my focus mostly revolved around getting inside, taking off this godforsaken bra, and releasing my poor feet from these freaking heels. I swear, besides sex with my husband, there wasn't any better feeling than taking off my bra and heels after a long day.

I tapped the garage door closed on the switch next to the entrance to the house and stepped inside. I hooked my purse on one of the fixtures by the door and headed down the hall, but I came to a halting stop when I reached the threshold of the kitchen and looked down toward my feet. Instantly, confusion urged a furrow in my brow as I stared down at the hardwood floor, a trail of red and pink that led from the kitchen and into the main hallway that led to the upstairs all I could see.

Rose petals.

So many rose petals.

A giant smile consumed my face as I set my keys and phone down on the counter right next to the heart-shaped card propped up on a bowl of fruit and waiting for me.

On the front, it read *Be My Valentine Forever and Always, Benny?*

I flipped it over, and on the back, a handwritten message in my husband's familiar scrawl stared back at me.

My Georgie,

Happy (*very* early) Valentine's Day, gorgeous.

If there is one thing I'm certain of, it's beautiful, amazing you and the fact that I want to spend the rest of my life laying the world at your adorable feet.

"*I vow to spend the rest of our lives laughing, smiling, going on crazy adventures, and most importantly, loving each other through the good times and the bad...*"

When I said those words to you, while standing at the altar and professing my love and eternal commitment to you in front of God and our family and friends, I meant them.

And that's exactly why, even though you think Valentine's Day holds some kind of curse over your pretty little head, I'm determined to find a way around it and spoil the hell out of you.

Pack your bags, Georgie.

Big-dicked Brooks has a special, *sexy*, romantic adventure planned just for you. And he's even agreed to let the rest of my body come too.

My heart is yours.
Always,
Kline

Happy early Valentine's Day?
Pack your bags?
A romantic adventure?
So many questions filled my head.

Completely puzzled, I had to place a hand over my mouth in an effort to stifle the shocked giggle that came out of my throat and the giddy emotions that rolled around in my belly.

What was happening?

When I read a little farther, I found the instructions for how to find out were waiting right there for me.

P.S. Follow the roses.

It didn't take long before I did just that, shucking my heels and taking off at a run down the hallway and up the stairs. Eventually, I reached our master bedroom, where my husband stood beside our bed with two glasses of wine in his hands and a glorious stripe of confidence painted across his perfect lips.

"Hello, wife."

"Well, hello, husband." I smiled back at him. "This is…uh…quite the greeting…"

His smirk blossomed into a megawatt smile as he handed me a glass of white wine, but he didn't say anything else.

"So…uh…mind telling me what's going on?" I asked, eyeing my husband inquisitively as I took a polite sip.

"Well…" Kline stepped forward and pressed a kiss to the corner of my mouth. "I know February 14th isn't your favorite day, but I want to make sure my beautiful wife still gets to enjoy getting spoiled for Valentine's Day, even if that means bending the rules a little bit."

I tilted my head to the side.

"So, Georgie, will you be my *really* early valentine?" He pretended to cough over the word "really," and my cheeks started to hurt with my smile.

"I want to say yes, immediately, but…" He furrowed his brow. "Given my history with this holiday, I'm hoping you won't mind if I request a copy of the fine print first."

"The fine print?" he questioned, a chuckle following his words.

I nodded. "The nitty-gritty. The details. The exact plan you have, so I know how to properly prepare myself in case of emergency."

He pulled me in suddenly, slamming a kiss to my lips and stealing my breath away. By the time he pulled away, I found I wasn't all that concerned with the details anymore.

"God, I love you, Benny. We leave on a secret getaway tomorrow morning. Far away from February, far away from your parents, far away from everything. Just you and me and time to ourselves."

"A getaway? Tomorrow?" I questioned, shock and awe in my voice.

He nodded, eyes shining with amusement.

"But it's Thursday. I have work—"

He cut me off by shaking his head. "I already talked to Wes and got the approval."

I stared at him for a long moment, excitement starting to build in my body. "Where…where are we going?"

"Cabo."

"Cabo, Kline?" I questioned on a shrill shriek that made me thankful we'd moved to the suburbs. In New York, at least five people would have either called the cops or put out a hit on me. "You're taking me to freaking *Cabo* tomorrow morning?"

Oh Mylanta, my husband was one swoony fucking bastard!

He nodded. "Beach, sun, and lots of delicious sex. You in, Benny girl?"

I almost opened my mouth to shout "Hell yes!" but one very important thought popped into my mind. I couldn't go through pet-panic again. "Before I answer that—first, tell me who is watching the boys?"

"Don't worry, baby, I did *not* put Cassie and Thatch in charge of supervising Walter and Stan," he answered, amusement shining in his voice. "I've hired a very qualified, fully vetted dog sitter to come stay at the house. Came highly recommended from Meryl."

Knowing full well that Meryl was the kind of woman who took zero bullshit, when he said that, I knew with certainty that my boys would be in good hands.

Thank goodness for that. A huge sigh of relief escaped my lungs.

"So, now that we have that settled, what's it going to be, baby?" Kline asked. "You ready to be my valentine and spend several fantastic, sun-filled days in Cabo with me?"

"Are you kidding me?" I exclaimed and jumped up into his arms, sloshing the white wine out of my glass and all over our clothes. But I didn't care, and neither did he. Lips to his, I kissed the hell out of my husband. "I'm in," I said, between kisses to his lips and cheeks and nose and forehead. "I'm in, I'm in, I'm in!"

Kline chuckled, took the now half-empty wine glass out of my hand, and set both his and mine on our nightstand.

His forehead, his nose, his cheeks, pretty much any part of his face I could get my lips on, they were all the subject of a very long and pointed attack.

Eventually, though, my lips found his again, and the kissing went from cute and adorable to deep and passionate and heated.

Hell's bells, I would never grow tired of kissing this man.

My legs were wrapped around his waist, and I pressed myself against him, grinding myself against the firm bulge beneath the zipper of his jeans.

Oh *yes.*

"Fuck, baby, you always make me so hard." Kline groaned.

I knew exactly what he meant. If women had dicks, I'd have been tenting the fabric at my crotch for a good long time now.

He laid me back on our bed and kissed a path of openmouthed kisses down my neck and chest, only stopping to move my blouse out of the way with his teeth.

Instantly, my eyes fell closed and a moan escaped my mouth.

"Shall we start our Valentine's celebration a little early?" he asked, blue eyes blazing as they looked up into mine.

"Yes, please," I begged desperately. Not one for sexual theatrics, my husband didn't waste any time removing my clothes.

And then his clothes.

Until finally, he was sliding inside me.

"God, Kline, that feels so good," I said, my voice more of a whimper than I'd ever heard it. "It always feels *so* good."

"Just think, baby. Tomorrow begins the start of *even more* of this," he said, pushing himself deeper on a heady groan. "Four days of me, you, and my cock inside your perfect pussy."

Oh, holy hell. I had a feeling I was going to have a much greater weekend than Thatch could ever have imagined earlier.

Chapter 4

Thatch

*A*nother *day, another dollar, another boring-ass conference.*
Sure, the men and women on the call included some of my most important investors and some of the biggest brains on Wall Street, but fuck, they all had a true talent for droning on and on and *on.*

It was a true wonder of the world how I, Thatcher Kelly, adrenaline junkie, adventure-seeker, award-winning prankster, and all-around larger-than-life, attractive-as-fuck, charming-as-hell man, ended up in the world of finance and investments with a bunch of pencil-sharpening number-crunchers, but it was my reality. On the plus side, they were less likely to fuck your sister—assuming you had one—or jiggle your girl's tits behind your back. I could appreciate the loyalty, and I'd noticed a sleeper-cell, nice-guy version of Mr. Steal Your Girl in one or two of them.

Maybe the next time Kline fucked me over by taking his wife on a second goddamn honeymoon, I'd enlist one of them as my backup wingman.

Eh, fuck. No way they'd be as good as Big-dick.

Oh well. At least they had helped make me rich.

The conversation veered toward upcoming quarterly earnings for corporations I'd already done my homework on, so when an email notification popped up in the right-hand corner of my laptop screen, in the name of softening the boredom blow, I clicked it open.

Fuck yes! It was the response I'd been waiting for with bated breath. Truly, the whole foundation of my best bro's marriage was on the line, and it was up to me to save it. I would go full-on Elizabeth Bennet on Kline "Mr. Bingley" Brooks if he didn't step up to the plate for my homegirl Georgia "Jane Bennet" Brooks if I needed to. Trust me, there was no length I wasn't willing to go to. I'd have to get it specially made—given my fantastically giantlike size—but I'd be a fucking stunner in a hoop dress.

To: Thatcher Kelly
From: Antonio Diamond
Re: Brooks Reservation

Thatch,
Confirming that I've set your plans in motion, and I've been assured by my staff that they will maintain the utmost discretion. As far as the Brookses are concerned, your kind gifts will be compliments of the hotel.
Call my cell if you need anything else.
-A.D.

Instantly, a smile formed at the corners of my lips.

Man, I loved when a plan came together. And I really loved that I had the capital to add in the romance Kline so foolishly left out, without financial burden or limitation. It made me feel all tingly inside to be able to donate so much so selflessly.

I pulled open the drawer on the right side of my desk and snatched the digital camera inside. One click to the power button and a glance at the screen assured me it was fully charged, so I shut it down with a smile and placed it back inside.

I was going to need it in a few days to snap a picture as the "Swoony Billionaire" himself fell at my feet and kissed them with his thanks for saving his Valentine's getaway—no, his *marriage*. Women liked pizzazz—they liked to be wowed—even when they said they didn't.

Only foolish guys didn't know how to read between the lines.

The sounds of Len Dodson's monotone-as-fuck voice continued to filter in from the speaker of my phone, and I tuned him out, my focus going straight to the priorities—ensuring that the plans in motion were foolproof and accurate.

Cell in hand, I shot a quick text to the one person who could assist with that confirmation. It was a gamble, bringing another person—especially a person without the foresight to see the value in a brilliant plan like mine—into my loop, but thankfully, I had the perfect set of "weighted dice" to ensure the odds didn't fuck me. Because when you tried to fuck Thatcher Kelly, he always fucked you harder. Always, no matter if you were a pussy-bearing friend or a dick-swinging foe. A sword of my stature was never unprepared.

Me: Georgia will be back to work on Monday, right? Just off Thursday and Friday this week?

A minute after I hit send, my phone vibrated with a response.

Wes: Yes, only two days off work for the second fucking honeymoon. I guess Kline told you too.

He told me, I dragged it out of him. Po-tay-to, po-tah-to.

Me: Um, yeah.

Wes: Wait…why do you care when she comes back to work?

Wes Lancaster was normally too involved in his own broody, sassy bullshit to have a sixth sense about me. If he was on the brink of figuring me out this time, all I needed to do was drag him off the scent a little bit.

Me: Because I'm a good fucking friend, that's why. I just wanted to make sure I have their itinerary in case something crazy happens while they're gone. You know, taking a trip to a foreign country is where most people get abducted. Mexico's got the cartel, for fuck's sake.

Wes: And what exactly are you going to do about the cartel from here?

Me: Nothing, specifically. I'm not the fucking Karate Kid, Whiny Whitney. Jesus. But at least I'll know where they were supposed to be if they go missing. Didn't your momma teach you to use the buddy system with your friends? You're ALWAYS supposed to let someone know where you are and when.
Wes: Not the Karate Kid? That's funny because I'm pretty sure you're trying to fucking Mr. Miyagi me right now. I wasn't sure, but then you brought my mom into it. What are you scheming, Kelly?

Damn, maybe the bastard does have a sixth sense?

Me: Cool the inquisition, Wesley. I'm not scheming shit. Just being a good friend and trying to make sure our buddy Kline and his wife Georgia are safe.

Wes: Right. And I'm Mother Teresa. You're up to no good, and I know it.

Me: May I suggest you consider upping your therapy hours to three a week, dude? I think your paranoia might be getting out of control.

Wes: Nice deflection, T, but it's not working. I'm onto you. For the sake of your balls, you better tell Kline NOW. Because the instant he calls to tell me something's not right, I'm gonna sell your ass down the river.

Wes Lancaster, ladies and gentlemen. The good-time fun-ruiner.

I mulled over my options for a hot minute before deciding that honesty was the best policy where Wes was concerned. At least then, I'd be able to blackmail him or something to keep the intel I gave him on the down-low. We'd been friends for years, and I had more than a few incriminating drunk videos of him saved up for a rainy day. Over the years, we'd taken far too many trips to Vegas for him not to be aware my phone was filled with embarrassing evidence.

If I tried to snow him, it'd just piss him off more.

Don't worry, I'm not talking hard-core blackmail.
More like, soft-core. The late-night Cinemax of blackmail,
if you will.
No X-rated money shots, just tits and ass and the illusion of sex.

Decision made, I typed out a response.

Me: Okay, fine, you prick. I AM planning something. A few things. Whatever. But it's only because K's supposed romantic plans sucked goat tits. You don't need to worry. It's all first-class shit. They're gonna have the time of their lives, and our tightwad billionaire bestie isn't even going to have to pay for any of it. It's the best of both worlds.

Wes: Fucking hell. I knew it. Kline is going to put your balls in a goddamn vise, and there's no way I'm letting you take me down as an accomplice.

Big surprise. Whiny fucking Whitney was already crying his little baby tears. It was time to set his ass straight.

Me: All right, sister. I know your panties are already chafing over this, but you're going to have to man up and get the hell over it. You can't tell him shit about this because if you do, I'll bury you in a shallow grave of amateur porn from all our wild years in Vegas. I'm sure the tabloids would have a field day with grainy sex videos of the steel-faced owner of the Mavericks.

Wes: Goddammit, Thatch. I don't want to be involved in your stupid shit.

Me: Yeah, well, you only have yourself to blame for that, son. You should probably remind yourself of this conversation the next time you want to ask questions…

Wes: I hate you so much right now.

Me: I love you too, buddy. And thanks for keeping this on the down-low. I'm so glad we were able to come to this agreement where we understand each other.

Wes: You are such an asshole, you know that?

Pfft. As long as he kept his goddamn mouth shut, I didn't care what he thought of me.

Come hell or high water, my best friend's wife was going to have a Valentine's getaway she'd never forget. *All because of me.*

Chapter 5

Georgia

"You almost ready, baby?" Kline called from the living room area of our far-too-big-for-two-people luxurious suite at the Diamond. Apparently, the resort was world-renowned and owned by Antonio Diamond, a wealthy man who just so happened to be a business acquaintance of my wonderful, surprise-getaway-planning husband. Upon our arrival, we'd been greeted personally, served champagne, and escorted to our room by a man who was to be our personal concierge.

I had to admit, my husband was off to a pretty dang good start in making formal celebrations of love a little less intimidating.

"Only a few more minutes!" I answered, carefully adding another layer of mascara to my eyelashes.

This was my first-ever visit to Cabo, and it had only taken one step out onto the balcony of our suite to understand the beauty of it. With white sand beaches and aquamarine water and refreshing saltwater air, it was downright breathtaking.

But I wanted to look hot enough tonight that Kline couldn't tear his eyes away from me to see any of it.

We'd only been in Cabo for a few hours, but I was quickly realizing that celebrating Valentine's Day in May was one of the best ideas my husband had ever had, reverse of the curse or not. We'd already had more hot sex than most of the married women I knew had had in the last two weeks combined, and there were still three more days left to set some kind of insane record that was worthy of a Reddit thread.

Once I finished with my mascara and added a hint of pink to my lips, I stepped back and gave tonight's dinner attire a quick once-over in the huge master bathroom mirror, making sure all the necessary things were in place.

Flowy white linen dress? Check.

Strappy nude heels? Check.

Blond hair sporting sexy beach waves? Check.

Enough visible cleavage to turn my ass man into a boob aficionado? Check, check.

I smiled at myself, did a little twirl, and strode out of the bathroom, through the master bedroom, and into the living room of the palatial suite. A mischievous grin crested my lips when I walked past our bed, still messy from our earlier hot afternoon sex romp after we'd arrived in Cabo via a private jet and a limo ride from the airport. And the delectable view that was my husband standing in front of the floor-to-ceiling doors that led out onto the balcony of the living room only made it grow.

Dressed in a black suit, crisp white shirt, and no tie, my man was *handsome.*

The instant he turned around and met my eyes, a slow, seductive-as-hell smirk formed at the corners of his lips and put my measly little smile to shame. When Kline Brooks looked at me like that, I knew he was thinking *dirty.* "Damn, baby. You look incredible," he said and closed the distance between us to press a delicious kiss to my lips. It was short but sexy, and the feel of his tongue swirling around mine made my knees wobble into each other.

As I carefully rubbed a lipstick smudge from the corner of his mouth, I smiled up at him. "And you, Mr. Brooks, look as handsome as ever."

"Shall we go enjoy some dinner downstairs?"

I nodded, more than a little bit enthusiastic to get the food show on the road. "After all that hot afternoon sex and no lunch, I am so hungry I could eat the asshole out of a dead monkey."

Kline's laugh was raucous enough to echo off the walls of our living room and out the balcony doors to the ocean. I swore there was a sea turtle out there somewhere falling in love at first sound. "You sure have a way with words, Mrs. Brooks."

I shrugged, admitting, "That's one I got from Cass, as you might imagine. But she's used it so much over the years, I guess it stuck."

He laughed at that, this time with a little less shock, and gently placed his hand at the small of my back, leading us toward the entryway of our suite. But just before we reached the door, three raps sounded against it and stopped our progress.

Kline tilted his head to the side in confusion but reached out to turn the handle and open the door anyway. My man, even in the face of uncertainty, was never one to beat around the bush. It was part of what I loved about him. He was the perfect amount of confident, stopping just shy of being cocky.

On the other side, smiling at us from the threshold, stood a friendly, fiftysomething man of Asian descent wearing a white chef's jacket and tall red chef's hat. From the look on my husband's face, I guessed he didn't recognize him either.

"Mr. Brooks?" the man asked, smiling back and forth between the two of us.

"That's me," my husband replied. "Can I help you with something?"

"Are you ready for dinner, sir?"

"Well…" Kline paused, and his gaze flitted down toward me for a quick moment before landing back on the man. "Yes. We were just on our way downstairs now."

"Oh, no, sir," the man interjected with a shake of his head. "No need to go downstairs. A very special evening has already been planned for you and your lovely wife right here in your room."

"What?" I questioned, a little bit of disappointment mixing with outrage. *Hell's bells, if I would've known that, I would've, you know, stayed in the cozy resort bathrobe after my shower and skipped these damn heels...*

"We're eating in the room?"

Kline started to shake his head, but before he could respond, Mr. Chef chimed in again.

"Yes, ma'am. I am Haruto, and it would be my greatest pleasure to serve you tonight."

Kline, never one for bullshit and a dab-hand at reading my face, cut right to the chase. "You'll have to excuse me, Haruto, as I'm sure your food is wonderful, but my wife and I did not plan this dinner. There must be some kind of mistake. Are you sure you have the right room?"

Haruto glanced to the side of the door to double-check the gold number plaque and then back my husband. "I am sure, Mr. Brooks. I am here to be at your service. I can see that this wasn't your plan, but I assure you, it will be my greatest honor to make this a meal you remember always."

Kline smiled, replying diplomatically, "We really appreciate that, Haruto. You'll have to excuse us. We're just confused. Do you happen to know who planned this dinner?"

"Actually, sir, it's compliments of the resort," he answered. I swear, for the briefest of moments, a secret smile sat behind his eyes, but it disappeared between one blink and the next.

"Mr. Diamond arranged this?" Kline asked, surprised. "I didn't even tell him it was a special occasion."

"Oh, sir. Any occasion with your wife is meant to be a special one, yes?" He offered a knowing grin. "The Diamond Resort just wants you and Mrs. Brooks to have the best stay possible."

My husband's eyes focused on me again, and I could see the wheels of his mind turning. He was skeptical; that much was apparent. I wasn't sure exactly why, since the people at the front desk had started fawning over us the moment we got here, but he was practical at heart. My dear husband had a tendency to forget that he was a freaking billionaire and that people loved to toss the world at his feet just for the hell of it.

I wanted to pull him to the side and explain it gently. Really, I did.

But, see, I was fucking hungry.

And food basically trumped everything. So, I was going to go with the KISS—keep it simple, stupid—method and get the hell out of Haruto's way so he could get to cooking.

"It was probably just your friend Antonio," I reassured in the name of my empty stomach. "I mean, think about everything that was waiting for us when we arrived."

"You are newly wedded, correct? The romance is very important," Haruto jumped in, obviously trying to help me hurry this decision along.

"Are you sure you're okay with the change?" Kline finally turned to me to ask. The relief that we would be eating soon made me want to fall to my knees and weep.

"Completely fine. I just want to eat." Lord knew, calling off Haruto would be a lengthy ordeal. The man was politely dogged, and I didn't think he would be giving up with a simple *No   thanks.*

Kline refocused his attention back on Mr. Chef. "Okay. Yeah. Dinner would be great."

Haruto bounced on his toes and clapped excited hands in front of himself.

"Oh, wonderful!"

I chimed in, offering a friendly smile. "We're very, *very* honored that you're going to make us dinner tonight."

"You are welcome, Mr. and Mrs. Brooks. If you don't mind, my two assistants, Kane and Yui, will also be joining me."

Promptly, his two assistants, a young male and female in matching white attire, appeared into view.

Both Kline and I stepped back to let them inside, both of us offering welcoming greetings and smiles as they wheeled two covered carts and what looked to be a sleek metal grill on wheels into the room.

Holy moly, talk about coming prepared…

"Please, Mr. and Mrs. Brooks, go enjoy a drink on the balcony while we set up," Haruto instructed us, and his assistant Yui wasted no time grabbing a bottle of wine from the bottom of her cart and pouring us each a glass.

"It shouldn't take us too long to set up, and then, I shall bestow the best hibachi-style dinner that will ever grace your taste buds upon you," Haruto said, graciously bowing toward us.

"Thank you, Haruto." Kline smiled and pressed his hand to the small of my back, leading me out onto the balcony.

The instant we were safely on the other side of the closed doors, I looked at him with wide, amused eyes. "I guess you're going to have to thank your buddy Antonio, huh? It seems like he's really pulling out all the stops to help you prove me wrong."

I giggled, and Kline smiled. "You seem excited."

Strangely, I was. It was all unexpected and a little confusing, but it was kind of exhilarating too. Before I met Kline, I never got this kind of specialty treatment when I went away on vacations. I was just a regular girl with regular money. I guessed I was still getting used to it all.

I nodded, and Kline's smile deepened as he leaned down to kiss the corner of my mouth. "Good. If you're happy, I'm happy."

"I am. Happy, that is. Especially since you knowing the owner of the hotel means there's only a small percent chance that this is actually the beginning of an international murder scheme, where we end up on the grill by the end of the night."

Knowing my penchant for dramatics and Netflix obsession with crime documentaries, Kline just chuckled and wrapped his arm around my shoulders, tucking me close to his side and turning us to face the ocean. The night he fell asleep to the TV on something other than the explicit details of human mutilation was the day he would actually worry.

The sun had just set beyond the horizon, making the sky dance with hues of pink and orange and red. And the waves crashed gently against the white sand.

"That view will never get old," I said and stepped up onto my tippy-toes to place a kiss to Kline's cheek. "Thank you for this. I had no idea I'd need a little getaway with you so soon after our honeymoon, but this surprise trip, well, it was much-needed."

"Anything for you," he said, pressing a gentle kiss to my forehead. "My gorgeous, beautiful wife and valentine."

My mouth, my eyes, my cheeks, even my heart smiled at that. "Always and forever, Kline."

"Ditto, baby."

Luckily for my stomach, the setup for our unexpected hibachi-style dinner hadn't taken long at all. Before we knew it, Yui opened the balcony doors and ushered us back inside, leading us toward the center of our suite's living room area, where a romantic table for two had been set up in front of the sleek metal grill Haruto stood behind.

Spatula and knife in his hands and a confident smile on his lips, the man was ready to hibachi rock and roll.

I couldn't deny it was a little odd to be in Mexico, and instead of eating, you know, like, fresh guacamole, we were about to dive into a Japanese-inspired meal, but I also couldn't deny that I was pretty damn excited for the delicious food about to head my way.

"Tonight, I will prepare a romantic feast of steak, chicken, shrimp, scallops, lobster, and the best rice you will ever taste in your life," Haruto announced, and my stomach growled in excitement.

Without delay, he showed off his impressive skills, tossing his tools around with precision while chopping up zucchini and carrots and onions and mushrooms.

By the time the shrimp and chicken and rice were placed onto the sizzling grill, my mouth was practically watering, while Haruto cheekily made a train out of sliced onions and moved it around the grill.

And let me tell you, I was all aboard on this food train.

Choo-mother-flipping-choo! Get in my belly!

"Mrs. Brooks," Haruto said, a grin on his lips. "Ready to play catch?" he asked and held up a shrimp on his spatula.

Immediately, anxiety clenched my stomach. I wasn't good with food-style games. Truthfully, I wasn't good with objects flying at my face, period. I needed to shut this down before things got out of hand.

"Oh *no*. No, no thank you," I responded through a nervous giggle. "Not me." I shook my head and held up both hands in a universal sign of *"Hi, I'm an anxious person who gets super awkward and weird when she's put on the spot. Please don't try to make me catch the shrimp in my mouth."*

Evidently, though, Haruto was determined. "You can do it, Mrs. Brooks! We believe in you!" He cheered me on. "Right, Mr. Brooks? We believe in her!"

"You got this, baby." Kline nodded, playfully oblivious to my internal state of impending doom, but the instant his eyes met mine and his brain registered my wide eyes and my irrational anxiety about catching a tiny piece of seafood in my mouth, he tried to divert the attention on to himself. "Actually, Haruto, why don't you toss that my way? Let me give it a shot first. Break the ice, so to speak."

"Ah, Mr. Brooks, but ladies first. *Always*," Haruto persisted.

"No, really. I don't need to be first," I protested. Haruto grinned, his spatula still aimed at me, and I shook my head. "Not me. Him." I pointed maniacally at my husband with one index finger. "Do him. Make him catch the shrimp. He loves shrimp. Right, Kline? You love them so much!" More nervous giggles spilled from my lips, and I swear to God, my cheeks were so red, I'd need no costume to audition for the role of a lobster.

"Open up and say *ah*, Mrs. Brooks!"

"No, no, no—" I tried to stop him again, but he was determined to toss that damn shrimp into my mouth. Haruto, the pushiest spatula-shrimp-pusher that had ever pushed shrimp.

Peer-pressured into an awkward corner I couldn't escape, I finally nodded like a bull rider in the chute, and no joke, he just let the sucker *fly*. Directly at my face without any prep or warning at all.

Like watching sand through an hourglass or water boil in a pot on a stove, it happened in slow motion at first. Hell, it was so slow, it gave time for a small part of me to woman up and believe that I could actually do it.

So, with my mouth open, I leaned back in my chair and tracked the shrimp as it floated through the air.

You guys, I swear, I'm trying. I really am. But it's not going to happen.

In an instant, I went from a woman on a shrimp-catching mission to a woman feeling said shrimp bounce off her forehead as her chair jolted too far back, causing an outright free fall toward the ground.

A squeal jumped from my lips, my stomach lurched, and my hands reached out to try to stop the momentum, but there was nothing I could do. As I flailed like a lunatic, my chair continued its descent toward the ground, and I slammed one of my strappy heel-covered feet on something so hard that it felt like I'd inadvertently amputated my toes from my body.

Pain shot behind my eyes like a bullet. "Ah, hell!"

But that pain was swiftly made second priority when *bam!*

Impact engaged.

In a crash-landing, my chair hit the floor with a harsh blow, and my whole body bounced out of it and onto the cool tile.

"Georgie! Shit!" Kline shouted, concern raising his voice as he jumped from his own chair to help me.

"Oh no, Mrs. Brooks!" Haruto's voice joined in. "Are you okay?"

Between the pain from banging my damn toes on something and the shock of my body smacking into the ground, I had to blink a few times before I could even register their questions. The wind had officially been knocked out of my lungs and, consequently, right out of my special hibachi dinner sails.

"I'm fine—" I started to reassure them, but Yui's panicked voice cut me off.

"Mr. Haruto!" She shouted at the top of her lungs. "The grill! The grill! Mr. Haruto, the grill!"

With me still on the ground, the sounds of panic and chaos erupted above.

"Oh no!" Haruto yelled, and hurried footsteps followed his voice.

With quick and strong hands, Kline helped me to my feet and ran his hands along my body to check for obvious injury.

The assessment didn't last long, though, before the real urgency of the other emergency set in.

"Fire!" Haruto shouted. "Fire!"

It only took one glance toward the grill to figure out what all the hullabaloo was about.

But this wasn't a hullabaloo.

It was the real emergency deal.

My eyes wide, flames filled my vision.

Actual flames.

From an actual fire.

Inside our suite, coming right off Haruto's grill.

Holy shit!

Not again!

Bright orange and red blazed off the grill to terrifying heights, and Haruto and his two assistants scrambled around our suite, trying to douse the fire with whatever they could find.

"Kane!" Haruto shouted to his other assistant. "The fire extinguisher! Where is it?"

Kane rummaged through their carts like a madman, trying to find it.

All the while, Yui filled up bowls with water from the small kitchen sink of our suite, but I'll be honest, with the height of the flames and shallow depth of those bowls, I knew they wouldn't do anything to help stop the fire I still wasn't even sure how had started.

That is, until the remnants of pain from my toes registered in my mind. *Oh my goodness, did I start the fire with my foot? Because I was trying to catch a piece of freaking seafood in my mouth?!*

Talk about a disaster. Accidental, of course, but still, a fucking disaster.

The curse, it seemed, was determined to continue.

"We need to evacuate!" Kline shouted, pulling me from my not-the-right-time thoughts and grabbing the dinner crew's attention. "Don't worry about the fire. We need to get out of here!"

Taking charge of the situation, he picked up the phone on the desk and told the front desk to call 9-1-1.

All the while, the damn fire waited for no one, causing so much smoke that it triggered the suite's alarms. Then, of course, that triggered the *whole* resort's alarms, because why not get the rest of the patrons involved, you know?

At Kline's urging, Haruto and Yui and Kane stopped trying to put out the fire and began to head toward the door, with us right behind them.

But just before we could actually get out of our suite, the sprinklers deployed with a hiss and a fizz, spraying water from the ceiling into our faces and onto every surface, every piece of furniture, pretty much *everything* inside the suite.

And because I hadn't even managed to catch the one piece of shrimp in my mouth, I still hadn't eaten even a freaking bite.

Chapter 6

Kline

"Sir, your new suite is ready, and the hotel concierge has already moved all of your belongings into it," Heather, the nice woman at the front desk, updated me. "It sounds like, besides the exterior of your suitcases and a few pairs of shoes getting wet from the sprinklers, nothing was ruined."

What a fucking night. The whole point of this getaway was to break the streak of Valentine's disasters for my wife—to prove that she didn't need to be worried about celebrating our love in any official capacity—and the first fucking day had gone up in literal flames.

"Thank you so much," I said, my voice a rush of tired, beleaguered appreciation. It had been a long couple of hours, we still hadn't eaten, and to top it all off, we'd done thousands of dollars of damage to one of Antonio's hotel rooms. "And again, I'm very sorry that happened in our hotel room."

"It was an accident, sir," she responded. "The fire chief even determined that, after examining the room once the fire was put out. We're just glad everyone got out safely."

"Yeah." I sighed and ran a hand through my hair. Even though I knew it wasn't my fault or Haruto's fault or even Georgia's foot's fault for banging into the grill and causing some kind of freak flame explosion, I still felt pretty fucking terrible that any of us was having to deal with this at all. "Your help and kindness with this are extremely appreciated."

Heather nodded and smiled. "It's my pleasure, Mr. Brooks."

I turned around and found Georgia standing in the middle of the lobby, her blond hair still wet from the sprinklers and a fire blanket wrapped around her shoulders.

"Did Haruto and Kane and Yui already leave?" I asked when I reached her.

"After apologizing to me a million times, yes. They just left a little while ago."

"And the fire department?"

"Also gone." She nodded.

"And what about your good mood?"

"Wavering slightly," she admitted, "but not gone entirely."

Well, that was good at least.

"Good." I smiled down at her, pulling her and the fire blanket into a tight hug. "What a night, huh?"

"Uh-huh." She snorted. "I'm pretty sure this makes it official, though. I'm not cursed on February 14th…" She paused and locked her half-amused, half-terrified gaze with mine. "I'm cursed when it comes to *anything* related to Valentine's Day. Hell, me just uttering those two words is probably putting everyone around us at risk for something insane to happen."

"Don't be ridiculous." A smirk found its way on to my lips. "It was just a freak thing, baby. Tomorrow will be better."

"You say that, but that's what we said about today. Given my current state…" She shrugged her shoulders to emphasize the fire blanket around them. "And the fact that I *still* haven't eaten anything, I'm not holding my breath."

I frowned. This was not at all what I had in mind when I planned this trip, and I hated to see Georgie looking so defeated.

"Hey, silver lining," I interjected, trying to lighten the mood. "At least neither one of us was standing in the lobby in *Mr. Handsome* red underwear while the fire department was putting out the fire, so that's something to be thankful for."

Giggles escaped her lungs. "Oh yeah, thank goodness for that. A real highlight of the night."

"C'mon, baby." I chuckled and wrapped my arm around her shoulders. "Let's go upstairs to our new suite, order some room service, have a little 'thank goodness we didn't die in a fire' sex, and call it a night."

She grinned over at me. "I'm on board with this plan."

It didn't take long before we were in the elevator and heading up the twenty floors to our new room.

"Just promise me something, okay," she asked as we rode upward. "Let's just keep things simple for the rest of our time here. No grand gestures. No sweetheart dinners. This is officially just a trip since anything related to…*you know*…is cursed."

Christ. Now she was even avoiding the words *Valentine's Day.*

"You're not cursed, baby," I reassured her. "Tonight was just a hiccup in what will be a fantastic, sex-filled weekend getaway. But yes. I promise, everything will be simple from here on out."

"A hiccup?" She burst into laughter. "I have to give it to you, Kline. Your faith and fortitude to disprove the curse are admirable."

"There's no curse!" I exclaimed, chuckles mixing with my words.

Georgia just rolled her eyes, but thankfully, didn't refute my proclamation.

One day, I would set her straight about this superstition.

The elevator dinged our arrival, and when we stepped into the hallway, my phone chimed from the back pocket of my pants.

As we walked down the hall and toward our suite, I pulled it out to find a new text.

Wes: Hey, man. How is Cabo treating you?

My eyebrows pinched together as I double-checked the sender. Wes was not the type of guy to check in after I'd forced him to give Georgia the time off. He was the type to grumble and ignore and make sure he got me back with subtle retaliation until the day I died. It was definitely him, though, and he *was* checking in, so maybe age was starting to soften him up a little?

Me: Hey, man. Well, considering Georgie and I are headed to our second room of the trip in less than 24 hours of being here because a fire broke out in our room, I'd say it could be going better.

His response chimed in mere seconds later.

Wes: A FIRE? What the fuck are you talking about?

Me: A hibachi chef came to our suite, and the damn grill caught on fire. The fucking fire department even had to come. It was nuts, man.
Wes: Tell me you're joking.

Me: From my lips to God's ears, Wes. The resort even had to evacuate temporarily while the fire department got it under control.

Wes: Holy fuck, man. Is everyone okay?

Georgie was sliding out of her heels and contorting her body to try to unzip her dress, and I had no doubt she was going to need my assistance soon. My fingers to the keys of my phone, I shot off one last text, eager to get this conversation over with and move on to the only good thing we'd been able to count on so far—really hot sex.

Me: Everyone is good, man. Not exactly the night we planned, but it's all over now. Talk to you later.

I dropped the phone on the table by the door to our new suite and unbuttoned the top of my shirt.

Then, I put all of my focus and attention on the most important thing—romancing my beautiful wife.

Chapter 7

Thatch

Drinks flowed from the bar.

Patrons danced and sang along to the live band.

And the beautiful women inside the establishment appeared ready and waiting for ole Thatcher to make his move.

There was no doubt about it; the Raines Law Room was hopping. But while I waited anxiously to hear how well all my plans for the lovebirds in Cabo had turned out, it all became white noise.

In no time at all, I excused myself from a conversation with a flirtatious, redheaded woman in a tight black dress and headed out of the bar to make a quick call away from the jovial commotion.

The second I stepped outside, warm night air brushed across my face, and I pressed my back up against the brick of the building as I hit dial on the call.

It took three rings before a greeting filled my ears.

"Mr. Kelly!" Haruto exclaimed into the receiver. "How are you?"

"Well, Harry, I'm a little concerned. I expected I would have heard from you by now about how the dinner went. Did they love it?"

"Ah, yes. Well…see…"

His hesitant, filibustering words urged my chest to expand with irritation, but I quickly forced a calming breath into my lungs. I refused to let myself go verbal Hulk Smash on my beloved Haruto. Not only had he agreed to take on the task of flying to Cabo last minute to help my best friend and his wife have an awesome getaway, but his restaurant in NYC was one of my favorite places to eat. And my father had always said, *Never shit where you eat, son. You never know when you'll accidentally take a bite.*

"Come on, Harry. Lay it on me. How'd it go?"

"Well…there was a fire," he replied, almost as if he weren't telling me some of the worst news I could get. "It was crazy, Mr. Kelly. I've never seen my grill have flames that high."

A *fire*? *Fuck.* That was not at all what was supposed to go down when I secretly hired Haruto and his assistants to bring their romance A game to Kline and Georgie's Cabo getaway. Kline was going to eat my goddamn balls in milk and call them cereal if he found out I was the culprit.

"Harry, when I said give them an exciting dinner show, the exciting part was more figurative than anything else."

"Mr. Kelly, you're a very funny man," he replied on a soft chuckle, his voice unconcerned with the fact that his hibachi grill set my best friend's suite on fire. "And don't worry, I was prepared to give Mr. and Mrs. Brooks an exciting dinner experience, but what can I say? Accidents happen sometimes."

"Accidents, Harry? A burned plate of rice is an accident. A fucking fire is a cause for alarm."

"Oh yeah, it was a very big fire," he added. "Mrs. Brooks's eyes looked like flying saucers."

Fucking great.

"Listen, Harry. Tell me you didn't tell them it was me who hired you."

"Oh no, Mr. Kelly. I did not. Your NDA was very explicit."

Thank fuck I'd had the foresight to make them all sign the damn thing. It probably wasn't great for Antonio that he was getting pegged as the source, but it sure took the sweat off my balls. Kline rode a pretty firm line with me. He was much more forgiving of other people.

"Which, by the way, while I have you on the phone, should I send the invoice for damages to your assistant?"

"Invoice for damages?"

"Yes," he continued. "My grill, carts, basically everything was destroyed."

Fucking hell. It had already cost me a mint to fix Kline's boring Valentine's plans, and now I was paying for the damages from his inability to conform to them.

Obviously, though, none of that was Haruto's fault.

"Yeah, Harry," I said through a sigh. "Send your invoice on over, and I'll make sure it gets paid."

"Thank you, Mr. Kelly. I will see you back in New York, yes?"

"Yes, Haruto. I'll come in soon."

"Good, good. Please do not bring Mrs. Brooks."

I laughed as Harry ended the call, and I tucked my phone back into the chest pocket of my suit jacket.

It buzzed nearly immediately, though, so I pulled it back out and read the screen.

Whiny Whitney, it seemed, was ready to weep again. *Fucking lightweight.*

Wes: You better pick out your casket now, bro. I just talked to Kline, and they had a fucking FIRE in their room. I can only assume you were behind it.

Me: Wow, calm down. What's with the dramatics? It's all been taken care of, and everything will be back on track tomorrow.

Wes: Back on track? You need to shut this shit down NOW. Kline was still in decent spirits, but I have a feeling that's only because he didn't know it was you who started this shitstorm. If something happens again, I will not hesitate to throw you under the bus, blackmail or not.

Me: Relax. Everything is under control.

And it was. Sure, I was a bit defeated that the first big event I had arranged for Kline and Georgie didn't exactly go as planned, but when I reminded myself of what was to come, I quickly realized that it was all good in the Valentine's Day hood.

Don't worry, Georgia girl. Ole Thatcher has made sure the best is yet to come…

Chapter 8

Cabo, Friday, May 26th

Georgia

The sensation of my hair being brushed away from my neck and soft kisses being peppered across my shoulders and down my back stirred me from the recesses of my dreamlike state.

Truthfully, I had no idea what I was dreaming, but I was certain it wasn't even half as good as what I was feeling.

Lips I knew belonged to the man who owned my heart continued their seductive path down, down, *down* my back, over my ass, and along the backs of my thighs.

Oh boy. This is niiiiice.

I fluttered my eyes open and turned over from my belly to my back.

Instantly, Kline looked up at me from his perch between my thighs.

Yes. This is definitely nice.

"Mornin', baby," he greeted, and I shivered.

"Morning," I whispered back, and my thighs appeared to have a mind of their own, already spreading wide open at his words.

The look on his face could make the panties of a million women fall straight off in a blink of an eye. Thankfully, though, I was the *only* woman on the planet who was lucky enough to be on the receiving end of one of Kline Brooks's signature sexy, swoony smirks.

I knew I was completely biased, but my husband, for all intents and purposes, was the king of swoon.

That expression of his turned downright salacious when his blue eyes flitted from my steady gaze to the spot between my thighs. The one place on my body that always seemed to ache for him.

"Damn, what a glorious fucking morning this is," he whispered, and his warm breath brushed across my skin in a way that urged what felt like an infinite amount of goose bumps to make their appearance on my body. He looked up at me and waggled his brows. "And after our wild and crazy adventure last night, I think it's safe to say this perfect morning is warranted."

"I second that thought." A giggle jumped from my throat. There was no denying our romantic getaway had hit quite the speed bump last night, but then again, unexpected fires and emergency evacuations had a way of changing up the plans.

Kline chuckled, but then, in a flash, his eyes turned hot and fiery. "Thankfully, I'm prepared to atone for last night. Four Georgie orgasms for every speed bump we've encountered."

I computed the math in my head.

One speed bump equals…

"*Kline.*" My jaw dropped. "But that's *four* orgasms…"

"It sure fucking is," he commented, eyes serious and head offering one curt nod.

No time to waste, he leaned forward to press his mouth against me.

I moaned and my back arched, and it was apparent my husband was a man on a fucking mission, eating and licking and sucking at me like he was trying to hit the Guinness World Record for quickest orgasm ever to occur.

"Oh my God, Kline," I whimpered, and my legs shook so hard I had to reach down and grip his hair with my hands just to give myself the illusion of steady.

But there was nothing steady about this. He was a man possessed by the sole intention of making me come, and I was at the mercy of his mouth.

And that intention of his came to fruition in warp-speed fashion.

"That's it, baby," he whispered against my skin. "Come on my tongue."

Between one breath and the next, my climax clutched me hard, wrapping me up so tight in a weighted blanket of intensity that I felt as if I would explode from the inside out.

Waves of pleasure chugged through my body like a fucking freight train.

"H-h-holy shit! Oh my God!" I moaned and whimpered, and God knows what other noises jumped from my lungs.

"That's one," he said, and I barely had time to catch my breath before he gripped my thighs, got to his knees, and slid himself inside me.

The glorious sensation of his cock filling me up made my eyes roll back, and more moans escaped my lips.

"That's it, baby," Kline said, his voice all sexy and raspy. "Let me feel that perfect pussy of yours tighten around my cock."

"You feel so good," I whimpered. "Keep going."

"Oh, trust me," he said, completely full of himself. "I'm not stopping until all four of your orgasms have been achieved."

And did he achieve his goal? Well, let's just say my husband is a man of his word.
When Kline Brooks says he's giving you four orgasms, he's going to give you four motherflipping orgasms.

Surely, this had to be a sign that my Valentine's curse had finally decided to leave Cabo and go bother someone else...*right?*

Chapter 9

Kline

At a little after one, freshly showered and sitting on the balcony, I was enjoying the soft sounds of the ocean while I scanned through a few work emails.

I'd woken up Georgie at eight this morning and commandeered her sexy little body for over four hours in the name of blowing her fucking mind.

Thankfully, it'd been a successful mission, and the horrors of last night had almost all been carried away with the wind.

And the seductive power my once-virginal-and-innocent Benny girl wielded over me evoked the kind of intensity and arousal that didn't require shit like Viagra to engage in hours-long, marathon sex, so it hadn't been even the slightest of a burden.

Obviously, we were currently in what most would call the "honeymoon phase" of our marriage, the phase in which most people wished to stay forever. But, if I was being honest, I was starting to get a little worried if we didn't move on soon, we'd end up fucking each other to death...

What a way to go, though, I thought, making myself laugh out loud. Handily, that was when my beautiful wife chose to make her appearance on the balcony, and her answering smile was worth more than the weight of my entire fortune in gold.

"Something got you in a good mood, Mr. Brooks?"

I beamed up at her. "Baby, I'm in Cabo with my beautiful wife. A good mood is a constant."

She was dressed in sandals and a simple white sundress, the vision of her made my brain short-circuit, dumping my thoughts right back into the bottomless pit of fantasies I'd barely chipped away at this morning.

You're hopeless, dude. Fucking hopeless.

My brain wasn't lying. I was hopelessly fucking in love *and infatuation and in lust* with my wife. As if my hand had a mind of its own, I reached out and slid my fingers up her thigh. Maybe if I convinced her just right, she'd let me take her back to bed for a little while before we went to eat.

"Kline Brooks!" She slapped me away on a giggle, squealing and jumping back a step. "You're insane!"

"Insane for you." I smirked up at her. "And you can hardly blame me for going on an exploratory mission to find out what you have on under that dress. I'm detail-driven—analytical—you know that about me. I'd even wager to say it's something you love about me."

She shook her head, pursing her lips in faux contemplation and tapping a finger on her chin. "Let's see. If I tell you—thus ending your quest for an answer—do you promise to take me downstairs to eat without delay?"

Desperate, I nodded like a little wooden marionette. "Of course, my love."

She hummed then, turning on her toe and spinning away before glancing back at me over her shoulder and popping her eyebrows coquettishly.

"Nothing."

Nothing? My jaw went unhinged. Surely, I misheard her. I must have passed out in the middle of a fantasy. Because the idea of my sweet, innocent wife *bare* beneath her dress—

"You heard me right." A coy little grin quirked up the corners of her lips as she read my mind. "I'm not wearing anything underneath this dress, but the only way you're ever going to see for yourself is to actually feed me something first. You promised."

"Georgie, you just told me you're not wearing any panties. How could you be hungry at a time like this?"

"Seriously, Kline?" She snorted and stomped one foot to the ground. "You just fucked me for, like, four hours! I need sustenance!"

"I *fucked* you for four hours?" I repeated her words, picking my ass up off the seat of my chair and stalking toward her. "Benny, that mouth of yours has gotten seriously dirty."

"And it's all your fault," she retorted back, jumping away from my groping hands and smacking at my wrists. "You've turned me into a sex-crazed, orgasm-craving, foulmouthed, scandalized harlot. I am the Wheorgie Cassie has always wanted me to be."

Her words spurred a chuckle from my lungs. "Don't worry, baby. It's not a bad thing. In fact, your dirty mouth and my endless stamina are the best things we've got going for us on this trip so far."

She laughed. "Well, that, I agree with. It's almost enough to make me count last night as a fluke."

"Really?" I asked hopefully. "You'll be my official valentine?"

"I said *almost*."

I pouted, and she giggled. "I tell you what… You take me downstairs and feed me, and I'll come back up here and feed *you*." My dick jerked in my pants. "And if you use your tongue the way I really like, I just might be inclined to give in." She winked, and I had to grab my chest to keep from fainting. Goddamn, this woman was definitely going to put me in an early grave.

Here lies Kline Brooks, husband, entrepreneur, and beloved friend. Don't be sad. He died from fucking.

"As always, your wish is my command." Sliding my phone back

into my pocket, I placed a swift kiss to the love of my life's lips and
wrapped one arm around her waist, leading us back into our suite and
toward the front door.

Hand to the doorknob, I twisted it open, holding it back for
Georgia to walk on through, but she froze at the threshold, eyes wide
as she looked toward the hallway.

I followed her gaze, and when I noted not one, not two, but three
men in sombreros holding instruments in their hands, my smile
melted like an ice cube on a New York summer sidewalk.

"*Hola*, Mr. and Mrs. Brooks!" the man with the guitar greeted us
through a cheerful bellow. "Today, it will be our pleasure to serenade
you!"

What? No.

"I don't think—"

Loud and enthusiastic and with complete disregard for the
words coming out of my mouth, they dove straight into the music.
The chords of the guitar riffed the accompanying instruments into
a soundtrack of classic mariachi beats, the volume of which was so
loud, it seemed to bounce off the stucco walls of the hallway.

"I'm Armando!" the man with the guitar shouted over their
music, introducing himself. "And these are my brothers, Juan and
Francisco!"

"*Hola!*" the brothers greeted in synchrony, Juan still playing his
trumpet on the necessary notes and Francisco never missing a stroke
on his violin.

"And we'd like to introduce you to two more *very* special guests
that will be playing with us today..." Armando paused and offered a
quick, sharp whistle from his lips.

"Here are Bobo Buttons and Mr. Boots!"

And right there, before Georgia's and my very confused eyes, two
small monkeys in little red vests appeared and hopped up onto Juan's
and Armando's shoulders.

Poised in their little fists were maracas, which they didn't hesitate to shake to the beat, teeth-filled little monkey smiles pasted to their faces.

With one glace to each other, it was clear there was only one thing running through both my wife's and my minds.

Was there really a Valentine's curse upon us? And would we ever be able to escape it?

Chapter 10

Kline

Armando and his brothers were committed to their task of serenading us. Even the monkeys hadn't stopped shaking their fucking maracas since we'd left our suite.

In the elevator.

Through the lobby.

Wherever we went, they followed.

I'd tried several times to get their attention to talk—to call them off, for the love of God—but they'd only sped up their tempo in response. I knew they spoke English—Armando had given away that fact right up front—but they were obviously experienced at pretending they didn't.

Luckily, it seemed their break time fell during our breakfast, giving us a few blessed moments of silence as we ate. Although, they didn't go far. In fact, they merely stood near our table, instruments still in hand, and Bobo Buttons didn't give one single fuck about keeping a polite distance.

I watched on as he snuck a piece of my wife's pancake from her plate, and I sighed. *This is fucking insane.*

It *was* insane. And, generally speaking, when insane shit went down in my life, it all revolved around one goddamn equally insane person.

I hadn't spoken to Thatch since we'd left, but a couple of vest-wearing monkeys, as it turned out, were the perfect watering can for my always-present seeds of doubt. In fact, with all the shit he gave me about not making a big romantic gesture this weekend, I was surprised I hadn't sniffed his scent at the first sign of disaster last night.

Frustrated and fed up, I set out to get to the bottom of the situation. Now that they weren't actually playing, maybe I'd be able to ask Armando a question without setting off a crescendo.

"Hey, Armando?" I inquired, instantly getting his attention.

Unfortunately, just like before, he took my question as the signal, and after one quick nod to his brothers, they were off to the mariachi races, filling the entire resort restaurant with their upbeat music.

Shit.

"Armando!" I whisper-yelled over the music, trying not to interrupt the other patrons' meals. But it was useless. The music was already fucking loud as shit.

Goddammit. If I found out Thatch was really behind this, I was going to take a couple of inches off his favorite appendage and shove them up his big, jolly ass.

Bobo Buttons and Mr. Boots joined in on the fun, and Georgia looked like she was two seconds away from burrowing herself into the restaurant floor.

"Armando!" I shouted again, louder this time, and I started to gesture my hand in the air in a universal sign to *cut it.*

But he was oblivious, his jovial face smiling and looking around the room while his fingers strummed at a quick pace across his guitar.

"Armando!" I tried again to get his attention.

This time, it worked. He met my eyes and bellowed back, "Do you have a song request, Mr. Brooks?"

A song request? I wanted to shout back at him. *Silence, Armando! That's my fucking song request!*

Thankfully, no matter how strong the urge to lose my cool, I stuck with my usual MO—a calm and clearheaded approach.

"Could you please stop playing for a second?" I questioned, making my voice the loudest it had ever been in the middle of a restaurant.

"What was that, sir?" he called toward me, his voice even louder than mine.

Jesus Christ.

"Stop playing!"

"Stop playing?" he repeated while he, in fact, kept playing.

"Yes! Stop playing the fucking music!" I shouted, bringing Armando, his brothers, and the monkeys to a screeching halt, and the eyes of every patron over to me.

I breathed a sigh of relief, no matter the sour reception from everyone around us at my uncouth yell.

"Listen, Armando," I said, my voice much quieter now as I gestured for him to come closer to the table. He did. "Who arranged this…lovely music for us?"

Armando simpered. "I wish I could tell you, Mr. Brooks, but we signed a contract *and* an NDA when we agreed to play for you and Mrs. Brooks this weekend. Both explicitly stated that we wouldn't reveal who hired us."

A fucking NDA?

That was it. I was convinced. *Thatch was definitely behind this, the fucker.* I was going to make him wish he'd never been born.

"Armando," I began, my voice as diplomatic as humanly possible for a man whose brain, right at that very moment, was plotting a gruesome murder. "While we've loved every minute of your music today, I can assure you that Mrs. Brooks and I do not need you to follow us around any longer." If they did this all weekend, I would drown myself in the ocean and take Georgia with me—obviously, as a sympathy killing.

"Oh, but we do, sir," Armando refuted. "Like I said earlier, we signed a contract and an NDA."

"Don't worry about those," I assured. "I'll make sure you're not held to them."

He grinned at that. "I was told you'd say that."

"Let me guess," I said, laying my cards out on the table. "A man by the name of Thatcher Kelly is behind all this?"

His grin only grew. "Good try, Mr. Brooks, but I cannot divulge—"

"Listen, Armando, we truly enjoyed the music," I lied, because let's face it, it was one thing to love mariachi music, but it was another thing to be stalked by an actual band. My fucking eardrums were already ringing, and it had been only a little over an hour or so since they showed up at our door. "But you don't need to stick with us any longer. Consider your talented job completed."

He started to open his mouth to refuse again, but I cut him off at the pass. I was done with Thatch's bullshit, plain and simple. I didn't care if it cost me a million fucking dollars to call it all off, this would be the end of it.

"Mr. Brooks, my brothers and I cannot back out of our agreement. That would be like getting paid but not doing our job."

I looked across the table at my wife, who was now feeding the rest of her pancakes to Bobo Buttons and Mr. Boots, and a tiny part of my brain exploded. I was going to call that big giant on his bullshit right now.

I grabbed my cell phone out of my pocket, scrolled into my messages with Thatch, and found three unread bubbles in the thread. I'd forgotten I'd set his contact to Do Not Disturb at the office and never turned it back.

Right there, in the messages he'd sent me after I'd hung on him, was the proof that I wasn't completely out of line. I read through them one by one, my anger growing with each successive text.

Thatch: Talk about being disrespectful, bro. Hanging up on me without warning? Not cool.

Thatch: I'm just trying to help. Trying to salvage your marriage before you shoot it into the dumpster like a flaming arrow.

Thatch: Ignoring me still? You're lucky I love you so much. If I didn't, I'd let you dig your own hole with your bomb-ass wife, and you'd be divorced by the end of the year. Not to worry, though. I'll make sure Georgia girl hangs around until your balls are saggy little prunes.

"Kline?" Georgia asked, handing a piece of pancake to Mr. Boots and glancing nervously between Armando and me. I held up a single pointer finger, hit send on a call to the only person who could be behind this fucking circus, and took a deep breath as Georgia turned worried eyes to her monkey friends.

It rang.

And rang.

And fucking rang until it went to voice mail, *"You got Thatcher, baby. Leave a message."*

I hit end on the call and switched communication modes, back to the string of texts.

Me: I know you're behind this goddamn monkey mariachi band AND the hibachi dinner last night.

I waited a few seconds, and when no response came through, I sent another. That fucker always had his phone nearby, and if he wasn't answering, it was because he knew he'd fucked up.

Me: Call it off, dude. Call it all off, the band and the monkeys and whatever other crazy shit you have planned, or I swear to God, I'm ready to go to jail for your homicide when I get home.

Still, no response.

Me: THATCH

Me: CALL

Me: IT

Me: OFF

No matter what I sent his way, the outcome stayed the same—radio silence.

So, in the name of covering my bases, I shot a text to the only other person who might be able to provide confirmation. If I was right, it was the reason he'd checked in on us last night in the first place.

Me: That big fucking giant cocksucking asshole is the one behind all of this, isn't he?

A minute later and my source didn't even question who or what I was referring to.

He only responded with one word.

Wes: Yep.

I fucking knew it. That sealed it. I was going to kill him.

Chapter 11

Cabo, Friday, May 26th

Georgia

Once Kline and I—*and Bobo Buttons and Mr. Boots*—finished our breakfast and my husband had tried to convince the mariachi brothers that their presence was no longer needed, to no avail, we tried to make the best of our day.

First, we attempted a little shopping in some of the resort's boutiques, but our music-playing entourage proved to be an annoying disruption to everyone else inside the shops.

The beach was our next destination, but it was hard to relax in the sun when a mariachi band was right beside you, playing their little hearts out.

From my lounge chair, I lifted my hand to shield my eyes from the sun and glanced over at my husband. Arms across his chest and his mouth set in a firm line, Kline was *pissed*.

So ticked off, in fact, that anger was literally vibrating off his body.

Though, it was hard to notice with, you know, the mariachi music surrounding us.

He was convinced that Thatch was behind it all, yet no matter how many times he tried to reach Thatch, he'd yet to receive any response. Which, understandably, only made him angrier.

Not to mention, one text to Wes and it had apparently been confirmed that Thatcher Kelly was the man behind the monkeys.

I glanced back and forth between my stone-faced husband and the jubilant men strumming their instruments and offered up a silent prayer. *Please, God, grant Kline some serenity before he explodes.*

My husband wasn't the kind of man who resorted to impulsive anger, but he also wasn't the kind of man who tolerated nonsense for an extended amount of time.

And if anyone was keeping count, the hourglass of crazy had just about run out.

Armando strummed the strings of his guitar, bringing their current song to a close, and an internal sigh of relief loosened up the tightness clutching at my lungs.

Though, the relief lasted all of two minutes.

Ba-ba-ba-bum! Ba-ba-ba-bum! The familiar, strong, and vibrant beats bounced through the air again, and it was the straw that broke the camel's back.

"Enough!" Kline shouted, jumping up from his lounge chair. "It's enough! I'm sorry, but it's enough!"

Uh oh. I cringed.

The music stopped, definitely, but crickets followed. Fellow beachgoers offered curious, shocked looks in our direction. And Armando and his brothers stared at Kline with dropped jaws and wide eyes.

Even Bobo Buttons and Mr. Boots hid their tiny maracas behind their backs. Truthfully, I was kind of starting to get attached to the two little guys.

"I'm sorry, guys," Kline backtracked, trying to calm himself down. "I really am. But I can't handle you following us around for the rest of the weekend. It's too much. No matter how great you guys are, it's way too much. My fucking idiot friend has basically hired you to stalk us. I know that's not your fault, but if you don't go away when I ask, my only real option will be to call the authorities, and I'm pretty certain I'd ruin my wife's surprise getaway if I called the police and your cute fucking monkeys ended up in handcuffs." He sighed. Ran a hand through his hair.

No response. No white flag waved. The brothers just stared at him, while their monkeys hid behind their legs.

All I could do was sit there on my lounger, while the tightness in my chest damn near squeezed the breath out of my lungs.

"I will pay you double whatever Thatch is paying you to make it stop!" Kline shouted finally, fed up with the stonewalling, and the tension in the air endured an immediate, lightening shift.

"Double, Mr. Brooks?" Armando asked.

"Yes. *Double*," Kline replied without hesitation. "And if that motherfucker even thinks about suing you for breach of contract, I'll gladly pay your legal fees to beat his fucking ass in court. Truthfully, at this point, it would make my goddamn day to watch him explain to a jury why he hired a mariachi band to stalk his friend for an entire fucking weekend."

Armando looked toward his brothers, and both Francisco and Juan shrugged, then nodded.

"Okay, Mr. Brooks," Armando eventually said, holding out his hand toward Kline's. "Consider it a deal."

A giant breath of air whooshed from my lungs.

"Thank fuck for that," Kline agreed, shaking hands and finalizing the verbal deal.

After my husband offered several apologies for his outburst and gave Armando and crew his secretary Meryl's contact information to get paid, I felt a little sad as I watched Bobo Buttons and Mr. Boots pack up their maracas and head off into the proverbial sunset.

Good luck, little buddies!

Obviously, though, in the name of my husband's sanity, I kept that information to myself.

On a huff, Kline sat back down on his lounger, staring out toward the ocean with his lips set in a firm line.

It was safe to say the monkeys had taken a toll on him.

"You okay?" I asked, and he shrugged.

"I've been better," he replied and met my eyes.

Yeah, he's definitely worn the hell out on the insanity that's been tossed our way the past two days.

I was almost tempted to remind him of my Valentine's curse.

The words were right there, sitting on my tongue.

Now isn't the time, I reminded myself. *Sure, the fire and the monkeys and the mariachi stalkers are more than just circumstantial evidence to plead my case, but it's not the time.*

Kline had scheduled this surprise getaway to romance me, swoon me, give me an awesome early Valentine's experience. Putting our lives and hearing and sanity in danger certainly hadn't been the intention.

He was the best husband, and he was in need of a distraction and relaxation and *fun*.

"I'm going to the bar to grab us some drinks. I think we could both use one right about now." Decision made, I hopped up from my lounger and leaned forward to press a kiss to his mouth. "Scotch or beer?"

"Beer." Kline looked up at me, and the hint of a smile touched his lips. "You want some help?"

I shook my head. "I got this, baby."

Destination in sight, I walked away from our loungers, across the sand, and up the wooden stairs that led to the pool deck. Once I reached the bar, a friendly bartender in a colorful bow tie and a name tag that read *Sam* took my order—beer for Kline and a piña colada for me.

While Sam made our drinks, I took a seat on an empty barstool and waited.

"Excuse me," a female voice said, startling me from my own little world of stress decompression. I looked to my right to see a fortysomething woman with long red hair grinning at me. I did my best to smile back.

"Um, yes?"

"Can I just say that I *love* your hair? I've always loved beachy waves, but I can never get them to look right."

"Oh wow, thank you," I answered, both surprised and delighted at the compliment.

"And your bikini," she added. "It looks fabulous on you. Actually, both my husband and I noticed you and your husband walking toward the beach earlier, and I told him then how much I envied your whole ensemble."

I smiled. Normally, it might be a little weird if someone had picked me out of a crowd on the beach and remembered me at the bar, but I knew we'd been leaving quite the wake of recognition this morning with all the commotion we'd caused.

"Let me guess. You noticed the mariachi band that was following us around?"

She grinned. "They did call a little bit of attention," she admitted with a laugh. "But you're a gorgeous couple."

"Oh my goodness, thank you. You are way too kind," I dismissed sheepishly.

"I'm Paula, by the way," she introduced herself as she closed the distance between us, moving from her barstool to the empty one beside mine.

"It's nice to meet you, Paula. I'm Georgia."

"That's my husband Frank over there near the pool," she added and pointed toward a bald man in blue swim trunks. She waved toward him, and immediately, he waved back. That was nice. I always loved to see other couples so happily in love. It gave me hope for the future.

"My husband Kline is back there on the beach," I said and then smacked my forehead. "I guess you saw him before, though, huh?"

I giggled, and her eyes sparkled, delighted.

"Are you guys enjoying your trip?" she asked and reached forward to gently place her hand over mine. "Cabo is absolutely gorgeous, right?"

"Oh yeah," I answered, lying a little bit. I mean, it wasn't exactly Cabo's fault our trip felt like a dumpster fire. Plus, I figured the less she knew, the less chance it would get out that our suite was the cause for the evacuation last night. "I mean, we've had a few speed bumps, but it's certainly beautiful here."

"Any big plans tonight?"

I shook my head. "I think my husband is just happy that mariachi band is no longer following us around."

Paula gently tapped my shoulder with her hand, and giggles fell from her lips. "That band was certainly something."

"They sure were." I snorted. "Very talented, but also very loud."

Paula burst into laughter, her hand brushing my shoulder again. "Beautiful *and* hilarious? Georgia, you're adorable."

"Thank you. You're such a sweetheart, Paula." Unsure of what else to say because compliments from strangers always tended to make me feel kind of awkward, I just grinned at her.

"You know what I think?"

"What?"

"I think you and Kline should come to a party with us."

I tilted my head to the side. "A party? What kind of party?"

"It's a couples party," she began to explain and proceeded to tell me all the details about it. It was at one of the private villas here at the resort, just after dinner, so we didn't have to worry about it starting too late. That sort of thing. By the time she finished hyping it up, I was honestly starting to feel like maybe it wasn't such a bad idea.

If there was one thing my husband needed, it was some fun to take his mind off the disasters that had occurred since we arrived.

She reached into her purse and handed me a fancy invitation.

"So, it's a masquerade ball?" I asked after scanning the embossed sheet of paper, and she nodded. "That sounds pretty fancy…"

"Don't worry about dressing up," she said, and a cheeky grin consumed her mouth. "Heck, you could show up naked, and as long as you have a mask on, no one would care."

I laughed. "And it's just for couples?" I didn't want to have to worry about some weird woman hitting on Kline when I went to the bathroom or deal with him getting jealous if some guy happened to pay me too much attention. We just needed to be able to enjoy each other.

"Yes," Paula answered. "It's actually an annual event for couples. Frank and I come to Cabo every year for it as a celebration of our anniversary. Fifteen years this year."

"Wow! It's that good that you guys go every year?"

She nodded again, eyes a complicated combination of serious and enthusiastic. "It is fantastic, Georgia. You will have the time of your life."

Man, maybe this was the kind of thing we needed to turn the whole trip around.

"You just *have* to go," Paula encouraged, gently tapping her hand to mine again. "You will love it."

I smiled. By the time the bartender set Kline's and my drinks in front of me, my mind was made up. We needed some fun and we needed it ASAP, and this sounded like just the ticket. Hell, even the invitation was gold, just like Willy Wonka intended.

"Okay, Paula," I said as I stood up from my barstool with the drinks in my hands. "We'll be there."

A few hours later, I found myself in the master bathroom of our suite, fresh out of the shower and thinking about all the events that had occurred since we'd landed in Cabo less than forty-eight hours ago.

First, a hibachi grill dinner and what was supposed to be a romantic evening with Kline had turned into standing in the hotel lobby for three hours while the fire department worked to stop our hotel room from spreading a fire that lit up the whole resort.

And today, my husband had to pay an obscene amount of money to a mariachi band that had been hired to stalk us.

Basically, if two plus two equaled four, then last night plus today equaled *shitshow*.

Truthfully, this morning at breakfast, when Bobo Buttons and Mr. Boots were stealing pieces of my pancakes and everyone in the restaurant was giving us strange looks, I wasn't sure I'd ever felt more embarrassed in my whole life.

And I was friends with Cassie Phillips.

So, that was saying a lot.

It truly felt as if the universe was giving us all the fucking signs that anything revolving around Valentine's Day was not for yours truly.

Frankly, I grew more and more convinced by the minute, but what could I do? Tell Kline to pack our bags and get us on the next flight home?

That option made me feel far too bad to consider.

Which explained why I was currently getting myself ready for a night out instead of curling up in the fetal position and trying to go into a hibernation coma until our flight departed on Sunday.

Plus, my new friend Paula *had* made this couples party sound like a good time...

I stared at my reflection in the mirror as I did my makeup.

Tonight's exciting plans called for sexy drama—smoky eyes and red lips.

I lined my eyes first, and then I finished my lips, turning them from a pale pink to a bright red in a matter of minutes.

Once my hair was perfectly in place, I added the final touch of a sexy, masquerade-style mask I managed to find in one of the resort's boutiques. It was completely black, only covered my nose and eyes, and had hints of shimmery gold. The mask paired perfectly with the floor-length black silk dress and strappy heels I'd chosen for tonight's shindig.

Once I was certain I was ready, I headed into the living room of our suite, where Kline waited for me. In another sharp black suit and crisp white shirt, he looked *good*. But then again, my handsome husband *always* looked good.

And the masquerade-style mask that covered his face—a completely black one—only added to his hotness factor. It was like freaking Christian Grey was standing right in front of me, ready to whisk me off to Escala with the sounds of Thomas Tallis providing the soundtrack.

"Baby, you look delicious," he said, setting his glass of scotch on the coffee table and walking over toward me. He wrapped both hands around my waist and pulled me tight against his chest.

"Likewise, husband." I grinned. "Are you ready to have some fun?"

He pressed a sexy kiss to my lips. "With you? Always."

"As long as it doesn't include a fire or monkeys, right?" I teased, and he waggled his brows.

"I like it hot, Benny, just not like that."

"Is that right?"

He beamed down at me, his blue eyes blazing behind the mask. And his hand reached down and slid a slow and seductive path up my thigh, taking the silk of my dress with it. He didn't stop until his hand was right there, right between my thighs, gripping me where an ache had already started to throb. "That's right. Mark my words. By the time we make it back to our room, you're going to be begging for my cock."

"You promise?" I asked, biting down on my bottom lip.

Kline winked. "It's a guarantee, baby."

Chapter 12

Kline

Once I helped my sexy-as-hell wife into the town car, I rounded the back and hopped inside.

Nico, our driver for the night, pulled out of the resort and onto the main road, taking us in the direction of tonight's plans—some kind of couples-only masquerade ball my wife had managed to get us invited to while getting drinks at the pool bar.

Initially, when she came back from the bar with our drinks and told me about the party, I wasn't really feeling it.

But the more Georgia talked about it and the more excited she sounded, I couldn't say no.

Apparently, this was a yearly tradition in Cabo, and this year, the event was being held at a swanky, million-dollar villa on the other side of the resort, that overlooked the beach. And like I said, my wife was pumped about it, rambling on and on about how this party was the exact kind of fun we needed.

And with the way my wife looked tonight, I had zero regrets about agreeing.

Black silk dress with a sexy slit up her right thigh, she looked so amazing, it was a damn shock I was able to control myself long enough to get us out of our suite. The temptation to remove said dress from her sexy body with my fucking teeth was nearly too much to bear.

But you can bet your sweet ass, that's exactly what I would be doing later when we got back to our suite.

"Where are you two headed tonight?" Nico asked, and I took one more lingering glance at my wife's sexy legs peeking out beneath silk before meeting his eyes in the rearview mirror.

"We were invited to some kind of masked ball," I answered.

"The Masquerade Entendre?" he questioned, and Georgia chimed in.

"Yes! That's the one! Have you heard of it?"

"Oh, yes." Nico nodded, keeping his eyes on the road. "Everyone in Cabo knows about that event." He glanced in the rearview mirror, and his eyes shone with something I couldn't discern. "It's a *very* famous yearly tradition. Although, only a select few get to experience it, if you know what I mean."

"Is it a fun event?" Georgia asked, and Nico offered a wink in her direction.

"Oh *yeah*, pretty sure everyone who attends the Masquerade Entendre loves it," he answered, turning into a long driveway that was highlighted by the glow of lamps that lined it all the way until the end.

"Have you ever been to it?" Georgie continued with her inquiry as he came to a stop behind a line of cars in front of the stately beach villa.

"Ha! I wish," he said through a laugh. "Sadly, my wife isn't as adventurous as you are, Mrs. Brooks. Although, I have had the opportunity to bring a few like-minded couples like yourselves to this event over the years, and everyone leaves this party satisfied."

Like-minded couples?

I tilted my head to the side, confused by his words.

But before I could try to decipher what he meant, the car gently rolled forward, came to a stop, and Nico hopped out to open my door.

I stepped out and held out a hand to help Georgie to her feet.

"Enjoy your evening, Mr. and Mrs. Brooks," Nico said, offering a smile that damn near bordered on devilish, and then he was back in his town car and heading down the long driveway.

"Okay…so, that was kind of strange…" I muttered, pausing to press a gentle hand to Georgia's back and walking toward the velvet-roped-off aisle that led inside the mansion.

"What was strange?" she asked, glancing toward me, her blue eyes flashing with confusion behind her mask.

"Our driver. Nico."

She quirked an eyebrow, and it just barely rose above the right side of her mask.

"It felt like he was talking in code, and my radar detector didn't like what he was implying."

"What are you talking about?" Still confused, she paused just outside the mansion doors, and the masked couple at our backs had to step around us to go inside.

"That conversation didn't feel odd to you?"

"Uh…no." She shook her head, and an amused smile formed at her lips. "It only made me more excited about tonight. I think Paula was right. We're going to have the time of our lives."

"Okay," I said through a sigh, just wanting to have something go right. I didn't want to be the stick in the mud that led to even more disappointment for my wife. "Let's do it, then. Let's go have some fun."

She laughed. "You seem like you're afraid Thatch is going to, like, pop out of the bushes or something with an entourage of clowns."

I shrugged. "I wouldn't put it past the bastard."

I mean, he did send an entire hibachi grill into our suite last night. And had a band stalk us today.

"You're just being paranoid," Georgie chastised.

Maybe she was right. Being best friends with the world's biggest prankster would make anyone jumpy after they had to suffer a five-alarm fire in the name of Thatch's idea of romance.

If that bastard ever decided to stop eating at the pussy buffet, good luck to the woman who married him. She either needed to be completely clueless or downright insane to willingly be a part of his craziness for the rest of her life.

Finally, Georgia and I stepped inside an entryway that felt as if it had been plucked right out of Versailles. Gilded pillars and marble floors and a Renaissance-style painted cathedral ceiling filled my view, and I immediately started to wonder about who was footing the bill for this place. I knew I was a billionaire, but a villa like this had to go for more than a hundred grand a night.

Surely, he or she was in the business of making money.

Lots of it.

And damn did they like showing it off.

"This place is insane," Georgia whispered toward me, and I nodded.

"Whoever is staying here really wants us to know they have money."

She snorted. "You do realize you're worth billions, right?" she tossed out, a giggle on her lips.

"Pretty sure you mean *we're* worth billions," I corrected her. "And the day I start renting mansions like this and gilding fucking everything like some kind of sixteenth-century king instead of donating money to charities that actually serve good in the world, divorce me."

"Don't be ridiculous." She slapped my chest. "That would mean I'd be going against my vows."

"Yeah, well, this is me giving you permission to go against your vows if I turn into that kind of megalomaniac moron."

She rolled her eyes and laughed. "How about we actually go inside the mansion and, I don't know, enjoy the party instead of balking at how much they spent on those gold pillars until your humble billionaire head explodes?"

I grinned down at her. "Good idea."

Once we reached the end of the entryway, the room opened up into a grand ballroom that was filled with about a hundred guests.

Everyone was dressed for the occasion in suits and gowns and masks adorning their faces.

Chatter and laughter echoed within the space, while a live band at the opposite end of the room played cover songs for the guests that had chosen to dance.

The modern music clashed with the Renaissance décor, but somehow, it also worked.

"I kind of feel like I'm Kirsten Dunst in that movie *Marie Antoinette*," Georgia said, a smile on her lips.

I chuckled at her adorable randomness and nodded toward the bar. "Do you want a drink?"

"Yes, please. And while you get the drinks, I'm going to run to the ladies' room really quick. The corset I'm wearing under this dress is about to squeeze the pee right out of me."

"Okay, baby," I agreed with a laugh and pressed a soft kiss to her forehead.

Once I reached the bar and noted from a distance that Georgia had safely found the restrooms on the opposite end of the ballroom, a bartender dressed in a tuxedo smiled toward me.

"What can I get you tonight, sir?"

"A scotch on the rocks and a glass of white wine."

While he made our drinks, I turned back toward the ballroom, resting a hip on the edge of the bar and taking in the view.

People chatting and laughing and dancing occupied the giant space.

Scanning the crowd superficially, I spotted a man and woman deep in a passionate kiss, their clinch so tight that the side of the woman's breast was only a scant millimeter from escaping her dress. *Damn, they're really going for it tonight, I guess...*

But that thought started to become a theme when I continued to look around the room and found not one, not two, not even three, but seven other couples involved in the same passionate display of PDA.

And then, when I moved my gaze to the far corner of the ballroom, where a sitting area of couches and chairs was located, alarm bells sounded in my head. Two women and two men went at one another ravenously, bouncing back and forth between partners with the kind of cozy familiarity I'd never had with any of my friends.

And by cozy, I mean I just saw tits.
Tits out in the open, getting a good old-fashioned
tongue-lashing world tour.
Georgia said the lady from the bar had said this party was fun, but I
don't recall her mentioning that Pornhub was sponsoring it…

Immediately, I looked toward the bathrooms and watched as Georgia stepped back into the ballroom, but she only made it halfway toward the bar before she was stopped by a male and female in purple masks. She smiled, and by her reaction to their presence, I had a feeling the woman was Paula from the bar.

"Here are your drinks, sir."

I turned around to find the scotch and wine sitting on the bar and the bartender smiling toward me. The niggling voice in the back of my head said I should leave them there and run, but not wanting to be unnecessarily judgmental, I forced myself to pump the brakes until I had a little bit more information.

"Thank you," I said and tossed a few bills into his tip jar.

"Appreciate it, sir. Enjoy the *pleasurable festivities.*"

Pleasurable festivities? Okay. The way he said it made me feel exactly like I had when our driver Nico said *like-minded couples.* Danger, Will Robinson. Danger.

"What kind of ball is this, exactly?"

The bartender looked at me, eyes slightly confused. "What do you mean, sir?"

I ground my jaw, not wanting to have to try to explain this shit aloud, and he seemingly caught on enough to give me an answer without it.

"Uh…" The bartender paused and leaned over the bar to get a little closer to me. "If you're wondering when partners are supposed to be selected, I'm pretty sure we were told that most couples will be heading toward the rooms upstairs around ten or so."

"Heading to the rooms upstairs?" I questioned. "What rooms?"

"You know, *the rooms*," he said, finally breaking into a kind smile. "Let me guess, this is your first time to a swingers event?"

Oh. Holy. Fucking. Shit.

"*Kline!*" A harsh whisper filled my ears, and I turned away from the bartender to see my wife standing there with huge, wide eyes. "I just saw two penises," she continued, keeping her voice low, but unable to hide the shock from it. "And I can't be sure, but I think Paula wants me to sleep with her husband!"

"Baby—" I started to say, but Georgia was too worked up as she glanced around the room, paranoia in her eyes.

"Oh my God!" she quietly exclaimed and buried her face into my chest. "Make that three penises! Why are there penises, Kline? And not a single one of them even has a mask on!"

"Baby—" I attempted again, but man, she was fired up.

"What is wrong with people?" she questioned more to herself than me. "Why does it feel like there are more dicks than people at this ball, and why on earth would Paula want me to sleep with her husband?"

"It's a swingers party, Benny," I said, finally getting a word in.

"What?"

"Swingers, baby. As in, people who bang one another's spouses."

"No, it's not," she whispered, horrified.

"Oh, but it is."

Georgia just stood there, staring at me and gulping like a beached fish.

I couldn't really blame her, though. I mean, this was completely unexpected and uncharted territory for a woman who'd kept her virginhood as long as she had, and all of it was happening on the heels of a day when she ended up feeding half her breakfast to two vest-wearing, maraca-shaking, begging monkeys.

The human mind could only take so much crazy before it started to shut the fuck down.

When I glanced over my shoulder and spotted a man in a neon-yellow banana hammock and a woman attempting to make said banana get hard with her hand, I made an instant executive decision—we had to go, and we had to go right fucking now.

No time to waste, I leaned down and tossed my wife over my shoulder like a fucking fireman and strode right toward the exit doors of the villa without looking back.

"Kline!" Georgia squealed, finally finding her voice. "What are you doing?"

"Baby, this is some crazy *Eyes Wide Shut* kind of shit, and I'm getting us out of here before a damn orgy begins."

"Yeah, that's probably a good idea," she agreed, accepting the circumstances for what they were with a sigh.

We both knew this party was heading down a path neither one of us wanted to tread, and the sooner we got the fuck out of there, the better.

I mean, a fucking swingers event? What the ever-loving-shit?

How, in the matter of not even forty-eight hours, could two people keep finding themselves in situations like this?

Thatch, my brain reminded me. *Fucking Thatch.*

That bastard was the reason for all of it.

The fire.

The band.

The monkeys.

And *this*.

I didn't know how the fucker did it, but somehow, he had even managed to plant someone at the bar to give Georgia that invitation.

He wasn't even in Cabo, but it felt like he was *everywhere*.

Lungs on fire with building rage, I stopped in the same spot Nico had dropped us off and set Georgia back to her feet.

Grabbing my phone out of my suit pocket, I sent our driver a text and let him know we were ready for him to come get us. His response was instant.

Be there in twenty minutes, Mr. Brooks.

And then I clicked out of that text box and into another.

Me: I will fucking kill you.

Me: First, a fire.

Me: Then, a monkey mariachi band.

Me: AND NOW? SENDING US TO A FUCKING SWINGERS PARTY? WHAT IS WRONG WITH YOU??? IS THERE AN ACTUAL SCREW LOOSE IN YOUR BIG, STUPID BRAIN?

Figuring the dickhead would continue to be MIA, I was shocked when my phone vibrated with a response.

Thatch: Wait…what? You guys went to a dick swap? Tell me I'm seeing things, Special K, because if not, I might just perish right here.
Me: SHUT UP! You know damn well you arranged this! Planted that woman so that Georgia would get the invitation and we'd end up here!

Thatch: K, I swear on my big cock, I don't know anything about a swingers party. Honestly, I wish I could take the credit for it. But it sounds like you and Georgia girl are getting wild and crazy in Cabo all on your own, huh? Good for you, dude. Maybe I was wrong. Looks like you've got the plans to keep your marriage hot and spicy under control.

Me: I don't think you're getting this, but I am so mad at you. SO FUCKING MAD. If I could reach through this phone and pull your heart out of your chest with my bare hand, I would right now.

Thatch: Geez. Chill, dude. The swingers party wasn't me, I swear on it. The other stuff, I might have had a hand in, but I was just trying to make your getaway awesome. Special. Memorable. I mean, you had zero plans. Someone had to do something. And you can't really deny your Cabo trip sounds like it's turned into something that will be downright unforgettable. Think of all the memories you can tell your grandchildren now.

All the memories I could tell my grandchildren? Was he fucking serious?

At his words, my chest constricted so tightly, I thought I might be having a myocardial infarction.

Georgie, apparently, had noticed. "Just breathe, baby. Relax."

Taking several deep breaths in and out of my lungs, I worked to calm myself down.

And after a few minutes, instead of responding, I shoved my cell back in my suit pocket and ignored him. No doubt, it was the safest, smartest thing to do until we were back home and I could beat his fucking ass.

Chapter 13

Georgia

After Kline and I had escaped a couples sex orgy before we had to witness money shots, we'd come straight back to our suite and called it a night.

We didn't even have sex. Just undressed, got into bed, and tried to sleep away the trauma of the past forty-eight hours' events.

Unfortunately, sleep didn't last long for me. At a little after six in the morning, I was up and wide awake.

Careful not to disturb Kline, I got out of bed and made myself a fresh cup of coffee before taking it out onto the balcony.

Eyes still bleary, I sat down in one of the chairs and stared out toward the beach, mindlessly taking sips from my mug.

By the time the sun started to make its debut over the horizon, I felt a little more alert and my eyes had managed to transition from squinty to fully opened.

I stood up from my chair and leaned my elbows on the balcony railing, taking in the way the waves crashed against the white sand beach. It was still pretty early for any action, but there were a handful of early morning people taking walks and going on jogs.

With my empty mug still in my hands, I started to turn toward the doors to go back inside and make my second cup of coffee for the day, but something a little farther down the coast caught my eye.

A team of three men was dragging something out of the back of a black pickup truck. And in a matter of minutes, a massive, colorful, plastic-looking cloth was completely stretched out across the sand.

What on earth is that?

It wasn't until the huge, vibrant mass started to inflate into a balloon-like shape that I realized it was connected to a basket. Immediately, my brain connected the dots and solved the mystery—*a hot air balloon.*

At first, I just curiously watched the men work from my spot on the balcony.

But eventually, my mind took its investigation further and started to remind me of all of the facts.

A hot air balloon.

On the beach.

Right near your resort.

Once I factored in all the crazy shit that had happened since we'd arrived in Cabo, panic seized my throat.

Oh, *hell* no. That was *not* going to happen. We would, without a doubt, crash and die.

At a damn near sprint, I ran back inside our suite and dove straight onto the bed, shaking my husband's shoulders. "Kline! Kline!" I shouted his name, too worked up to gently ease him awake. "You have to get up, and we have to get the fuck out of here!"

"W-what?" he questioned, groaning and blinking his eyes open.

"Baby, someone is getting a hot air balloon ready on the beach!"

"Okay?"

"Kline, you need to wake up and understand what I'm saying," I said, voice still gripped by anxiety.

"What is happening right now?" he questioned, rubbing at his eyes, clearing his throat, and sitting up enough to rest his back against the headboard.

Once his still-sleepy eyes met mine, I reiterated my point. "There is a hot air balloon being blown up just outside our resort."

"Okay?" He was still confused. "What does that have to do with us?"

I just stared at him and gave him a moment to put the pieces together.

"Wait...you think Thatch is behind this?"

"Just...think about the past two days. *Really* think about them."

He blinked again.

"Baby, I love you, and I'm so thankful for this trip you tried to plan for us. But it's time we get away from this fucking getaway. And we need to do it before we end up thousands of feet in the sky in a fucking wicker basket," I said, my voice rising octaves with each word. "We'll die, Kline!" I exclaimed and hopped up from the bed, pacing the floor beside it. "If we stay here, we'll literally die in that hot air balloon."

"Fuck," Kline muttered and ran a hand through his hair. But to my surprise and relief, he got out of bed and tossed on a pair of boxer briefs. "You start packing, and I'll handle getting the flight home."

He grabbed his phone from the nightstand, scrolled through his contacts, but before he hit send on a call, he paused. "*Shit.* We can't fly on the private jet, baby." He looked at me, eyes serious. "We have to fly commercial!"

"What?" I asked as I grabbed our suitcases out of the closet.

"Thatch has infiltrated every goddamn aspect of this trip," he explained. "Who knows if he has some of the flight staff in his pocket, too? I mean, fuck, Georgie, there could be a fucking petting zoo or something waiting for us on the jet."

Holy hell.

This getaway had been such a shitshow that my calm, clever,

incredibly rational husband had officially become a conspiracy the-
orist, paranoid that Thatch was like some corrupt politician, buying
favors from his own staff. *Yeah, it was time to get home.*

"Okay. A commercial flight it is." It wasn't like I hadn't been flying
coach for my whole life.

"I'll let the flight staff know they can head back without us," he
said, voice determined. His fingers tapped across the screen of his
phone in rapid succession.

A few moments later, he had us two last-minute seats booked on
a flight to Newark.

And it didn't take long for us to pack our bags, put on our best
disguises in the form of sunglasses and hats, and get the fuck out of
Dodge.

The magnificent, five-star *Diamond* resort had officially lost its
luster.

Chapter 14

Twenty-four hours earlier than I'd planned, Georgia and I found ourselves at home, sitting on the couch, with Walter and Stan cuddled up on either side. A just-delivered pizza and breadsticks and drinks sat on the coffee table in front of us, and Georgia scrolled through the latest Netflix releases, trying to find a movie to watch.

We'd left Cabo in a rush this morning, all in the name of getting away from our "perfect little getaway" before more disaster occurred. *The fucking irony.* We'd literally had to escape the early Valentine's surprise that I'd planned to show Georgie that her supposed curse wasn't real, and in the process, I'm pretty sure that shit had blown up spectacularly—right in my face.

The only way our trip could have gone any worse was if we'd stayed to finish it.

Other people could call us paranoid all they wanted, but until they'd experienced being stalked by actual mariachi monkeys and doused by the sprinkler system in their hotel room in the name of Thatch's idea of romance, they had no right to comment on the matter.

"What do you feel like watching?" Georgia asked, still determined to find a movie that fit both the criteria we always strove for—neither of us had seen it, and both of us wanted to see it.

But fuck me, it was a tall order to carry out.

Truthfully, this was a common theme and conundrum with us.

We always *wanted* to find a new movie, spent a shitload of time trying *to find* a new movie, but in the end, we ended up watching a movie we'd both already seen or reruns of *The Office*.

In the digital age of technology, with everything at the tips of our fingers, how could it still feel like there was nothing to watch? Your guess was as good as mine.

I grabbed a slice of pizza and took a bite, but before I could manage a second bite, my phone chimed from the coffee table.

Thatch: You still mad at me?

He'd been demon-texting me the same sentiment all day. I'd been ignoring every single one. I tossed my phone back on the table, and Georgia sighed.

She didn't like discontentment in the friendship circle, even if she'd been the victim of this particular friend's stupid schemes.

"You're still not going to answer him?"

I shook my head. Not yet. Not if there was going to be any chance of letting him live.

Georgie sighed as my phone vibrated on the table again. I picked it up and read it—for some reason, I hadn't been able to help myself—but I tossed it back down without responding again.

Thatch: C'mon, K. Don't be mad. You know I was just trying to help you make Georgie's getaway fun.

Make Georgie's getaway fun? *Ha.* By the end of his attempts at helping with the fun, my wife was convinced we had to leave Cabo before we died in a hot air balloon.

Thatch: Also, for the fortieth time, I'd like to swear on the most perfectly perfect set of tits in the world, I did not send you and Georgia girl to a beat-the-meat market. If I'm lying, may they deflate right this moment, never to be fondled again.

Swearing on the destruction of tits was a pretty big deal for the giant bastard, so chances were, he was telling the truth about the swingers. But he was still behind everything else, so he could stew in his nerves while I enjoyed a fucking quiet night of pizza with my wife. Of course, my cell chimed a few more times, but *fuck that crazy fucker.*

"Oh, Kline! I've got it!" Georgia exclaimed, pointing the remote toward the TV.

I looked at the screen and saw Tom Hanks and Meg Ryan and the title *You've Got Mail.* "Baby, we've seen this movie a thousand times."

"Because it's the best rom-com movie ever! And oh my gosh!" She bounced up and down on the couch. "It reminds me so much of how our relationship started. We have to watch it." she begged. "Please, please, *please!*"

Her enthusiasm made me grin. "You really want to watch it?"

"Yes!"

"Then, by all means, hit play."

"Woo-hoo!" she exclaimed and leaned forward to press a smacking kiss to my lips.

Thank God she was so fucking adorable. It was like a balm to my constantly simmering anger.

Too tempted by her cuteness, I reached out and pulled her back toward me for another kiss. This time, though, I made damn sure it lasted longer than a second. Lips to hers, I coaxed her mouth to follow my soft, tender movements.

"I love you," I whispered against her lips once I slowly ended the kiss. "Every part of me loves every part of you, baby."

"Do you know what I realized?" She smiled, and her eyes searched mine.

"What?"

"I'm not cursed when it comes to Valentine's Day."

I furrowed my brow at her surprising admission. "And what makes you say that? Now? After the weekend we've just had?"

"Because I'm not destined to have this fantastic, awesome Valentine's Day. I don't need it. Because every single day with you *is* Valentine's Day."

"Georgia." Her words hit me square in the chest and officially smothered the withering flame.

"I love you," she said and pressed a tender kiss to my lips. "I love everything about our life. I don't need or want anything else in this world besides you and the perfect little bubble we've created for ourselves."

"Ditto, baby."

Goddamn. My woman. She was the best.

"So, husband of mine, are you ready to enjoy our perfect evening of pizza and rom-com on the couch?"

"Count me all in."

Once she hit play on the movie, she cuddled up close to me, her fingers mindlessly strumming through Walter's fur as Tom Hanks appeared on the screen.

All the while, I couldn't stop thinking about how fucking lucky I was.

With my arm around my wife's shoulders, I tucked her closer to my side before grabbing my phone to shoot out a text. My wife was right. Lingering grudges didn't have any place in a fairy tale like ours.

Me: I should be mad at you, dude. I really should.

His response was instant.

Thatch: But you've forgiven your ole buddy Thatch?

Me: Yeah, I guess I have. Just count yourself lucky that I'm in love. If I weren't, I'd be a lot less forgiving.

Thatch: Aw, Kline. You know I love you too, right?

Me: *extends middle finger*

Thatch: Oh, sweetie, you shouldn't have. *kisses*

I tossed my phone down on the table again and tucked my wife even closer. Even though my best friend was a fucking lunatic and the getaway I'd planned for my wife turned into a goddamn disaster, I'd never been happier in my whole life.

Georgia and I didn't need fancy getaways.

We just needed each other, and about that, I would always be certain.

THE END

Love Kline, Georgie, and the crew and ready to officially dive into Thatcher Kelly's book?
Read **Banking the Billionaire**, the next stand-alone romantic comedy in the *Billionaire Bad Boy Series*, right now!
You really don't want to miss Cassie making good on her promise, right?
#IdThatchThat

BEEN THERE, DONE THAT TO ALL OF THE ABOVE?
Never fear, we have a list of over THIRTY other titles to keep you busy for as long as your little reading heart desires!
Check them out at our website: *www.authormaxmonroe.com*

WHAT'S NEXT FROM MAX MONROE?
Stay up-to-date with our characters and our upcoming releases by signing up for our newsletter on our website:
www.authormaxmonroe.com/newsletter!
We'll be announcing our NEXT new release soon!

You may live to regret much, but we promise it won't be subscribing to our newsletter.
Seriously, we make it fun!
Character conversations about royal babies, parenting woes, embarrassing moments, and shitty horoscopes are just the beginning!
If you're already signed up, consider sending us a message to tell us how much you love us. We really like that. ;)

Follow us online:

Facebook: www.facebook.com/authormaxmonroe

Reader Group: www.facebook.com/groups/1561640154166388

Twitter: www.twitter.com/authormaxmonroe

Instagram: www.instagram.com/authormaxmonroe

Goodreads: https://goo.gl/8VUIz2

Acknowledgments

First of all, THANK YOU for reading. That goes for anyone who has bought a copy, read an ARC, helped us beta, edited, or found time in their busy schedule just to make sure we stayed on track. Thank you for supporting us, for talking about our books, and for just being so unbelievably loving and supportive of our characters. You've made this our MOST favorite adventure thus far.

THANK YOU to each other. Monroe is thanking Max. Max is thanking Monroe. *Blah, blah, blah.* We do this every book. Seriously. *Every* book. And there was no way we were going to start the first book of 2021 without continuing the tradition!

THANK YOU, Lisa, for accepting our 2021 "let's always be on a deadline" challenge! Or maybe…we shouldn't be thanking you? Maybe we should be concerned that you've enabled us? Just kidding! Well, sort of. LOL. Cheers to lots of projects this year! And thank you for always being our ride-or-die editor. Even when our schedule forces you to drink more wine.

THANK YOU, Stacey, for making the insides of our book look so damn pretty and rolling with the crazy schedule punches we throw your way. You are the absolute best!

THANK YOU, Peter (aka Banana), for rocking our covers. And for spending lots of time covering nipples and enhancing crotches when we ask you to. It's a tough job, but somebody's got to do it.

THANK YOU, Social Butterfly PR, for doing So. Many. Things. You make our lives so much easier. If you were one of our kids, you guys would be our favorite child.

THANK YOU to every blogger who has read, reviewed, posted, shared, and supported us. Your enthusiasm, support, and hard work do not go unnoticed. We love youuuuuuuuuuuuu!

THANK YOU to the people who love us—our family. You are our biggest supporters and motivators. We couldn't do this without you. Although, it should be noted, sometimes you guys are hella distracting. But the ones who are the most distracting are under the age of eleven, so we're not going to hold that against you. HAHA.

THANK YOU to our Camp members! You guys are the best! THE BEST, we tell you! You've made Camp the coolest place to be and one of our favorite places to go to procrastinate.

As always, all our love.
XOXO,
Max & Monroe

Made in the USA
Las Vegas, NV
04 November 2022